LISA JACKSON

WHISPERS

KENSINGTON BOOKS
www.kensingtonbooks.com

KENSINGTON BOOKS are published by

Kensington Publishing Corp.
119 West 40th Street
New York, NY 10018

All Kensington titles, imprints, and distributed lines are available at special quantity discounts for bulk purchases for sales promotion, premiums, fund-raising, educational, or institutional use.

Special book excerpts or customized printings can also be created to fit specific needs. For details, write or phone the office of the Kensington Special Sales Manager: Kensington Publishing Corp., 119 West 40th Street, New York, NY 10018. Attn. Special Sales Department. Phone: 1-800-221-2647.

Kensington and the K logo Reg. U.S. Pat. & TM Off.

ISBN-13: 978-1-4967-0052-0
ISBN-10: 1-4967-0052-X

First Zebra Mass Market Printing: June 1996
First Kensington Trade Paperback Printing: November 2015

10 9 8 7 6 5 4 3 2 1

Printed in the United States of America

OUTSTANDING PRAISE FOR THE NOVELS OF LISA JACKSON

Close to Home
"Jackson definitely knows how to jangle readers' nerves. . . .
Close to Home is perfect for readers of Joy Fielding or
fans of Mary Higgins Clark."
—*Booklist*

Tell Me
"Absolutely tension filled . . . Jackson is on top of her game."
—*Suspense Magazine*

You Don't Want to Know
"Lisa Jackson shows yet again why she is one of the best
at romantic suspense. A pure nail biter."
—Harlan Coben, # 1 *New York Times* bestselling author

"Shiveringly good suspense! Lisa Jackson ratchets up the
tension as one woman's desperate search for her missing son
takes her to the very brink of losing her husband, her sanity,
her very self. Each chapter will leave you wondering who
to trust. The answer: You don't want to know. . . ."
—Lisa Gardner, *New York Times* bestselling author

Devious
"Terrifying . . . a creepy thriller sure to please Jackson's many fans."
—*Publishers Weekly*

Without Mercy
"Her latest whodunit hits all the marks, taking readers on
a nail-biting roller-coaster ride."
—*Library Journal*

"A juicy creep-a-thon . . . builds to a surprising cliffhanger ending."
—*Publishers Weekly* (starred review)

Malice
"Taut, twisty . . . *Malice* displays the skilled Jackson at her best yet."
—*The Providence Journal*

Books by Lisa Jackson

Stand-Alones

See How She Dies
Final Scream
Running Scared
Whispers
Twice Kissed
Unspoken
Deep Freeze
Fatal Burn
Most Likely to Die
Wicked Game
Wicked Lies
Something Wicked
Wicked Ways
Without Mercy
You Don't Want to Know
Close to Home
After She's Gone

Anthony Paterno / Cahill Family Novels

If She Only Knew
Almost Dead

Rick Bentz / Reuben Montoya Novels

Hot Blooded
Cold Blooded
Shiver
Absolute Fear
Lost Souls
Malice
Devious
Never Die Alone

Pierce Reed / Nikki Gillette Novels

The Night Before
The Morning After
Tell Me

Selena Alvarez / Regan Pescoli Novels

Left to Die
Chosen to Die
Born to Die
Afraid to Die
Ready to Die
Deserves to Die

Published by Kensington Publishing Corporation

To Anita. Agent. Mentor. Friend.
You will be missed but never forgotten.

PART 1

1996

PROLOGUE

"Bitch." Harley Taggert was drunk, but not drunk enough. He needed another bottle of champagne to dull the pain cutting through his soul and he stumbled as he walked along the deck of his father's sailboat. The night was clear, the salt smell of the ocean invading his nostrils, the boat gently rocking against its moorings. How could she do this to him? How could she give him back the goddamned ring?

Because she's a heartless bitch. She gave you back the ring didn't she?

He glanced down at his curled fist and saw the diamond ring winking in his sweaty palm and remembered pieces of her rehearsed speech about their relationship not working and her wanting to be "friends" or some such rot. Yeah, right. Like she was "friends" with Kane Moran, that two-bit hoodlum? She was probably on her way to screw Moran's brains out right now.

He squeezed his eyes shut and saw her face in his mind's eye. God she was beautiful, but then all the Holland women were.

Claire. Jesus. Why?

Damn it, he'd loved her.

More than he'd realized. More than he thought possible.

And she'd cheated on him.

With that low-life poor bastard.

Harley swayed a little as he reached the prow and looked skyward to the skeletal masts rising into the starry night. He felt tears sting his eyes and was ashamed. It was the champagne. Had to be. Because he was a man and men didn't ever cry—especially not the sons of Neal Taggert. Never them.

"Shit," he muttered and looked westward past the bay to the open sea. He should leave. Forever. Or . . . do as he threatened and end it all. Just jump into the frigid water and breathe deep. That would show 'em. Or else he should have another drink . . . but first . . . he needed to get rid of the ring. With all his might he pulled his arm back and heaved the sickening diamond as far as he could throw and fell against the railing with the effort just as he heard a distinctive plop as the damned engagement ring settled into the depths of the bay. "Good riddance," Harley muttered, pulling himself onto his feet as he felt rather than saw someone with him.

He turned quickly, but he was alone. No one had climbed aboard. No one lingered on the dock. It was just his mind playing weird games with him. The hot summer night was getting to him. Even the breath of wind rolling in from the Pacific was warmer than usual for summer in Oregon.

Another noise. From the dock. Fear zinged up his spine. He squinted but saw no one lingering beneath the lights strung over the worn planks. He was alone. Aside from the old coot dozing in the marina office and the people playing some old Eagles album . . . he was just jumpy—too many emotions and too much booze. Or not enough.

From the corner of his eye he saw movement and he twisted his head around in time to see a bony cat slip around a lamppost.

Get a grip. You're losin' it, man. Either jump into the water and end it or go back into the cabin and raid the old man's liquor cabinet. There's a fifth of Black Velvet with your name on it.

He took one step toward the cabin when he saw her . . . just a quicksilver image of a woman sliding quickly through the shadows. Every hair on the back of his neck rose. Had Claire returned? Rethought her heartless decision to cast him aside? Well, it was too fuckin' late . . . but . . . there was something wrong about her. It didn't seem right. Or was the champagne clouding his judgment.

He blinked and she seemed to have disappeared. But he knew better. Felt her eyes—hidden condemning orbs. Whoever it was seemed used to slinking around and hiding in the shadows, someone who loved to spy. Someone who wasn't quite right. Someone like his sister.

Swallowing back his fear, he took a tentative step forward, toward the prow, easing closer to the railing. "Paige?" he called, hoping to sound steadier than he felt. "Is that you? Come on outta there—"

Something flashed by the side of his head and he turned quickly to see a gloved hand raised high. "What the hell?"

Bam!

"Die, bastard," an evil voice snarled.

He caught a glimpse of a rock hoisted high.

Before he could move, it crashed down.

Bam!

Pain exploded in his skull.

White light flashed behind his eyes.

Harley staggered backward, blood running in his eyes, fear sliding down his spine. His hips hit the railing and he tried to catch himself, but it was too late. Momentum pitched him over the side of the sleek craft and he was falling . . . falling.

Thud!

The back of his head cracked the dock.

Pain screamed through his skull. His body convulsed. Blindly he groped, reaching, scrabbling for anything to hold on to, his fingers scraping the side of his father's boat only to lose their grip as he hit the icy water.

You're going to die. Right now . . . Fight, Harley, fight!

He tried to scream. Saltwater filled his nose and throat. His reactions were slow, out of sync. *Help me, please, someone help me!* But the words were lost in his mind. Pain ricocheted through his brain, through the dark frigid water. His lungs burned. He flailed wildly, thrashing and churning as his clothes weighed him down. Sluggishly he tried to kick upward but his foot was held tight, tangled or . . . or gripped by someone under the dock. His lungs were on fire, threatening to explode. Frantic, he fought, kicking, looking up to the surface where, beyond the rippling veil of the waterline he caught a glimpse of his attacker as she stood beneath a lamppost on the dock.

The surface was so far away . . . he was going to die . . . she'd killed him. *Why? Oh, God, please help me! Jump in here, call nine-one-one, do* some*thing.* He tried to swim upward, but whatever was holding his foot wouldn't let go! His entire body screamed in agony. The image overhead rippled before his eyes as he struggled, a pale watery face illuminated by the lights of the dock, a face twisted in horror while the manacle on his ankle seemed to tighten, as if the Grim Reaper himself were holding him fast, ensuring his horrid death.

There wasn't any more time. In one last effort, Harley kicked and tried to scream.

His tortured lungs shattered. Air spewed, bubbling upward, taking with it any chance of survival. Saltwater flooded his throat. Cold as death it burned like hell. Wave after wave of burning water crushing him from the inside out . . . and then it came . . . the blackness, an eerily seductive calm teased at the edges of his brain, closing in on him as he quit struggling and the last bit of air bubbled up from his lungs. His eyes rolled up in his head, offering him one final glimpse of the world through a watery curtain where he saw the ghostly face of his killer as she inched backward, away from light and into the darkness.

CHAPTER 1

All's fair in love and war.

Or so the old saying went. Kane wasn't entirely sure he could adopt the adage, not when Claire Holland's future was at stake, but then what the hell, she'd never cared for him anyway. Never given him the time of day except once, when she'd let her tightly laced guard down. He stepped hard on the emergency brake as he cut the engine and reminded himself that she was married, separated but married, and her name was now Claire St. John.

Rain peppered the windshield, drizzling down the glass in jagged streaks as Kane stared at the shack he'd inherited—a three-room cabin on the shores of Lake Arrowhead. Shingles were missing from the roof; two windows were covered with plywood now decorated with graffiti; rust ran in orange stains from downspouts clogged by years of leaves, needles, and dirt; and the front porch sagged like a broken-down cart horse's back. Stumps, mutilated by a chain saw and blackened from years in the rain, had toppled over long before they became his father's works of Northwest art. The attic window—the only source of natural light in the cramped space that had been his bedroom—had been smashed, and pieces of glass still littered the porch roof.

Welcome home, he thought sourly as he climbed out of his rig, threw his duffel bag and bedroll over one shoulder, and ducked against an icy blast of wind. Hot pain shot through his hip, compliments of a stray piece of shrapnel he'd collected on his last assignment overseas. He winced and hitched the bag higher on his shoulder as he cursed the fact that he still limped a bit, enough to throw off his gait when he wanted to move fast.

On the stoop, he inserted his key into the old lock, and the latch gave way completely, the door opening with a groaning creak, sawdust filtering down from the useless dead bolt.

Years of dust, dead air, and the general feeling of lost dreams crowded around him as he walked over the threshold. Second thoughts were his companions for the first time since deciding upon this mission. Maybe moving back here was a bad idea. Maybe the guy who came up with the phrase "let sleeping dogs lie" knew something Kane didn't.

Too bad. He stepped over an upended coffee table. Now wasn't the time for turning back. He dropped his duffel and sleeping bag onto a couch in the corner—a once-rose-colored contemporary sectional, now a dingy pink-gray, with the stuffing exposed in several spots. The windowsills were dry and peeling, covered with the remnants of spiders' meals, brittle carcasses of insects. In one corner of the ceiling, where the tiles drooped, a half-decayed yellow jacket's nest hung loosely. The knotty pine walls were mildew-stained, and the dank smell slipped through the cabin like a fetid shadow.

He'd camped in worse places than this over the years, seen hovels in the Middle East and Bosnia that made this old cabin look like a palace, but none of those wretched abodes had he ever called home. Only in this place was his soul stripped bare and bleeding, this run-down cottage where he'd been reared in his earlier years by a mother whose shoes had wafer-thin soles because she walked so many miles behind the counter of the Westwind Bar and Grill.

"You take care of yourself, honey," she'd said, touching him lightly on the shoulder and slanting him a sad smile. "I'll be home late, so lock the door. Your daddy, he'll be home soon." A lie. Always a lie, but one he never questioned. She'd brushed a kiss across his cheek. Alice Moran had always smelled of roses and smoke, a mixture of cheap perfume and bargain brand cigarettes. For years the top drawer of her dresser had been filled with coupons from the backs of cigarette packs, collected and used to buy something special other than the barest of necessities. Most of the Christmas and birthday gifts Kane had received had been compliments of his mother's nicotine habit.

But that had been a long time ago, when life, though lean, had been simple for a boy of eight or nine. Right around the time of Pop's accident, when their sorry lives had changed for the worse.

There wasn't much reason to dwell on the past, so he ignored the raw anger in his gut as well as the pain in his hip. He found a yellowed newspaper from fifteen years ago and felt like he had as a gawky, rebellious teenager—horny as hell and burning with a need for more from life, a taste of better things, a desire to be as good as the Hollands and the Taggerts, the richest families on the lake, the social elite of this tiny coastal burg as well as the city of Portland, some ninety miles to the east.

And he'd wanted Claire. With a brain-numbing lust and a fire between his legs he'd fantasized about her—the rich, unavailable daughter of Dutch Holland.

He wadded the old newspaper in his fist as he remembered how many nights he'd lain awake, trying to devise plans to be with her, none of which had materialized into anything more than a frustration that had caused sweat to bead on his upper lip and his cock to become stiff as a flagpole on a windless day.

He didn't want to think about Claire. She'd only complicate things, and he'd never been good enough for her anyway. No. She'd had her adolescent sights set on Harley Taggert, son of her father's biggest competitor. Except for one time. One magic morning.

"Hell," he growled, trying to chase her image from his mind. Despite the rain, he threw open the windows, letting in a harsh, wet breeze that carried the scent of the Pacific Ocean. Maybe the cold air would blow away the lingering sense of despair and lost hopes that clung, like stubborn cobwebs, to the faded curtains and scattered pieces of cheap furniture in this dump.

He let the door stand open as he made one more trip to the Jeep for his briefcase, cell phone, laptop computer, and pint of Irish whiskey, the label of which boasted his father's favorite cheap blend. It was ironic, him drinking the same liquor as Pop, a man he'd detested, but it seemed fitting somehow. Hampton Moran had been a miserable son of a bitch, mean to the bone and, after the accident that had left him wheelchair-bound, he'd become a violent drunk, filled with self-pity and seething rage. Before the fall that had crippled him, he'd drunk too much and beaten his wife and boy. Afterward with only Kane to take care of him, Pop had been reduced to a bitter shell of a man who sought solace and relief from the bottle. Black Velvet, when he could afford her, became his favorite lady, Jack Daniel's a sometime but too expensive friend. More often than not he was left with rotgut Irish whiskey to fuel his broken dreams.

No wonder Kane's mother had left after a while. She'd had no choice. A rich man had wooed her, promised her a better life as long as she left Hampton and her son. The man didn't need the extra baggage of a wild boy; he had half-grown kids of his own. And a wife. Kane had never known the bastard's name, but every month, like clockwork, a money order for three hundred dollars in Kane's name arrived in the mailbox. Hampton, sober for the first time in thirty days, would wait for the mail carrier, have Kane retrieve the letterless envelope, and force him to cash the anonymous check. Pop was generous. He gave Kane five dollars, and the remainder would tide him over for the rest of the month.

"You've heard of blood money, haven't you boy, well this is jizz-money—earned by your mother for spreading her legs for that rich son of a bitch. Remember that, Kane; no woman is worth losing your heart or your wallet. Scourge of the earth they are. Whores. Jezebels." And then he'd begin to quote scripture, mixed-up verses that made no sense.

Kane remembered the day his mother had left. "I'll be back," she'd promised, tears running down her cheeks as she'd hugged her son, clinging to him as if she knew she'd never see him again. "I'll be back to take you away from him."

Pop had been sleeping, snoring away last night's bender.

Kane hadn't so much as lifted his hands to hold her or wave good-bye. When she stepped into the long black car with its grim-faced driver, Kane had only stared at her with eyes accusing her of being a failure and a traitor.

"I promise, honey. I'll be back."

But it hadn't happened. Her untruth had been just one more link in the tarnished chain of broken promises that had been Kane's life. He'd never seen her again, never bothered to find out what had happened. Until now.

And the truth stung—it stung like a bitch.

He didn't bother with a glass, just opened the bottle and took a long pull, then brushed off the chipped Formica with his coat sleeve, plugged in the computer, and sat at the metal-legged table where he'd taken most of the meals of the first twenty years of his life. The electric company must've come through and reconnected the old wires because the screen flickered and the laptop hummed in readiness.

Snapping open his briefcase, he pulled out a file, thick with notes, clippings, and pictures of the Holland family. He dealt the photographs out like cards from a well-worn deck. First card faceup was the king of diamonds, old Dutch Holland, patriarch and would-be governor of the state, a man who claimed to be of the people, but, Kane knew, was more twisted than a sailor's knot.

Second was a picture of Dutch's ex-wife Dominique, still model-beautiful, but living out of the country these days and, presumably, a source who might, for the right amount of cash, help him with his quest. Then there were the glossy prints of two of Dutch's daughters, Miranda and Tessa. The final photograph, a snapshot, was of Claire.

Too bad she was involved, and, he guessed, involved to her teeth.

His jaw hardened at the two faces staring sightlessly from poses encouraged by some nameless but expensive photographer. He dropped the pictures of Miranda and Tessa, the oldest and youngest onto the table's surface to join their parents, but he studied Claire's picture more closely, a snapshot that he'd committed to memory long before. She was astride a painted pony, only the back and neck of which were visible. But Claire was caught square in the camera's lens. His camera's lens.

Clear eyes, straight nose, wide cheekbones, and loose cinnamon brown curls framing an oval face. God, she was beautiful. Her smile was shy and enigmatic, a naive turn-on. Hell, he still felt it, that slightly elevated beat of his pulse whenever he thought of her, the girl who had everything, who had looked at him with disdain and pity.

But not anymore.

Now the tables had turned. He was the one in control. A twinge of conscience spiked his brain because he knew that what he was about to do might expose Claire to the most brutal of scrutiny. Her life would be turned inside out and shaken until all the dirt fell out, all the hidden secrets exposed like the bleached bones of a desert carcass.

Too bad. If she got hurt, well, that was just part of life. The breaks. Sometimes pain couldn't be helped. A man was dead, sent to a watery grave years before by someone who had lived in the house of Holland. Kane was determined to find out who had crushed Harley Taggert's skull and hidden the crime for over sixteen years. He had personal reasons for this vendetta, reasons that went far beyond his pressing need to make a living, reasons that included his sincere belief that Harley might not have been the only victim in the lies and deceit that were hidden beneath the still surface of Lake Arrowhead.

He flipped through a few pages of notes, then positioned the computer in front of him. Fingers moving deftly, he typed out the first page:

Power Play:
The Murder of Harley Taggert
by
Kane Moran

He took another swig from his bottle and started writing. Even though his investigation into all the skeletons tucked discreetly away in the Holland family closets was just beginning, he realized that before he was finished, Harley's murderer would face charges on a sixteen-year-old crime. Dutch Holland, the bastard, would have no chance of becoming governor of Oregon, and every single member of the Holland family, including Claire, would despise Kane Moran.

So be it. Life wasn't easy, and it sure as hell wasn't fair. He'd learned that painful lesson years ago, and Claire had been one of his teachers. Besides, this, his exposé of the Holland family, was to be his revenge and catharsis.

A new start.

He tipped the bottle back again. A swallow of whiskey burned a fiery path to his stomach, and Kane wondered why, instead of a sense of elation, he felt a premonition of dread, as if he'd unwittingly taken his first step into hell.

"I don't care if you have to kiss Moran's ugly ass or tie him up in lawsuits for the rest of his life. Find out something that we can use against him. Bribe him or kill the stupid bastard with your bare hands, Murdock! Just find a way to squelch the damned book!" Dutch slammed the car phone into its cradle. "Spineless cretin," he growled, though in truth, Ralph Murdock, his attorney and campaign manager, was one of the few people in this world whom Benedict Holland trusted.

Clamping down on the cigar jammed between his teeth, he floored the accelerator and his Cadillac shot forward, tires skimming on the narrow road winding through this stretch of old growth timber. The speedometer inched past sixty and mossy-barked fir trees swept by in a blur.

Who would have thought that the ghost of Harley Taggert would rise now at this critical point in his life? And who the hell did Kane Moran, the man penning the story surrounding Harley's death, think he was? The last time Dutch had seen him, years ago, Moran had been a mean-tempered kid with a chip on his shoulder the size of Nebraska, a hoodlum always in trouble with the law. Somehow he'd scrounged his way through college and he'd become a risk-taking fool of a journalist who, because of some damned wound, had decided to settle down back home in Oregon to write a book about Harley Taggert's death.

As his car shot over the summit, Dutch experienced the tightening in his chest again, that same old sense of panic that squeezed him whenever he thought of the night the Taggert kid died. Deep in the darkest reaches of his heart he suspected that one of his daughters had bashed in the boy's skull.

Which one? Which one of his girls had done it? His firstborn,

Miranda, a lawyer working for the district attorney's office, was ambitious to a fault, her pride unbending. She looked so much like her mother it was spooky. Randa had inherited Dominique's thick dark hair and sultry blue eyes. He'd heard comments that Miranda was haughty, that she had ice water running through her veins, but she certainly wasn't cold enough or stupid enough to have murdered the Taggert kid. No, Dutch wouldn't believe it; Randa had been too self-possessed, a woman who knew what she wanted out of life.

Claire, his secondborn, had been the quiet one, a romantic by nature. As a kid she'd been gawky, plain in comparison with her sisters, but she'd grown into her looks, and he suspected that she would be the kind of woman who, as the years passed, would look better and better. At the time of Harley's death she'd been a soft-spoken athletic girl, the middle sister, one to whom he hadn't paid much attention. She never gave him any trouble except that she'd fallen in love with Harley Taggert. Then there was Tessa. The baby. And the rebel. There was no reason she would have wanted Harley Taggert dead. At least no reason Dutch knew about. And even now that thought settled like a stone in his gut.

Until recently, Dutch hadn't lost much sleep over the Taggert boy's demise.

Now, his fingers grew sweaty around the steering wheel. Claire, with her haunted eyes and smattering of freckles, wasn't a killer. She couldn't be. Christ, there wasn't a mean bone in her body. Or was there? What of Miranda? Maybe he didn't know his eldest as well as he thought he did.

The sun was hanging low over the western hills, blinding him with its bright rays. He flipped down the visor. The road split and he turned toward the small town of Chinook and the old lodge he'd bought for a song.

The Caddy shimmied as Dutch took the corner too fast, but he barely noticed as he slid over the center line. A pickup going the opposite direction blasted its horn and skidded on the gravel shoulder to avoid collision.

"Bastard," Dutch growled, still lost in thought. His youngest daughter, Tessa, was and always had been the maverick in the family. Blond and blue-eyed with a figure that, at twelve, had been obscenely curvaceous, Tessa had forever been the wild card in the deck that was the Holland family. Whereas Miranda had tried to please, and Claire had faded into the woodwork, Tessa had brazenly and willfully defied Dutch whenever she could. Knowing she was his favorite, she'd rebelled at every turn. Trouble—that's what Tessa had been, but Dutch couldn't believe, wouldn't, that she was a killer.

"Damn it all to hell," he muttered as he chewed on the end of his cigar. If only he'd been fortunate enough to have sired sons. Things would have been different. Far different. God had played a cruel trick on him with these girls.

Daughters always gave a man grief.

Easing off the accelerator at the crooked pine tree, the one he'd planted a lifetime ago, when he'd bought this place for Dominique, he guided the car into the private lane leading to the estate. He'd been a lovesick fool at the time he'd set that little pine into the ground, but the years had changed him, worn that love so thin it had shattered like crystal hurled against stone.

He unlocked the gates and drove along the cracked asphalt of the once-tended drive. The silvery waters of the lake winked seductively through the trees. How he'd loved this place.

Nostalgia tugged at his heart as he rounded a final bend and saw the house, a rambling old hunting lodge that, nestled in a stand of oak and fir, rose three stories to look upon the lake.

Home.

A place of triumph and heartache.

Thinking his wife would love it as much as he did, he'd bought the vast tree-covered acres for Dominique. From the moment she saw the rough timbers and open beams, she'd hated everything there was about their new home. Her appraising eyes had studied the steep angle of the roof, the cedar walls, plank floors, and pitched ceiling. She touched the wooden railing of the stairs, with its hand-carved banister and posts decorated with handcrafted Northwest creatures, and her nostrils had flared as if she'd suddenly come across a bad smell. "You bought this for *me?*" she'd asked, incredulous and bitterly disappointed. Her voice had echoed through the cavernous foyer. "This . . . this monstrosity?"

Miranda, barely four, the spitting image of her mother, had eyed the old house solemnly as if she'd expected all manner of ghosts, goblins, and monsters to appear at any given second.

"I suppose this"—Dominique pointed a long finger at the salmon carved into the lowest post—"is considered art?"

"Yes."

"For the love of God, Benedict, why? What possessed you to buy it?"

Dutch had felt the first premonition of dread steal through his heart. He spread his hands. "It's for you and the girls."

"For *us*? Out here? In the middle of nowhere?" High heels clicked indignantly as she walked through the foyer and into the living room, with its vaulted ceilings and three chandeliers created by nesting dozens of deer antlers together. "Away from my friends?"

"It's good for children to grow up—"

"In the city, Benedict, where they can meet other children their age, in a house that does them justice, where they'll be exposed to culture and the right people." She sighed, then, spying Claire toddling through open French doors where the back of the house flanked the lake, Dominique started running, heels clipping ever faster. "This is going to be a nightmare." Snagging Claire from the covered porch before she was anywhere near the shoreline, Dominique turned and glared at her husband. "Living here won't work."

"Of course it will. I'll build tennis courts and a pool with its own house. You can have gardens and your own studio over the garage."

Tessa, the baby and always a fussy thing, gave out a lusty cry and wriggled in the nursemaid's arms.

"Shh," Bonita, barely sixteen and illegally in the States, whispered to the red-faced cherub.

"I can't live here." Dominique was firm.

"Sure you can."

"Where will the girls learn French—"

"From you."

"I'm *not* a tutor."

"We'll hire one. The house is big."

"What about piano, violin, fencing, riding . . . oh, dear God."

She looked about to break down, her huge blue eyes suddenly moist, her manicured fingers pressed to her lips.

"It will work, I promise," Dutch insisted.

"But I can't possibly . . . I'm not cut out to be a maid . . . I'm going to need more help than just Bonita, here."

"I know, I know. I've already talked to a woman—Indian woman by the name of Songbird. You'll have more than enough help, Dominique. You'll be able to live like a queen."

She'd made a deprecating sound deep in her throat. "The Queen of Nowhere. Has a nice ring to it, don't you think?"

From that day forward, she'd hated living here, despised the lake, predicted that nothing good would happen anywhere near the sandy banks of Lake Arrowhead.

As it turned out, she'd been right.

Now Dutch cracked the window a bit farther, letting in the moist summer air. The water, spangled by the hot summer sun, appeared placid, incapable of causing so much heartache and agony.

"Son of a bitch," he muttered, cigar firmly between his teeth as he grabbed the bottle of scotch he'd brought from town, climbed out of his car, and waded stiffly through the thick layers of cones and needles to the front door. It opened easily, as if he'd been expected. The soles of his shoes slapped against the dusty floorboards, and he thought he heard a mouse scurrying to a dark corner.

In the kitchen he rummaged through the cupboards and found a glass, dusty from years of neglect. He'd called ahead and the electricity, phones, gas, and water had been turned on. In the next few days the house would be cleaned from top to bottom, and his grown daughters would arrive, whether they wanted to come back or not.

Wiping the glass with his fingers, he poured himself a generous shot, then climbed the stairs to his bedroom—the one he'd shared for years with Dominique. The bed, a massive four-poster was stripped bare, the mattress covered in plastic. He walked to the windows, opened the drapes, and, sipping his drink, glanced at the swimming pool, long dry, a nest of leaves and dirt clogging the drain. The pool house, positioned near the diving board, was locked up, had been for years. Then he looked past the pool to the lake he loved. Staring at the tranquil water, he felt dread, like the ticking of a clock, pound ceaselessly in his brain.

What had happened so long ago? What would he discover? A shudder coursed through him. He tossed back his drink, felt the fiery liquor splash the back of his throat and warm his belly as he headed downstairs, away from this morgue, with its dark memories of old, disappointing sex and so little love. Christ, Dominique had turned into a bitch.

In the den, he fished his wallet from his pocket, extracted a single page he'd ripped from the notepad on his desk, and stared at the three telephone numbers of his daughters. None would be glad to hear from him, but they'd do what he asked.

They always did.

He picked up the receiver, heard a click and a dial tone, and set his jaw.

Damn Harley Taggert. Damn Kane Moran. And goddamn the truth, whatever the hell it was.

CHAPTER 2

"It's not fair! *We* shouldn't have to move. *We* didn't do anything wrong. *We're* not the perverts!" Sean glowered at his mother, his eyes partially hidden by his shaggy hair, his jaw tight and strong. A spattering of freckles bridged his nose despite his summer tan. Rebellion radiated from him in indignant waves, and his hands opened and closed into fists of frustration. In the glimmer of a moment he looked so much like his father, Claire wanted to fold him into her arms and never let go.

"It's just better this way." She dumped the contents of the top drawer of her dresser onto the bed and stuffed her socks and underwear into an empty cardboard box, all the while wishing she believed her own words. The pain would eventually go away—it always did—but it would take time. Lots of time.

"Dad's the one who should be leaving!" Sean slumped onto a packing crate and frowned through the open bedroom window to the gnarled apple tree, where a tire swing swayed slightly in the breeze. The old whitewall was suspended by a fraying, blackened rope, a sad reminder of her children's youth and innocence; innocence that had recently been destroyed. The kids hadn't used the swing in years, and thin yellow grass had finally grown back in the ridges where their sneakers had once scuffed the earth bare. But that seemed eons ago, in a time when Claire had convinced herself that she and her small family were content, that the sins of the past would never invade their lives, that she could find happy-ever-after in this sleepy little Colorado town.

How wrong she'd been. She slammed the empty drawer shut and started working on the next with a vengeance. The sooner she was out of this room, this house, the whole damned town, the better.

Standing, Sean fidgeted and shoved his hands into the ragged back pockets of cutoffs that looked as if they might at any moment slip off his slim hips. "I hate Oregon."

"It's a big state—a lot of country to hate."

"I won't stay."

"Sure you will." But she detested the sound of determination in his voice. "Grandpa's there."

He made a deprecating sound of disdain.

"I might have a job there."

"As a substitute teacher. Big deal."

"It is. We can't stay here, Sean. You know that. You'll adjust." She glanced up to the dusty mirror, where she could see his reflection, tall and muscular, a few hairs beginning to sprout over his upper lip and chin. Defiance edged the corners of his mouth and his jaw, once soft with childhood, had begun to take the hard, forceful shape of a man's.

"All my friends are here. And Samantha, what about her? She doesn't even understand what's going on."

Neither do I, son. Neither do you. "I'll explain it to her someday."

He snorted in disbelief. "What're you gonna tell her, Mom? That her freak of a dad was balling a girl only a few years older than her?" Sean's voice was a harsh, disbelieving whisper. "That he was screwing my girlfriend?" He hooked his thumb to his chest. *"My* goddamned girlfriend!"

"Stop it!" She tossed her nightgowns into the box with her socks. "There's no reason to swear."

"Like hell! There's plenty of reasons. Admit it. This is why you finally divorced Dad after all those years of separation, isn't it? You knew!" His face had turned scarlet, his eyes filled with tears that he wouldn't shed. "You knew and you didn't tell me!"

Fury and humiliation burned through Claire, and she stepped

over to the door and shut it so that the latch clicked softly. "Samantha's only twelve; she doesn't need to know that her father—"

"Why not?" Sean demanded, angling up his chin. "Don't you think she's heard things—all our dirty little secrets, from her friends?" Then he smiled without a trace of humor and shook his head. "Oh, that's right, she doesn't have any, does she? Lucky for her. Then she doesn't have to listen to 'em tell her that her old man's a perverted rapist—"

"Enough!" Claire cried, her voice strangled as she shoved hard on the second drawer of her bureau and it shut with a bang. "Don't you think this bothers me? He was my husband, Sean. I know you're hurting, you're embarrassed and mortified, but so am I."

"So you're running away. Like a chicken-shit dog with her tail tucked between her legs."

So cynical for one so young. She grabbed him by both of his shoulders, her fingers digging into his muscles, her head tilted back so she could look squarely into his angry young face. "Don't you ever talk to me like that again! Your father made mistakes, lots of them and . . ." She saw the wounded look in his eyes and something inside of her broke—a fragile dam she'd tried so hard to erect. "Oh, Sean." Folding his stiff unforgiving body into her arms, she wanted to break down and cry. But falling apart wouldn't do any good.

She whispered, "Oh, honey, I'm so sorry. So sorry." Sean remained immobile in her embrace, a statue who didn't dare hug her back. Slowly she released him.

"It's not your fault, is it? You . . . you didn't drive him to—" He looked away, bright color climbing up his neck.

The insinuation ricocheted through her brain. She'd asked herself the same question a thousand times over. Was she not woman enough to keep her man? Her man. What a joke! Deep inside she knew that what had happened wasn't her fault. She only wished she'd seen it coming so that the ugly accusations, the whispered rumors, the dark soul-scraping pain hadn't blindsided her children. All her adult life she'd only wanted to protect them. "Of course not," she answered shakily. "I know this is hard for you. Believe me, it's hard for me, too, but I think it's best for all of us—you, me, and Samantha—if we start over somewhere."

"We can't hide." His gaze was hard and had seen far too much for his tender age. "It'll catch up to us. Even in some little backwater town in friggin' Oregon."

Rubbing the back of her neck, she shook her head. "I know. But by the time it does, we'll be stronger and—"

"Mom?" The door creaked open and Samantha, lines of worry marring her smooth forehead, slid into the room. At twelve she was gawky, her arms and legs a little too long, her body lanky and athletic rather than curvy. For nearly a year she'd been hoping to grow breasts, but the little nubs on her chest barely filled out the training bra she disdained to wear. Most of the girls in her class had already developed, and everyone seemed to know who wore a B cup, who filled out a C and, God forbid, who was cursed with a double A. Samantha was a late bloomer. A curse as far as Samantha was concerned; a blessing to her mother's experienced eyes. "What's going on?"

"Just packing up," Claire said brightly—too brightly. Her cheer sounded as false as it was. Sean rolled his eyes and flopped onto the bed—stripped of sheets and blankets and now covered with belts, T-shirts, shorts, slips, and pajamas. Claire tossed a mateless shoulder pad into the throwaway bag near the door.

"You were yelling." Samantha's worried gaze moved from her brother to her mother.

"Not really."

"I heard you."

Not now; I can't deal with this now. "Sean doesn't want to move," Claire explained, frowning at a purse that she tossed into another bag with items to be given to the Salvation Army. "He doesn't want to leave his friends."

"His friends are all jerks and stoners."

He sat bolt upright. "You don't know anything!"

"Benjie North's mom found his stash—right in a fake mailbox in his bedroom. Marijuana and hash and—"

Claire's gaze fell on Sean, her worst suspicions confirmed. She could barely breathe. Her fingers curled around the strap of a second purse. "Is this true?"

"It was a setup."

"A setup. By whom?"

A beat. Just a moment of condemning hesitation. "His older brother," Sean lied. "Max hid his stuff in Benjie's room to fake out his parents. Benjie's clean. I swear." He shot his sister a look that could cut through steel.

"Max is only seventeen."

"You can do dope at any age, Mom."

"I know." She let go of her death grip on the purse's handle. "That's what worries me."

"Worries you?"

"What about you, Sean?"

"I've never done anything!" Defiance sparked in his eyes.

Samantha started to open her mouth, thought better of it, and sealed her lips.

Sean swallowed hard. "Well just cigarettes and some chew, but you already know about that."

"Sean—"

"He's telling the truth," Samantha said, her gaze meeting her brother's, a secret hanging between them. With a chilling start, Claire was reminded of the secrets she'd shared with her sisters.

"How would you know?" Claire asked her daughter.

"I go through his room."

"You what?" Sean whispered in quiet fury.

Samantha lifted a shoulder. "All he's got is some condoms, a couple of *Playboy*s, and a lighter."

"You sneaking little creep!" Fists clenched in frustration, he crossed the room and loomed over her. "You had no right to go through my things! You stay out of my room, or I'll read that damned diary you think is so secret."

"Don't you ever—"

"Stop it!" Claire ordered, realizing they were getting nowhere. "Enough! Both of you—stay out of each other's things." Then, to lighten the mood, she added, "That's my job. If there's any snooping, I'll be the one to go through drawers and closets and secret hiding places—"

"Oh, sure," Sean mocked.

"Try me."

Yanking the rubber band from her ponytail, Samantha checked her face in the mirror and scowled at a pimple as she shook out her hair. "Well, I'm glad we're moving. I'm sick of everyone staring at me and saying all those lies about Dad."

Give me strength! Crossing her arms under her chest, Claire leaned a hip against the bureau for support. "What lies?"

"Candi Whittaker says that Dad is some kind of weirdo, that he did something nasty with Jessica Stewart, but I told them they were wrong; that Jessica used to be Sean's girlfriend."

Sean groaned and turned his back on his sister.

"And what did Candi say to that?" Claire hardly dared ask.

"She laughed—a real creepy laugh, it gave me the willies—and then she told Tammy Dawson that I was in a classic case of denial and that she should know because her father's a psychiatrist." Samantha's gaze was troubled, but she lifted her chin, refusing to be beat down by what she assumed were lies about her father. "It's not true, is it?" Her voice was suddenly so small, her fingers lacing and unlacing in worry. "Daddy didn't do something awful with Jessica, did he? That isn't why you left him?"

Claire's heart sank. Biting her lip, she fought an onslaught of fresh, hot tears and took Samantha into her arms. Sick inside, she admitted the truth. "Daddy and I had lots of problems, you know that."

"Everyone does. You said so." Doubt cracked Samantha's voice. Her blond head, so recently proud, bowed.

"That's true, honey. Everyone does. But—"

"No." She tried to wiggle away, to hide from the truth, but Claire decided that there was no time like the present, especially if Samantha's friends were giving her a bad time.

"But it's also true that Jessica says she and Daddy were . . . well, were intimate."

Samantha's body began to tremble violently. "Intimate?"

"Meaning that he fucked her," Sean clarified.

"No!"

"Sean, hush!" Claire clung to her daughter. "Don't use that kind of language around this house—"

Samantha's eyes were wild. "But he didn't, did he? Daddy would never, ever—"

"Whatever happened, you have to have faith in your father," Claire heard herself saying, though the words rang like the hollow sound of a lonely bell. She'd lost faith in Paul a long time ago; she'd given up on him and their sham of a marriage years before. She'd only stuck it out for the kids. Now that seemed like a cruel, disgusting joke. Her children would forever bear these scars. "Daddy and I were already separated when . . . well, when Jessica said that it happened."

"You're saying that Jessica lied?" Samantha asked, hope in her tiny voice.

"No way!" Sean sneered. "I walked in on them. They were humping like dogs in heat!"

"Stop it, Sean!"

"No!" Samantha shook her head violently. "No! No! No!"

"Honey, I'm just telling you what Jessica is saying." Claire's throat was suddenly raw with the pain her daughter felt.

"But why?" Samantha's voice was an octave higher than normal.

"Because she's a slut, and he's a pervert."

"I don't know," Claire said. "Sean, I don't want to hear another word—"

"No! It's not true!" Samantha's body stiffened, and she pushed Claire away. "I don't believe you!" She ran to the door. "You're a liar, Sean, a creepy, lowlife liar!"

The door banged shut behind her, and Claire whirled on her son. "That was uncalled for."

"That was the truth."

"There are kinder ways—"

"Yeah, like letting Candi Suck-Up Whittaker rub Sam's nose in it! Face it, Mom, Dad's a sex fiend who likes young girls. Samantha's better off knowing the truth. That way she won't get hurt anymore."

"Won't she?" Claire whispered under her breath as she ran after Samantha through the house, out the front door, and down the street. A hot breeze turned the leaves of the aspen trees, causing them to shimmer in the sunlight, and somewhere behind the neighbor's house a dog was barking fiercely. Claire dashed down the sidewalk, dodging a tricycle and a bump in the walk where the roots of a tree had buckled the cement, all the while chasing after her daughter. Samantha was sobbing, her golden hair streaming behind her, her long legs running fast, as if she could leave the horrid words and accusations back in the house.

Running away. Just like you, Claire. But you can't run. Sooner or later the past catches up to you.

At Center Street, Samantha ran against the light and a pickup squealed to a stop, narrowly missing her. Claire's heart stopped and she screamed. "Watch out!" *No. No. No.*

"Hey, kid, watch where you're goin'," the driver barked, a cigarette wobbling in the corner of his mouth.

Heart pumping with fear, Claire held out her hand and ran in front of his rig.

"What the hell—"

"Samantha, wait, please," Claire yelled, but Samantha didn't even glance over her shoulder.

"Friggin' idiots!" The truck roared off.

Breathing hard, Claire caught up with her daughter a block away from the park. The sun was blistering, blinding as it reflected off the sidewalk and fenders of cars parked along the street. Tears tracked down Samantha's red cheeks.

"Oh, baby," Claire whispered. "I'm sorry."

"You should have told me," Samantha charged.

"I didn't know how."

"I hate him!"

"No, you can't hate your father."

"I do! I hate him." She swallowed hard, and as Claire reached for her, she yanked away. "And I hate you, too."

"Oh, Sami, no—"

"Don't call me that!" she nearly squealed and Claire realized Paul had always called Samantha by her nickname.

"All right."

Sniffing loudly, Samantha rubbed the back of her hand under her eyes. "I'm glad we're moving," she said, blinking rapidly. "Glad."

"So am I—"

"Oh, no!" Her face suddenly drained of color. Abruptly Samantha turned around, facing the other direction, willing her body to stop shaking. Claire glanced over her shoulder and saw Candi Whittaker, a slim girl with a tiny waist and breasts no decent twelve-year-old should own, sauntering up the street with another girl Claire didn't recognize. At the sight of Samantha and her mother, both girls stared, swallowed smiles, and began to whisper. Claire used her body as a shield, blocking the little snips' view of her daughter, waiting until they'd taken a path that wound past the tennis courts and stopped looking over their small, self-righteous shoulders.

"It's all right. They won't bother you. Come on." Claire ushered Samantha back along the street, leading her home. Sean was probably right; moving wouldn't solve their problems. They couldn't run away. She'd tried that once before a long time ago and the past seemed to forever chase her, nipping ferociously at her heels.

Now, it had finally caught up to her. She didn't tell Samantha or Sean that there was another reason they were moving back to Oregon, a reason she didn't want to face. But she had no choice. Her father, a rich man used to getting his way, had called last week and demanded that she return to Lake Arrowhead, a place that brought back so many nightmares she couldn't begin to count them.

She'd protested, but Dutch hadn't taken no for an answer, and she had no choice but to agree. He knew of her trouble with Paul and had promised to help her relocate, put in a good word with the school district, let her live rent-free in the huge house where she'd grown up, give her a hand as she struggled to find her footing as a single mother.

She would have been a fool to say no, but there was something more that bothered her, a dark tone in his voice that caught her attention and caused the hairs on the back of her neck to rise.

Dutch had intimated that he knew something about the past—not all of it—but enough to convince her that she had to face him as well as what had happened sixteen years ago. So she'd agreed to meet with her father, though her stomach revolted at the thought.

"Come on," she said to Samantha. "Everything's going to be okay."

"It can't be," Samantha grumbled.

You're so right, sweetheart. "We'll make it right. You'll see." But even as she said the words, she knew they were lies. All lies.

Tessa flipped on the radio and felt the warmth of summer stream through her short hair as her Mustang convertible raced through the Siskiyou Mountains near the Oregon border. The northern California landscape was sun-bleached and desolate, the hills dry. She'd been driving for hours and would have to stop soon, or her bladder would burst from the beer that she'd sipped all the way from Sonoma. An icy bottle of Coors was cradled between her bare legs, the sweat from the glass cooling her skin and soaking the hem of her shorts. Open containers of alcohol were illegal. Drinking and driving was illegal. Well, for that matter most of the fun in life was either considered illegal or immoral. Tessa didn't really care. Not now, when she, at her father's behest, was returning to Lake Arrowhead.

Dread skittered down her spine. The old man had always tried to put the fear of God into her and sometimes succeeded. Nonetheless she rebelled. Just wait 'til old Dutch caught a glimpse of her latest tattoo.

"Bastard," she muttered as the radio crackled and groaned. She punched button after button and heard only screeches and static, as the canyons were steep, the stations distant, the only station she could get played oldies, ancient rock and roll. Right now Janis Joplin was screeching through the speakers. My God, the woman had been dead for years, had passed into the next world, whatever that was, long before Tessa had any interest in music, but today the hard-driving rock and gravelly voice of Joplin touched Tessa in a dark, private spot. Janis sang as if she knew pain—real gut-wrenching agony. The kind of anguish Tessa lived with daily.

Music pounded through the car.

Tessa took a long tug from her bottle and reached into her fringed purse for a pack of cigarettes.

Take a,
Take another little piece of my heart now, darlin'
Break a,
Break another . . .

That's it, she thought. Break another piece of my heart. Hadn't all the men she'd ever trusted? Tessa slid the Virginia Slims between her lips and punched in the lighter. Images of her past drifted behind her eyes and her adolescence crept into her subconscious. Her foot eased down on the gas pedal and the speedometer needle crowded ninety, way over the legal limit, but she didn't notice, didn't care. She was swept away in the tormented current of the past, dammed so long in her subconscious that she wasn't really sure what was real and what was fantasy.

The lighter popped out and Tessa lit up, smoke curling from her nostrils to be sucked away by the racing wind as the Mustang roared up the freeway.

Didn't I make you feel . . .

Janis was still wailing as Tessa drained her beer, chucked the bottle out of the car, and heard glass shatter over the thrum of the engine. Joplin's voice faded. Jesus, if only she could find another station. One with music from the *current* century. Hip hop or rap or techno. Too bad her CD player was busted.

Shoving her sunglasses onto the bridge of her nose with one finger, Tessa drove with her knee. Then she steeled herself. In less than six hours, she'd have to face her family for the first time in years. Her stomach knotted. Dutch, when he'd called her apartment, had sworn that both Tessa's sisters would be waiting for her at Lake Arrowhead.

"Prick," she mumbled, flipping the butt of her cigarette onto the freeway. Claire and Miranda. The romantic and the ice princess. It had been years since Tessa had seen them together, since they'd huddled, shivering and dripping, as they'd sworn that they would never divulge what had happened in the murky waters of the lake that night.

Shaking, she reached behind her, snapped open the lid of the cooler, her fingers surrounding the neck of another bottle of Coors standing at attention in the packed ice. Then she thought better of drinking any more alcohol. Soon she'd reach the border. It was time to sober up. And, she decided as another morbid song from the sixties cranked up, time to face the damned music of a song that was written long ago and just kept playing over and over in her head.

"He was here again," Louise announced as she stuck her head into Miranda's tiny office.

Miranda's skin crawled. "Who?" But she knew the answer and it bothered her. A lot. Despite her outward bravado, she had her own fears, her own demons to deal with and the thought that she could possibly have a stalker struck to the very core of her terror. Though she appeared tough on the outside, Miranda knew that any psych student who took a peek at her relationships with men would note that she had "issues." Make that "major issues." Her back teeth gritted though she managed a smile.

"The same creep who's been dogging you for the past three days." Miranda's stomach tightened as Louise edged in, straightened Miranda's framed law degree that forever tilted on the wall, then slouched against the single file cabinet jammed into the corner. A smooth-skinned black woman with almond eyes and a keen intelligence, Louise had been working as a secretary in the Multnomah County DA's office for the past four years. Now, Louise's eyes were dark with concern.

Which only upped Miranda's fear factor.

She hadn't set foot in her cubicle of an office all afternoon and had only stopped by to pick up some papers. For most of the day, she'd been talking with the medical examiner or briefing Denise Santiago on the Richmond murder case. It was funny how she could deal with crimes on a daily basis, brutal, horrible crimes against people and property with a fierce doggedness that didn't expose any of her own personal fears, but the thought of one man following her brought images from her past, painful, severe images that she had buried for years, straight to the fore.

"Who is this guy?" she wondered aloud and fought the dread that settled like lead in her stomach as she packed away a sheaf of handwritten notes in her briefcase. She caught a glimpse of a picture she kept on the corner of her desk—her favorite snapshot of her two sisters and herself. It had been taken long ago, when she had been an innocent fifteen. Three girls at the brink of adolescence, their arms linked together as they stood on a windswept boulder high above the angry gray waters of the Pacific Ocean. Their faces were ruddy, their smiles sincere, their spirits as free as the gales that had tugged at their hair, blowing the strands in front of their eyes. A lifetime ago. A naive age that could never be recaptured. She snapped her briefcase shut.

"I wish I had some idea who he is."

Louise lifted a shoulder. "Don't have a clue. But my guess is he's bad news."

"This is the district attorney's office for crying out loud. We're not that far from the police station. There are dozens of cops all around. How does he get in?"

"Like everyone else—through the front door. That's the trouble with a public building, you know. It's bought and paid for with tax dollars and allows any idiot inside." Louise crossed her arms over her ample chest. "Petrillo doesn't like this guy nosing around any more than I do. He told me to contact him the next time the mystery man shows up."

Frank Petrillo was a detective who had been with the department for more years than Miranda. Recently divorced and the father of two kids, he didn't see as much as he wanted to, he'd been asking Miranda out for the past three months. So far, they'd only shared a pizza after working late one night. That was as involved as Miranda wanted to be. She didn't date anyone she worked with. It was her personal, unwritten but never-broken law.

"I just don't understand why he doesn't leave his name or number—why he keeps missing me." Her desk was still messy, a few files piled on one corner, reference books open near her computer monitor, a half-full cup of coffee gone cold where she'd left it near her calendar.

"You ever thought he's one of those stalkers?"

Of course she had. "He's too close. Taking too many risks."

"Fits a stalker's M.O., if you ask me."

Miranda plucked her raincoat from a hook on the back of the door and slung the coat over one arm. "Tell me about him."

"This is the third time he's been in." Louise held up three slim fingers. "He was here yesterday and the day before. Won't leave his name, and when I suggest he talk to someone else, he seems to disappear."

"What's he look like?" She'd never asked before; hadn't had the time or the interest, but the man was starting to get on her nerves— worry her a little.

"That's the kicker," Louise said, showing off even white teeth in her first smile of the afternoon. "He looks like he could have stepped off the pages of a Marlboro ad. You know the kind. Rugged, not polished, black hair, gray eyes that don't smile much. Intense. Six feet, maybe six-one or -two, lean and always dressed in jeans and a shirt—no tie, just some kind of leather jacket that's seen better years."

"So he doesn't scare you?"

"Not really, but then I don't scare easily," Louise said, her smile fading. Miranda thought about Louise's ex-husband, a man who had battered her, threatening her life for several years, before Louise had found the strength to get out and walk away from a violent marriage. "But there's something about him I don't trust. When he couldn't get past me, he stopped by Debbie's desk, leaned his hips against it, smiled, and turned on the charm."

"He had some?" Miranda asked.

"Yeah—a little. If you like men who can turn it on at will—crooked smile, dimple, all at once Mr. Hard-As-Nails is the Boy Next Door. That's what's scary about him, if you ask me. Anyway, he started asking Debbie all sorts of questions. About you. Personal questions. She couldn't answer 'em, of course, was practically tongue-tied around the man, and when I strolled over, he made a quick exit."

"Maybe he's a reporter." Slinging the strap of her purse over her shoulder, Miranda hauled her briefcase from the desk.

"Then why not leave a card? A phone number? Make a damned appointment? Huh? I'm telling you, girl, there's something not right about this guy. He's not on the up-and-up."

"We get a lot of those around here."

Louise shook her head. Black curls glistened under the harsh fluorescent lights. "No, we don't, honey, not in the DA's office, and even though the guy doesn't look like a crazy with a gun, you can't be too careful these days."

"Petrillo's checking him out, though, right?"

Louise lifted a shoulder. "Trying to."

"Don't worry about it," Miranda said, pausing at the door. "I've got a few days off. Maybe whoever he is, he'll give up and crawl back under the rock he calls home."

"Like Ronnie Klug did."

The muscles in the back of Miranda's neck tightened, and she nearly missed a step. Inadvertently, she touched her throat, felt the tiny trace of a scar, then let her hand drop.

"I don't think—"

"This could be another guy you sent to prison, Randa. You've been at this job long enough that some of those boys are getting out now."

"The man who was here is an ex-con?"

"I don't know. Doesn't look like it, but you can't ever tell. Remember Ted Bundy? Good-looking. Charming. A real lady-killer."

Couldn't argue with that kind of logic. "Point well taken."

"Okay. So Petrillo's looking through mug shots of every guy or boyfriend of a woman you sent away. Trouble is, the list is pretty long."

"Besides, you can always reach me on my cell phone or e-mail."

"By then it might be too late."

"Look, Louise. Don't lose any sleep over it, okay? Just because a guy comes snooping around—"

"Is reason enough to be worried. This man looks determined, the kind of person who doesn't give up without one helluva fight. I'm telling you, Miranda, watch that back of yours while you're on vacation."

Vacation. If Louise only knew what Miranda was really doing— where she was going.

Miranda wasn't usually a woman prone to a case of nerves, but Louise's worries, plus the mention of Ronnie Klug, had gotten to her. Ronnie Klug and his twelve-inch knife.

The fact that she was leaving town for a meeting—no, make that command performance—with her father didn't help ease the knots in her stomach as she made her way to her car. Dutch Holland was used to getting his way, from his ex-wife and children as well as his hundreds of employees. And now, for some unknown reason, he wanted to see his firstborn.

Throwing her briefcase and coat into the trunk, she took one sweeping glance around the parking garage, then peered through the window and into the backseat of her Volvo. No one appeared to be lurking in the corners. No sinister figure in the shadows. Thank God.

Miranda slid behind the wheel and tried to ignore a blistering headache that was beginning to pound at her temples.

Within minutes she edged into traffic crawling steadfastly out of the city. The air-conditioning unit in the car was on the fritz, so she rolled down the window and studied the trunk of a Buick she was following. A gust of breathless summer air raced into the warm interior. She caught a glimpse of her reflection in the rearview mirror. Not a pretty sight. Her lipstick had faded, her mascara rubbed off, and a network of tiny red lines was visible in her eyes. Her hair, pulled back into a tight knot at the base of her skull, was beginning to come loose. "Great," she muttered, switching lanes as she yanked her hair free and tossed the thick rubber band onto the seat next to her. "Just great."

Who was the guy who'd been asking questions about her, and why was he nosing around now, when all hell seemed to be breaking loose? When her father, curse him, had decided to yank on his patriarchal strings again? When her life was falling apart?

"Pull yourself together," she told herself; she couldn't afford to fall apart. Not now. She'd worked too hard to get where she was, climbed up the ladder in the DA's office one hard-fought rung at a time and suffered her share of emotional as well as physical hardships in the process. One mysterious guy loitering around wasn't going to get to her. She wouldn't, couldn't allow it. She'd spent too many years feeling victimized, spent too much money on shrinks to finally put her past behind her, kept her secrets far too long to lose it all now.

Nor was the summons from dear old Dad—a curt phone message left on her answering machine going to be her undoing. Running the fingers of one hand through her hair, massaging her scalp and letting the wind unwind the tangled strands, she drove steadily west, into the setting sun.

Dutch Holland had ordered her to meet him at the family home by the lake of all places. She had thought that the old lodge had been boarded up for years, hoped that the slipcovers and sheets that had been draped over the furniture would never be removed, prayed that the secrets hidden away in that monstrosity of a cabin would be buried forever.

"Too bad," she muttered under her breath as she braked for a road construction crew that was packing up for the day. She maneuvered around the orange cones as one of the crewmen tossed a shovel into the back of a tar-spattered truck. A flagger—a woman in a fluorescent orange vest— paused to light a cigarette before stepping into the vehicle.

Miranda squinted against the sun. A bothersome thought bored its way into her mind. Was it possible that the mystery man who had shown up asking questions in her office was somehow connected to the summons from her father? Or was it just a coincidence that he appeared about the same time her estranged family began making demands again?

No way. Miranda Holland had been working for the law too long to believe in coincidence.

CHAPTER 3

"It's now or never." *So why not never?*

Miranda turned off the Volvo's engine and heard it tick as it cooled. Through the bug-spattered windshield, she saw the placid water of the lake and she bit her lip. In her mind's eye she was eighteen, dripping wet, scared to death, and lying through her chattering teeth. "Oh, God," she whispered, and dropped her head for a second, resting her forehead on the steering wheel. She hadn't been back here since that summer.

"Get a grip." She couldn't fall apart now. Not after all the years she'd spent making something of herself, proving to her father and the world that she was more than Dutch Holland's daughter.

Grabbing her purse and coat, she climbed out of the car, then walked along the path leading to the wide front porch that skirted the lodge. She rapped sharply on the front door, then didn't wait for a response. She tried the knob and the latch gave way. Suddenly she was in the house where she'd grown up, and dozens of memories tripped through her mind. Innocent memories of a pampered childhood with her two sisters, absent father, and distracted mother. Darker images from her adolescent years when she alone knew that her parents' marriage was disintegrating, that whatever love they'd shared had slipped through their fingers. And finally that dark, fateful night when all their lives had been altered forever.

As she walked through the foyer, she was assailed by the scents of pine and solvent, wax and detergent. Hardwood floors gleamed to a soft patina as lamps, freshly dusted, cast pools of light on the newly waxed oak.

"Dad?" she called, running her fingers along the railing of the stairs that climbed three floors. There had once been a graceful wooden salmon arching upon the final post, but the fish, and all the other creatures that were carved into the railing, had been hacked away years before. Now only the scarred post remained.

"Back here." Just the sound of his voice caused her throat to constrict a little. For the first eighteen years of her life it had been her mission to please him, to prove to him that she was just as good as any son he might have sired. He had never bothered to hide the fact that he'd wanted boys—strong, strapping sons to someday take over the business—and Miranda had attempted to fill the void caused by the lack of male heirs. Of course, all her attempts had been a futile waste of time.

Fist clenched around the strap of her purse, she marched through the wide front hallway toward the main room in the back of the lodge, a room with a ceiling that soared three stories and boasted a wall of glass that overlooked the smooth waters of the lake.

Her father was seated in his favorite chair, a leather recliner placed strategically near the cold hearth of the fireplace. Dressed in a suit and tie, crisp white shirt, and shoes polished to a blinding gloss, he didn't bother to rise, just cradled his drink as he leaned back and watched her enter. A newspaper lay open on the table next to his chair, and all the furniture, long draped, was uncovered. Even the grand piano on which she'd taken years of lessons was poised in the corner, as if ready for gifted hands to float over the keys and fill this old lodge with music again.

"Miranda." Dutch's voice was rough and cracked a little. "You look just like—"

"I know, I know." She forced a smile. "More like Mom every day."

"She was—still is, I imagine—a beautiful woman."

"Should I take that as a compliment?" she asked, and wondered what it was he really wanted after all these years, when her contact with him had been sporadic at best.

"Do."

His eyes were serious, but sparkled just a little as he waved her toward one of the high-backed chairs facing him. "You were always the prompt one. Pour yourself a drink and sit down."

She wasn't so easily put at ease. "The prompt one?" Tossing her coat over the back of the couch, she asked, "What's this all about?" Crossing her arms under her breasts, hoping to appear cool and professional, not a little lost child of twelve who had overheard the horrid arguments between her parents, she wondered why, when she wasn't intimidated by harsh judges, oily defense attorneys, or hardened criminals, this one man could shake her confidence as no one else ever could. Most of her life Miranda had tried and failed to please her father. Only recently had she quit beating her head against the wall by seeking his approval. Only in the past few years had she finally come to terms with her relationship with him and become her own woman. She didn't really give a damn if he approved of her or not.

But still she'd come running. And she was nervous.

"I need to talk to you girls."

"Girls? Plural?" She lifted an eyebrow. This was news. Worrisome news.

"Claire and Tessa will be here shortly."

"Why? What's going on?" A prick of guilt pierced her brain. What if he were dying? Struggling against disease? But as she stared down at the robust man in the oxblood recliner, she dismissed her concerns. His face was tanned, his blue eyes clear as a June morning as they looked at her above half-glasses that sat on the end of his nose. His hair, thick and always coarse, was no longer brown, but peppered with gray that lightened perceptibly at his temples. Aside from a thickening of his waist, he appeared as healthy as ever. And just as untrustworthy.

Twin car engines whined. Tires crunched on old gravel. Doors slammed in unison.

Dutch's smile was tight. "Your sisters."

He was right. In a clatter of footsteps and a murmur of hushed voices, Miranda's two siblings entered the house and, soon thereafter, the living room. Claire, tall and thin, with reddish-brown hair clipped away from her face, jeans and a cotton sweater, looked anxious, as if she'd lost more weight. Tessa, the youngest and always the most daring, wore a cocky smile. Her tangled blond hair was spiked and way beyond sun-bleached. A long voile dress—dark purple that was sheer enough to show off her legs when she walked in front of the light—billowed around her. Suede boots decorated with beads encased her feet and climbed halfway up her calves. Around her right forearm a band of barbed wire had been permanently tattooed or burned into her skin. A dozen earrings glittered along one ear.

"Randa!" Claire's smile was filled with relief, Tessa's suddenly more guarded.

Hugging her sister close, Claire whispered, "What's up?"

"Beats me," Miranda mouthed back.

Claire, nervous to the point that she hadn't been able to eat, rubbed the chill from her arms. The last few days had been torture. She wondered about Sean and Samantha—tucked in a tiny motel room in a town even smaller than the one they'd left in Colorado. Worried, she glanced at her watch and hoped to God that whatever Dutch had planned wouldn't take long.

"How are the kids?" Randa asked, as Tessa paced the perimeter of the room.

If I only knew. "As well as can be expected, considering." Claire had never been much of a liar. "To tell you the truth, it's been hell. Paul was involved—"

"It'll be all right," Miranda said. Just like Randa. Always in charge. Always cool. Always soothing troubled waters.

"I hope so." Claire pushed her hair away from her face. "Sean isn't crazy about moving away from his friends."

Tessa snorted. "He'll get over it. I did."

"Did you?" Dutch snapped the recliner up and climbed to his feet. He didn't so much as lift a finger to touch his daughters.

Theirs had not been a demonstrative family; the girls hadn't hugged or brushed a kiss across his cheek in more than a decade. Which was just fine with Claire. "Now that you're all here, we may as well get down to business," he said, motioning toward a portable cart laden with unopened bottles. "The bar is stocked if you're thirsty, and there's some sort of tray in the kitchen—fruit, cheese, smoked salmon, and crackers, that kind of nonsense."

No one took a step toward the swinging doors that led out of the room.

"This place gives me the creeps," Tessa announced, eyeing the paneled walls now barren of any decoration. Their mother's artwork, so liberally sprinkled throughout the house while they were growing up, had disappeared. And the heads of wild beasts— cougar, buffalo, antelope, wolf, and bear— so proudly displayed in bygone years, must have migrated upstairs to the attic or been sold. No snarling animal dared gaze through glass eyes from these old walls any longer.

Impatience marred Dutch's expression. "The lodge gives you the creeps?" he growled. "Hell, Tessa, you grew up here."

"Don't remind me." She flopped onto the couch, dropped a huge leather purse into her lap, and scrounged around for a pack of cigarettes.

"If you're not going to have a drink or some food, you may as well sit down." Dutch waved his other daughters into chairs, and Claire reminded herself that she wasn't a girl of ten getting a lecture. She was a full-grown woman, an adult, with a life of her own, in shambles though it might be. "You probably want to know why I asked you all to come here."

"Not me. I know why." Tessa shook out a cigarette and lit up. She shot a stream of smoke from the corner of her mouth. "This is some kind of power trip." Leaning back on the couch, she flung one arm over the soft cushions. "It always is with you."

Claire inwardly cringed. Why did Tessa make everything a battle? From the day she'd been born, she'd challenged her parents. Didn't she notice the wash of color ride up her father's neck and stain his cheeks, the sharpening of his gaze?

"This time, Tessa, you might be right," he conceded with a wide, well-practiced grin; the same smile Claire had witnessed as a child whenever he had come home and told his wife about his most recent deal, a scheme that was certain to make him millions, a business venture that would put that bastard Taggert in his place. Dutch took a sip of his drink. "I've been approached to run for governor come the next election."

The news settled quietly.

No one said a word.

Smoke curled to the ceiling from the cigarette momentarily forgotten in Tessa's hand.

Claire could barely breathe. An election? Complete with staff, reporters, and voters examining every minute of Dutch's life—his children's lives? Prying into any rumor, any bit of gossip? Oh, no, not now . . .

"This has been coming for quite a while. Several people want me to run and are willing to back me. I've only held off because . . . well, frankly, I'm not sure what I'm up against— not my opponent, you understand, but what kind of a toll an election will take on the family, on you girls, on your mother, and on me. But that's not really what's stopping me. It's the scandal that worries me."

Miranda, perched stiffly in an overstuffed chair asked, "What scandal?"

Claire swallowed hard and focused on her older sister. *Don't do this!* She shook her head slightly, barely moving, just enough to get Miranda's attention and silently beg her not to push the issue. Clearing her throat, Tessa stared off into the distance, as if looking through the sun-glazed windows, but was, Claire suspected, lost in her own memories—her own private hell.

Dutch sighed. "You know what scandal," he said. "Look, I'm not lily-white myself—got a few skeletons in my own closet, but nothing like the one you girls have been hiding for the last sixteen years."

Claire's blood turned to ice. So this was it. Her palms began to sweat.

Dutch settled back into his chair and tented his fingers under his chin. "Like it or not, the whole sordid mess is going to come out. Besides, I have personal enemies who will do anything in their power to see that I fail in my run for governor: enemies like Weston Taggert. There's another problem. His name is Kane Moran—you all probably remember him." He didn't wait for an answer, but Claire's heart already pumping fast, began an irregular cadence fed by fear. *Kane?* What could he have to do with anything? This was getting worse by the minute.

"Anyway, Mr. Moran is kind of a drifter, used to live around here as a kid. His dad was a mean son of a bitch who worked for me a long time ago and had an accident that put him in a wheelchair. The kid scraped by somehow, became a hotshot freelance journalist who's been all over the world, reporting on hot spots. He quit that kind of work last year after he was wounded and nearly killed in Bosnia, I think it was. So he's back."

"Here?" Claire asked, barely breathing.

"Now he's taken it upon himself to become a—" he waved impatiently. "Well, I'd call him a novelist because sure as I'm standing here he's going to be creating fiction, but he seems to deem our family important enough to write about. His book is gonna be one of those unauthorized exposé types."

"On us?" Miranda clarified.

"Well, yes, but specifically on the death of Harley Taggert."

Claire nearly swooned. She gripped the back of the couch for support. Thunder pounded in her ears.

Dutch's face lost all trace of humor. Lines of strain gouged the skin around his eyes as he settled back into his recliner. "So I don't want to be caught off guard, if you know what I mean. I've got to know what I'm up against here."

Don't lose it, Claire. Not now. Not after all these years. She swallowed hard. "I—we—don't know what you're talking about." She forced her gaze to meet her father's steadily even though inside she was withering like a vine deprived of water. Silently she cursed herself for never having learned the art of lying, a characteristic that would have come in handy over the years.

Dutch rubbed his chin. "I wish to God I could believe you, but I can't."

Here it comes. Claire braced herself, met her father's condemning stare, and forced herself to breathe.

Dutch gazed at each of his daughters in turn, as if looking long and hard enough, he could crack through the veneer of their innocence and see the ugly truth. "I want to know what happened on the night the Taggert kid died."

God help us. Sweet, trusting Harley.

"I think one of you girls was involved."

Claire let out a whimper of protest. "No—"

Dutch loosened his tie, but his gaze was fixed steadily upon his middle daughter. "You were going to marry him, weren't you?"

"What's the point of this?" Miranda cut in.

"Shit." Tessa drew on her cigarette. "I'm not going to sit here and listen to this crap." Hauling herself to her feet, she grabbed her purse, flung the butt of her Virginia Slims into the fireplace, and started for the door.

"Sit down, Tessa. We're all in this together." Dutch's jaw was rock-hard. "All I'm talking about now is damage control. I was hoping you girls would finally be straight with me, but I suspected you might not be, so I hired someone to help."

"What?" Miranda froze and Claire saw the fear on her sister's face. Miranda had worked so hard to protect them all. She'd come up with the story, the lies. Claire swallowed hard. Surely her private father couldn't have, wouldn't have brought an outsider in on this . . . oh, God . . . all of her hard-fought plans, all of the desperate nights, all of the tightly wound lies. They would all be found out and then . . . Oh, God, she couldn't think what would happen if the truth, so dark and murky, would ever see the light of day.

"You did what?" Miranda, ashen faced, demanded of Dutch.

Claire's head began to thunder again, echoing with a dizzying rush of sound.

"Denver Styles." He let the name sink in, though it held no meaning for Claire. But Miranda stopped short and for a second a shadow of fear passed behind her eyes. Quickly it disappeared as she seemed to get a grip on herself.

"Styles is a damned good private investigator. He'll find out what happened sixteen years ago and help me do whatever I have to do to keep it quiet, or at least tone it down." He reached for his drink. "So you girls have a choice. Either you come clean with me now, or you let Styles dig it up on his own. The first way will be the most painless, believe me." He swallowed the last of his scotch.

"You're out of your mind." Miranda shot to her feet. "The sheriff 's department concluded that Harley Taggert had a boating accident—no foul play, no suicide."

"'Course they did," Dutch said, his face mottling in anger. "Didn't you ever wonder why?"

Claire's stomach dropped to the floor. She didn't want to hear this. Not now. Not ever. Harley was gone; nothing could bring him back.

"Suicide? No one would have bought that." Dutch snorted at the absurdity. "The kid didn't leave a note and had no history of depression, so, you're right, the suicide idea didn't stick." His lips thinned.

"Didn't stick?" Claire repeated, suddenly catching a glimmer of what her father was hinting.

"Wait a minute. Are you suggesting that—what?" Miranda's eyes were wide and she slowly sat down again. "There was foul play and we"—she made a sweeping gesture to include her sisters—"were somehow involved?"

Dutch crossed to the bar and poured himself another drink. "The reason Taggert's death was ruled an accident was because I paid the sheriff's department off—a bribe not to investigate a possible homicide."

"What?" Claire's voice came out in a rush.

"Don't start talking like this," Miranda said.

"Worried?"

"You bet I am." Miranda, visibly bristling, walked to the windows and balanced her hips on the sill. "Accusations like this could ruin the reputation of the local sheriff's department."

"You're worried about Sheriff McBain losing his job? Hell, he retired, full pension, three years ago."

"It's more personal than that, Dad, and you know it. A story like this, linking my name to a . . . what, murder? Is that what you're really saying? It could jeopardize my career."

Ice clinked in his glass as he swirled his drink. "Possibly."

"And what about you? If you're serious about running for office, this could kill it. If anyone got wind that you tried to fix the Taggert case—"

"I'll deny it." Dutch's eyes blazed. "As for your precious career, it's already in jeopardy. Something about a botched prosecution of a known rapist?"

Some of the starch seeped out of Miranda. She felt her shoulders sag. Her father was right—at least partially. Bruno Larkin should be behind bars instead of walking free because of testimony that hadn't held up in court. The woman who had been raped, Ellen Farmer, a shy thirty-year-old who still lived with her parents, never dated, attended church regularly, and believed that sex outside of matrimony was a sin, had committed suicide after the second day of court. Miranda should have seen it coming. Without Ellen's testimony, the case was dropped, a sweet woman was dead, and Bruno walked. "You've made your point."

Dutch's gaze moved to include his other daughters. "Okay, now that we understand each other, let's get down to it. Which one of you was involved in the Taggert kid's death?"

"Oh for God's sake!" Tessa slung the strap of her purse over her shoulder. "As I said, I'm leaving."

Just then, the sound of an engine rumbled like damning thunder through the night.

Claire, pale, looked about to keel over. She cast a furtive glance in Miranda's direction and wiped her palms against the faded fabric of her jeans.

"This Denver Styles," Miranda said, still shaken. "Has he already been checking around? Has he stopped by my office asking questions?"

Dutch lifted a shoulder. "Don't know."

"I don't appreciate my private life being turned inside out by you or anyone else," she said, her stomach knotting so painfully she could barely breathe. "There was a time when you could tell us what to do, who to see, where to go, but that's over, Dad—"

A loud rap interrupted her, and she turned toward the sound.

"Door's open," Dutch yelled.

Miranda felt as if a vise were tightening over her lungs as footsteps rang through the hall and a man appeared: a tall, rangy man with wide shoulders, faded jeans, and a cocksure attitude that was evident in his walk. Beard stubble darkened his jaw and sharp cheekbones that hinted at some Native American ancestor slashed upward to eyes that were deep-set and eagle-sharp. In one swift glance, he had probably looked over the three women, sized them up, and pigeonholed each one.

"Denver!" Dutch rolled onto his feet, his hand outstretched.

The hint of a smile touched Styles's lips as he clasped Dutch's hand, but there was no warmth in his eyes. " 'Bout time you showed up. I'd like you to meet my daughters." He motioned to the sisters. "Miranda, Claire, Tessa, this is the man I told you about. He's going to ask you all some questions and you, girls, are going to tell him the truth."

CHAPTER 4

Miranda sized the guy up. She'd seen more than her share of lowlifes in her years with the department, and could smell a con man within seconds. This guy, hard-edged and quietly condemning, didn't have the usual odor, but there was something about him that smacked of insincerity and something else—something even more disturbing. She felt a touch of familiarity, as if she'd seen him before, but she couldn't place his face, and the feeling disappeared like morning fog touched by the warmth of the sun.

"I think Dad brought you into this on false pretenses," she said, crossing her legs and clasping her hands on her knee. His eyes flickered for a second to her calf, but his expression didn't change a bit. So he wasn't completely impervious. Good. "The story is—"

"I'm not interested in the story, Ms. Holland." His smile was coldly patient as he leaned a shoulder against the dark timber of the mantel. "I just want the truth."

Miranda matched his cool attitude with her own. "I'm sure you've already read the police reports and newspaper clippings or Dad wouldn't have hired you."

His black eyebrows rose a fraction.

A dark, numbing fear settled deep in the pit of her stomach as she repeated the story she'd told over and over again—to the deputies of the sheriff's department, to the nosiest reporters, to her family and friends. It was forever branded in her memory even though it was a bald-faced lie. She glanced at her sisters; Tessa, blond and belligerent, insolently smoking another cigarette while Claire's expression was hard to read, her skin pale. "The three of us"—she motioned to her sisters—"were on our way home from the drive-in movie on the other side of Chinook. We'd gone together to see a trilogy of old Clint Eastwood movies. It was late, after midnight. The movies hadn't started until sunset, which was after nine o'clock, I think. We left before the last picture was over. I was driving and dead tired and . . . I guess I fell asleep at the wheel, I don't remember skidding off the road, but the next thing I knew, the car was in the lake." She stared straight into Styles's disbelieving eyes. He wasn't buying this—not for a second. Still, she plunged on, stepping deeper into the muck of half-truths and lies. "The impact woke me up and Tessa and Claire were screaming their heads off. Water was filling up the inside of the car and we all had to swim out in the pitch-black . . . it was . . ." She shuddered and her voice became a whisper. "We were lucky, I guess. My car went off the road in only six feet of water, so we were able to help each other out and swim to shore."

Styles didn't say a word.

"It's not a mystery, Mr. Styles—"

"Denver. You'll be seeing a lot of me. No reason to keep tripping over names." A half smile, a false grin meant to disarm and encourage her to keep talking tugged at his lips, but those gray eyes never warmed to her, never so much as flickered with a touch of understanding. "I suppose your sisters would repeat, nearly word for word, the same story."

"It's not a story," Tessa interjected with a toss of her head.

"No one saw you at the drive-in." His dark eyebrows drew together, as if he were deep in thought. "Isn't that strange considering that you three are pretty high-profile, what with being from one of the wealthiest families in the area?"

"We didn't talk to anyone."

"No? Not even in the snack bar?"

"There wasn't a lot of people there. It was right before the drive-in theater closed for good."

"We took our own sodas," Claire said, her voice thin.

He rubbed his chin. "And you didn't get out of the car for what? Three or four hours? Not even to use the ladies' room?"

"I don't think so," Miranda replied before Claire could say anything else and get them all into bigger trouble.

"That's pretty unbelievable, don't you think?"

Her voice was calm, smooth as glass. "That's the way it was. Obviously there were a lot of other cars there, families and teenagers, but none around us that I recognized. As I told the sheriff's department a long time ago, there was a white station wagon with wood on the side—I don't know the make—with a family of kids, parked next to us. The space on the other side of my car was empty. In front of us was a pickup—dark-colored with a bank of spotlights stretched across the cab, and other than that I don't remember any other vehicle."

"And you were driving a black Camaro."

"That's right. It was totaled later that night. Just because no one the police spoke with that night had seen us doesn't mean there wasn't someone there who had. They just didn't look hard enough."

"The guy who sold tickets didn't remember your car."

"He was probably stoned. His memory wasn't all that great. If you read his deposition you'll see that he hardly knew the names of the movies that were playing." Her fists clenched and she had to force her fingers to straighten. If she'd learned anything in her years as a lawyer, it was how to hide emotion when necessary, how to bring it to the surface when needed. Right now the less knowledge Denver Styles scraped up about her and that hellish night, the better.

Dutch winced as he stood, then rubbed his knee. "The reason the police didn't find out much that night is because I bought 'em off."

"Dad, don't," she warned, incredulous even though he had already alluded to tampering with the investigation. To what lengths would her father go to get his way?

Claire let out a tiny, disbelieving gasp, and Tessa, always the cynic, rolled her eyes. "You never stop, do you?" Tessa demanded. "Jesus, Dad, you bribed the police?"

"I did what I had to do," he snapped as he walked across the room, his pace evening out as he reached the French doors and opened them, letting in a warm breeze. "I figured this was probably the single most important moment of all our lives and I thought—hell, I hoped I was saving you girls, your mother, yes, and me, a pile of grief."

"You didn't believe us." Miranda felt empty inside. Drained. The truth was sure to come out, every last painful and ugly detail.

"I couldn't and I wasn't about to take the risk that one of you would be exposed as that Taggert boy's killer."

Miranda's insides shook.

"His name was Harley," Claire said, lifting her chin. "It's been sixteen years, Dad. You don't have to refer to him as 'that boy' anymore." Standing proudly, she stared at her father, then her gaze moved past him, through the open door to the lake, and focused on whatever she saw in the distance, on the opposite shore.

"All I wanted to do was save your skins."

"And your reputation," Tessa said. "That's about the time Stone Illahee was opening the second phase, wasn't it? You couldn't risk that your new resort would be tainted with some sort of scandal. New golf course, indoor tennis courts, Olympic-size pool, gorgeous views, and major debt. What would happen if the word got out that Benedict Holland's, the owner's, daughters were involved in—"

"In an accident," Miranda said quickly. "You had so little faith that you bought off the investigation."

"That's right." Dutch was defensive, his bushy gray eyebrows pulling together. "Paid the sheriff's department to downplay the whole incident."

"Not smart," Styles observed.

"Hey, look, I wasn't planning on running for office then."

"But now you are and you want to dredge all this up again." Claire rubbed one temple with her fingers as she tried and failed to stave off a headache. "Why?"

"To beat Moran to the punch and divert him if I have to." He walked to the bar and motioned to the full bottles. "How about a drink?"

"Another time." Denver eyed Tessa. "You want to elaborate?"

"How?"

"See anyone you know at the movies?" His tone wasn't the least bit imperious, and yet Miranda felt an underlying challenge in his words.

"While you're pouring, Dad," Tessa said, as if sensing trouble, "*I'll* have a drink. Vodka straight up."

"I already told you," Miranda said, standing and crossing the room so that she could meet Styles's gaze more evenly. "You don't have to try and trip us up by pitting one of us against the other."

"Is that what I was doing?"

"You tell me."

"I just thought I should hear your sisters' sides of the story even though you've already primed them."

Claire, too, was on her feet. "Look, I don't really have time for this. I've got kids waiting for me. Miranda told you the truth, I don't have anything else to add."

"Oh, hell, Claire," Dutch growled. "Tell the man about Taggert. You ran around here mooning over the guy and had just announced that you were going to marry him. You've got a helluva lot more to say." He handed a drink to Tessa, who, a stubborn set to her jaw, walked to the window and rested her head against the glass.

Claire's stomach clenched. "It's true. I had hoped to marry Harley, though . . . it . . . it wasn't working out." She rubbed the back of one of her hands with the thumb of the other. "Everyone was against it because of a feud that existed between our families."

"He knows about the damned feud." Frowning darkly, Dutch fell into his chair again, raised the leg support, and took a sip from his glass.

Claire felt a chill even though it was still warm. Through the open door she noticed the sun was beginning to set, fiery pink-and-orange beams fractured against the underbelly of a few high clouds. She knew that Miranda had spoken first to remind her younger sisters of the lie they'd concocted, the altering of the facts to protect them all, but suddenly it seemed that their secret, woven tightly by each woman's determination to put that dark, ugly night behind them, was beginning to unravel and fray. "When I first met Harley, I mean, I'd known him all my life, but when I realized I was attracted to him, it was at the lake. He was going with another girl, Kendall Forsythe, at the time."

"The bitch," Tessa interjected, and received a harsh, warning glare from Miranda.

"Kendall—as in Weston Taggert's wife."

"Yes." Claire nodded. She wasn't going to let anyone, either her father or her older sister, dictate how she felt or what she said. Things had changed over the last decade and a half, and if she'd learned anything, it was that she had to speak up for herself and rely on her own judgment. For too many years she'd trusted other people—first her mother, then Harley, eventually Miranda, and finally Paul. "Dad might have told you that he thought the Taggerts had moved here with the express purpose of running him out of business, but that wasn't true."

Her father snorted. "Neal should have stuck to shipping up in Seattle."

"They moved down here in the fifties, I think," Claire continued, glancing from Miranda to Styles.

"Nineteen fifty-six." Dutch opened a glass humidor and fingered a cigar.

"Anyway, Dad took it as a personal insult that he'd have some competition."

"I knew it, that Harley brainwashed you!"

"Jesus, Dad," Tessa said, as Dutch bit off the end of his cigar and spit it into the fireplace. "You called us all up, insisted that we show up here and spill our guts, then when Claire tries, you start insulting her. I'm outta here." She tossed back her drink, snagged her purse, and headed for the door.

"No, wait—" Dutch shoved himself out of the recliner and wincing as he put weight on his bad knee, hurried after his youngest, bullheaded, daughter. But Tessa wasn't about to stay and be insulted. Within seconds an engine fired to life. Tessa's Mustang roared away.

"Go ahead," Styles said to Claire. His hands were forced into the pockets of his beat-up jacket, and he seemed less stiff and unbending than he had when he'd first entered. "What about the Taggerts?"

"They're originally from Seattle. As Dad mentioned, the family had some kind of shipping operation up there started by his great-grandfather, I think."

"Old Evan Taggert, Neal's grandfather," Dutch said, puffing on his cigar as he strode into the room again. Agitation caused a tic to quiver near his temple. "Sorry about Tessa. Sometimes she's a hothead, but she's staying at the resort—a suite in the north wing. You can call her later."

"I will," Denver said, then nodded toward Claire, urging her to continue.

"Anyway, Harley's dad wanted to do something different."

"Making millions shipping out of Puget Sound wasn't good enough, I guess," Dutch grumbled. "So he started buying all the cheap land on the Oregon coast he could get his hands on. You can't buy much beach property in Washington, it's all owned by the Indians—reservations, so Neal decided to horn in on my territory. The bastard envisioned himself as the premier developer of this stretch of land, settled himself and his family around Chinook."

"And in direct competition with you."

"You got it." Scowling, Dutch finished his drink and set the glass onto the table by his folded newspaper. "Scammed me out of a prime piece around Seaside. Built himself Sea Breeze right after I'd started construction of Stone Illahee." Dutch drew on his cigar until the ash glowed red. "Bastard."

"So how did you feel about Claire marrying into the Taggert family?"

"I hated it."

"How badly?"

Dutch's eyes narrowed on Denver. "Look, I didn't hire you to insinuate that I had something to do with the kid's death. Believe me, if I would have killed him, no one would think it was anything other than an accident."

"Stop it!" Miranda ordered.

"I can't listen to this another second." Claire was on her feet, her insides quivering. "I don't know what you thought you'd accomplish by hauling us all up here, but as far as I'm concerned it's over. Past history." She scrounged in her purse, found the keys, and started for the door.

"We have more to discuss," Dutch insisted, rising again from his chair.

Claire held a hand up as she left, cutting off any further protests. "Later."

"But I want you to stay here, at the house. I thought we'd agreed."

"It was a bad idea."

"Your kids need a home, Claire, not some cheap apartment that has no meaning for them. Here they can have the run of the place, we can get some horses again, they can canoe and swim. There's the lake, tennis courts, pool—"

"I can't be bought, Dad." But she hesitated. Her weak spot was her kids, and Dutch knew it.

"I'm not buying you. I'm just offering to help out. For Sean and Samantha's sake." She wanted to trust him, to believe that he was developing some latent grandfatherly feelings for his only grandchildren. "Your mother never liked it here, but you did. Of all the kids, you enjoyed living in this place."

That much was true. Still . . . she didn't want to take any handouts. They always came with a hidden price tag. For the first time in her life she was standing on her own two feet. "I don't think so, Dad."

"Well, don't make up your mind tonight. We'll talk later."

Turning, she let her gaze sweep through the house with its warm cedar walls, massive fireplace, and winding staircase with its mutilated posts. The house was stark now, only a few basic pieces of furniture and no decor, but she'd always felt a kinship with this old building; it had weathered more storms than she. "I'll think about it," she promised, hating the way the words seemed to give her father the upper hand again.

Miranda watched her sister leave and felt a withering sense of despair before she turned to face Dutch. "I think you're being a stubborn old fool."

"Good to know some things never change."

"Look, I agreed to come here even though I didn't have a clue as to what you wanted. Now, I think I've made a big mistake. This morbid fascination you have with Harley Taggert's death is beyond me. Let Kane Moran dig up whatever he can find and let it go." Turning slowly to face the latest in a long string of her father's yes-men and errand boys, she said, "Now, Mr. Styles, I have a question for you."

"Shoot." He didn't so much as smile.

"Someone's been hanging around my office, missing me but bothering my secretary and the receptionist."

"Have they?" He crossed his arms on his chest. His leather jacket creaked softly, and there was the glimmer of something other than grim determination in his eyes, a flicker of a deeper, more frightening emotion.

"Was it you?"

"You get straight to the point. I like that."

"You haven't answered my question," she reminded him, stepping closer, refusing to be intimidated. "Were you in the DA's office today?"

"Yep."

Disappointment burrowed deep into her heart. For some unnamed reason she didn't want this rangy, arrogant son of a bitch to be part of anything remotely sinister.

"Why didn't you wait or leave your name?"

"I thought it would be inappropriate."

"But hanging around the courthouse wasn't?"

His gray gaze, so like a winter storm brewing over the ocean, penetrated deep into hers. "What your father has me looking into is highly personal, don't you think? Something you wouldn't want your coworkers, subordinates, or supervisors to know about. I figured you wouldn't meet me at home, so I dropped in at your office."

"And grilled the receptionist."

"Just asked a few questions."

"Debbie talks too much," Miranda snapped, venting her anger. She didn't know who to start with. She'd just as soon wring Denver

Styles's neck as deal with him, and she felt an overwhelming need to tell her father to use his thick-skulled head and let sleeping dogs lie. As for Debbie . . . well, Debbie, sweet thing, couldn't help herself. Chitchat and flirting were ingrained deep into her personality. She'd never change. But what about Kane Moran? Why had he decided to come home now to stir up all this trouble?

"Randa—" Her father's voice, filled with a quiet reproach, caused her to second guess herself. As it always had. "I know that you're upset, expected you to be, but it's important that I know what I'm dealing with. A lot of people are banking on me. They've donated thousands of dollars to my campaign. I can't let even the breath of a scandal touch me."

"Then give it up, Dutch," she suggested as she plucked her coat off the back of the couch. "Because you and I both know there are so many skeletons rattling around in all the Holland family closets it's impossible to keep them locked away, let alone keep track of all the keys. Sooner or later, one of those scandal-riddled secrets is going to escape."

"Maybe, but everything else that's happened over the years is less distasteful—a dalliance here, a bad investment there, nothing substantial," he allowed, taking off his reading glasses and buffing them with the edge of his sleeve. "But when we're discussing the night Harley Taggert died, the night that Kane Moran is going to scrutinize, unfortunately, we're talking about murder."

If nothing else, the old man was predictable, Kane thought. He strode along the shores of the lake. Bleached wood and rocks were interspersed by sand that was cast silver with the faint glow of the moon. Clouds gathered, threatening to break into a storm. He brushed aside the branches of a few fir trees that hugged the shoreline and slapped him in the face.

Not a hundred feet ahead stood the Holland lodge, several windowpanes glowing brightly in the summer night. Just as Kane had expected, Benedict, Dutch to his "good ol' boy" friends, had rung up his daughters and dragged them back to their old lakeside home, probably to warn them of him, to tell them that whatever they did they were, at all costs, to keep their mouths shut. Kane had no idea how the old man had convinced the girls to return—probably it had to do with bribery, that was his usual M.O.—but judging from the cars that had come and gone, they were all back home, returning like the prodigal daughters they were.

Son of a bitch, his plan was working.

CHAPTER 5

"You really lived here when you were growing up?" Samantha eyed the old lodge as if it were a castle from a fairy tale. She ran up the stairs, explored each room, then stole up to the attic, where the servants had once lived, and clambered down the back stairs to the kitchen. "It's . . . it's wonderful." She grinned from ear to ear as Claire unpacked groceries.

"Tell it to your brother." Claire hitched her chin toward the kitchen window, where she watched Sean, who was flopped on an old porch swing, one toe touching the floorboards, his scowl dark as he squinted across the lake. Claire, too, stared across the blue water, and her heart skipped a beat as she recognized the cabin where Kane Moran had grown up. Someone had taken the trouble to reroof the cottage and give it a new coat of gray paint, and the sunlight glinted off some kind of vehicle parked haphazardly in the drive.

Claire's throat tightened. Was it possible that Kane had moved in? Her father hadn't mentioned where his nemesis had put down roots, but *someone* lived across the water. "Stop jumping at shadows," she reprimanded, and Sam, who was reaching for the doorknob, stopped short.

"What?"

"Just talking to myself. Go out and see if your brother's hungry. I can whip up a turkey sandwich or heat some pizza."

"He won't say anything," Sam said with a lift of her slim shoulder. "He's just a big grouch."

Amen, Claire thought, reaching into one of the sacks and stuffing a pint of strawberries into the refrigerator. At first she'd hesitated, not wanting to take her father's charity, but then she'd decided she was being selfish, that her children could heal here in this rambling house in the woods, perhaps even thrive. So she'd taken Dutch up on his offer and moved in. The house still looked bare. Her small amount of furniture plus what had been left years before couldn't begin to fill over twenty vast rooms. In the distance she heard the trill of a meadowlark and the soft rumble of a boat trolling in the lake.

"Well, here goes nothing." Samantha, having easily shaken the Colorado dust from her heels, was enthusiastic, glad for a change, whereas Sean hated his new life in Oregon and treated Claire as if she were an enemy, the person responsible for all his misery, which, of course, she was.

"I'll make some lemonade."

"It won't do any good, Mom," Samantha said with a knowledge far too wise for her tender years. "He *likes* being a jerk." She sauntered through the door, walked up to Sean, and though Claire couldn't hear the exchange of conversation through the closed window, she got the idea. Sean, arms folded over his chest, jaw thrust forward in silent accusation, didn't respond. Samantha threw a look over her shoulder and met her mother's gaze. She didn't have to say "I told you so." Claire read it in her eyes.

Great. Claire attempted and failed at avoiding hateful thoughts directed at her ex-husband. Sean needed a father figure in his life right now, a man who could straighten him out, and definitely not someone who thought any female over the age of fifteen was fair game. Shuddering, Claire put away the rest of the groceries and, from the corner of her eye, watched as Samantha skittered off to explore the woods near the lake. Sean stretched, cast his mother a bitter glance through the glass, and, as if he didn't want to be within ten feet of her, sauntered toward the stables, where three horses, two geldings and a mare, now resided, compliments of Dutch Holland.

She shut the refrigerator as someone rapped loudly on the front door.

Claire wiped her hands on a towel. Maybe Tessa or Randa had stopped by. It had been several days since the confrontation with Denver Styles in this very house, and she hadn't heard a word from either of her sisters. "Coming!" she yelled as she hurried through the hallway to the foyer. She threw open the door.

Kane stood on the porch.

Claire held on to the doorknob for support. Her heart took a fateful, stupid leap.

"Claire." One side of his mouth lifted in an arrogant but hauntingly familiar smile. Taller than she remembered, his features hardened by the passing years, he would never again be considered a boy. A breeze had the nerve to ruffle his hair—light brown, sunstreaked, and in need of a cut—while he stood, arms crossed over his chest, stretching a wheat-colored cotton sweater at the shoulders.

A vise seemed to clamp over her stomach, slowly turning and squeezing so hard she could barely breathe. He was the one man she had no right ever to lay eyes upon again, and he was here, standing on her front porch, as bold and brash as the wild, rebellious teenager he'd once been. "What're you doing here?"

"I thought I'd welcome you back to the old neighborhood."

"But you . . . you . . ." She caught hold of herself before she came across as the tongue-tied adolescent she'd once been— the rich girl he'd adored, the girl who had scorned him . . . well, for a while. She licked her lips and crossed her arms over her chest, as if protecting her heart. "Dad says you're writing some kind of tell-all book about him, about us, and about Harley and the night he died."

A dark cloud passed behind his gold eyes but was gone in an instant. "That's true."

"Why?"

His lips twisted cynically. "It's time."

"Because Dad's thinking of running for governor?"

A slight elevation of his eyebrows. "That's one reason."

"And the others?" Her hands were beginning to sweat.

His gaze narrowed, shifting for a second to her lips before returning to her eyes and settling there. Claire's heart thumped mercilessly. "I think I—we—owe it to Harley."

"You were hardly best friends."

Again that chilling smile. "The reasons for that run too deep to mention, don't you think?"

She swallowed hard against a throat so dry it ached. "What happened between us—" she said, then stopped, gathering herself. *Don't let him get to you. Not again.* "Was there something you wanted to say to me?"

"More than you'd want to hear. I figured your old man told you what I was up to and tried to make it look like I was on some kind of witch-hunt."

She nodded. "That's about the gist of it."

He snorted. "Okay, so there's some truth in the fact that I'd love to show good old Benedict that he's not above the law, that he can't always bribe his way out of a mess, that he's not goddamned royalty around here."

"Is there a point to this?"

He fingered the rough post that supported the roof. "I thought you should know that things have changed around here. Significantly. For one thing, Neal Taggert suffered a stroke a few years back. He's stuck in a wheelchair. Weston's in charge now."

Claire shuddered inwardly. Weston Taggert was the opposite of his younger brother. Tall, athletic, cocksure, and mean-tempered, Weston was the antithesis of all that was good in Harley.

"It's no secret that Weston's worse than Neal when it comes to hating your family. And his wife . . ."

"Kendall," Claire said, feeling as if the weight of the world had been dropped on her shoulders. They had a past, she and Kendall, a link because of Harley. And now Kendall Forsythe was married to Harley's older brother, a man who had stated publicly as well as privately that he'd like nothing better than to embarrass the hell out of Dutch Holland—then run him out of town.

"Seems like you and Weston are cut from the same cloth."

Kane's eyes flashed dangerously, and the skin over the bridge of his nose tightened a bit. He leaned closer to her and she took a small breath. "I have nothing against you or your sisters, you know that."

"I don't know anything about you, Kane, or why you're on this mission to destroy my family."

"Not the family. It's your father—"

"Who had nothing to do with Harley Taggert's death. You know, Dad thinks you're being paid by the Taggerts, and it wouldn't surprise me a bit." She tilted up her chin and gazed defiantly into eyes the color of expensive scotch. "I assume you're being paid a lot of money to paint my father as an ogre."

"This isn't about money."

"Sure it is. Big book deal, kickbacks from my father's political opponent, and a little pot sweetener from the Taggerts. Looks like you finally got what you wanted, Kane."

"That, darlin', is where you're wrong." He stared at her so intently she wanted to back away, was certain he'd reach out and grab her, yank her hard against him, but he didn't move. Instead his pupils dilated and the corners of his eyes squinted ever so slightly. "You know what I wanted a long time ago, what I couldn't have."

Her throat caught.

"That's right, Claire. Back then, I wanted you. I would have laid down and died if you would have just looked at me—really looked at me—as a person who loved you rather than as a curiosity, a onenight stand to experiment with, a tiny step onto the wild side when you had no one else to turn to—"

"Stop it! I don't know why you're here, why you've started dredging all this up again, but it's a mistake. Believe me. Leave this alone. Find some other dirty little scandal to expose, but just . . . just don't do this."

"Too late, darlin'. I've already got myself a deal."

"As I said. 'Money.'"

"Mom?" Sean, hearing the end of the conversation, appeared around the corner of the house. His eyes centered on the intruder before settling on his mother. "You okay?"

Oh, great! How much of the discussion had he heard? As if suddenly jolted by a current of electricity, she stepped away from

Kane, put much-needed distance between her body and his, and forced her quivering insides to settle. This was no time to lose a fraction of her composure. Not in front of her son. Not with Kane Moran.

"Your boy?" Kane asked.

"Yes, uh, this is Sean. Sean—Mr. Moran." Her voice sounded so much calmer than she felt.

"Glad to meet you," Kane said, walking up to Sean with his hand outstretched. "I knew your Ma when she was about your age."

"That's right. Kane was a . . . neighbor."

"My dad worked for your grandfather."

"So?" Sean wasn't impressed and his insolent *I-don't-give-a-damn* attitude was firmly in place.

"Lived right across the lake in that old cabin over there."

Sean couldn't help himself, his gaze wandered over the water to the thicket of fir trees and the tiny cottage nestled therein. "Doesn't look like much."

"Sean!"

"Well, it doesn't."

Kane didn't appear to take offense. He gave a stiff nod of agreement. "You're right. It wasn't then and isn't much better now. In fact I grew up humiliated and embarrassed that I lived in that dump. Avoided being there as much as possible."

Suspicion tightened the corners of Sean's mouth. He hadn't expected Kane to see things as he did.

"My old man was a cripple and a mean son of a bitch. I found ways to avoid being around him or hanging out at home, and usually managed to get myself into a mess of trouble. But I didn't really give a rip. I figured fate had given me a bum deal, and I spent a lot of time being angry at the world and a royal pain in the butt."

"All I said was that it doesn't look like much," Sean mumbled.

"And I agreed with you." He clapped Sean on the back, and the boy visibly jerked away. "You, now, you're lucky, living in a great big house like this."

Sean made a disbelieving sound in the back of his throat. "Yeah, right," he grunted as he glanced at his mother, seemed satisfied that there wasn't any serious trouble brewing, and vaulted over the rail to disappear around the corner of the house.

"What is it you want from me?" she asked when Sean was out of earshot.

"Same thing I've always wanted."

Her pulse jumped a little, and she had to remind herself that she was a grown woman, divorced, mother of two, someone unaffected by long-forgotten emotions. "I think you'd better go."

His lips clamped together in a hard, thin line. "You're right. I should. But I thought I'd give you the chance to tell me your side of the story."

"My side?"

"About the night Harley Taggert died."

"So we're back to that."

"Never left it. Despite everything that happened between us, you never told me the truth."

"Oh, God, Kane, I can't."

He pinned her with a hard glare, then, fleetingly, a hint of regret softened the edge of his jaw. "Look, Claire, I know this will be rough. Okay, so I'm the bad guy, but I'm doing this because it's time, and I've been given the opportunity, okay? Whatever happens, I want you to know that I'm not trying to hurt you or your sisters."

"Oh, thank God. *Now* I'm relieved," she said, unable to hide the sarcasm that crept into her words. "I'll finally be able to sleep at night."

"I thought you should know."

"And I think you should go to hell."

"Been there." Scratching his jaw, he eyed her for a long second. "See ya around, Claire. If you decide you want to tell me anything about that night, just give a yell. I'm right across the lake." Turning on his heel, he jammed his hands into his pockets and sauntered down a path to the boat dock, where tied to one of the bleached moorings was a small motorboat. Kane stepped aboard, cast off, started the engine, and, with a final wave, gunned the motor. The boat made a wide arc, leaving a frothy wake as it curved near the shoreline and headed back to the far side of the lake.

Claire's insides felt as if they were made of jelly. Why was Kane so insistent to dig up the past, why did he move back into the cabin he'd sworn to hate as a kid, and why, for God's sake, why did her traitorous heart beat a little faster just at the sight of him?

As it always had.

Because you're an idiot around men. Always have been, always will be.

Guilt caused her teeth to dig into her lower lip as she watched the wake disappear into the smooth, glassy surface of Lake Arrowhead.

Kane Moran had always been a thorn in her backside, a poor wild kid who'd once had a crush on her, and she'd spent most of her adolescence avoiding him. But it hadn't always been possible, and there had been times when she'd wondered if her devotion to Harley was the result of fear—a gnawing worry that she should cling to good and decent Harley because the Moran boy with his hang-the-law attitude and air of invincible recklessness had appealed to her on a baser, more primitive, level.

Kane Moran was bound by no rules.

He hated authority and spit in its face.

He was the ultimate rebel.

He was bad with a capital B.

And deep in her heart, Claire had found him irresistible. She'd spent nights on her knees praying that this indecent attraction to him, one that caused her blood to heat and her heart to trip-hammer, would pass before anyone—especially Kane himself—noticed. She told herself that when she woke up from dreams where Kane was performing all sorts of wildly delicious ministrations to her body, it was only whimsy, nothing to worry about. She swam lap after lap in the pool, trying to force him from her mind. But late at night, when the moon rose high, its silvery light spangling the black waters of the lake, Claire had sat on the window ledge in her bedroom with the sash thrown wide so she could feel the salt-laden breeze off the Pacific rush through her hair and press her nightgown to her body while she gazed across the dark expanse to the single light burning in the attic window of Kane's house. She had closed her eyes and imagined his hands and tongue caressing her sweat-soaked body. Stirrings deep inside her made her restless, and she knew that despite her vows to herself otherwise, making love to him would be an experience worth any risk on earth, a once-in-a-lifetime chance that would condemn her forever.

Now, years later, she looked across those same shadowy waters and felt long-buried yearnings deep inside, the pulsing want that had, as a girl, kept her from sleeping. She clutched a hand to her throat and hoped history wasn't so foolish as to repeat itself.

Once with Kane Moran was bad enough; twice would surely damn them both.

PART 2

SIXTEEN YEARS EARLIER

CHAPTER 6

"I don't know what you see in Harley Taggert." Tessa wound another clump of blond hair around a heated roller. Wearing only a bra and panties, she was sitting at the vanity in her bathroom, her face drawn in concentration as she met Claire's gaze in the mirror. "If you ask me, Weston's the interesting one."

"And a jerk." Claire didn't trust the older Taggert boy. Weston was smooth as a perfectly tuned engine and twice as oily.

"Yeah, but you have to admit Harley's kind of a wimp. Damn!" Tessa sucked her breath through her teeth, shook her hand, and dropped the roller. "I always do this."

Gingerly, Claire picked up the hot roller and dropped it onto a heated spindle in Tessa's case.

Licking her finger, Tessa scowled. "The problem with Harley—"

"There is no problem."

"Sure there is. He's a dishrag. He'll do anything his old man says."

"No way." But Claire felt a smidgen of doubt in her own convictions. *If* Harley had a fault, and that was a pretty big "if," then it was that he didn't have as strong a will as Claire would have liked.

"Then why hasn't he broken it off with Kendall?" Tessa asked, finely arched eyebrows lifting a fraction higher as she reached for another roller. "You remember her, don't you, Kendall Forsythe from Portland, daughter of one of the biggest real estate moguls or whatever you want to call them in San Francisco before the family moved up here and—"

"I *know* who Kendall is."

"Harley was engaged to her."

"It was never official." Claire hated the feeling that she had to defend him. Harley was good and sweet and kind and so what if he wasn't the athlete or student or ladies' man that Weston had been? Who cared that he sometimes had trouble making up his mind? It was just that he was thoughtful.

"Kendall seemed to think it was official. I talked to Harley's kid sister at the beach yesterday, and she said that Kendall's all broken up and refuses to believe it's over. Paige says that Kendall's been spending as much time as she can at her parents' beach cabin in Manzanita, just so she can be close to him."

"Paige Taggert is a pain in the backside." Claire had bent over backward to try and make friends with the only Taggert daughter, but Paige had turned up her recently reshaped nose and wouldn't give her the time of day.

"Well she adores Kendall and thinks that whatever Kendall says or does is the gospel truth." Furrows sliced across Tessa's smooth forehead as she secured the final roller. "If you ask me, it's kind of sick. Like *she's* got a crush on Kendall or something."

"You're the one who's sick."

"I'm tellin' ya, it's weird." Tessa blotted her face with a tissue. "Harley hasn't called today, has he?"

"No, but—"

"Or yesterday?"

"He's been busy—"

"Or the day before that?"

"I don't keep track."

"Sure you do. You've been hanging around the house, jumping every time the phone rings, hoping that Harley's on the other end of the line. Why don't you just call him?" Tessa asked as she adjusted the strap of her bra, then reached for a tube of coral lipstick. "That's what I would do."

"I know it's what *you* would do, but I'm not like you."

"That's the problem, isn't it? Because there's no way, *no way* I would ever mope around for a boy, not even *Weston* Taggert. It's just not healthy. Believe me. No boy, especially not Harley Taggert, is worth it."

Claire rolled her eyes and decided the conversation wasn't worth having. Everyone, including Tessa and Randa, disapproved of her seeing Harley. Like he was Judas or something. The atmosphere in the house seemed cloying, and she decided, as she always did when her sisters bugged her, that she'd leave Tessa to her makeup and Randa to her books and go for a ride in the hills. She'd always loved the outdoors and sometimes couldn't stand being cooped up.

Passing by Miranda's doorway she spied her older sister tucked in a corner of the window seat, a book in her hands, but her eyes turned toward the open window, as if she were looking for someone. Lately Miranda had been different, not quite so bossy, and there were times when she disappeared for hours. No one knew where she went, but she always had a book with her and Claire assumed she'd found a secret spot in the woods where she read. The strange thing was that Miranda was still reading the same novel, *The Clan of the Cave Bear,* that she had been reading for weeks. Randa could usually knock off a book in a few days. Something was going on with Miranda, but Claire didn't have the time or inclination to wonder what it was as she hustled down the back stairs.

It was a muggy day, all the windows were flung open, and the strains of some love song from a Broadway musical echoed through the halls. No doubt her mother was at the piano again, adding music to a house that she hated.

Oh, Dominique tried. There were always freshly cut flowers in the foyer and dining room, classical music often wafted from hidden speakers, the silver was polished each week and used, with the crystal and gilt-edged china, at every evening meal. Tutors of French and violin, teachers for ballet and fencing, instructors for riding English style all paraded through the hallowed halls of this old house.

Claire ran her fingers down the smooth stair rail to stop at the bottom step, where the top of the final post had been rounded and worn from the touch of loving fingers. But not Dominique's. She thought everything about the house disgusting; the rock fireplace, charred by years of blazes in the grate rustic; the antler chandeliers barbaric.

Claire loved them all.

Wearing only shorts and a T-shirt, she dashed down the back hallway and through the kitchen. Ruby Songbird was kneading bread with her thick fingers while quietly humming in soft counterpoint to the piano's sorrowful notes. Ruby was a statuesque woman with a smooth flat face, dark flashing eyes, and a rare smile that could light up the room. Her hair, if ever unbound, would probably fall to her knees, but as it was, the gray-streaked black strands were wound in a tight bun at the base of her skull, where, Claire was certain, she had a second set of eyes. Nothing seemed to escape Ruby's detection.

In Claire's opinion, not that anyone else seemed to notice, Ruby had changed a little, and lately seemed preoccupied as she went through her daily tasks of cooking or cleaning or keeping "that miserable caretaker and his stepson" in line. She had help, of course, but Ruby was in charge of seeing that the old lodge was kept the way Dominique demanded.

"Hi," Claire said, snatching an apple from the fruit basket that had been left on the kitchen island.

"You're going off riding again?" Ruby asked as she slanted a glance over her shoulder, her fingers never losing their rhythm in the soft dough.

"I thought about it."

"Hmm."

It was unnerving how the woman could guess her thoughts. Sometimes Claire wondered if she had ESP or something. Ruby claimed to be a descendant of the last shaman or chieftain or some bigwig of her tribe, and maybe she'd inherited some of his magic. Not that Claire really believed in all that stuff.

"Be careful."

"I'm not going far."

Ruby clucked her tongue. "But sometimes these woods . . ."

Her lower lip protruded and she stopped herself, as if she'd said too much.

"What? What about the woods?" Claire took a bite, and the apple cracked.

"They're haunted."

"Oh, sure."

"This was once sacred ground."

"I'll be fine," Claire said, refusing to be baited and drawn into an argument. Ruby insisted, and maybe rightfully so, that the Indian tribes around these parts had suffered mightily at the hands of the white man. Claire didn't want to argue the point. She'd read enough history to know that atrocities had been waged against the tribes, but she didn't really feel it was her responsibility to right some age-old wrong, even if her ancestors had been bigoted rednecks. Fortunately Ruby's kids, Crystal and Jack, didn't seem to feel as persecuted as their mother. A pretty girl and free spirit, Crystal didn't wear her Native American heritage as if it were some kind of badge of honor. Neither was it her personal burden. As for Jack— he was a hellion, pure and simple. The color of his skin didn't have a whole lot to do with it.

"Just take care," Ruby warned over her shoulder again as she deftly rolled the dough and split it into two loaves.

On the porch, Claire stepped into her favorite pair of boots and noticed a mud dauber building a tiny nest under the eaves. The wasp worked feverishly, its shiny black body in constant motion, its jaws chewing endlessly.

What did Tessa know about love, Claire thought, as she tossed the rest of her apple aside, followed a flagstone path to the stables, and slung a bridle over Marty's wide head. Her father had bought the horses already named, and the two geldings—a pinto and a paint—had already been christened Spin and Marty after the heroes of some old TV show that Claire had never seen or even heard of before. The bay mare was Hazel, after an old character from the comics as well as a television show. Dumb names, Claire thought as she clucked her tongue and led Marty out of the stables and through a gate.

She didn't bother with a saddle, just flung herself over Marty's broad back. His ears pricked forward eagerly as they trotted through the stands of old growth Douglas fir. Shafts of sunlight pierced through the canopy of thick boughs, dappling the shadowy hills as they followed an old deer trail that snaked upward along the Illa-hee cliffs.

The air was thick and breathless, smelling of salt and seaweed and, motionless in the sky overhead, a few gossamer clouds clung to the tops of the coastal hills. Claire tried to shake off Tessa's warn-ings about Harley, but couldn't. Her sister's observations lingered stubbornly in her mind, echoing her own worries.

Since when did she care what Tessa thought? Chiding herself, she slapped the reins against Marty's shoulder. The horse re-sponded, his legs stretching into a quick gallop that snatched Claire's breath and caused her eyes to tear. With pounding hooves, Marty sprinted through the trees, vaulting fallen logs that had top-pled across the path, shying only once when a startled grouse, wings flapping wildly, flew out of a clump of ferns.

Marty stumbled, regained his footing, then lengthened his strides as he raced ever upward. At the summit, Claire pulled on the reins as the gelding snorted and fidgeted, sweat staining his coat. "You're a trouper," she said, patting his shoulder as she stared across the narrow bridge of land. To the west, the Pacific Ocean stretched in deepening shades of gray. To the east, the serene wa-ters of Lake Arrowhead reflected the sky's dusky blue. Between the two was this forested ridge, a place she often visited when she wanted to be alone.

Clucking her tongue, she urged Marty to the edge of the cliff so that she could catch a glimpse of Stone Illahee, her father's resort that rose from a crescent of sandy beach. Craning her neck, she stared down the steep ridge to the ocean below the jagged rocks. Thunderous waves pounded the shore, crashing wildly against the stony bluffs while shooting frigid white spray high into the air.

Claire sighed. Her worries melted away. Things would work out with Harley. They had to.

A quiet cough broke the stillness.

The hairs on the back of her neck rose, and, heart hammering, she twisted on Marty's spotted back. This was private land, owned by her father, and no one who valued his life would be trespassing. In the span of a heartbeat she thought of Ruby's warning.

Frantically, she searched the woods until, through a copse of trees she spied the Moran boy, a wild juvenile delinquent who had dropped out of school, worked as a gofer for a local paper owned by one of his relatives, and was always a suspect when any crime was committed near the small town of Chinook. His hair was too long, uncombed, his chin in need of a shave, his jeans nearly white from too many washings and now covered with dust. He was squatting near the remains of a dead campfire, a stick in one hand as he scattered the black embers and ash, but his eyes, the color of the brandy her father sipped after dinner each night, never left her.

Despite his dark reputation, Kane Moran intrigued her a little, teased at her curiosity, and she knew, from the few times that she'd run into him and felt his gaze move slowly up her body, that he found her just as interesting. Maybe more so. He was the kind of boy to avoid, one who would only cause a girl deep emotional pain.

"I didn't know you were here," she said, as she guided Marty closer to the camp.

"No one does."

"You know this is my father's property."

He raised a golden eyebrow. "So?"

"There are no trespassing signs posted."

His smile was wicked as he rocked back on his heels to stare up at her. "Oh, I get it. You're part of the Stone Illahee police department. It's your job to go around"—he motioned widely with his charred stick—"and throw people off."

"No, but—"

"Just me?"

"I'm not throwing you off."

He snorted. "I wasn't leaving anyway, Princess."

The endearment—if that's what you'd call it—irritated her. "My name's Claire."

"I know. Everybody around Chinook knows."

"What're you doing here?"

"Getting away from it all," he said, his eyes glinting a bit.

"Couldn't afford the rates down at your father's resort, so I thought I'd spend some time here."

"Do you honestly expect me to believe that?"

"Nah." He shook his head as he stretched to his feet and she realized how tall and rawboned he was. "I don't really care what you think."

She eyed his camp—old sleeping bag, expensive camera, knapsack, and empty bottle of sour mash whiskey. Nearby, glinting behind a clump of brush, was a motorcycle, a huge chrome-and-black machine that he used to speed down the highway or squirrel around town. But what was odd—or vaguely appealing to Claire— was that he'd spent the night out here alone, near the fire, staring up at the stars and listening to the never-ending roar of the ocean. Not what she would have expected from a small-time hoodlum.

"So, now it's your turn," he said, striding to Marty's side and touching the animal's soft nose. "What are you running from?"

"I'm not running from anything."

His eyes accused her of lying. "Whatever you say."

"I just wanted to get out of the house."

"Your old man give you trouble?" He bristled a bit, the corners of his mouth twisting downward.

"What? No. No, everything's fine . . . Sometimes I need to get away from the same old four walls."

"So where's Taggert?"

"What?" The question surprised her. Though she and Harley had been dating for a couple of months, she didn't think it was common knowledge or anyone's business, especially not someone's who really didn't know her.

"Your boyfriend, Princess. Remember? Where is he?" He reached into his shirt pocket and found a pack of cigarettes. Shaking out a couple, he offered one to her, and when she declined with a shake of her head, one side of his mouth twitched, as if she somehow had amused him. With a click of his lighter, he lit up and inhaled deeply.

"What do you care?"

"I don't," he said in a cloud of smoke. "Just making polite conversation."

He was mocking her, she just knew it, but she couldn't help rising to the bait, like a salmon to a fisherman's lure. "Impolite conversation."

He shrugged. "Whatever."

"Look, I don't like discussing my private life with strangers."

"I'm not a stranger, Claire. Lived across the lake from you all my life."

"You know what I mean—"

"I sure do, darlin'." He took another drag on his cigarette and shot smoke from the side of his mouth. "I sure do." He didn't elaborate, just patted Marty on the shoulder near her bare leg and turned. Without another word he gathered up his things, such as they were, swung the strap of his camera over his neck, rolled the rest of his belongings into his sleeping bag, and hooked it by elastic cords to the back of his motorcycle.

"Want a ride?" he asked, and again she shook her head.

"Got one." She motioned to Marty.

To her surprise Kane lifted his camera, took several shots of her astride the horse, then snapped the thirty-five millimeter back into its case, tossed his cigarette butt into the cold ashes of the fire, and started the big bike's engine. Marty reared as the cycle sparked to life, but Claire clung on. Then Kane Moran was gone, vanishing into a plume of blue exhaust that chased after him as he raced his bike along the rocky trails.

Claire was left with a vague feeling of disappointment and a welling sense of despair. Why this was she didn't understand, but it definitely had something to do with Kane Moran.

"For the love of Jesus, son, stay away from Claire Holland!" Neal Taggert tossed a file onto the corner of his desk in disgust. Papers flew, scattering like a flock of startled birds to land in disarray on the plush carpet. Neal didn't seem to notice. Or maybe he just didn't care.

Harley wanted to run away and hide. His father's tantrums had always been a source of fear to him, but he held his ground, standing in front of the polished mahogany desk, spine stiff as a drill sergeant's, back unbending, as he stood in the den. Let the old man rant and rave. This time, Harley wasn't backing down. "I'm in love with her."

"Holy Christ. *Love?*" Neal let out a stream of oaths that brought warmth to the tops of Harley's ears. "There is no such thing as love and let me tell you"—he pointed a fleshy finger at Harley's nose as he stood and glared at his second-born son—"the very notion of love is overrated."

"I'm not going to stop seeing her."

"Like hell." The old man swept around the desk more quickly than Harley had expected. Five-nine and topping two hundred pounds, Neal was amazingly agile. "Listen to me, kid. You'll lose interest in that girl fast"—he snapped his fingers— "or you'll be cut out of my will, ya hear that?"

Harley's heart stood still for just a second, and in an instant he saw his life, his and Claire's, flash before his eyes. They would be strapped, no money, no frills, living in a tenement of an apartment over a garage or cheap Italian restaurant where the sounds of patrons and loud cooks rattling pans and barking orders filtered through the floorboards, along with the stench of too much garlic and heavily spiced tomato sauce. He'd have to give up his Jag. His fists clenched, and the back of his jaw ached from the clamp of his teeth.

As if reading his mind, Neal grinned, showing off one gold-capped tooth. "Ain't a pretty picture, is it?"

"Doesn't matter. I'm not giving her up."

Neal sighed and ran a hand through the sparse strands of hair covering his balding pate. "Shit, son, you don't have to pretend with me. Oh, sure you'd like to think you were noble and romantic and all that crap, but the truth of the matter is you're no better than me or Weston. You like the good life more than you love"—again he snorted—"any woman."

"But Claire—"

"Is a Holland. Just like her old man." He rested a hip on the corner of the desk and sighed as if from his soul. If he had one. The jury was still out when it came to matters of Neal's conscience or spirit. "I tried to cozy up to old Dutch, y'know. When I came here, I suggested that we form . . . well, an alliance if not a partnership, but Benedict Holland is nothing if not territorial, and he couldn't see how much money could be made if we worked together instead of in competition with each other. Ever since your mother and I moved here, Dutch has been chewing on his tail, trying to think of ways to get rid of me, your mother, and anything to do with Taggert Industries. If you ask me—and I know you didn't—Dutch is probably paying his daughter to make eyes at you just to get back at me."

"You're incredible," Harley said, his voice a low whisper. "You're so damned self-centered that you think everything is about you. This is different, and I'm going to see Claire whether you approve or not."

"Then you'd better be ready to move out and forget about going back to Berkeley in the fall. And the car . . . it's only leased, you know, so I'll be expecting you to turn over the keys."

Harley swallowed the fear that crept through him, the fear that he'd fought ever since he was a kid, the fear that somehow he wasn't good enough. For years he'd lived in Weston's shadow. Weston, the tall and athletic god of the football field as well as the backseat. Weston, who breezed through high school and entered Stanford on a goddamned scholarship. Weston the great, the king, the pain in the ass. "You can't bully me, Dad," Harley insisted and felt his damned Adam's apple bob.

"Sure I can, son." Neal seemed relaxed, his hands clasped, as if he were *savoring* this little power play. "How long do you think you'd last in the real world, with a two-bit job and a pile of bills? Claire Holland has expensive tastes, just as you do. She wouldn't be happy 'living on love' or whatever the hell you want to call it. Neither would you."

"Kendall's here!" Paige, Harley's dip of a sister, didn't bother knocking, just threw open the door and swung into the room.

Heart sinking, he glanced out the front window of the den and spied Kendall's little red Triumph skid to a stop near the garage. She alighted, a frail-looking girl with pale skin, paler hair, and wide blue eyes that had the habit of accusing him of betrayal, deceit, and all manner of sin.

Harley's day went from bad to worse.

"I hope you can explain this better to her than you did to me," Neal said, straightening as Harley walked through double doors to the foyer and the front door that Paige was flinging open.

"I thought you were in Portland," Paige said, beaming at the older, prettier girl. Paige adored Kendall the way that she'd revered the girls who had made the cheerleading squad or who were elected homecoming princess or queen of the prom or some other juvenile fluff—the same way she'd paid homage to her stupid Barbie dolls when she'd been a few years younger with an overblown, exaggerated, and downright obsessive passion.

Kendall had the decency to blush a little. "I, um, came to see Harley." She glanced at him with sorrowful eyes that made him cringe inside.

"Oh." Paige's face fell, and the smile that was wired with braces disappeared.

"But I'll stop by and see you before I go." Kendall added a smile to her promise, and Harley braced himself.

"Kendall!" Neal boomed with a grin any Cheshire cat would envy. "How are you and your folks?"

"Fine."

"Your old man's golf game?"

"As bad as ever if you believe him."

"That sandbagger? No way." With a hearty chuckle, Neal gave her a fatherly clap on the shoulder, ignored his own daughter, and glared at Harley without saying a word. The message was clear: *This, son, is the woman for you.*

Harley knew differently. While his father returned to the den, and Paige reluctantly made herself scarce, Harley and Kendall walked through the house. "I don't know what you're doing here," he said, as he opened the heavy sliding door. He held the door open for Kendall, then followed her onto a wraparound cedar deck that was poised high above a canyon. Far below the Chinook River sliced through the ravine on its furious path to the sea. The uppermost branches of fir trees offered shade from the summer sun, and the sound of the swift current muffled their voices.

Taking in a deep breath, Kendall said simply, "I love you."

"We've been over this."

"I want to marry you." Kendall seemed haunted, her white skin even more translucent.

"You don't."

"For God's sake, Harley, you know I do." She stepped closer to him so that the fragrance of her perfume competed with the dank scent of the encroaching forest. "We made love. Right here on this deck. In your car. In your bed. I was a virgin, and you . . . you told me you loved me then . . ."

His jaw clenched and his fingers curled over the rail as the first tears rained from her eyes.

"What if . . . what if I got pregnant?" she said, and Harley's heart stopped for a second before beginning to beat again. *Pregnant? Kendall?* The world pitched beneath his feet. There was no way she was knocked up. They'd been careful. *He'd* been careful.

"You're not pregnant."

"No." She shook her head, sunlight playing on her pale blond crown. "I wish I was."

"So I'd marry you."

"Yes! I'd make you happy, Harley," she vowed, stepping forward, taking one of his hands in both of hers. She started to raise it to her lips, and he drew away, didn't want to see her grovel, felt enough like a heel as it was.

"It's over, Kendall. I don't know what I have to do or say to convince you."

"You still love me."

"No."

She flinched as if she'd been hit with a spiked two-by-four. Tears fell in earnest, and she sniffed back a sob. Harley had never been heartless. Stupid, yes. Naive on more than one occasion, but heartless? Never. And he couldn't stand to see her cry.

Knowing he was making a mistake of gargantuan proportions, he sighed and folded her into his arms. "I'm sorry, Kendall," he said against her hair. "I really am."

"Just love me, Harley. Is that too much to ask?" She lifted her face and blinked, then kissed him with a passion that surprised him. The kiss was hot, wanting, and tasting of the salt of her tears. For a second he surrendered, his bones beginning to melt before he stepped back quickly, his arms dropping to his sides.

"I'm sorry." He meant it. He'd never meant to hurt her or lead her on; it was just so damned hard to make up his mind. Now that he had, he felt like a bastard.

"This is all because of Claire Holland," she said around a hiccup, as a flimsy cloud blocked the sun before floating slowly inland.

"What happened between us had nothing to do with Claire."

"Like hell." Swiping at her eyes with her fingertips, smearing mascara already beginning to run, she inched her chin up a notch or two. "If I have to fight for you, I will."

"This isn't a battle."

"Not to you, maybe, but to me."

"Kendall?" Paige's voice echoed through the canyon, and, squinting upward, Harley caught a view of his sister sitting on the seat of her open window. Stringy brown hair hung down, and her eyes, when she glanced at her brother, were murderous. She'd probably heard the whole argument, witnessed the entire ugly scene. Great! Just what he needed. More pressure, this time from his kid sister.

"I'll—I'll be up in a minute," Kendall said, smiling brightly though her eyes were red, her face streaked, her shoulders slumped. As Paige disappeared into the room, Kendall whispered, "That kid should keep her nose in her own business."

For once Harley agreed and wondered how many other pairs of eyes had watched his exchange with Kendall through the three stories of windows that looked over this ravine and were cracked open for ventilation. He thought he caught sight of another image lurking behind a pane of glass that reflected the sunlight, then told himself he was jumping at shadows.

"Just give me one more chance," Kendall pleaded, grabbing his hand and pulling him toward the stairs at the north side of the deck where a clematis trailed, huge purple blossoms nodding in the heat. Still looking over his shoulder, he descended, Kendall in the lead, and told himself that this was dangerous. She was taking him along the path that cut through the forest, following the course of the river, and she was sure to stop where they had a dozen times before—at a shady glen where sunlight stabbed through the trees and tall, sun-bleached grass bent with the breeze.

"I think you'd better go, Kendall," he said, but his heart began to pound, and when she threw her arms around his neck to kiss him, male instinct overcame rational thought. "Don't," he whispered, without much conviction, as her fingers reached under his sweater. "No, Kendall . . ." He gripped her shoulders as his belt clinked open and her deft fingers slid down the zipper. Then she slithered down his body to kneel before him and he was lost, his fingers twining in her blond hair, his mind screaming that he was surely damned.

CHAPTER 7

Paige opened the window a little wider and bit her lower lip until it hurt. Harley and Kendall had been gone for half an hour, and she was getting anxious. The good news was that Kendall must be convincing Harley that she was the only girl for him; the bad news was she probably wouldn't so much as glance Paige's way when they returned.

Sighing, Paige doodled on the notepad resting on her lap and frowned when a yellow jacket swept in through the window, buzzed loudly, and bounced against the glass in its failed attempts at freedom.

Paige wrote Kendall's name over and over again, practicing a signature that could never be hers and silently wished she was more like the older girl. Kendall, thin to the point of seeming fragile, had grace, natural beauty, and knew how to flirt. She had a way of turning boys' heads without trying.

So why was Kendall so stuck on Harley? Jeez, he was a wimp. And what did he see in Claire Holland? She'd rather ride a horse than shop for designer clothes. Kendall Forsythe, with an hourglass figure, to-die-for straight hair, and a face right out of *Seventeen*, lived in Portland, went to a private school with other rich kids, and drove her own Triumph. She'd been a cheerleader and actually modeled.

Sighing, Paige crossed the room and opened her scrapbook to the section she'd reserved for Kendall. There, in grainy black and white, was her idol, dressed in a lacy half-slip and bra that were half-price because of an anniversary sale. Paige closed her eyes and wished for a minute that she was Kendall Forsythe even though she knew it would never happen. All the diets, braces, and nose jobs in the world would never give her a bit of Kendall's grace or sophistication.

She'd caught a glimpse of Kendall naked once, when the older girl had changed into a swimsuit, and Paige had walked into the bathroom just as Kendall had stepped into the one-piece. Her skin was white above and below her tan lines, her navel an "innie," her waist so small it couldn't possibly hold all her insides—liver, spleen, kidneys, and all the other things Mr. Minke had tried to teach them about in biology—but what was the most astounding aspect of Kendall's incredible body was her boobs. Perched high on a rib cage that showed her bones a bit, two white globes with big disk-like nipples swung free for a second before they were quickly hidden by red-and-white spandex.

Paige had blushed and apologized all over herself, but Kendall had only laughed and waved off her embarrassment as if she were used to people seeing her in a state of undress. Even now, Paige's cheeks turned hot at the thought of Kendall's beautiful breasts.

Harley was so stupid.

Paige's own boobs were dismal creations. Small, with tiny nipples that were too dark for the rest of her skin. Those breasts, if you could call them that, weren't her only bad feature. For some reason she'd lost out when it came to the Taggert good looks. She took after heavy Aunt Ida, with her hooked nose and beady eyes. But Paige was smart—probably smarter than Weston because he was such a jerk, and a lot smarter than Harley—which wasn't such a great feat in itself.

Weston, the oldest Taggert child, was nearly a god he was so good-looking. Wavy brown hair, eyes as blue as Delft china, a jaw-line Harrison Ford would envy, and a body sculpted by lifting weights and boxing. Harley, he was an idiot—but handsome in his own way, Paige thought grudgingly. His hair was straight and black, his eyes, fringed by straight dark lashes that Paige would die for, were a hazel hue that was close to green and sparkled easily. His skin was clear, without a single zit, and often dark with a beard shadow.

By the time Neal and Mikki Taggert had gotten around to having their third child, all the good genes seemed to have been used up on their sons. Mikki had often complained that her last pregnancy had nearly killed her. Maybe the fact that she was just plain worn-out chasing two active boys had robbed her daughter of the looks and energy that were Taggert trademarks.

Paige didn't even want to glance in the mirror to see the evidence that her parents shouldn't have had her. She was dorky and dumpy and nothing worked. Expensive clothes and makeup looked all wrong on her. Whenever she tried anything new with her lank brown hair, it turned into a mortifying disaster. If only she could be like Kendall . . .

She heard voices and dashed to the window again. Harley and Kendall were climbing up the stairs to the back deck. Both were red-faced, and Harley looked as if he could spit nails. Kendall had been crying. Tears streaked her cheeks and she was clinging to Harley as if she were desperate.

Shit a brick, was Harley blind as well as dumb as stone? What did he see in Claire Holland that wasn't ten times better in Kendall?

"But I love you," Kendall was saying while vainly trying to hold back tears. Her blond hair was mussed, her skirt grass-stained.

Paige swallowed hard and felt that particular tingle deep inside her when she realized what had just transpired. Kendall and Harley had *done it!* Even though he was supposed to be dating Claire.

"I've always loved you."

"Stop it," he growled.

"But you love me, too."

"Shut up!" Harley said and Kendall gasped. "Christ, I'm sorry— I didn't mean—" He stopped, closed his eyes, and tipped his head back as if stretching the tension from his spine while searching for the right words in that thick skull of his. "It's over, Kendall. Just accept it."

"I can't. Not when I know you love me." She sniffed loudly and lifted her chin the way that Paige had so often emulated in front of her mirror.

"I *don't* love you."

"Then you used me, is that it?"

"You seduced me."

"And you couldn't stop," she reminded him, a note of triumph in her voice only to disappear when she asked, "What if you just got me pregnant?"

What? Paige got goose bumps. *Pregnant? Kendall?* As in fat with big, sloppy boobs? Yuck!

Harley had the decency to turn white. "You're not— You couldn't be—"

"We won't know for a few weeks, will we?"

Harley sagged against the rail, his fingers gripping into the wood, his jaw rigid. The spineless creep. "Then . . . then you'll have to get rid of it. I'll help. I've got money—"

"If you're talking about aborting our baby, *ours,* Harley, then forget it. I'd never do anything like that."

"But I can't—we can't—"

With a sad sigh, she shook her head slowly side to side, as if finally seeing him for the gutless jerk he was. "Things will work out, honey," she said, as if *she* had to console *him,* when she was the one who might be knocked up. Oh, jeez, what a mess. Kendall slipped her arms around Harley's waist and rested her head against his chest. He didn't move, just stiffened. "You'll see."

Paige slid away from the window and sat on the floor, her back propped by her bed, her chubby white legs stretched in front of her.

"Kendall—for the love of God—we can't let this happen." Harley's voice sounded strained, as if he were afraid. What a coward! Kendall was just too good for him. Paige reached up to her nightstand for her pencil and notepad again, but her fingers encountered the tangle of wires that was her headgear, meant to fix teeth that refused to grow straight. She hated the appliance; it made her feel as if she were some alien from outer space, and she refused to wear it at school. Her hand stopped moving when she heard Kendall's voice.

"Look, Harley, I can't see Paige like this . . . tell her I had to leave; I was late for an appointment or something."

"You tell her."

"I can't deal with her now. Come on, Harley," Kendall cajoled, as disappointment wallowed deep in Paige's guts. Her fingers encountered her pad and pencil and she drew the writing tools onto her lap. "It's the least you can do. I don't want to hurt her feelings."

"Why?"

"Because she's a nice kid. Misguided but nice."

Paige brightened a bit. Kendall still liked her.

"She's weird."

Kendall's laugh was brittle. "All you Taggerts are weird. That's why you're all so adorable."

Paige's stomach turned over.

"I love you," Kendall said, and Paige squeezed her pencil so tightly, her knuckles turned white.

"Just don't be pregnant."

Harley's words still hung in the summer air as Kendall's footsteps retreated. Paige's buckteeth sank into her lip and she started writing, practicing Kendall's signature in her big, loopy handwriting. In her mind's eye she saw Kendall as a famous model, strolling gracefully down a fashion runway, her arms swinging, her eyes blue and sexy as cameras flashed to catch her come-hither smile and the play of light on her sequined designer gown.

I can't deal with her now. What was that supposed to mean?

She's weird. Harley didn't know up from sideways.

All you Taggerts are weird. That's why you're all so adorable.

Is that what Kendall thought? What everyone thought? She peeked out the window and saw Harley, hand planted on the deck rail, shoulders hunched as he glared down at the canyon. His face was so white Paige thought he might puke.

"Scared another one off, eh?" Weston's voice rose up to Paige's window like oil when poured into water.

"What's that supposed to mean?" Harley turned, his face set in a snarl.

"Kendall nearly ran me down when she took off." Weston came into view. Taller than Harley, better-looking by most people's estimations, he hoisted himself up and onto the rail. One little push and he'd fall thirty feet or so to the river. He didn't seem to notice, and his smile was as cocky as ever. "You sure have a way with women, little brother."

Harley didn't respond, just glowered at Weston as he tugged

thoughtfully on his lower lip. "Can't seem to make up your mind between Kendall or that Holland girl."

"Her name's Claire."

Weston's grin twisted a bit. "I gotta tell you, I don't know what it is you see in that one."

"You wouldn't."

"She's pretty enough, but she doesn't have the ass or the tits of her sisters. Not worth tossing over Kendall Forsythe. Now Kendall, there's an interesting one . . ." He leaned forward a bit. ". . . I've heard that her cunt is like hot honey—sticky, sweet, and moist."

Paige gulped.

"She doesn't let just anyone get into her pants, either, so consider yourself one of the chosen few."

"Shut up, Wes."

"I'd give half my trust fund just to see if it's true. But I didn't come looking for you to discuss your love life."

"Good."

"Dad's going to the attorneys' office in the morning and redraw his will."

"So—?"

"He's not happy that you're consorting with the enemy, so to speak. It could cost you."

"He can go to hell."

Weston shook his head. "You don't get it, do you? You could be cut out of millions because you're obsessed with Claire Holland."

A muscle worked in one corner of Harley's jaw, and he had the decency to look awash in guilt. Good. He deserved to feel lower than a slug's belly.

"You know, I understand your fascination with becoming the rebel and dating the daughter of Dad's enemy, but you'd better learn to play your cards right. Your timing's all wrong. I'm telling you, Dad will cut you off."

"So what do you care?"

"Me?" Weston's lower lip extended thoughtfully. He shoved a hunk of shiny hair from his eyes. "I don't really give a flying fuck what you do."

"Then why're you here?"

"I don't like any of us being duped by the Hollands or anyone else for that matter."

"I'm not."

"Claire Holland has you wound around her finger so tight it's turning red and threatening to fall off."

"Bull."

"Get smart, Harley. It doesn't help any of us if you look like a lovesick, pussy-whipped fool."

"What about you and Crystal?"

Crystal Songbird? The Indian girl who worked for the Hollands? Weston was dating her?

"Crystal's safe."

"Why?"

"She knows all I want is a good lay. Nothing more. She's willing to give it to me."

"And what does she get out of it?"

"Besides the best sex she'll ever experience? Trinkets."

"Trinkets?"

"You remember, like the beads that were used to buy Manhattan? I buy her earrings and clothes and whatever she wants."

"She's your whore." Harley's voice was filled with disgust.

"Don't let her hear you say that. She's part of a very proud people, you know." Weston's laugh was nasty.

"Proud enough that her old man would probably cut off your balls before he scalped you. You're sick, Weston."

"No, Harley. Just smart. Crystal's a good choice. Not because she's a descendant of the local chief, but because she's poor. You'll find that women without money are willing to do whatever you want just for a few nice words and a gift or two. Poor women are simple."

"Christ, Wes, that's pathetic."

"It's the way the world works."

"As I said before, you're sick."

"Not all of us can be monogamous, Harley. In fact only a damned few of us feel the need to be that noble. You, apparently, are . . . right?" There was enough guileless innocence stamped over Weston's face to suggest that he was tormenting his younger brother in his own unique way. "You're true to Kendall, I mean Claire."

Paige tensed.

Harley seemed to have had enough of his brother's advice—bad or good. Red-faced, he turned, but not before Weston caught his arm. "Hold on a minute. I didn't mean to insult you, not really. I even understand about the Holland girls being fascinating in the forbidden fruit kind of way, and once the old man changes his will and I know my inheritance is secure, I might just want me a piece of Holland ass myself."

Harley yanked his arm from his brother's grip. "Stay away from Claire."

Weston rubbed his chin and his eyes narrowed. "How about a wager?"

Harley's expression was incredulous. "You want to bet?"

"Mmm. That I can get one of the Holland girls to bed before the end of summer."

"Leave them alone."

"All of them?" One of Weston's eyebrows rose a fraction. He loved a challenge. "Don't tell me you're banging all the sisters," he accused. "Wouldn't that get old Dutch's goat if all of his precious daughters were fucking a Taggert?"

"What the hell are you talking about?"

"The old man. He would absolutely piss his pants, wouldn't he?" Weston's grin was pure evil and Paige realized again what a mean bastard he really was. His sexual fascination with the Holland girls bordered on sick, but then that wasn't really a surprise.

Harley lunged, reaching for Weston's neck, but he missed as Weston sidestepped him, grabbed an arm, and twisted it around his back, causing Harley to grimace in pain. "Don't be greedy, Harl. There's more than enough Holland cunt to go around."

"You're a perverted bastard."

"Probably. It runs in the family, though, doesn't it? At least I'm not swearing undying love for Lady Claire while balling Kendall out in the woods." He shoved Harley away, and Harley stumbled against the rail. Shadows from the branches overhead crossed his face.

Paige's stomach turned. Poor Kendall.

"You'll get yours," Harley warned.

Weston laughed. "I hope so. And yours as well. Wouldn't it be something to be able to say that I'd gotten three pieces of Holland ass? I wonder what old Dutch would think about that?"

Disgust and humiliation contorting his features, Harley walked under the deck's overhang and out of Paige's view. "Watch your back, Wes."

Paige heard the sliding door whoosh on its track only to shut with a hard thud that shook the house. He was *such* a wimp! He should have punched Wes's lights out for all his comments about Kendall. Weston was one of those egomaniacs who Kendall said thought with their dicks instead of their heads. Squinting against the afternoon sun, Weston slowly lifted his head and before Paige could duck inside, his gaze touched hers. "Get an earful?" he asked, clucking his tongue and shaking his head as a malicious grin stretched wide across his face. "Vicarious thrills, Paigie?"

Paige wanted to tell him to go to hell, but she knew better, had seen the blistering side of Weston's anger more than enough times. As a younger boy he'd beaten the tar out of Harley, lured squirrels with peanuts only to shoot them with slingshots, and kept track of how many cats, raccoons, and possums he'd killed with his car. Weston had a mean streak that ran deep and scared Paige. Rather than dig herself a deeper grave by arguing, she slid down the wall, her cheeks burning. He'd known she was listening all along, and he'd ridiculed Harley anyway. Her fingers curled against the baseboard.

"You know, Paige, eavesdropping can only get you into trouble. 'Course that's probably what you want, isn't it? Some kind of trouble to liven up that dull life of yours?"

She swallowed back the urge to cry. How many times had he humiliated her while she was just a pudgy kid who thought her older brothers were gods? Well, she knew better now. Weston was a cruel son of a bitch and Harley—he needed a spine transplant in a big way.

She heard Weston's laughter, aimed straight at her, and she cringed inside. She knew that she was often the butt of his jokes, had seen his friends try to repress grins when Weston had whispered something ugly and they'd all turned to look at her, realized that he was saying filthy things about her. Just a few weeks ago he'd even made the comment in her earshot, that she was probably the reason his father had strayed. Neal had taken one look at his pathetic daughter and decided never to risk having any more kids with Mikki, so he'd started "screwing around." Weston's friends, college men who had once been members of Weston's high school football team, didn't know that Paige was hovering on the stairs, listening to them as they played pool in the basement recreation room. They'd laughed at her expense and one of them had made some comment about how no boy would ever want to get into her pants and fuck her unless he put a bag over his head first.

Paige had slunk up the stairs and cried for over an hour, her only retribution being to steal a sick porno movie that Weston had hidden in the bottom of his athletic bag, under his football shoes. Paige had swiped the tape and left it where her mother was sure to find it. There had been hell to pay and Mikki had smashed the tape with Weston's favorite golf club, then broke the pitching wedge for good measure.

Paige had, in her own way, triumphed. She'd learned over the years how to deal with her perverted older brother, but never before had his poison extended to Kendall. Now that Weston had targeted her, things had changed.

And Kendall might be pregnant.

Gnawing on her lower lip, Paige scooted to the far side of her room where her stuffed animals, legions of them, stood guard in a built-in cupboard. The largest was a panda bear that flopped over in a little chair. Paige slid her hand behind the panda's back to a small slit in a seam behind one black leg and there, buried deep in the stuffing, she felt the cold hard muzzle of a small gun, the pistol she'd swiped from her mother's room weeks before.

She'd been snooping in Mikki Taggert's bedside table when she'd come upon the gun, tucked beneath tissue boxes, sachet packets, a bundle of sickening old love letters, and two pairs of reading glasses. At the time she didn't know why she'd felt a need to own the small weapon that seemed forgotten, though loaded.

Paige had felt a thrill at the pistol's cold touch, a sensation of power she'd never before experienced. At that moment, she knew that gun had to be hers. Over the years she'd stolen other items, a ring from Nana when she was still alive, a key chain from a local store just to see if she could shoplift and not get caught, a lighter from Harley, a tube of lipstick from Kendall, but never a weapon. This was different. She fingered the smooth barrel a second, licked her lower lip, then propped the panda back in his chair.

She had no use for a gun. No need of a weapon. No reason to keep the little pistol, but, she decided, hearing the rush of the river slicing through the canyon and smelling the acrid scent of smoke as Weston lit up, hell would freeze over before she'd give up the gun.

For the first time in her miserable life, Paige Taggert felt as if she had the upper hand.

CHAPTER 8

If he had any brains at all, he'd leave her alone. The Hollands were trouble, and Kane didn't have to look any farther than his old man to see what could happen if a person were to become involved with them. Squaring a chunk of fir on the old stump he used for splitting kindling, Kane raised his ax, swung down hard, and cleaved the wood into two pieces that spun onto the ground.

Sweat ran down his back and his shoulders began to ache, but he picked up another piece of green wood and settled it onto the stump. Pa's old dog gave a halfhearted woof from the front porch as the mail truck slowed at the end of the lane.

"Go fetch the mail!" Hampton, unshaven, his gray hair down to his shoulders, rolled his wheelchair onto the porch, sending the old hound through the rails as he grabbed the cane he left near the door and pounded on the ancient floorboards.

With a final swing of his ax, Kane split the knotty fir and headed off to the main road. Today was the fifth of the month, just about time for the monthly anonymous check to be waiting in the box. He felt his father's gaze, angry and unforgiving, boring into his naked back and heard the slap of the arthritic dog's gait behind him. Hampton's jealousy was an emotion he didn't bother hiding from his son.

"You've got two strong legs," he often said, glowering from the confines of his wheelchair, his eyes red from drink. "Get me another bottle." Or, on other occasions, he'd be more scathing. "If I still had my legs, I'd do twice the work you do around here, boy." Then there was the maudlin. "I loved her y'know, your ma, that is. Loved her more than any man has a right to love a woman, but I wasn't good enough. Not without my legs. Nah, she didn't want to be married to a cripple. Would rather be a rich man's whore."

Kane gritted his teeth time and time again and suffered his father's insults because he felt sorry for the old man who was forever reliving the accident that altered the course of his life.

"It's all Dutch Holland's fault y'know. The cable snapped on my harness while I was topping up on the south ridge. Faulty equipment, if you ask me, and that paltry little settlement wasn't enough." Hampton had stared across the lake to the Holland lodge, always lit like a damn Christmas tree. "Him and all his money. Fancy wife and three snotty-nosed girls. And what do I get out of workin' my butt off for him, eh? A broken back, a pissant parcel of land, and this!" he'd said, banging his useless cane against the metal frame of his wheelchair. "I hope Benedict Holland roasts in hell."

It never ended, Kane thought as he opened the mailbox and disrupted an industrious spider trying to spin a web in the shade between the box's flag and latch.

The envelope was there. Flat and thin, it was tucked into a stack of bills that would probably go unpaid for another forty-five days. But tonight Hampton Moran would dance with Black Velvet and tomorrow he'd get drunk with Jack Daniel's. By Wednesday he'd be back to his cheap rotgut, which would last until the fifth of August.

Kane scooped up the mail as the hound sniffed in the brush. It was time to leave Chinook and a thankless father. He lifted the envelope to his nose, hoping for the scent of perfume or the faint whiff of cigarette smoke, anything that might remind him of his mother, but smelled nothing. Scowling, he set off for the front porch, knowing full well that he'd have to help his dad to bed tonight.

"Come on, boy." He whistled to the dog and knew that Pop was right about one thing. Benedict "Dutch" Holland was one miserable son of a bitch. But that bastard had somehow sired the most interesting girl Kane had ever met.

* * *

Something was wrong. Claire could feel it in her bones; hear it in the words Harley hadn't said. Hanging up the phone in the front hallway, she felt empty inside and wondered, not for the first time, if her sisters and father had been right in warning her against dating him.

"Trouble in paradise?" Tessa asked as she breezed toward the stairs. A Diet Pepsi dangled from her fingers, and her skin was tanned and oily from the past two hours sunbathing near the pool.

"Everything's fine," Claire muttered, irritated that her sister seemed to read her thoughts at all the wrong moments. The house smelled of Ruby Songbird's barbecue sauce, and she could be heard humming while working in the kitchen.

"Is it really, fine, I mean?" Tessa's eyes sparkled with mischief. "You know I saw Harley with Kendall the other day."

Claire's heart sank, and she wanted to scream at Tessa that she was lying, but she bit her tongue. "You did?"

"Mmm. Down at the marina. If it's any consolation, it looked like they were fighting, but they were definitely together." She took a swallow from her soda and continued up the stairs, nearly running into Miranda at the landing.

"Are you giving her a bad time again?" Randa asked, eyeing Tessa with the older sister glare Claire recognized. It had been focused often enough in her direction.

"Just a little advice."

"Maybe she's had enough."

Claire couldn't believe her ears. Randa was always worrying that her younger sisters were flirting with danger, that they didn't use the brains God gave them, that they were forever getting themselves into trouble. Today she seemed carefree as she slipped down the final few steps. Dressed in shorts and a sleeveless top, she had a beach bag slung over her shoulder. Peeking from the open bag were a beach towel and her dog-eared copy of *The Clan of the Cave Bear*.

Tessa leaned over the rail from the stairs above. "I just think that if Claire's going to date one of the Taggert boys, she should concentrate on Weston."

Miranda stopped dead in her tracks. "You're kidding."

"No way. Weston Taggert's everything Harley's not—handsome, athletic, sexy—"

"—trouble of the worst order," Miranda filled in through suddenly tight lips.

"Maybe I like trouble," Tessa teased, lifting her soda to her lips and drinking.

"Not his kind. I'm not kidding, Tess."

"You don't even know him."

Miranda flushed. "He's a bastard with a capital B."

"Oooh," Tessa said, grinning that she'd managed to goad ever-cool Miranda.

"Believe me, he's bad news."

"Oh, that's enlightening!" Tessa took another pull from her drink.

"Harley's a sweet kid," Miranda clarified, touching Claire on the arm. "If you like him, okay, I can maybe understand it, even if dating him is a big hassle here in this house, but Weston . . ." Her eyes, cold as an arctic sea—found her youngest sister. "He's the worst kind of trouble a woman could possibly find. It has nothing to do with Dad's stupid feud."

"So look who's suddenly the goddess of love. The one of us who doesn't date."

"Low blow, Tessa," Claire said.

"Well, it's true." Tessa leaned over the rail, her breasts propped on the smooth banister, the fingers of her free hand clinging to the carved wooden bear standing on a nearby post. "What would Randa know about men, or boys, for that matter?"

Miranda opened her mouth, then snapped it closed and shook her head as if she couldn't fathom how stupid her youngest sister was.

"The bottom line is that Weston Taggert's a hunk." Tessa started up the stairs again.

"Stay away from him," Miranda warned, then checked her watch and flew through the front door.

"What got into her?" Claire asked as she watched Randa dash across the sprinkler heads spraying water over the lawn.

"Who knows and, frankly, who cares? Randa's always such a downer."

"She's just serious."

"But not today," Tessa observed from the second-story landing as she stared through the soaring windows of the foyer. Miranda's spotless Camaro roared down the drive. "She's been different lately." Tessa's lips puckered thoughtfully. "Do you think she's meeting some secret boyfriend?"

"Miranda?" Claire tried to picture her older sister in some kind of romantic tryst. "Nah. Probably late to pick up a book at the library."

"I don't think so," Tessa said, licking her upper lip thoughtfully as the dust settled in the drive. "No one is in that much of a hurry unless a boy's involved."

Claire didn't believe Tessa, but then that wasn't so abnormal. Claire discounted anything her younger sister said. While she looked upon Miranda as a fount of knowledge in all things except the male of the species, she thought Tessa was incredibly shallow. Tessa was too self-involved to realize there was more to life than Hollywood gossip, boys, and the small town of Chinook, which had become the center of her universe despite their mother's insistence that they learn the social graces needed in the right circles of Portland, Seattle, and San Francisco.

Miranda spent her life gaining knowledge, while Tessa tried desperately to lose any she might have picked up along the smooth path of her fifteen years of life. She never doubted she was born to be rich or spoiled. She believed that the people her father employed, from Ruby Songbird to Dan Riley the caretaker, should be her personal servants. She was royalty, a fairy-tale princess with a defiant streak, though, Claire was certain, Tessa had no idea why she should rebel against a father who gave her everything she wanted.

While Miranda worried about nuclear disasters, farm price supports, endangered species, and women's rights, Tessa didn't know they existed. Claire was somewhere in the middle, as always, caught between her two polarly opposed sisters.

Still brooding about Tessa's comments, Claire walked outside and away from the argument. She jogged along the path to the pier. Her father's motorboat, tied to the pilings, rocked gently. Claire untied the craft and settled behind the wheel. Without so much as a cough, the engine started, and Claire angled the boat's prow to-

ward the island at the far end of the lake. It wasn't much of an island really, just a rise of land dotted with a few sparse trees and a
sprinkle of beach grass growing between an outcropping of boulders. But it was isolated and uninhabited and sometimes, like
today, when her family and Harley were bothering her, it was a
place she could go to think.

Fish jumped and seagulls cried as the boat sliced through the
glassy water. The wind teased at her hair and she sighed, smelling
the fresh scent of water. Slowing the boat, she guided it into a sandy
cove and cut the engine. As she had dozens of times before, she
tied up to a twisted tree whose branches spread over the lake.
Splashing to the shore, she saw a hawk circling high above, his reflection darting on the lake's surface. She shielded her eyes for a
second to watch the bird before following an overgrown path and
kicking dust onto her wet legs.

As she climbed the trail, she thought about Harley. Ever since
she'd started seeing him she battled constant rumors that he was
still involved at some level with Kendall. "Hogwash," she muttered, but she couldn't shake the little doubt that was drilling
deeper into her heart. For all she knew the innuendo could have
been started by her father, a man who made no bones about the
fact that he wanted her to stop seeing anyone named Taggert. Only
her mother seemed to understand.

"Harley Taggert is handsome and well-off. He'll always be able
to take care of you," Dominique had said as she'd arranged roses in
a tall crystal vase on the dining room table one early summer morning. "A woman could do worse." Her hands had stopped moving
for a second as she'd stared at the wall where some of her paintings
graced the aged cedar panels. "It's not a matter of love so much as
survival."

"What?"

"I know, I know. You think you love the Taggert boy." Dominique's smile had been sad and world-weary. "Probably for all
the wrong reasons. The fact that your father forbids you from seeing him makes the boy all the more attractive."

"No, Mom, I love—"

"Of course you do. But let's be practical, shall we? If you marry
Harley, or a boy of his station, you'll never have to lift a finger,

never have to hold down a job, never worry about where your next meal is coming from. Even if the marriage doesn't work out, you'll be fine."

"It's not like that."

"No?" Dominique's long fingers plucked a brown leaf from the stem of one of the roses. "Well, good. But it doesn't hurt. Your sisters could take some advice from you, Claire. Miranda—well, she's just plain odd, studying all the time to what end I'll never know, and Tessa, oh Lord, that girl needs Valium, I swear. She's so . . . well, wild and rebellious, doesn't know what she wants in life." Lines of strain marred her mother's forehead. "I worry about Tessa—about all of you, but at least you seem to have a purpose and understand that marrying well defines a woman."

"I take it you're not a member of NOW." Miranda had walked through the room at just this moment, and her jaw was clamped so tight, the bone bleached her chin. Her fingers tightened over the smooth back of one of the Thomasville chairs. "You remember, the National Organization for Women."

"A pitiful organization made up of whining women who don't know their place."

"Haven't you ever wanted to be liberated?"

"Heavens no!" Dominique laughed at her eldest daughter. "You'll understand someday, Miranda, that men and women aren't equal."

"But their rights should be."

"Not if you ask me. All those women's libbers are doing is stirring up trouble. What happens to me if your father divorces me? Would I get alimony? Not if those screaming feminists have their way."

"I can't believe this," Miranda said. "Mom, we aren't living in the Dark Ages, for crying out loud!"

Dominique wasn't convinced. "Women will always need men to provide for them."

"Save me," Miranda whispered.

"Women, if they were smart, would give themselves better lives by choosing their partners more carefully."

"Like you did," Miranda shot, and Dominique's eyes flashed with a private pain that turned Claire's stomach.

"Yes," she said, pride in her voice.

"And you're miserable." Why was Miranda being so blunt and

hurtful? "I've heard you crying at night, Mom," Randa said gently. "I know it hasn't been easy." Dominique's spine suddenly looked as if someone had just poured starch down it.

"Neither is being poor and having to do anything to survive." Her lips pursed and she blinked as she turned back to the vase. "If you don't believe me, then think about Alice Moran—you know, the woman who lived with the foul-mouthed cripple across the lake."

"You know her?" Claire asked, dumbstruck. She didn't think either of her parents were aware of Kane's family.

"I knew *of* her. Her husband—well, I think they're still married even though she abandoned him and their son—anyway, Hampton's forever trying to sue your father because of the accident.

"Alice Moran is just one example of a woman who married poorly and paid the price."

"And you're an example of someone who married well and paid the price," Miranda said as she pushed through the swinging doors to the kitchen.

"Don't listen to her," Dominique had warned. "I'm afraid poor Randa is going to have to learn the hard way. You keep seeing Harley Taggert. Things will work out."

But they hadn't. Nothing seemed to be working. Claire didn't know how long it had been since she'd been with Harley, but it seemed like forever. She'd even seen Kane several times since she and Harley had been together. Kane Moran seemed suddenly to be everywhere she was, and she hated to admit it, but he intrigued her—well, just a little. He was everything Harley wasn't—poor, cocky, born with an I-don't-give-a-good-goddamn attitude and eyes that seemed to see past her facade and search for the real person buried deep inside. It was scary how he made her feel—all jumpy and nervous and defensive. She'd even wondered what it would be like to kiss him, but stopped herself short because of Harley.

The boy she loved, she reminded herself.

The man she was going to marry.

Gritting her teeth, she was determined to push all her wayward thoughts of Kane Moran out of her mind.

But she couldn't.

Because he was there, on the island.

She rounded a corner in the path and directly in front of her, on the highest point on this little rocky piece of ground, was her nemesis, the boy who caused her to question everything she'd ever dreamed of: Kane Moran.

Naked except for a pair of worn cutoffs, his hair still damp from a swim, he was stretched lazily over a smooth boulder.

Her throat closed for a second and she considered running away, but he'd already spied her, his eyes squinting at her as if he'd expected her to appear. She wanted to demand to know what he was doing here. After all, this was still her father's property, but she didn't want to sound petty. Besides, she'd seen him trespassing before. It was as if he felt no need to observe any man-made boundaries.

"If it isn't the princess," he drawled, and she felt the muscles in her back tighten. Propped on his elbows, sunlight playing across his tanned, taut skin, his eyes the pale hue of ale, he assessed her.

"I told you before I'm not a princess."

"Yeah, right." He rolled onto his bare feet.

"What're you doing here?"

"Contemplating my life," he said seriously, then allowed one side of his mouth to lift in a crooked, off-center grin that she found much too sexy.

"Really," she persisted, and stood in the shade of a solitary cedar tree. He made her nervous, and she wondered if he was suddenly everywhere she was, pretending interest and making conversation, because he hoped to find out about the latest lawsuit his father had filed against the Holland family.

"To tell the truth, I'm wondering if Uncle Sam really does want me."

"For the army?" The thought was chilling though she didn't understand why. She rubbed her arms and was aware of the way he was studying her, so intently she wanted to move away from his steady gaze. "You're going to enlist?"

"Why not?" he asked, lifting one muscular shoulder. "It's peacetime."

"For the moment, but things change, especially in politics."

He laughed. "What do you know about politics?"

She swallowed. "Not much, but . . ." He'd always lived across the lake, and though she barely knew him, she considered him a fixture of sorts in the little town of Chinook. People left all the time. Kids graduated from high school and went to college or got jobs. Some married and moved on. But for some reason she didn't want to examine too closely, Claire had thought, well, hoped, that Kane would always be around. Knowing he lived across the lake was as disturbing as it was comforting.

"Why the army?"

"Isn't it obvious?" he asked, his smile disappearing as a jet sliced the sky above, leaving a trailing white plume. "To get out of this place." He squinted against the lowering sun. "I get to see the world, earn money for college, all that bullshit that the recruiter shoved down my throat."

"What about your dad?" she asked without thinking.

"He'll get along." But two deep grooves appeared between his eyebrows and he looked away. "He always manages." He shoved a pebble with his toe, and it rolled and bounced downhill to plunk into the water. "So where's lover boy?"

"What?"

"Taggert," he clarified.

A slow burn climbed up the back of her neck. "I don't know. Working, I guess."

"If that's what you call it." Kane shook his head and laughed without any mirth. "Everyone else at the Taggert job site or lumber mill works his tail off—hard, physical labor, but Harley and Weston, the sons and heirs-apparent, already have offices with their names written in gold leaf on the windows of their doors.

"Weston is telling fifty-five-year-old supervisors how to do their jobs on the green chain. And Harley—" Kane rubbed his chin and shook his head. "What exactly is it he does for the company?"

"Don't know," Claire admitted.

"I bet if you asked Harley, he couldn't tell you, either."

"We don't talk about his work."

"No?" he asked, one eyebrow lifting as he crossed the sun-spangled space between them and stood toe to toe with her in the shade, his face so near she smelled a faint scent of aftershave mingled with smoke. She couldn't look away from the hard angle of his jaw and noticed a drip of water running from his hair down his neck. Her stomach squeezed, and she could barely breathe. "So what do you talk about—you and Prince Harley?"

"It's really none of your business. Harley—"

"I don't give a rip about Harley." His breath, warmer than the air, caressed her face. "But you . . ." He reached up and twined a curl of hair around a callused finger. ". . . for some damned reason I can't explain, I do give one about you." One side of his mouth lifted as if he were mocking himself. "It's this special curse I carry around with me."

She licked her lips, and his eyes caught the movement. With a string of oaths, he dropped his hand and turned away, as if in so doing he could break whatever spell had been cast around them in the shadow of the solitary tree. Tense muscles moved in his back as he walked away.

"Kane—" Oh, God, why did she call out? She wanted nothing to do with him, and yet there was a dark side to him that spoke to her, that reached forward to find a like part of her soul.

He glanced over his shoulder and her heart twisted at the confusion in his gaze. Gone was the arrogant, insulting cocksure hellion and in its place was a puzzled boy who was nearly a man. "Leave it alone, Claire," he said, and walked to the edge of a cliff, where, in one clean movement, he lifted his tanned arms, sprang from the ledge, and dived twenty feet into the still waters of the lake.

Shading her eyes with one hand, Claire watched as he surfaced and began swimming in steady, sure strokes to the shore where the dingy little cabin and his father waited.

CHAPTER 9

Harley glanced at his watch, then drummed his fingers on the desk in his office, a room he hated. Located in a single-story building across the road from the actual sawmill, filled with files and cheap, functional furniture, the room was cramped and tight. He tugged at his tie and felt sweat drip down his neck even though the air conditioner located in the window was going full throttle, wheezing and belching cool air through the tiny chamber his father had insisted was his. Damn it all, he still felt out of place, and would have had to have been blind not to notice the men in hard hats continually casting smug looks in his direction as they caught sight of him during the change of shift or on their breaks. They tried to swallow their smiles around thick wads of chewing tobacco, but Harley saw the amusement, and yes, disgust, in their gazes. They *knew* instinctively that he wasn't cut out to be their superior.

Once on his way to his car after work he'd caught Jack Songbird, one of the local mill workers, using a pocketknife to try and pry open the lock on the soda machine located behind one of the drying sheds. Harley had met Jack's eyes, frowned, then rather than cause a scene, looked in the other direction as the lock gave way.

The machine had been vandalized and robbed of less than twenty dollars and from then on, every time Harley had been forced to face

Jack, he'd spied the mockery, laughter, and disdain in Songbird's dark eyes. He should have fired the bastard right then and there. It would have been over. As it was, Jack's insolent presence reminded Harley just how weak he was. He couldn't even keep a small-time employee from penny-ante larceny. So how was he supposed to ride roughshod over the workers, any of whom could pick him up and snap his back like a brittle twig.

No, he wasn't cut out for this job. He yanked harder at the knot on his tie and slid the Best Lumber file back into a slot in his out basket. He'd spent hours poring over the invoices, staring at the figures on the last three months of shipments of raw lumber to Best's five outlets around Portland, and he couldn't figure out why Jerry Best was pulling his account from Taggert Industries. Best had been a customer for years, but, for some unfathomable reason, was determined to take his business elsewhere.

Probably to Dutch Holland. The son of a bitch had probably undercut their prices even though Dutch only owned a few sorry mills near Coos Bay. Hell, what a mess!

Now it was Harley's job to try and sweet-talk Jerry into staying with Taggert Industries—a name to be trusted. Christ, it was so much horseshit. He fingered the telephone, dialed, connected with Best's secretary, and felt an overwhelming sense of relief when he was told that Mr. Best wouldn't be back in the office until Monday. As he set the receiver down he noticed the sweat he'd smeared over the handle.

Glancing at his watch again, he wiped his palms on his slacks and thought the hell with it. Weston came and went as he pleased, never seeming to punch in. The old man handled it, but with Harley it was different. Never having shone as much as his older brother, whether it be on the football field, in school, or at the job, Harley was expected to try harder, spend more hours at the desk, kiss more asses.

Too bad. Tonight he was going to see Claire, and he didn't give a damn what his father had to say about it. He was on his feet and had reached for the door when his father's secretary's voice called over the intercom. "Mr. Taggert?"

"Yes."

"You have a call on line two." Harley's insides congealed. What if it was Jerry Best? What could he say to the man? How could he save the account? He wasn't a salesman; never would be. "It's Miss Forsythe."

Harley wanted to climb into a hole and die. This was worse than pretending he cared about the price of milled lumber. Why did Kendall keep chasing him? Didn't she understand that it was over? He snatched up the receiver and barked out a greeting. "Hi."

"Oh, Harley, I'm so glad I caught you." He imagined her face— all blue eyes and pink cheeks, pouty lips turned down at the corners.

"What's up?" Not that he cared. He flicked a piece of dirt from under one fingernail.

"It's—it's that I have to see you."

"Kendall, don't, I already told you—"

"It's important, Harley. I wouldn't have called you at work if it wasn't."

Holy shit, she was pregnant. Hadn't she said she wanted to be? Harley's knees went weak and he sagged against the desk for support. His stomach cramped so hard he thought he might lose his lunch. "What is it?"

"I don't want to talk over the phone. Meet me at my parents' beach house tonight."

"I can't."

A beat. "Please."

"I have plans."

Her voice sounded strangled. "Harley, listen, this is a matter of life or death."

The baby. She was pregnant and considering the abortion.

"I'll see you at eight."

"I can't."

"You really don't have a choice," she choked out, then slammed the receiver in his ear. For a second he thought he might pass out, the blackness in the corners of his vision threatening to blind him, but slowly he caught his breath. Kendall was right—he had to meet her. With shaking fingers he smoothed his hair from his face and tried to appear calm.

As he left the office he managed to wave to the woman in the steno pool who was assigned to be his secretary. Linda Something-

Or-Other. Fair, fat, and forty, but pleasant and efficient enough to make him feel foolish, that her smile was often at him not with him. *Stop it, Taggert, you're the boss.*

His Italian loafers crunched on the gravel of the washed-out parking lot. Potholes scarred the dusty asphalt, and no tree dared offer shade in an operation that was meant to reduce forest giants to two-by-fours. The fresh scent of sawdust mingled with the overpowering odor of diesel, and Harley hated every second of it.

His father, like Dutch Holland, was president of a corporation made up of many divisions. This sawmill was only one of the small companies under the umbrella of Taggert Industries. So it seemed ridiculous for Harley to be stuck in the mill when there were resorts and restaurants to operate.

"It'll do ya good," Neal had explained when he'd told Harley about his summer job. "Mix with the men who are the backbone of this company. Next year you can work at the resort in Seaside."

An empty promise, Harley thought as he pushed a pair of sunglasses onto the bridge of his nose and Weston's Porsche convertible roared into the parking lot.

Crystal Songbird, Jack's younger sister and a girl Weston dated off and on, was slouched in the passenger seat of the convertible, her fingers tapping the rhythm of Bruce Springsteen's "Hungry Heart." Her black hair shimmered blue in the afternoon sunlight. If she saw Harley, she didn't acknowledge him, but Weston was out of the car in an instant and bore down on him as if with a single purpose. Jaw set and hard, fists clenched, he crossed the parking lot.

Got a wife and kid in Baltimore, Jack . . .

Wes looked angry enough to spit nails.

Harley braced himself for what appeared to be a showdown. Weston's lips were white with determination.

"Where's Dad?" he demanded.

"Not here."

"You're sure?" Weston asked, then muttered under his breath, "Son of a bitch. I called the office in Portland and . . . oh, hell, they said he was here."

"What's got into you?"

Weston ran the fingers of both hands through his hair, then glanced over his shoulder at Crystal, but she didn't seem to pay him any attention as she studied her reflection in the rearview mirror and applied another layer of glossy lipstick.

Everybody's got a hungry heart . . .

"It's the same damn thing it always is." Weston swiped the sweat from his brow with his bare hand.

"What thing?"

Weston's eyes narrowed into slits. "The rumor."

"The wha—oh. That one." Harley finally understood. "The one about Dad having other kids—illegitimate ones?"

"Just one. A son."

"If you believe the rumors, yes." Harley didn't give two cents about the old lie that had been attached to Neal Taggert and his womanizing. Who cared?

"It doesn't bother you?"

"I don't lose any sleep over it."

"Don't you realize if it's true and this guy—this bastard of a half brother—ever steps forward, he might want a cut of everything?"

"So?"

"Christ, Harley, are you really that much of a moron?"

Harley's blood ran hot. "I just don't let things I can't control bother me. Where'd you hear it this time? From some guy three sheets to the wind at the Westwind Bar and Grill? Or over at Stone Illahee—Dutch Holland is always ready to spread a rumor about Dad? Or maybe from one of the gossips who hang out at the coffee shop?"

"No," Weston drawled, his lips thin with disdain for his younger brother. "This time I heard it from Mom."

Harley laughed. "Oh, great. Like she's never trying to get your goat. I don't know what happened between you, but Mom likes nothing better than to irritate the hell out of you and send you off on some wild-goose chase."

"Jesus, Harl, you're beyond hope!" Weston squeezed his eyes shut and shook his head, as if wondering how they could possibly be related.

"And you're jumping at shadows. What were you gonna do if Dad was here? Accuse him of having another little family tucked away?"

"I'd just ask for the truth."

"A good way to get cut out of the will, Wes, and we all know that no matter what, you'd never do anything to jeopardize getting your rather substantial piece of the Taggert financial pie."

"At least I don't sit around on my ass doing nothing, *nothing*, and just expect to inherit money."

"I don't expect anything."

Weston slid a glance at Harley's Jaguar and the fine layer of sawdust that had settled on the car's sparkling paint job. "Yeah, right. Look, it doesn't matter. I'll catch up with Dad later."

"Do that. And tell him to say 'Hi' to our half brother, would ya?"

"Go to hell, Harl."

Harley chuckled as Weston turned back to his sports car and Crystal. It was so rare that he could get one up on Wes, that watching his older brother's frustration warmed the dark cockles of his heart.

A shrill whistle blew as Weston wheeled his Porsche out of the parking lot. Across the street, behind tall mesh fences boasting signs about worker safety, it was time for the shift to change. Harley hurried to his car. He didn't want to have to make small talk with any of the workers. It wasn't that he was a snob, he told himself. He just didn't have anything in common with them.

Over the scream of saws, shouts of foremen, and rumble of trucks arriving with raw timber or leaving with stacked lumber, men in clean flannel shirts and dungarees put on hard hats and replaced their counterparts who were covered with sawdust and grime.

Harley unlocked the door of his pride and joy—a forest green Jag XKE that could go from zero to sixty in less time than it took to catch your breath. Parked between a beat-up Dodge pickup and a dusty station wagon with the words "Wash me" scribbled on the back window, the Jag sparkled like an emerald cast in gravel. He slid behind the wheel and flicked on the engine.

Packed with horsepower, his car was ready to roar down the road. For the next few minutes as the sleek car's tires sang against the asphalt, Harley would be in control of his destiny, his own man.

Then, damn it, he'd have to meet Kendall.

CHAPTER 10

"God help me," Kendall muttered, holding her abdomen and pacing on the deck of her father's beach house. Why couldn't she just let Harley go? What was this obsession with him? Paige was right, she could have had nearly any boy she wanted, but the only one worth having was Harley Taggert.

It wasn't just that he was a Taggert, but he was kind and sweet—well, he had been. Until he'd met Claire, that mousy, useless Holland girl. What, what did he see in her?

Kendall, when she realized that he was going to break up with her, had become desperate. She wanted to marry Harley Taggert and wasn't used to not getting her way.

Her stomach churned, tears threatened her eyes, and she placed her hands against the rail to stare past the shifting dunes with their clumps of beach grass to the darkening waters of the Pacific. This view of the sea, stretching for miles to the horizon, had always had a calming effect upon her, had helped her put her life into perspective. But not this evening. Not when everything was so out of control. A couple walked by, holding hands, laughing, their bare feet making impressions on the wet sand as the frothy tide eddied and swirled around their ankles. Their dog—a rangy, red Irish setter—frolicked in the surf, chasing after sticks that the man threw, then bounding back.

The lovers seemed so happy. As she and Harley had been. Before Claire. Her throat closed in on itself, and she fought the urge to break down and cry. Never in her life had she felt so helpless, never had she wanted anything so badly.

She heard a car stop in front of the cottage and opened the sliding door when she heard footsteps on the stairs to the deck. Her heart leapt. He'd come. He still cared.

"Harley—" she cried, only to have his name lodge in her throat as Weston appeared, big as life, an easygoing grin stretching over his square jaw. "Oh." Disappointment lodged deep in her soul.

"Thought you might be here."

"Did—did Harley send you?"

Weston's smile, one that had melted more female hearts than it should have, curved easily upward. "Nope. Came on my own."

"But how did you know that I—"

He leaned a hip against the railing of the deck and folded his arms over his chest. "When you leave a message at the office, word gets around."

"I didn't leave—"

He waved off her explanation. "Doesn't matter. I just came by with some advice."

The muscles in her back tightened. "I don't remember asking for any."

"Believe me, you need it." Weston glanced at her and sighed. "You know, Kendall, I'm surprised at you. I always thought you were a smart girl, one who knew what she wanted and figured out how to get it."

"With Harley it's different."

"Why?"

"It's just not so simple."

"Sure it is."

She ran frustrated fingers through her hair. "How?"

"Well, take advantage of the fact that he's not all that smart— don't argue the point, okay," he said, holding up a palm when she tried to protest. "We both know his limits." Weston's grin bordered on evil.

"What are you suggesting?"

"Trap him."

"What?" Had she heard him right?

"Get pregnant."

Her lips pursed. "I would never—"

"Sure you would," he cut in, looking suddenly bored. "I overheard your last conversation with him. You've got him on the ropes, now finish it." He hoisted himself onto the rail, back to the ocean, and stared at her. "Don't tell me you don't have the guts Kendall, because I don't believe it. I think you're a woman who knows what she wants and how to get it."

She bit her lip and considered. "What—what if there's no baby."

"Then make one."

She'd never thought Weston was an idiot, but he acted as if all she had to do was wave a magic wand and . . . "I can't just pretend."

"I didn't say to pretend. I said make a baby."

"I think I'll need Harley for that."

Weston stared at her as if she were incredibly dense. "Come on, Kendall. Harley's weak. Everyone knows it. All you've got to do is seduce him."

"Seduce him? Just like that?"

"Trust me, he won't be able to say no."

She considered his proposal. It had merit, true, but she didn't want to take any advice from Weston. He never did anything without a purpose—his own purpose. Eyeing him as she adjusted the umbrella sprouting from an outdoor table, she asked, "Why do you care?"

He glanced over his shoulder to the ocean, as if weighing his answer. "Don't suppose you'd believe me if I said that I was doing it because I cared about my brother."

"Nope. Try again. What's in it for you?"

"Okay. Harley's a pain in the butt. Now he's mooning around about Claire Holland, talking about marrying her—"

Kendall gasped, a pain sharp in her heart. Never once had he mentioned marriage to her.

"—and that would be a disaster."

"For you?"

"Yeah, and the whole damned family. Dad's so worked up about it, he can hardly concentrate on running the business. Going to give himself a heart attack or a stroke. Paige is upset, and I'll bet my eyeteeth old Dutch doesn't like it any better than the rest of us. This whole feud thing will start up again, and it will probably kill Dad."

His argument didn't ring true. Weston had never cared about anyone in his family. He'd always been out for number one, and there had never been a number two or three in his life. "There's more to this, isn't there? This is personal."

A muscle worked in Weston's square jaw. "Harley can't have a Holland," he said bluntly.

"Why not?"

His gaze narrowed as it slid back to her. "Because he doesn't deserve any one of them—even Claire."

"But he does deserve me?" Had he come here just to insult her?

"Look, I'm offering you a way to get what you want, that's all."

"So that Harley doesn't marry Claire and mess up whatever plans you've got."

"That's about the size of it."

"What if he won't be seduced?"

"Get a phony pregnancy test result, marry him, and get pregnant on the wedding night. Figure it out, Kendall, this isn't exactly brain surgery."

She gnawed on her lip. "What if it takes three or four months to get pregnant? He'll know—"

Weston swore under his breath, and when he looked at her it was with a new high-powered intensity. "You want a baby to seal this deal?" he asked.

"I—I guess."

"Then I'll give you one."

"What?" The saliva dried in her mouth. She couldn't believe she'd heard correctly.

"I'll get you pregnant." He dropped to the deck and advanced on her. Despite her loathing for him, she felt a thrill slide down her spine.

"You?"

"Same gene pool as Harley. Same blood type. There wouldn't be any question of paternity."

"Oh, God." Her heart was racing as her gaze locked with his. "What . . . what would you get out of this?" She swallowed hard as his gaze slid slowly down her body, then returned to her face.

"Your undying affection and gratitude."

"I don't think I can—"

"Not even to be Harley's wife?" He reached for her hand, drew it up to his lips, and kissed the inside of her palm.

Her knees went weak, but she yanked her hand back quickly, as if his kiss had seared her skin. "This is nuts. No way—"

"Think of it. You'll be Mrs. Harley Taggert."

"With your baby."

"You could miscarry . . ."

She nearly threw up, and one hand shot up to cover her mouth. "You're beyond perverted."

"Just trying to help." She turned away, but he was quick and wrapped strong arms around her middle so that her breasts were resting on his forearms. "Think about it, Kendall," he whispered into her ear as the ocean rumbled on the other side of the dunes and a hot July sun slowly lowered on the horizon. "We could have a little fun and then . . . bingo, you get Harley. What could it hurt?"

"Everything," she said, disgusted, though her skin, where he touched it, tingled. "You could ruin everything."

He laughed against her ear. "Don't think so, babe. You've done a good enough job of that yourself." He released her and headed for the steps. Before rounding the corner, he called over his shoulder, "But if you're content to let Harley slip through your fingers so that he can marry Claire Holland, don't blame me. Nope, honey, you'll only be able to blame yourself for that one."

Harley's voice had a definite edge to it. "I'm sorry, Claire, I'll call you later, but something's come up. Business. Dad won't let me out of it."

Closing her eyes, Claire wrapped the phone cord around her fingers and fought the urge to scream. Something was wrong, definitely wrong, and all those doubts she tried so valiantly to hold at bay continued to inch closer, crowding her. "He's just trying to keep us apart."

"I know, but I'll see you later. You know I will."

"It's been over a week."

"I know, I know," he said, and Claire could almost hear the

wheels turning in his mind. Was he lying to her? Avoiding her? Why not just break it off? Despair clutched her soul. She loved Harley, adored him and yet . . .

"We'll meet later—well, probably not tonight but soon. I swear. Claire, I miss you."

Do you? Do you really? "Harley—?"

"What?"

Was there the hint of irritation in his voice? She was going to tell him that she loved him, but thought better of it. He was too distracted—too distant. "Nothing."

"Good. Look, we should go sailing—at night."

"I'd . . . I'd like that."

"Meet me at the yacht club at ten—no ten-thirty. You know which berth."

"Yes, but—"

"I'm sorry that I can't see you sooner. I . . . I love you. You know that."

"I love you, too," she said, but the words sounded hollow and false, said on cue because they were expected.

Fighting a headache, she stared out the window and watched as the sun sank behind the western ridge of mountains. Where had Harley been when he'd called? Who was with him? Why had he canceled again?

He doesn't love you, not really. That thought was a bitter pill to swallow, one that would take gallons of self-esteem to wash down. She poured herself a glass of lemonade and pressed the cool tumbler to her forehead.

The house was hot and empty. With summer temperatures soaring and Dutch's steadfast refusal to add air-conditioning to the old lodge, the kitchen had collected a week of ninety-plus days' heat and trapped it. Even with the windows open it was hard to breathe.

Aside from the ticking of the grandfather clock in the front hall, the gentle hum of the refrigerator, and an occasional creak of ancient timbers, the rooms were silent. Miranda had left earlier without an explanation, as she often did these days. Dominique had insisted that Dutch spend the weekend with her in Portland, catching up with old friends, taking in a play, and enjoying the city. Tessa had escaped earlier with some friends who claimed they were going to see a movie, but it was probably all just a lie—everything was these days.

Shadows of the oncoming night stretched through the windows. Claire walked outside to sit in an old rocker that swayed on the back porch. As the sunset gave way to the purple of twilight, a few bats skimmed the lake's surface and fish jumped noisily in the water. One at a time the stars began to reveal themselves, and Claire wondered again what Harley was doing and with whom. His excuses were far too many and she was beginning to think that he was involved with another girl—probably Kendall Forsythe.

"Idiot," she muttered, loathing her romantic tendencies as she pushed against the floorboards with her toe. Hadn't everyone told her she was being stupid? Hadn't her father and sisters warned her not to get mixed up with Harley? But she'd been stubborn and intended to prove them all wrong.

She'd been played for a fool.

The old rocker creaked as it moved. Left alone, she might be maudlin enough to cry and feel sorry for herself, but she wasn't in the mood for tears and didn't like the scene it painted in her mind. She loved Harley, she was sure of it, but she wasn't going to be his—or any boy's—doormat.

She climbed out of the chair, walked through the kitchen to the hook by the back door where the keys were kept, and found the extra ring. Her father owned a bevy of vehicles, so she chose a Jeep painted army green, climbed inside, and headed into Chinook. It was a small town, hardly more than a stoplight, two taverns, a couple of restaurants, a few motels, and a grocery store, but it was more interesting than sitting around home and moping about a boy who couldn't seem to make any time for her.

Pushing the speed limit, she drove past the Methodist church—the only one in town with a spire—and discovered a group of kids hanging out at the local pizza parlor. Motorcycles and old pickup trucks were scattered throughout the parking lot, and, as she pocketed her keys and walked into the establishment, the scents of baking bread, garlic, tomato sauce, and cigarette smoke greeted her.

Families were clustered around tables, groups of teenagers claimed spots near the fake fireplace, but the first person her gaze landed upon was Kane Moran. Seated in the corner, long jean-clad legs stretched in front of him, torn black T-shirt stretched across his shoulders, he rested on the small of his back and studied the door. As if he'd been expecting her.

Great! The one guy she wanted to avoid. To her horror, her pulse quickened.

Self-conscious, she ordered a Coke at the bar, then, gathering her rapidly shredding bravado, walked up to him.

Within a day's growth of beard, his lips curved into a dark, dangerously welcoming smile. A half-drunk glass of cola sweated on the table and a cigarette, as if forgotten, burned in a tin ashtray. "If it isn't the princess," he drawled, nudging out a chair with the toe of a battle-scarred boot. "Slumming?"

"That's me. Princess Claire." She took the seat he offered and eyed him over the rim of her glass, hoping the cola would wet her suddenly parched throat. Leaning across the table, she asked, "But no, I'm not slumming any more than you are."

"This is my crowd."

"Is it?" she countered. "The way I hear it you run with the local hoodlums and thugs."

His sexy grin stretched a little. "Touché, Ms. Holland." With a wink, he added, "But I think it's the other way around, they run with me."

At least he had some kind of twisted sense of humor. "So why do you seem to think it's your personal mission to try and bother me?"

"Is that what I do?" He took a drag from his cigarette and washed it down with a swallow from his drink. "Bother you?" His gaze drilled into hers and she felt as if the room had suddenly shrunk, the air sucked out, and she was alone with him though the restaurant was filled with patrons and employees. The way he was looking at her—as if she were the last woman on earth and he'd been forced into celibacy for years. A trickle of sweat slid between her breasts.

"I, uh, just dropped by for a drink."

"Alone?"

She lifted a shoulder and fought a wave of embarrassment.

"Where's your better half?"

"I'm not married."

"Coulda fooled me." He drained his glass, and she wiped the beads of moisture from the outside of hers. If only he'd quit staring at her with those narrowed golden eyes. "Anyway, it's just a matter of time."

"How would you know?"

"You've made up your mind—right or wrong."

She rolled her lips over her teeth. "You don't know anything about me."

"Is that right?" Snorting in amusement, he rubbed the whiskers on his chin. "I know more than you think, Princess. Probably more than I should." It was his turn to lean closer to her, to pin her in his gaze as he studied every inch of her face. "You're the kind of woman who makes up her mind and does what she wants. Loyal and true-blue to a fault, you won't believe a bad word about anyone you care about even if it's as obvious as the nose on your face that you're being used."

She wanted to slap him. "I'm not—"

"Wake up, Claire. You're way too clever for this." Quick as a tiger pouncing, he reached across the table and his fingers curled over her wrists—warm, possessive manacles surrounding her skin. "So where is he?"

"Who? Harley? Working late." The excuse sounded so trite.

"Taggert hasn't done an honest day's labor in his life. Try again."

"He's . . . he's doing something for his father. Business."

"Harley Taggert involved in some big business deal? You don't believe that any more than I do."

Her chin lifted a bit. "He wouldn't lie."

"Of course he would, Claire," Kane said, his fingertips warm against the sensitive skin on the inside of her wrist. His face, so near, was etched by far more years than he'd lived. "Any man would."

"He called me and—" Why did she have to justify herself to Kane Moran? He wasn't even her friend, not really. He was just a near-grown man with a chip the size of Stone Illahee permanently attached to his shoulder.

"And he canceled."

"I'm meeting him later."

A flicker of emotion flared in his eyes for a heartbeat, only to fade so quickly she was certain she'd only imagined that tiny glimpse of raw pain and suffering. Moran was hard as nails, tough as rawhide, impervious to any emotional scarring, a mixed-up kid destined to become a criminal. Or so she'd heard from her father and some of the other men who gathered in the den for poker every Tuesday night. But this boy seated on the other side of the table, the one clamping her wrists in his warm, callused hands, the would-be man who knew so much about her, was no more a bad seed than she. Her heart clutched as she wondered what it would be like to kiss lips that were blade-thin and forever cynical. Slowly, embarrassed at the wayward turn of her thoughts, she withdrew her hands.

"I think I'd better go." She was too aware of him, too darkly fascinated.

"Pizza to go for Brown," a server called over the mike. The cash register dinged, conversation buzzed, and beneath it all the strains of an old Buddy Holly classic poured from hidden speakers attached to the jukebox and struggled to be heard over the din, yet Claire barely heard anything but the erratic beat of her own stupid heart.

He stood, took a final drag from his cigarette, and stubbed it out in the tray. "Want to go for a ride?" he asked in a cloud of smoke and unspoken innuendo.

"No, I should leave—"

"And go where? Wait by the phone for Taggert to call?"

"No, but—"

"It's just a ride, Claire."

"I know."

His eyes, beneath thick brows, flickered with a challenge.

"I don't think—"

"It's up to you." He slid his arms through the sleeves of his leather jacket and turned up the collar. "What's it gonna be?"

Why not? For all she knew Harley was with Kendall or some other girl. She swallowed back the quick "no" that leapt to her lips. "Okay," she finally said, tossing her hair over her shoulders.

His smile was dangerous. He grabbed her hand. "Come on."

Out the door, across the parking lot, and onto the chrome-and-black motorcycle. All the way Claire second-guessed herself. What if someone saw them, what if they were in an accident, what if Kane took her somewhere and refused to return her by ten-thirty? What did she know about him anyway? That he was a part-time hood, a suspect in most of the crimes around town, a boy who was burdened with a crippled father and a burning desire to shake the dust of Chinook from his leather boots. And the gut feeling that he wasn't as bad as he'd been painted.

Ignoring her thoughts, she wrapped her arms around his waist as he kick-started the bike. With a sputter and a roar the big machine caught fire. "Hang on," he yelled over his shoulder, and she buried her face between his shoulder blades. The smells of leather and smoke assailed her. Gravel sprayed from beneath the cycle's back wheel.

Within seconds they were across the parking lot and into the thin stream of traffic flowing through town. Neon lights of vacant motels and bars flashed by as the headlights of oncoming cars bore down on them only to pass by in an eye-stinging blur. The sound of the bike whining through its gears reverberated in her head, low at first and then screaming higher until he shifted. In a flash the town was behind them and they flew down the road, tears filling Claire's eyes only to be whipped away by the wind that pressed against her face and tangled her hair.

This is insane! she thought, realizing that she had to have been out of her mind to agree to taking this mad moonlit ride. And yet she felt lighthearted and free as they cruised past the rock and wrought-iron gates of Stone Illahee, her father's resort. Her guilt for being with another boy dissipated as she leaned against Kane's back. Poor and rebellious, headstrong and sarcastic, he was as far removed from Harley Taggert as any boy could be.

Defying the law, they sped along the beach, then back to the road and upward through the dark forest. Pale light from a moon not quite full was blocked by a canopy of branches. The only illumination was the steady beam from the bike's single headlight as it bounced against the road, which began to narrow. He shifted down as asphalt gave way to gravel that spun beneath the bike's wheels.

"Where are we going?" Claire asked, her voice caught on the wind. Suddenly this didn't seem like such a good idea.

"You'll see."

Maneuvering the cycle around the rusting posts of a gate to an abandoned logging road, Kane headed high into the mountains, the bike speeding up one of the twin ruts of a rock and dirt trail that cut through fields of white, rotting stumps that stood like ghostly sentinels on the once-forested ridges. Old growth timber had been stripped bare, clear-cut to leave scarred and naked hillsides. Claire's heart pounded and she felt a sense of dread steal through her blood. Agreeing to go with him, hopping on the motorcycle had been a mistake.

The bike screamed up the hill to a peak where a single stand of fir, somehow saved from the lumberjack's blade, remained intact. Kane slowed and cut the engine.

"Know where we are?" he asked as he took her hand and led her to a wide rock ledge with a view in all directions. Far below they saw the winking lights of Chinook and to the west a few campfires on the beach near the black, rolling waves of the ocean.

"The woods. An abandoned logging camp—"

"Your father's."

"Oh." Why did his voice sound like the knell of death?

"Over there." He wrapped one arm around her waist, rested his chin on her shoulder and pointed with his free hand across a small valley to a hill scraped clean of fir trees. "That's where my old man had his accident."

Claire's stomach turned over. Despite the warm, starlit night and the closeness of his body, she felt a chill slide down her backbone. "You brought me here to show me the place where your father got hurt?"

He didn't respond, just released her and settled onto the ledge. Rummaging in his jacket for a new pack of cigarettes, he closed his eyes and tilted his head back, as if to clear his mind. "I come up here to think sometimes." He rammed a Camel into his mouth, struck a match across the boulder, and, in a sizzle of phosphorus, lit up. The match's small flame tossed gold shadows against his rugged features for a second and he drew in a deep lungful of smoke.

"What do you think about?" she hardly dared ask.

Waving out the match, he grinned, his teeth a slash of white, the tip of his cigarette a single red coal glowing in the dark. "You, sometimes."

She swallowed hard. "Me?"

"Once in a while," he admitted, his eyes finding hers despite the night. "Don't you ever think about me?"

Standing near the bike, she rubbed the tips of her fingers with her thumbs. "I, uh, I try not to."

"But you do."

"Sometimes," she admitted, and felt like a traitor.

"I joined the army."

"What?" Her heart nearly stopped. His words seemed to echo off the surrounding mountains. "You did what?"

"Signed up. Yesterday."

"Why?" A little part of her seemed to wither and die—a part she didn't want to examine too closely. He would be leaving, not that she really cared, she told herself, but the town would somehow be emptier, less vital without him.

"It was time."

She bit her lip. "When—when do you leave?"

He lifted a shoulder and drew hard on his Camel. "A few weeks." An arm thrown around his raised knee, he stared to the west. "Sit down," he said without a smile. "I don't bite—well, not on a first date."

"This—this isn't a date."

He didn't comment, but she knew he was silently calling her a liar as he smoked.

"You think I'm afraid of you," she ventured.

"I think you should be."

"Why?" Nervous as a frightened colt and just as ready to bolt, she walked to the ledge and sat next to him.

"I've got a bad reputation, or so people tell me." His thoughtful gaze centered on her mouth and her lungs stopped taking in air. "You don't, Claire. At least not yet." He ground his cigarette out in the dirt.

"I don't think being with you alone this once is going to change that." Sitting so near to him, Claire told herself she could hold her own, that she wasn't nervous, that her palms were sweating because the night was sticky and humid, that her heart had a tendency to sometimes beat irregularly when she least expected it.

"You have more faith in me than you should."

"I don't think so."

He didn't respond, just stared at her with an intensity that heated her blood. A breeze, soft as the night, caressed her face and ruffled his hair. She couldn't help wonder what it would be like to kiss this hellion, to feel his arms around her, to close her eyes and lose herself in him. But she would never. She loved another boy. "Why did you bring me up here?" Her voice sounded so low and breathy it scared her.

Frowning, not touching her, he studied her face for a long heart-stopping second. "It was a mistake."

"Why?"

With a sigh, he leaned back on his elbows and cocked his head to look at her. For the first time since she'd met him, his hard-edged mask slipped, his face was raw with an unnamed pain. "You don't get it, do you?"

"Get what?"

His jaw clamped tight.

She wasn't about to be shut out. "You started this, Kane," she reminded him. "You talked me into coming here with you—"

"It didn't take much persuading, now, did it? I didn't exactly twist your arm."

He leaned closer to her, and she swallowed against a suddenly dry throat. "Admit it, Claire, you wanted to find out just what it is that makes me tick. You're bored with your predictable and dull life, tired of always doing what's expected, that's why you took up with Taggert, to get your old man's goat. But Harley Taggert doesn't exactly make your blood pump, does he?"

"Leave Harley out of this." Her heart knocked crazily against the confines of her ribs.

"Why? Afraid he'll find out that you think he's dull?"

"He's not—" She bit her tongue. Defending Harley wouldn't change anything. Besides, Kane was twisting her words around, manipulating the course of the conversation. "You brought me up here, Kane, and, without trying to psychoanalyze my reasons for coming, I want to know why."

He lifted a skeptical eyebrow.

Without thinking, she reached forward, dug her fingers into the leather sleeves of his jacket, and felt his muscles stiffen. Slowly, he glanced at her hands, then let his gaze move deliberately up to her face, where the depth of his eyes made breathing impossible. Perspiration clung to her skin.

"You're playing with fire, here, Princess," he warned, his gaze dark with forbidden promise as he inched closer to her.

She licked her lips nervously and he groaned.

"I'm going to regret this in about two minutes," he said, his face so close to hers she could smell the smoke lingering on his breath, see the doubts clouding his eyes. "But since I'm leaving town anyway, I guess it's time to own up to the truth."

She was shaking inside. Afraid of what he might say, desperate to hear it.

With both strong hands he took hold of her shoulders, his hot fingers clutching her desperately. "I'll never say this again, never admit it to anyone else, you understand?"

She nodded.

"The hell of it is, I love you, Claire Holland," he said flatly. "God knows I don't want to. Truth of the matter is, I loathe myself for it, but there it is."

She couldn't speak, was afraid to move, and felt like a frightened doe caught in headlights. Her heart hammered and she stole a glance at his lips, wondering if he was going to kiss her or if she should be the one to press her eager lips to his.

"There's something else you should know. If you were mine, I wouldn't keep you waiting. Harley Taggert's a fool, and you're an even bigger one to let him treat you this way. The reason I call you Princess? It's because that's the way you should be treated. Like goddamned royalty."

"Oh, God," she whispered, her perfect world shattered. He loved her? Kane Moran *loved* her?

"My sentiments exactly. Helluva mess, isn't it?" He let go then and she, too, dropped her hands. "Come on, Claire, I'll take you back to your car." His jaw was hard as granite. "We wouldn't want to keep Harley waiting, now, would we?"

He was on his feet in an instant and striding to the bike.

"Kane—"

He stopped dead in his tracks, glanced over his shoulder.

She swallowed hard. "I, uh, I don't know what to say—"

"Nothing. No lies. No excuses. Just say nothing." He swung one long leg over the bike, switched on the ignition, and threw his weight into the kick-start. The big machine's engine fired and growled, the noise ricocheting off the surrounding hills. "We're both better off if you don't say anything."

But she wasn't sure.

Throat as dry as dust, she walked on legs that didn't seem to touch the ground and settled behind him on the bike. It felt natural—so right—to wrap her arms around his waist. Over the roar of the engine, she thought he muttered, "Let's just forget this night ever existed." But she couldn't be sure. In her heart, she knew, she would treasure these past few hours forever.

CHAPTER 11

Dropping the mainsail and securing the boom, Weston felt the cooling spray of the ocean upon his face. There were times when he enjoyed sailing, being alone on the vast expanse of water, challenging the elements while feeling the pitch and roll of the sea. But not tonight.

Lights from the marina reflected on the dark, ever moving water. Using the power of the motor, he guided the sleek sailboat across the bay and into her berth. He tied up by rote, thought for a second about Crystal, then discarded the idea of seeing her again. She was warm and willing, a girl who would do anything to please him, and she bored him senseless. He needed a new conquest, a challenge.

The dismal part of it was, he knew that he'd never be satisfied, not with some new innocent conquest, not with an easy score, not even with Kendall if she accepted his offer. Christ, what a bastard he'd been to her—offering to screw her and impregnate her as if he were being noble. The truth of the matter was he'd just like a taste of Forsythe pussy. Besides, the thought of siring a child and having Harley raise it appealed to the perverse side of his nature. Not only would Kendall be forever in his debt, but he'd have one over on his stupid ass of a brother.

He locked the cabin and realized that even more than Kendall, he wanted one of the Holland girls.

Why? Because they'd been thrown in his face for nearly twenty years, described by his father as off-limits, the enemy, Dutch Holland's evil, if beautiful, spawn.

Which made them all the more interesting. And now that Harley had the balls to date Claire openly, Weston saw no good reason not to act on his male impulses. Oh, he talked a good story with all that bullshit to Harley about being cut out of the will, but the old man would never be so rash, and Weston would never do anything to upset his place as primary heir. He'd worked too many years sucking up to his father, playing Neal's games, shining at everything he did to blow it now. Neal Taggert made no bones about the fact that Weston was his favorite and as such would inherit the lion's share of the family fortune. Weston would never blow it and lose out.

But what if that son steps forward, the other one, the one no one acknowledges—the bastard?

When Weston had mentioned that the old rumor was rearing its ugly head again, Neal had sworn and blamed Dutch Holland for spreading lies. For some unknown reason Dutch hated Neal and would stop at nothing to ruin him.

Weston had been placated, at least for the time being, and had even stolen a copy of his father's will from the old man's office in Portland. Neal had just altered the document, but he hadn't lied. When his father kicked off, Weston was set for life.

If he didn't screw up. He wouldn't. He was too farsighted to mess up something important, but oh, he had an itch in his pants for Miranda Holland. What he wouldn't give for one night to show that icy, sharp-tongued woman what hot-blooded, snarling, pure animal lust was all about. He was a good lover and he could show her things that would leave her sweating, heart pounding, and begging for more.

That thought brought a smile to his lips. Every time he'd so much as smiled at her, she'd looked down her nose at him, and the thought of her pleading with him, her hair wet with perspiration, her face flushed, her supple fingers reaching for his zipper brought his cock to attention.

"Someday," he said under his breath. Someday she'd find out what a real man could reduce her to. Smiling, he adjusted his pants, and left the sailboat and the pier behind him as he walked under the arched neon Illahee Yacht Club sign and paused to light a cigarette. Another vision of Miranda Holland stole through his mind, as it had while he was out in the ocean and about a dozen times a day. For Christ's sake, he was getting as bad as Harley, except, unlike Claire, who was apparently willing to warm his younger brother's bed, Miranda would rather spit on him than talk to him.

Climbing into his convertible he imagined again what it would be like to make it with Miranda. Tall, long-legged, with eyes as cool as blue ice, she'd disdained most boys' advances, burying her straight, nearly perfect nose in a book more often than not, but Weston sensed that beneath her frosty composure was a hot-blooded woman who could be an animal in bed.

Sharp-witted and rapier-tongued, an unapproachable woman who had her entire future mapped out for herself, she would like the world to believe that she had no time for any attention from the opposite sex.

But she was handing out false advertising.

Weston remembered following Miranda in her black Camaro just last week. A guy had been with her, Hunter Riley, the stepson of Dutch Holland's caretaker. In Weston's estimation, Riley was a big-time loser. Miranda and Hunt had probably known each other for years, of course, and she could have been giving him a ride into town, but there was something a little too familiar in the way she had turned and smiled at him, or the casual toss of his arm around her shoulders, his fingers gently rubbing the back of her neck.

"Son of a bitch," he muttered, suddenly furious with Riley. Who was he? A nobody who worked for Weston's old man's logging company setting chokers part-time and for the Hollands tending the garden with his old man. A zero. Hunter Riley had barely scraped together enough credits to get through high school and was now struggling through classes at a local community college.

So what did sophisticated Miranda see in the roughneck?

Women, he thought as he took a corner a little too fast and the tires squealed, he'd give an inch off his dick just to understand them.

With the top of his Porsche down, he sped toward Stone Illahee, the resort his father disdained. He needed a lay and a good one. So he was on the prowl. Again. Itching to score. The hard heat between his legs a driving force. He didn't know if it was his incredible sex drive that egged him on or if it was his sharply honed competitive streak that urged him into sometimes poor choices of partners. Not that it mattered.

"Miranda," he muttered. She would be the one, although Claire was more woman than he'd first imagined. He'd once thought her dull as a church mouse, but as she'd grown and matured, he'd seen a tougher side to her. She was the most athletic of Dutch's daughters, forever on a horse or boat, swimming or rock climbing, a shy girl who'd turned into a daredevil of sorts. Probably why she was dating Harley.

Harley! What a pathetic excuse for a man he was. Always whining. Weston could hardly believe they were brothers. Harley was too sensitive, too easily manipulated ever to become a real man. Shifting down at the entrance of Stone Illahee, he grinned to himself and, on impulse, drove through the massive gates guarding the exclusive resort. Past the golf course and tennis courts, around a fenced area of dense, flowering shrubbery that screened the pool from the main parking lot. It wasn't quite ten, but he'd heard that old man Holland was out of town for the weekend and wouldn't be hanging around the resort. None of Dutch's workers, if they noticed a Taggert in their midst, would dare try and throw him off the property.

He was safe.

So why did he feel the touch of worry? Why did he sense that coming here was a mistake of immeasurable and irrefutable proportions?

He rounded a corner, and the smooth gray stone and dark timbers of the main lodge came into view. Splashed by hidden spotlights, five stories of irregular stone, glass, and cedar rose upward along the rocky ledge near the beach. Near the front door, an illuminated waterfall rushed and tumbled noisily through stands of contorted pine and rhododendron.

Feeling like an interloper, Weston parked his car, pocketed his keys, and headed inside. Music from the bar was flowing through open windows, calling to him like a siren's song. He didn't expect to see any of Dutch's daughters tonight, but there might be some willing female hanging out in the bar. His conscience pricked a bit as he remembered Crystal. They'd made love in the sailboat earlier in the afternoon before he'd dropped her off so that she could go to work. She was beautiful with her smooth golden skin, dark eyes, and incredible black hair, but she was too willing, too easy, a sex slave to him. Anything he wanted from her, she'd give. *Anything.* She acted as if he was her lord and master and sometimes he played the role to the hilt, but she was beginning to bore him with her acquiescence. He needed more of a challenge, a woman with a little more fire. One who would fight him for a while before lying down for him and finally spreading her legs.

He wanted Miranda Holland.

"You're as much a fool as Harley," he muttered under his breath as he pushed open the oak and glass door and headed into the bar. Down a short hallway he followed the scent of cigarette smoke and the tease of throbbing music.

A Portland band with a female lead singer in a tight leather minidress was playing some jazzy number he didn't recognize— one with too much saxophone and not enough bass. Weston settled into a booth as far from the stage as possible. Drumming his fingers nervously on the table, he stared at the cedar walls covered with fishing nets, Japanese floats, stuffed and mounted fish from all over the world as well as the weapons used to kill them. Harpoons, spears, poles, and tackle boxes were interspersed between the glassy-eyed salmon, marlin, and sharks.

A waitress in a black skirt, white blouse, and red tie floated over to him. He ordered a beer and grinned when she asked him to show his ID, proving that he was twenty-one.

"Weston Taggert," she said, her lips curving into a wider smile as she recognized his name. "I'll be back in a minute."

Several women caught his attention and smiled, but he wasn't interested. They were too easy and, from the looks of the desperation in their eyes, had played the barhopping game too long.

No, he wanted something different tonight. The ache in his groin wouldn't settle for an easy lay.

"There ya go, hon," the waitress said as she deposited a glass of light malt on the table.

The beer was cold, but didn't do much to cool his blood, and Weston drained his glass quickly, realizing that dropping by on Dutch Holland's sacred property wasn't all that much of a thrill. He left a five-dollar bill on the table and was walking across the lot to his car when he saw her—the youngest of Dutch's daughters, her blond hair shimmering silver under the lights of the parking lot. Tessa. Dressed in a pair of ragged cutoffs, a skimpy T-shirt, and a short-cropped leather vest decorated with rhinestones that sparkled under the security lamps, Tessa looked far from one of the richest girls in this stretch of country.

Rumor had it that she was a hot pants, always strutting through town in tight shorts and tiny sweaters that showed off her incredible breasts and slipped up to reveal the taut skin of her tanned abdomen. Oftentimes she flung a leather jacket carelessly over her back, but she never zipped it up, never gave up a chance for anyone to catch a glimpse of her incredible figure. Like now.

She was sitting on the ledge surrounding the waterfall, smoking a cigarette and staring at the fountain with disinterested eyes.

She wasn't the woman he wanted. She wasn't Miranda.

But she was here, and Weston was horny.

"You know, I was just thinking about you and your sisters and here you are," he said, shoving up the sleeves of his jacket and playing with the truth just a bit.

She glanced up sharply, startled, to stare at him hard for the span of a heartbeat, then turned her attention back to the swirling water. "Does that line ever work?"

"It's the truth."

"Right. And I'm the queen of England."

"I don't think so. Rumor has it she's a little older than you."

Tessa rolled her eyes and took another drag. "What're you

doing here? I thought this place was off-limits to the Taggerts. Anyone with your last name who drives through the gates takes the chance of being drawn and quartered."

Weston laughed. At least she wasn't dumb as a stone. "Maybe it's time one of us checked out the competition."

Again she looked at him with those incredible blue eyes, then lifted a shoulder as if she didn't really give a damn what he or any of his family did. "Suit yourself."

"Waiting for someone?" He sat next to her on the ledge and expected her to move a little, to put some distance between her body and his, but she didn't. Instead, she sucked hard on her cigarette, then shot smoke from the corner of her mouth.

"I guess."

"You don't know?"

"That's right. I don't know." Defiance hoisted her chin upward a notch, and he saw beyond the false bravado and pride to a younger and more vulnerable girl, an instant of insight into what made Tessa Holland tick. She blinked, and her hard shell was back in place, an armor in which there was a tiny chink.

"Is someone coming for you?"

"Maybe."

"Do you need a ride?"

She smiled and flicked her cigarette into the lit pool. The butt sizzled, bounced in the foamy swirls, and disappeared beneath the waterfall. "I might."

"Where do you want to go?"

She hesitated a second, then arched perfectly shaped blond brows. "Maybe I don't care."

His mouth twitched into a smile. She actually had the balls to defy him. "Maybe you should."

"What do you have in mind?" Her voice was low and intimate. She was playing with him, and he loved the game. It was one he understood, one he performed well, one in which he was always the victor.

"That depends on you."

"Does it?" She stood suddenly and hauled a fringed black bag over her shoulder. With a final glance of disdain at her father's resort, she said. "Okay, then let's go. You can give me a ride up to Seaside."

"What's there?" he asked and her smile brightened the night.

"What isn't?"

Harley was late. Claire, pacing on the dock where his father's sailboat was moored, was just about to give up on him, not just for the night, but possibly forever. That thought caused a chill in her heart and raised goose bumps on her arms.

"Oh, Harley," she whispered, feeling like the fool her sisters had accused her of being.

Sweet, perfect Harley had changed. He'd become distracted lately, willing to call and change their plans. When they'd first started dating, he couldn't get enough of her, and nothing, *nothing* had been able to stop him from being with her. His father's ranting, when Neal had found out, had fallen upon deaf ears; his older brother's warnings had only made him bolder; and his sister Paige's whining complaints had seemed to add fuel to the fire of his passion.

Claire, too, would have done anything to be with him in those first few mind-spinning weeks. He was kind, sweet, charming, and he adored her. He'd given up everything, his old girlfriend included, and suffered his father's wrath and his brother's taunts because, he'd vowed, he loved her. And she had believed him with all her young, naive heart.

But things had changed, she thought now, as she leaned against the rail of the pier and looked into the dark water where the string of lights suspended overhead was reflected in bright bobbing pinpoints on the inky surface. She felt it in the air, that change, like the turn of the wind, a quiet alteration in his need to be with her.

Her mistake had been making love to him. Ever since that one afternoon when they'd crossed the invisible line of true lovers, a barrier they'd sworn not to step over, their relationship had changed.

They'd been alone, canoeing, and had stopped at a small cove on the north shore of the lake. Harley had brought along a bottle of wine he'd swiped from his father's cellar. Together, with the summer sun warming their skin, they'd drunk, toasted each other, swam, splashed, laughed and kissed, delirious in their love.

Claire had never felt so light-headed, never so much as tasted any alcohol before, but there was something magical about that late afternoon, and she'd thrown caution to the soft wind that had brushed against her cheeks and ruffled Harley's black hair.

Harley was bolder, more intense than he had been, and Claire's thinking was a little muddled. His kisses had deepened, become demanding, and she'd willingly opened her mouth to him, let him skim her slick body with his hands. His fingers slid brazenly beneath the top of her swimsuit, and he'd discarded the scrap of fabric in a quick, deft move, as if he'd done it a hundred times before. Holding her close, treading water, he kissed her breasts above and beneath the surface. She tingled and a warm ache spread deep inside her.

"Put your legs around my waist," he'd ordered gently against her skin, his eyelashes studded with droplets of lake water. When she'd complied, wrapping her thighs around his muscular torso and lying on her back, her breasts bare to the warm summer sun, he'd whispered, "That's a girl," and kissed her abdomen. She was floating, drifting on a cloud of sensation as he carried her to the shore and began nuzzling her breasts in earnest, touching, sucking, creating a hot whirlpool deep in her center. He guided her hand to his crotch, groaned, and swore his undying love. He kicked off his trunks and she saw him naked for the first time. His erection was stiff and ready and scared her a little, but he was already peeling off the bottom of her suit.

Then they were naked, blissfully kissing, rubbing against each other, aching and wanting. He didn't ask, and she didn't object when he rolled her onto her back, parted her legs with his knees, and, in one quick thrust, stole the virginity she'd so valiantly guarded for seventeen years.

There had been pain, yes, and a few tears, but he'd kissed them away after three quick thrusts and his release. He'd fallen against her and, gasping in ecstasy, sworn he would love her until his dying day.

They hadn't planned on going all the way, she thought now, as she ran a hand along the weathered railing and a skinny black cat darted into the shadows. They had discussed the possibility, of course, as they'd experimented with making out and petting, but had agreed to wait until they were married for the ultimate act of consummation.

But that afternoon with the hot sun urging them on and the wine clouding their judgment, they'd made love.

Her fingers curled over the rail, and when she closed her eyes, she still remembered him, sweating hard, his muscles straining, his face set in a look of triumph as he'd entered her. She'd been blind with desire, hot with a yearning she was certain only he could fill. She'd been blissfully, foolishly in love.

They'd sworn then to always be together, to marry, to have children, to heal the scars that existed between their families, but lately Harley had changed. He didn't smile as easily and he wanted to have sex all the time. Whenever they were together, which wasn't often in the past few weeks, he expected her to make love to him. It seemed that since that day at the lake all he wanted from her was her body.

Which was crazy. He loved her. Or did he?

She heard his car and her heart leapt because a part of her had wondered if he'd stand her up again. Footsteps clattered on the dock and she smiled when she saw him running toward her.

"Sorry I'm late," he said, as he swept her into his arms and buried his face in the bend of her neck. "God, I've missed you!" His hands tangled in her hair, and he sighed more loudly than the wind chasing over the bay. Her heart kicked over and she forgave him. This was her dear, sweet Harley, the boy she loved with all her body and soul.

Closing her eyes, she held him close, ignoring the doubts, the fears, the worries that had tried to undermine their love.

"I've missed you, too," she said, her voice husky, tears burning in her eyes.

"Forgive me."

Her heart nearly stopped. "I don't need to forgive you."

"Oh, Claire, if you only knew." The despair in his voice echoed in her soul.

"Knew what?"

His entire body clenched, and he held her so tightly she could barely breathe.

"Knew what, Harley?"

He hesitated a beat too long. "That I love you. No matter what happens, please believe that I love you."

"Harley . . . nothing's going to happen," she whispered, but even as she clung to him, she felt a chill as cold as the sea in winter burrow deep in her heart.

"I hope you're right," he said, lifting his head to stare into her eyes. "I hope to God you're right."

CHAPTER 12

Checking her watch, Miranda felt her heartbeat quicken. It was nearly time to meet Hunter at the cottage, just as they'd planned. Her mouth went dry at the thought.

For the first time in her life, she was in love, and though she knew it was crazy, that she and Hunter Riley had no future together, she couldn't ignore the attraction she felt for him, the conviction in her soul that he was, at least for the moment, the man for her.

She'd seen enough of Claire's heartache to realize that she, too, was walking a dangerous path, a thin tightrope guaranteed to snap and only bring her pain, but for over eighteen years she'd trod carefully, never straying from the straight and narrow, hell-bent to prove herself as worthy as any son, any male heir, Dutch Holland might have spawned.

But for all her efforts, her father hadn't been impressed, nor had he even noticed, and soon she'd be off to college. She snatched a sweater from the foot of her bed and tucked her purse under her arm as she headed down the back stairs.

Hunter was older, and though he'd dropped out of high school, he'd gained his equivalency diploma and was taking classes at the local community college while working part-time logging for the Taggerts, and helping his aging father with odd jobs around the Holland estate.

Miranda had first noticed him—really noticed him—late in the spring when he and his dad had been clearing brush from one of the picnic spots on the shore of the lake. She'd been sitting on the back porch, reading as clouds had stolen over the sky and fat rain-drops had begun to fall.

Beneath the roof of the porch, she'd been dry, but Hunter and his father had worked on, even when the sky had opened and the spring shower had come down in earnest, curtains of water soaking the already wet ground. Throughout the downpour, Hunter had continued to slice away the scrub oak and hazel brush, uncaring that rain ran down his chin and plastered his T-shirt to his back. Miranda saw through the thin cotton, watched in throat-dry fascina-tion as his smooth muscles worked rhythmically, in a fluid motion that caused butterflies to flutter wildly in the pit of her stomach.

Sandy blond hair turned dark in the rain, and when he looked over his shoulder to pin her with eyes as gray as a winter storm, she had to look away. Heat climbed up the back of her neck and some new feeling, a mind-stripping sexual awareness found its way to a spot low in her belly.

She hadn't said a word to him that day, nor the next when, as the sun warmed the damp ground, creating steam and a sultry heat, she'd sat on the porch again, pretending interest in her book, while never taking her eyes off a man she'd known all her life but had never really seen.

"You were watching me," he'd accused her in the stables later in the week when she, not knowing that he was helping his father shore up the empty hayloft, had walked inside looking for Claire. The elder Riley was nowhere in sight, but Hunter stood at the top rung of the metal ladder of the loft, ripping off a floorboard that must've rotted through.

Sweat trickled down his neck and dampened the strands of hair at his nape.

"Me?" She stared up at him, past long legs tanned by hours of hard work in the sun and dusted by golden hair. Above his knees a tattered pair of cutoffs hung low on his hips and seemed barely supported by a disreputable tool belt. The rest of his body was naked, smooth sun-bronzed skin, sinewy muscles, chest hair that was a rich red-blond. Determined not to prove the jackass right,

Miranda looked past all his purely male features to the back of his head. He tossed the rotted board onto the floor at the base of the ladder. Crash! Dust motes swirled upward, a horsefly buzzed wildly, and Miranda coughed as Hunter slid a new piece of planed lumber into place.

"No reason to deny it," he went on. "The other day while I was clearing brush. You were watching."

"No, I—"

"I thought you were the smart one. The one that never lied." His voice was a low, sexy drawl that teased her even as his words condemned. "Don't tell me all those rumors are wrong."

"Excuse me?" she said, bristling. Who was he to talk to her as if she were a sneaky, untrustworthy child trying to pull a fast one on him?

He slid some nails from a pouch in his belt and shoved them into a corner of his mouth. Around the stainless steel toothpicks, he said, "Everyone in town seems to think that you're the smart one of the three Holland sisters. Ambitious and driven. You know, the oldest, most responsible kid, and all that shit." He slid a look down the ladder and grinned around the damned nails. "Come on, Randa, don't try to convince me that you don't know your own reputation."

"I don't listen to gossip."

"Right." He slipped a hammer from its loop.

Folding her arms under her breasts, she gave up all pretenses and leveled her gaze up at him. "You presume to know me."

"Just your type." He placed a nail on the board and slammed it three times with the hammer. Bam! Bam! Bam!

"I'm not a type."

"No? Admit it, you get off watching peons labor for your dad while you sit around and let your nail polish dry." He cast a look over one muscular shoulder, and his gaze was as hot as it was condemning.

"You know what? You're just another arrogant, self-serving jerk. There's plenty of those in this town."

"You were watching me."

"My mistake."

"Sure."

He turned back to the task at hand and banged another nail into place. Fluid muscles rippled with the effort. "And, just for the record, I'm not a jerk."

"Just like I'm not a self-centered rich bitch."

A low chuckle filled the barn. "No?"

"No." Miranda headed for the door, and he dropped lithely to the floor to land in front of her.

Startled, she couldn't help but take a step back. He smelled of sweat and musk and he was so close—so half-dressed, so blatantly sensual, she lost her breath for a second. His jaw was hard, softened only by a day's growth of golden whiskers and his eyes, darker in the shaded barn, were the color of gun-metal. He was staring at her so intently she wanted to back away, but there was a post from the hayloft already brushing her back, and she wouldn't give him the satisfaction of backing down, not even when she glanced at his mouth and her stomach curled in on itself as she saw the edge of white teeth against the hard seam of thin, dangerous lips. She licked her own and he stepped closer still, only the barest of space between the tips of her breasts and his naked chest.

"I heard you wanted to be an attorney."

"That's . . . that's right."

Flat nipples were partially hidden in the swirls of chest hair. Rigid abdominal muscles flexed as he breathed.

Her knees were suddenly less than dependable.

"Big ambitions?"

"No . . . yes, I guess so."

"What're you trying to prove?"

The question pierced through her consciousness, and when she raised her eyes to his, she saw that he was no longer mocking her, just curious and, from the dilation of his pupils she guessed, he was as sexually aware of her as she was of him.

"Nothing. I don't have to prove anything."

"But you want to." He lifted his hands and grabbed the post behind her, pinning her within the span of his arms, but not touching any part of her.

"Yes."

"Why? So your old man will quit spouting off about not having any sons?"

"I don't know," she said, her voice breathy with the lie. Of course she wanted to prove to Dutch Holland that she was as good as any son he might have sired.

"Or because you want to compete in a man's world?"

"I just want to be the best that I can."

"And to that end you'll deny yourself any simple pleasures."

"You don't know anything about me."

"I know that you eat carefully, exercise regularly by doing calisthenics in your room, read whatever you think will expand your mind, and try your damnedest to prove that you're everything Dutch should want in a child."

"How do you know—"

"I've been watching you, too."

Her throat closed, and she wondered if he'd peered through her windows at night, seen her look at her body, touch her breasts and smooth her hands down her abdomen while wondering what a man's touch would feel like. "You had no right—"

"No, just a desire. The same as yours."

"I don't have any de—"

"Don't lie."

He was too near; the stables too close and tight. "Get out of my way."

"If you're ever going to be worth your salt as a lawyer, you're going to have to learn how to handle people as well as insults and arguments. Even compliments upon occasion." His gaze lowered to her breasts rising and falling rapidly beneath her shirt.

"Oh, I get it," she mocked, unable to keep the sting out of her words. "This was a test. So now you're my teacher."

"Just making conversation."

His eyes centered on her mouth for a heart-stopping second, and something inside her, a part of her that was warm and vital and wanting, responded. She loathed him and yet was attracted to him on a level that she didn't want to admit existed. "Make conversation with someone who's interested."

"You're interested."

"I don't think so."

His smile said he didn't believe her. He stepped aside and, as she tried to pass, grabbed hold of her wrist. With a quick tug he spun her around and suddenly all those rock-hard muscles surrounded her. She couldn't move, could barely breathe, and her heart was knocking so frantically in her chest she was afraid she might pass out.

"Don't—"

His lips crashed down on hers in a kiss that was hard and punishing and ripped the breath from her lungs. She struggled but knew the effort was useless. Her rational mind swore and screamed silently to be set free while that wanton unknown womanly part of her that was just emerging wanted desperately to kiss back, to explore, to feel the excitement of pure, unfettered sex.

His hands were big and strong, his body hot and sweating, and he smelled of male and sawdust. He groaned deep in the back of his throat, and his tongue rimmed her lips to part them easily.

"You're interested," he repeated into her open mouth as he released her. "When you're woman enough to admit it, call me."

Stumbling backward through the door, she shook her head. "You'll rot in hell first."

"I don't think so."

And, damn him, he'd been right. For two weeks, she'd ignored him, looked through him whenever he was working on the estate, took great pains to remove herself whenever he was around, but each time her mind had spun back to that one, soul-wrenching kiss in the stables, her heartbeat had elevated, and she had begun to sweat.

At night, lying in her bed she'd thought of him, her body hot from the lingering summer heat, or during the day when she was supposed to be studying for the night classes she took, college courses through the local community college, another place she'd bumped into him in the small quad.

After two weeks, she'd abandoned her stand and thrown away her pride. She'd picked up the phone and called him. That night they'd spent hours on the beach, walking near the tide, watching as foamy surf licked the sand. He hadn't so much as touched her.

The next time was no different, nor the next. It was as if that one kiss had been all Hunter would ever share with her. Finally, she'd laid a hand on his wrist, tilted her head, and sighed. "Are you afraid of me?"

He laughed, a deep rumbling sound that echoed through her heart. "Afraid? Don't be ridiculous."

"But—" She felt like a fool. What could she say? He was leaning against the fender of her car and the sun was blinding and hot. She'd parked on a secluded stretch of beach miles away from her father's resort.

"But what?"

"We never . . . well, you know."

"Couldn't begin to guess," he drawled, but a smile tugged at the corners of his mouth.

"Don't be coy, Hunter."

"Then spit it out. What's on your mind?"

She swallowed and dropped her hand at a loss for words.

"Come on, counselor," he goaded. "Anyone who thinks she's gonna be some big hotshot attorney should be able to say what's on her mind."

"You never touch me," she blurted, feeling her face turn a dozen shades of red.

"And it bothers you." He fiddled with his ring, a gold band set with an onyx stone, while waiting for an answer.

She wanted to lie, but didn't. "Yeah, it does."

"Maybe I think you're untouchable."

"No, there's something else. What is it, Hunter?"

He eyed her up and down and then, muttering an oath under his breath, grabbed her. Hungry lips crashed down on hers, big hands spread over her back, and she melted against him, her body molding to his as she kissed him with the same urgency and fire that seemed to consume him. She opened her mouth eagerly, accepting his tongue and sagging against him, hungry for the touch and feel of him.

Waves pounded the beach, sand brushed up against her legs, the sun warmed her back and she felt as if they were the only two people in the universe.

"This . . . this is what you want?" he asked, pushing a strand of hair from her cheek.

I want you to love me! she thought wildly. "Yes."

"And this?" he kissed her again, and one hand reached under her blouse to touch her breast.

"Y-yes."

Hard fingers delved into the plain white cotton cup and brushed against her nipple.

Her breath died as he teased her breast, and she began to ache from the inside out. "More?" he asked, the single word ragged.

"Yes—no. Oooooh." Leaning against the car, he shifted, spreading his legs and dragging her between them. Her shorts were pressed into that intimate V of his crotch, the denim of his fly raised and stiff as he kissed her and unhooked her bra. Her breasts swung free and his hands, his rough, hot hands, were everywhere—touching, caressing, fondling.

"This could be trouble," he said, as he toyed with the zipper of her shorts.

"For you?"

"For you."

"Oh." She kissed him with the eager anticipation of a virgin flirting with her first real attempt at lovemaking.

"There's a point where I can't stop."

"Then don't stop. Ever—"

"Oh, Randa." He kissed her again, his lips demanding, his fingers touching her abdomen, and then as suddenly as he'd pulled her to him, he pushed her away. "No," he growled to himself. "No, no no. This is no good."

"Wh-what? Of course it's good."

"You don't get it, do you?" He shook his head and ran stiff, frustrated fingers through his hair. "You and I—we're worlds apart, Miranda, and there's nothing, not one damned thing, we can do about it."

"I don't understand."

"You will," he said, squinting fiercely at the horizon.

She'd refused to be put off and had called him boldly, brazenly, becoming one of those girls she detested, the ones who chased after boys. And it had worked. He'd agreed to keep seeing her, but only on the condition that they keep their relationship a secret.

"I don't want to deal with all the fallout and shit that might come down if your old man finds out," he'd said when they were alone by the stream. "Let him have a coronary over Taggert and your sister, but keep my name out of it."

"Why?"

"It's just too damned complicated, okay? Trust me on this one."

And she had. No one knew that they were seeing each other, their meetings were secret rendezvous that added to the mystique and romance of it all. As she drove to the cottage on the north side of the property where they'd agreed to meet, she knew that they would probably make love. They'd come close before, but he'd always held back, and she'd begun to trust him with her heart. Tonight, with a spattering of stars flung over the dark heavens, she expected that they might not be able to restrain themselves, and, damn it, she didn't care.

She turned into the overgrown lane that led to the cottage and heard the sound of dry weeds scrape the underside of her car. Grass as tall as the windows of the Camaro waved in the wind and ancient, untended roses gave off their sweet fragrance as they tangled in long vines along with the berries that grew wild in this part of Oregon.

No one used the cottage any longer. It had been built before the lodge, around the turn of the century, and had been long forgotten. Berry vines climbed over the porch rails, several bricks had fallen from the chimney, but inside it was warm and dry and tonight, though the temperature was hovering near sixty-five, a fire glowed through the windows.

Hunter was waiting.

Miranda's heart knocked wildly as she hurried up the front steps and pressed on the door.

"You're late." His voice surprised her for she hadn't heard him on the porch. She jumped, startled, then felt his strong arms wrap possessively around her.

"You're early."

"Couldn't wait."

"No?" She laughed as he swept her up into his arms and kicked open the door. Like a groom carrying his new bride over the threshold, he kissed her as he walked inside. Her head swam as he laid her on an old iron bed covered with quilts and pillows that he'd brought. The fire crackled in the grate, mossy logs being devoured by eager flames, and Miranda looked up at the man she'd come to love.

Never predictable, he could be cruel one minute, kind the next. He'd shown her how to shoot a bow and arrow, how to make a stone skip on the surface of the water, confided that boys at fourteen would rather eat than do anything and at sixteen wanted to screw anything that moved. He didn't suffer fools and refused to date her openly. "No reason to get tongues wagging," he'd said. "Believe me, you don't want to be the topic of conversation."

"I wouldn't mind," she'd argued, but he'd hear none of it, and the argument was their one source of friction.

Now, as she lay in his arms, staring up at his strong jaw and eyes dark with passion, she wondered if she'd marry him someday. For the first time she saw beyond their stations in life—the privileged daughter of a millionaire and the poor stepson of the caretaker. What did it matter?

He kissed her and her blood raced. The old mattress sagged. Miranda wrapped her arms around his neck as he began to stroke her, touch her, cause her skin to come to life. Never had she felt so alive, so wanted.

Desire uncoiled deep inside her, stretching and yawning, clawing her gently in the deepest, most feminine part of her body.

"Hunter," Miranda whispered, her voice a rasp, her blood hot and wild. He was kissing her, lowering her bra strap, touching his wet tongue to skin that had never seen the light of day. The stubble of his beard was rough, his breath hot, his flesh, like hers, on fire.

Her fingers curled into his thick hair and she gasped with want as firelight flickered and danced in coppery shadows on his skin.

He unhooked her bra and let it drop to the floor, watching in silent fascination as her breasts, so tightly bound, fell free. "You're so damned beautiful," he finally said, his breath fanning her skin. "It should be a sin." He touched her nipple and it hardened expectantly before he slid lower and began to suck.

"Oh . . . oh . . ." His hands were in her shorts, skimming them off her buttocks, touching her suddenly moist curls, sliding intimately on the inside of her thighs, rubbing up against her, probing into the most secret of her places.

She couldn't help herself. She, who had always been cool and aloof, who, some boys had said, had ice water running through her veins, arched against him, silently begging for more. She was in a tiny room in a dilapidated cottage, on a bed that had cradled lovers for nearly a hundred years, and she was kissing a man she barely knew, a man who refused to be seen in public with her, a man who was about to become her first and only lover.

Afterward, in the sheen of afterglow, he held her close and stroked her face. His ring reflected the flickering flames of the fire. She touched the black stone. "Is this significant?" she asked.

"It's the only thing I'm wearing."

Chuckling softly she smiled up at him. "I know. I just wondered if it was significant." She twisted a finger in the coarse hairs of his chest. "You know, did some girl give it to you?"

He snorted. "Hardly." He took off the circle of gold and stared through its center. "This is all that I have of my natural father—the guy without a face who impregnated my mother and took a long hike. I should throw it away, I suppose, but I keep it to remind me that the bastard didn't want me, didn't want my ma, and I was lucky enough to have Dan Riley as a stepfather."

"What was his name?"

"My *real* father?" He sighed. "Don't know. No one ever said, and there's no name listed on my birth certificate."

"Don't you want to know?"

"Nah." Sliding the ring back on his finger, he pulled her closer and she nestled against the hard muscles of his naked shoulder. "It doesn't matter." Pressing a kiss to the top of her head, he added, "Right now, all that matters is you and me."

"Forever?" she asked.

"Forever is a long time, but maybe. Yeah, maybe."

Miranda tilted her head upward, waiting for the kiss she knew would come. She'd finally found a little bit of heaven right here on earth.

"You were with Weston Taggert last night?" Miranda whispered, feeling her face turn pale as she poured water into the Mr. Coffee machine and heard the first gurgling sounds as the coffeemaker began to heat. Her sister's surprise announcement ricocheted off the walls of her mind as she was still coming to terms with the fact that she and Hunter had made love. The soreness between her legs this morning was a constant reminder of last night. She cleared her throat and tried to concentrate on the problem at hand. The problem, as always, was Tessa. "For God's sake, Tessa, why?"

Tessa lifted an insolent I-don't-give-a-damn-what-you-think shoulder as she strolled to the table and stifled a yawn. "Why not?"

"You know why not, the guy's bad news."

"Because he's a Taggert? Ah, ah, ah, Randa, you're starting to sound like Dad."

"Give me a break, this has nothing to do with him being a Taggert and you know it. The guy's got a reputation." *And what about Hunter? Why won't he let anyone know that you're a couple? Is he ashamed of you, trying to protect you, or, like Weston, just plain bad news?*

The radio was playing and an ancient Kenny Rogers song wafted through the room.

"Ruby . . . don't take your love to town . . ."

Before she could hear any more of the song, Miranda snapped off the radio.

Tessa kicked out one of the café chairs and sank into it. Holding her chin in one hand, she offered Miranda a smile that was patently coy. "Weston's considered the most eligible bachelor in Chinook."

"Listen to you! What are you talking about—eligible bachelors?" Miranda opened a loaf of bread and slapped two slices into the toaster. "You're only fifteen, for crying out loud. *Fifteen!* A baby! It's not like you need to find a husband!"

Petulance thrust out Tessa's lower lip. She rubbed her eyes and last night's mascara discolored her cheeks. "Well *I* don't plan on being a wrinkled old maid."

"Is that a jab at me?"

"Take it any way you want it." Tessa was playing with the salt and pepper shakers, staring at the ceramic strawberries as if they held all the secrets of the universe.

The toast popped up and Miranda threw in another couple of slices before buttering the first two with a vengeance that nearly tore holes in the bread. "I'm not planning on being an old maid, but neither am I going to be some rich boy's toy. Weston Taggert is a user." She used the butter knife to punctuate her words by wagging it in Tessa's direction. "He takes what he can get from girls. Then, when he's bored, he throws them away like empty beer cans."

"Says who?"

"Anybody with any brains!"

Tessa slumped lower in her chair and ignored the plate of toast Miranda set on the table beside her.

"Look, he's been coming on to me for years," Miranda admitted.

Tessa laughed. "You?" She eyed her straight arrow of a sister. "I don't think so."

"It's true."

"Yeah, well, I'm not buying it. We got anything to drink around here? Juice?"

"In the fridge." Miranda would be damned if she'd pour Tessa a glass of anything. The toast was good enough.

She wanted to warn Tessa about Weston again, but it would only be an exercise in frustration. There was just no arguing with her. What a disaster! Tessa and Weston. Dutch would have a heart attack. Miranda only hoped that this thing with Weston was a one-night stand.

"Where's Ruby?" Tessa asked as she reached for a piece of toast and began peeling off the crust.

Miranda checked her watch. Nearly ten o'clock and Ruby Songbird still hadn't shown up. Miranda couldn't remember a day when Ruby hadn't been in the house before eight, washing windows, scrubbing floors, baking bread, and stoically giving orders that she expected to be unquestioned and obeyed. Miranda disregarded any thought that something might be wrong and focused her attention on her youngest sister. Tessa had a way of getting into trouble. Big life-altering trouble. "Look, I don't know what you're thinking, Tess, but getting involved with Weston is all wrong, believe me."

"Just like Harley and Claire are all wrong?" Tessa asked, her gaze skating to the doorway as Claire walked in, taking in the tail end of the conversation.

"It's different." Miranda felt trapped, cornered by her cunning fox of a sister.

"How?" Tessa demanded.

Miranda silently counted to ten and gazed directly at Claire. "Harley and Claire think they're in love. They've dated a while, seem committed to each other and—"

"What about Kendall Forsythe?"

Claire turned as pale as winter sunlight, and her fingers coiled tightly. "What?"

"Harley can't seem to really break it off with her." Tessa scraped back her chair and if she was conscious of the pain in Claire's eyes, she didn't show it.

"That's a lie," Claire said firmly. "He and Kendall are history."

"I don't think so." Tessa swung open the refrigerator door and rummaged inside until she came up with a jar of Ruby's homemade raspberry jam and a pitcher of orange juice.

Ruby? Where in the world was she? Miranda walked to the windows and stared at the path to the driveway, the one that curved around the back of the garage and cut between the lake and swimming pool, the one Ruby used each morning.

"You shouldn't believe anything Weston tells you." Claire, finding some steel for her spine, strode across the kitchen and poured herself a cup of coffee even though the pot wasn't finished filling. Hot drops sizzled on the warming plate before she placed the glass pot back in its spot. To her credit, her hands barely shook.

Tessa was unconcerned. "Why not?" She grabbed a teaspoon from the drawer and plunged it into the jam.

"He's . . . he's not trustworthy."

"And Harley is?" Tessa arched a disbelieving brow as she dipped a spoon into the jam and leaned a hip against the cupboards.

"Yes!"

"Look, Tess, there's no reason to argue, just be careful, okay?" Miranda suggested.

"Like you are?" Tessa's smile, like that of a cat who'd swallowed the pet canary, didn't falter as she licked the spoon clean. "You know, when you're with Hunter."

"Hunter? Hunter Riley?" Claire asked, a crease forming between her eyebrows as she turned to her older sister.

"According to Weston, Randa's been seeing Hunter on the sly."

"We're friends," Miranda said. That much wasn't a lie.

"And so much more."

"Really?" Claire, always the romantic, seemed intrigued.

Damn Weston Taggert and his big mouth.

"What's it they say about people who live in glass houses?" Tessa asked as she plopped down in her chair again and spread a thick layer of jam onto her toast. "Something about not throwing stones?"

"You and Hunt?" Claire was still digesting the information and Miranda was certain her face, suddenly hot, had betrayed her. "For real?"

"It's not that big of a deal."

Tessa rolled her eyes.

"You *are* seeing him!" Claire's lips twitched into a small smile. "I don't believe it."

"Don't. It's nothing." Now, *that* was a lie. Her feelings for Hunter were important, a very big deal, the single most meaningful relationship in her life.

Tessa made a disparaging sound in the back of her throat. "What would Daddy say, hmm? His oldest daughter, the serious, *good* girl, the one who plans on going to—where is it?—oh, yeah, either Radcliffe or Yale or Stanford, right?"

"Willamette."

Tessa rolled her eyes. "Such lofty ideals, when really she's out doing God only knows what with the caretaker's son." Clucking her tongue, Tessa wagged her head dramatically from side to side. "And Mama, oh, Randa, think what she'd say about dating someone beneath your station."

"He's not beneath—" Miranda snapped her mouth shut. "I can't believe we're having this conversation."

"You started it."

"And I'm ending it right now!" She glanced at her watch again. "Where is Ruby? She's never late."

"Cut her a break, will ya? Mom and Dad are in Portland. She's probably just sleeping in. You know what they say. When the cat's away . . ." Tessa licked the corner of her lip.

"You're just full of old-time sayings, aren't you?"

"If the shoe fits—"

"Oh, stop it!" Claire took a long swallow of her coffee. "I think you two should be the first to know."

"Know what?" Miranda felt a niggle of fear climb up her spine.

"Uh-oh." Tessa's grin faded.

"I've made a big decision." Claire took a deep breath.

"About?" Miranda prodded.

Tessa shook her head as if she'd already guessed.

Claire set down her cup, managed a rather weak-looking smile, and held out her left hand. On her ring finger a diamond winked proudly in the morning light. "It's official," she said, her voice trembling a bit, uncertainty written all over her even features. "We don't care what anyone else thinks. Harley and I are getting married."

CHAPTER 13

Kendall's tears were real and bitter. They rained from her porcelain blue eyes and drizzled down her chin. "You can't," she whispered, her fists balling in his shirt, her body limp with grief. "You can't marry her."

She was standing on the deck of her parents' beach house, the winds off the Pacific fierce, sand blowing through the dunes and onto the floor. The morning sun was weak, and Harley felt cold as death. He'd come to tell Kendall because he thought she should be the first to know. Now he realized what a mistake he'd made.

Through sheer curtains, he saw Kendall's mother seated in a leather recliner, smoking a cigarette and sipping coffee as she read the morning paper. If she had the least bit of interest in what was going on between her daughter and the boy who had dated her for nearly a year, she didn't show it.

Thank God.

Harley wanted to comfort Kendall, to tell her she'd get over him, to help her through this pain, but how could he when he'd been the cause of it? Her breath, wet from the wash of tears, was hot against his neck and he felt like a heel. Whereas Weston triumphed in breaking girls' hearts, Harley hated it. "Look, I didn't want you to hear it from someone else."

"But what—what if I'm pregnant?" she choked out and fear, real and dark, clawed at his sense of decency.

"You're not."

"I—I don't know." She sniffed, tried to pull herself together, but, giving up, flung herself against him. His arms, of their own volition, surrounded her. He moved slightly so that the umbrella of the deck table, flapping in the stiff breeze, partially hid them from the bank of windows, just in case Kendall's mother looked their way.

"We'll take care of it. I told you—"

"And I told you I'd never have an abortion," she vowed with so much passion it scared him. "My father will kill me." She sagged against him and he smelled her skin and the scent of the elusive perfume she wore, some fragrance that her aunt sent her from Paris each Christmas.

"Things will work out."

"How?"

"I—I don't know," he admitted, feeling too young to deal with all this. He didn't really believe that Kendall was pregnant. It was too convenient, suited her purposes too well and yet how would he know? "I'll go to the doctor with you," he offered.

"Would you?"

Damn! She sounded hopeful when he'd intended to call her bluff. Could it really be true? Was he going to be a father? Oh, shit. "Of course."

"The appointment's in three weeks."

"Three weeks?"

"It's the first I could get with Dr. Spanner in Vancouver. I tried one of those in-home pregnancy tests and . . . and it looks like . . . like I'm pregnant, but I want to check with a doctor."

"Oh, God." So it was true. Harley felt a noose tightening around his throat. She smiled up at him. "Please, until we go check this out, don't make any rash announcements about getting married to Claire." She nestled her head against his chest and he knew in his heart he couldn't say no. Just as he never had. Christ, why was he such a baby?

"Harley?" she said, and her voice was so small he could barely hear it over the roar of the surf. Salty air clung to his skin.

"Yeah." Harley had never been so scared in his life.

"I love you." She sighed against his shirt. "No matter what, I'll always love you."

"Don't. Please, Kendall—"

"I'd do anything not to lose you."

"This is crazy talk."

"Maybe." She looked up, her face innocent, her lips, long bleached of any lipstick, beckoning. "I'm serious. Whatever it takes, I'll make sure that you love me again."

And she meant it.

Weston lit a cigarette, then let it burn in the ashtray by his bathroom sink as he soaked his beard and smoothed on shaving cream. He felt the edge of a hangover burning his eyes and pounding in his brain. His mouth tasted like shit and his muscles ached a little, but he was one who believed in the old adage that if you soared with the eagles at night, you had to rise with the sparrows in the morning.

With practiced hands he shaved off a day's worth of stubble and saw the dark spots on his neck—hickeys of all things—where Tessa Holland had pressed her hot little lips against his skin and sucked like no one he'd ever been with. Hell, he got hard just thinking of her.

Who would have thought she was a virgin, the way she'd been strutting her stuff around town for the past couple of years? She'd been hot and willing when he'd driven her to the cabin he kept for just such times; she hadn't shown any fear. She'd kissed and touched like a woman of the world instead of a naive schoolgirl. Instead of jailbait.

He nicked himself, swore, dabbed at the wound, and rammed his Marlboro into the corner of his mouth as he continued scraping his beard away. He should have been more careful, at least used a damned rubber, but he'd been swept off his feet by the thought that he was actually scoring on one of Dutch Holland's daughters.

Tessa wouldn't have been his first choice, of course. That particular obsession belonged to Miranda, but he hadn't been too choosy last night. Tessa had sighed when he'd kissed her, mewed when he'd stroked her breasts, cried out as he'd nipped at those glorious globes with his teeth and teased her with his tongue. She'd gone down on him as if she'd done it regularly, so it was a shock to him when he'd spread her willing legs, thrust into her wet cunt, and felt resistance.

Not that he'd stopped. She'd wanted it, begged for it—or had she?—seemed as determined as he about making it. At first she'd cried out, shifted away from him on the bed where he'd scored so often, but then she'd given into the hot-blooded animal she was.

Shooting a stream of smoke, he crushed his cigarette and rinsed his face. At times he wondered why his damned sex drive was always in fifth gear. He couldn't look at a woman without fantasizing about bedding her and when it came to the Holland girls, it was worse. He didn't want to think it was because of some twisted condition because he'd seen his mother's treachery . . . No, that couldn't be it. Nor was it because of the feud between the families, not really. It was the challenge of it all. Miranda, Claire, and Tessa were so damned arrogant and their better-than-thou attitude coupled with their beauty got to him. Big-time. So he'd scored with Tessa . . . one little virgin down, two to go, though he doubted the other two were innocents. Claire was doing it with Harley, Weston was sure of it, and Miranda, ice princess that she appeared, was surely all fire below the surface.

He wanted to bed all three Holland girls in the worst way. But those thoughts were normal, the quirk he dealt with was that he was forever acting on his impulses, even when he instinctively knew he should be more selective, probably because of all his mother's sermons. As if she knew anything about virtue.

His jaw tightened, and as he frowned at his reflection the years rolled back and he was a boy again, no more than ten or eleven. He'd climbed his favorite oak tree and was on the lookout for squirrels, his slingshot ready while he wished that he had a BB gun like some of his friends. Settled onto his favorite branch, eyes trained on a hawthorn tree where a family of squirrels usually nested, he heard music coming from the second-story window of the guest house.

Mick Jagger—his mother's favorite in recent years, she'd seen him in person, even gotten his autograph—was singing about brown sugar again. Jeez, Weston was sick of that song. He'd heard it for years, watched in stunned awe as his usually conservative mother would close her eyes, wag her head, and swing her hips to the music. He just didn't get it. And he didn't like the noise now. It was bound to drive the squirrels away.

He was about to shimmy down the tree when he heard laughter—his mother's tinkling, and rare laughter—coming from the open window. Another voice, deeper and male, said something indiscernible, and Mikki Taggert giggled like a schoolgirl again. A sense that something was wrong settled over Weston, and though he knew he shouldn't, he inched farther onto the branch that brushed against the guest house.

"I can't believe you're here," Mikki said, whispering in delight again as the song ended.

"Couldn't stay away."

"I'm glad." Her voice had lowered an octave and Weston, his hands sweaty as he looked down toward the ground that looked so far away, closed in on the open window.

"Looks like you were ready for me."

"No, silly, I was going to work on my tan."

A rumble of laughter. "In September?"

"Why not?"

"I think we can work on something else."

"You're evil," Mikki insisted, though she didn't sound scared. Her voice was breathy and low; the tone made Weston's skin crawl—like the sound of fingernails scraping against a chalkboard. Something in the back of his mind cautioned him to scramble back down the tree, to run as fast and as far away as his legs would carry him, but it was as if he were drawn by a magnet, pulled closer to that open window by an irresistible and probably malignant force.

"Evil?" the man repeated, and Weston thought he heard the sound of ice cubes tinkling in a glass. "I don't think so."

"What would Neal say?"

Yeah! What would Dad say?

Laughter. Deep and dark and dangerous. "Now that's an interesting question, but let's not think about him right now."

"Shouldn't we?" Mikki Taggert's question hung in the late summer air. "I thought this was all about him, that he was the one really getting screwed, so to speak."

The window and edge of the curtains were near. Weston craned his neck and squinted. As his eyes adjusted to the dark interior his stomach, already churning, turned over. His mother was standing on her tiptoes, her arms thrown around the thick neck of a big man, his fingers moving against her bare back, untying the string to the top of her bikini. Oil gleamed on her already-tanned skin.

The man kissed her, and with a quick movement, pulled the red bra down. Weston swallowed as he saw his mother's breasts, white where the sun hadn't touched them, dark huge disks for nipples, stretch marks marring their beauty. He squeezed his eyes shut and nearly fell off his perch. His brain thundered. What was his mother doing with this guy—this stranger with the thick neck and brown hair just starting to gray?

His stomach convulsed and it was all he could do not to retch and throw up. Sweat slid down his nose and he wished to God he'd never climbed the tree, never crawled near this damned window, but still he stared, unable to drag his gaze away, watching in morbid fascination as his mother, the woman he'd looked up to all his life tipped her head back and let the guy kiss her, his hands finding those big pillowy breasts as they tumbled onto the antique quilt Grandma had stitched. Mikki made deep, ugly sounds in the back of her throat and arched up against the man—rubbing his crotch.

Bile tickled Weston's throat as the man stripped himself of his shirt. The slingshot in Weston's back pocket pressed against his butt and he thought of aiming through the window and shooting a rock right at the guy's head. Why not? The bastard deserved it. He reached for his weapon as his mother let out a long, low, "Ooooh, that's it baby."

Weston's heart shriveled. How many lectures had his mother given him and his little brother about being good, playing fair, never cheating, always being loyal? He couldn't count the times that Mikki had smoothed his cowlick with loving fingers, straightened his tie, and driven Harley, Baby Paige, and him into town to the Second Christian Church where from high in the pulpit Reverend Jones, the most boring minister in the world, went on and on about the wrath and power of God.

Mama had always told him to be true to himself, to his family, to

God and Jesus. She'd told him over and over again that the Ten Commandments and the Golden Rule were never to be broken, and yet there she was, stripping some guy of his clothes, *humping* him for God's sake.

Still it was too dark to see the man's face, but Weston had the sickening feeling that he should know him as he stared at his freckled hairy back. There was a mirror across the room, facing the bed, but the guy never looked up, and all Weston viewed was the top of his head as he straddled Mama, his back to the window. Weston heard the distinctive metallic hiss of a zipper being lowered. "You want me, baby?"

That voice! Weston had heard it before.

"Yes."

"How much, baby? Show Daddy how much."

He couldn't stand it another minute. Yanking the slingshot and a sharp-edged rock from his back pocket, he took aim. Through the open window, right at that white, freckled back he sighted his slingshot, drew back on the thick rubber band, and with a thwang, let his sharp little missile fly.

Crash! The mirror over the bureau shattered and the man, startled, yelled and looked over his shoulder. Oh, shit! He was in for it now. As he swung down from the limb and landed hard on the balls of his feet, Weston caught a glimpse of Dutch Holland's red face.

Dutch Holland. Dad's rival. Mom's been fucking Dutch Holland?

Betrayal screamed through Weston's brain.

"Was that your kid?" Dutch demanded.

Weston rolled into the undergrowth, startling a rabbit that dived into the bracken. Agilely, Weston scrambled to his feet, but the burning image of his mother, *his mother!* screwing her brains out with Dutch Holland burned through his mind, clouded his vision. How could she? How? With that mean son of a bitch? Without so much as a glance over his shoulder, Weston ran. Faster and faster. Nearly tripping over dirt clods and potholes. Branches slapped his face, brought tears. Because he couldn't be crying over his mother. No way. *Jezebel. Cunt. Whore.* He tore through the forest, putting as much distance as he could from the nasty, ugly, horrible scene that was jammed into his brain. Mikki singing. Mikki smiling. Mikki moaning while that bastard rutted on her.

His stomach heaved and Weston had to stop to puke. Then he was running again, splashing through the creek, rocks slippery under his feet. Scrambling up the far bank, berry vines tore at his pant legs, spiderwebs and leaves brushed his tears away. Sobbing, scared and angry he ran farther and farther into the forest. As far as he could go until he collapsed on the ground and pounded a fist into the earth. How could she do it? How? He gasped for breath and thoughts of his mother, his friggin' *mother*—his good, church-going, pious mother—tore at his brain.

He hated her.

He hated fucking Dutch Holland.

And he'd get back at them both. Someday. Some way. That was it. He'd show both of 'em. And he'd start by staying away. Making his bitch of a mother worry about him . . . if she did . . . maybe she didn't even care. Maybe she never had.

He stayed out all night, hiding in the forest, crouched under a rocky ledge where he imagined cougars and bears and coyotes lived. He spent the next day tired, hungry, and sick with thoughts about his whore of a mother. He didn't want to live and hoped she was sick with worry about him. As night fell again he slept outside, closer to the house this time, near enough to see the warm patches of light glowing through the trees, beckoning him home.

On the third day his stomach was cramped from lack of food. He sneaked into the kitchen to grab a couple of Cokes from the back porch and a box of Hostess cupcakes from the pantry when she caught him. Dressed in a beige pantsuit, her purse over her arm as if she were running to the market, she spied him from the hallway.

"I think we need to talk, Wes," she said. Her eyes were cool and blue, without emotion. "Your father is very angry that you ran away."

He didn't say a word, just stood at the sliding door, ready to escape to the forest.

Clucking her tongue, she shook her head. "Look at you. You're filthy. Now, if you come upstairs and clean yourself up, I think I can work things out so that your father doesn't beat the tar out of you."

Weston's eyes narrowed. This was all wrong. Everything she was saying was wrong.

"I told him that you broke the mirror in the guest house, that you ran away from me, and that it was best to let you come back on your own rather than have the police hunt you down, but your father . . . well, you know how he is. As I said, he's angry with you, son. Very angry."

"And how about you? Is he mad at you, too?"

"Why would he be angry with me?" she asked as if she really didn't understand. She'd screwed his father's enemy and was playing the part of the innocent.

"Because of the guy."

"What guy?"

"Mr. Holland. You were in bed with Mr. Holland. Fucking him!"

"What?" She crossed the room and slapped him so hard his head slammed against the wall. "Take that filthy talk out of here."

"But you were—"

Smack! Her hand caught his cheek again. "Don't you ever spread lies about me, Weston. I'm your mother, and I deserve some respect. Now, I'll plead your case with your father. I'll ask him not to punish you too severely for breaking the mirror and running away, but if you start telling these lies about me, there's nothing more I can do for you."

"I'm not lying."

"Oh, yes you are," she said, leaning down so that her nose was nearly touching his. "You've been a liar from the day you were born, Weston. Always making up stories, but until now they weren't particularly harmful. But this . . . this lie . . . is malicious. If you breathe one word of it, just one, I swear I'll tell your father, and he'll make your life a living hell. You know he can do it, Weston. He's done it before. So what's it going to be? Are you going to take the punishment for breaking the mirror and running away, or are you going to keep lying about me and force me to have your father put you in isolation down in the cellar? Remember the cellar? You saw a rat down there the last time, didn't you? And spiders."

"Spiders don't scare me." But he shuddered. And he remembered being locked in the basement. It had been cold, damp and dark. His backside burned from the welts of his father's belt and he could remember Neal Taggert's taunts from the other side of the door. "Watch your goddamned mouth, Wes, or I'll leave you in there forever. You'll never get a piece of my estate. No, siree, I'll cut you off and leave you in there to rot."

His mother was watching him. She lifted a dark skeptical brow. "They don't scare you. Good. But what I really hope is that you'll prove to be the smart boy I've always thought you were. The good, intelligent, loving son." Straightening, she crossed her arms under her breasts and he blocked out the image of her nipples and white skin and Dutch Holland's thick fingers touching her.

He had no choice. The Coke bottles slipped from his fingers and rolled across the hardwood floor. "Okay," he whispered, rubbing the side of his face.

"Okay what?"

"Okay, I won't say anything about Mr. Holland."

"You mean you won't lie about me."

His eyes looked up and caught the cold determination in hers. "I'll say what you want."

"I only want the truth, Weston," she said. "Now, run upstairs and clean up. Throw those awful clothes and your slingshot into the trash. You'll have to be punished, of course, but it'll only be a little grounding, a week or so, and I'll tell your father how sorry you are. How's that?" Her smile was bright and false as fool's gold.

"I won't forget," he said sullenly.

"Forget what?"

"I won't forget ever," he said, and took off up the stairs. His relationship with his mother had never been the same and his feelings for all people bearing the name of Holland had been colored forever.

So he couldn't feel too badly about taking Tessa's virtue. She'd practically served it up to him on a silver platter. As far as he could see, it was tit for tat. Or maybe tit for tit. Dutch Holland had bedded his mother, and now Weston had returned the favor by making it with daughter number three. It felt good. As if he was getting a little of the Taggert pride back.

He'd learned from his mother. For the first decade of his life he'd thought his father was the shrewd one in their marriage, but Mikki Taggert had talents even her husband didn't appreciate.

Weston dried his face, picked off the toilet paper he'd dabbed on his wounds, and told himself to savor Tessa Holland for as long as possible. Then, maybe, he'd get lucky enough to have his way with Miranda. Stepping into slacks, he thought about the eldest Holland daughter. Statuesque and dark-haired, with intelligent eyes and a biting tongue, she was a challenge. Oh, how he'd love to seduce her.

With Tessa there had been no seduction. It was almost as if *she'd* decided that he was going to be the one. Miranda would prove more difficult. Smiling as he buckled his belt, he didn't let it bother him that maybe, just maybe, Tessa Holland had manipulated him instead of the other way around.

He reached for his jacket and walked out of the bathroom to find Kendall Forsythe, looking for all the world like a rag doll who'd lost half her stuffing, seated on the corner of his bed.

"What are you doing here?" He glanced to the doorway. Christ, he hoped no one had seen her.

"Paige let me in."

"She knows you're in *my* room?"

"I—I had no choice." She ran a shaky hand over her mouth, glanced at him, then looked quickly away. "I know this is awkward. Oh, God, I can't believe I'm actually doing this."

"Doing what?" He was mystified, but an inkling of what was going on in that gorgeous head of hers began to reach him.

Fists clenched, she rose and walked to the open window. "I—uh—I think I want to take you up on your offer," she said so quietly he barely heard the words.

"My offer?" Then he remembered. "Oh."

"That's right." She stiffened and turned to face him, her smooth skin the color of chalk. "I need to get pregnant and fast."

He couldn't help the smile that inched up one side of his mouth. Thoughts of Miranda and Tessa Holland slipped away. "You know me, Kendall," he said, walking slowly across the room, sizing her up as a predator might a wounded bird. "I'm always willing to oblige."

CHAPTER 14

"So it's finally official, the two richest families in the whole god-damned state are going to merge." Jack Songbird lifted his rifle to his shoulder, narrowed an eye, and pulled the trigger. A tin can hopped off the bale of hay he'd set on the far side of a field of bent beach grass. Overhead the sky was cloudy, dark with the promise of a storm. "Harley Taggert's gonna marry Claire Holland."

The news settled like lead in Kane's stomach, and he closed his mind to the thought of Claire spending the rest of her life with a spineless dishrag like Taggert. Hell, what did the guy have besides money and more money? "It'll only happen if the families allow it." He'd heard the local gossip, running like a prairie fire through the beauty shops, groceries, Bible study groups, taverns, cafés, diners, and liquor stores from one small town to another up and down the coast.

"What can they do?"

"Claire's too young. She'll need Daddy's signature."

"Unless they wait until she turns eighteen."

Every muscle in Kane's body was suddenly tight as a bowstring. What did he care? Claire Holland could marry anyone she damn well pleased. She was a snooty rich girl with an attitude, and his feelings for her were just plain stupid—a schoolboy crush that he'd nurtured over the years. Yet he couldn't just roll over and play dead, not when he felt as he did. It had been nearly two weeks since he'd last seen her, and soon he and Uncle Sam had a date. Time was running out.

Kane tipped his bottle back, drained it, and let it drop to the ground. Then he hoisted his own .22 and took careful aim. He squeezed the trigger and missed. Jack let out a whoop reminiscent of Indians in old black-and-white movies. "Pathetic white man," he taunted. It was their running joke.

"Yeah, well let's see how you do with a bow and arrow."

"A damned sight better than you." He checked his watch and swore. "Son of a bitch. Son of a goddamned bitch." Then he grinned. "Late for work again."

"You shouldn't have lost track of time."

"How would you like working for Weston Taggert?" Jack's lips curled into a snarl and hate tightened the skin over the planes of his face.

"I wouldn't."

"Neither do I. Already had a fight with my ma about it, just this morning. Told her I was gonna quit, and she said I'd never get another job around these parts. Made her late for work. Boy, was she pissed!" He tossed a hank of jet black hair off his face and a sly expression crossed the bladed features of his face. "You know what needs to happen to Weston Taggert?"

"I can think of a lot of things."

"Someone needs to sneak into his room at night and scare the living shit out of him by taking off some of his scalp—at least his hair. Just for fun." He aimed quickly and got off three shots. Two cans danced, and a bottle shattered.

"Dead eye," Kane remarked, looking at Jack's handiwork. Three broken bottles and umpteen cans littered the ground by the target.

"I just wish I was aiming at Taggert's ugly head."

You're not the only one, Kane thought as he steadied himself and sighted the last bottle, but didn't squeeze the trigger. "Be careful what you say around these parts."

"Yeah, it could get back to him, through my sister." Jack saw a hawk circling and aimed straight up, as if he intended to blow the bird out of the sky. "Why she wants to be that bastard's whore is beyond me." Blade-thin, Jack's mouth was suddenly cruel. "He's just using her."

"He uses everyone."

"Maybe I should start screwing his little sister and see how *he* likes it."

"She's just a kid. And a funny one at that. An oddball." In Kane's estimation Paige Taggert wasn't playing with a full deck, but then what did he know, he was just poor white trash. Poor white trash with a crush on one of the local princesses. If he had a lick of sense he'd blow town now, insist on joining up this week instead of wait-ing . . . for what? He squinted up at the threatening sky and felt the same premonition of evil that he had for the better part of a week.

Jack was still ranting. "Yeah, well Crystal's just a kid, too, but she'll lie on her back for that lowlife son of a bitch and turn a blind eye when he screws around on her."

"She'll wise up."

"Or get knocked up," Jack growled, as Kane took another shot at the last bottle and it remained standing, taunting him.

"You'd better give this up," Jack said, swinging his rifle around and snapping off a shot. Glass shattered and sprayed. "You're just no damned good at it." Slinging his rifle over his back, he started off at a trot through the fields. "See ya later. Maybe if I'm lucky, I'll get fired."

"You're not marrying anyone, especially a Taggert, and that's final," Dutch said at the dinner table, his lips barely moving, his rage pulsing in an irritated throb under his jaw. "Hell, I'm only out of town two nights and what happens? You"—he swung cold blue eyes on his youngest daughter—"are seen drinking, *drinking, mind you, when you're six years underage,* at the resort, *my* resort, and then spotted later with Weston Taggert, and you"—his attention landed with full hostile force upon Claire again—"are stupid enough to plan to marry the Milquetoast of that damned family." He shoved his plate away from him in a fit of fury. Juice from his slab of baron of beef splattered over the linen tablecloth as he reached into his inside jacket pocket for a cigar.

"For the love of God, Benedict, control yourself." Dominique's face was taut and white, her mouth puckered in disgust. "At least the Taggert boys have some respectability."

"You mean money," Tessa corrected, and Miranda wished her youngest sister would just shut up. When their father was in this kind of mood, there wasn't any talking to him.

"There isn't a respectable bone in the whole stinking family." Dutch was on his feet, jamming the cigar between his teeth. "I knew this would happen, you know," he said to his wife as his hand rested on the handle of the French doors. His cigar wagged in his mouth. "Didn't I tell you? When each of them was born. Trouble."

"You wanted sons," Dominique said, defeat and disappointment edging her words.

Claire bit her lower lip, Tessa rolled her eyes, and Miranda, who had heard this argument before, felt a headache beginning to build at the base of her skull.

"You bet I wanted sons. Big, strapping boys who would inherit everything I've worked for. I came from a family of men, Dominique."

"This isn't about her," Tessa cut in.

"Sure it is. It's about all of you. I feel like a fish out of water in my own damned home. Girls! I've been threatening to send you to boarding schools. Hell, your mother here would love it if you would study in Switzerland or goddamned France and, believe me, I'll send all three of you abroad if there's any more talk about marrying a Taggert."

"But—" Claire said, rising.

"I'm not fooling around. Push me and you'll be on the next flight out of Portland."

"I love him!" Claire announced, shaking as she faced her father, defying him for the first time in her life. Miranda wished she could kick Claire under the table. This wasn't the time to push it with him. Give him some time to cool off.

"You love him," Dutch muttered. *"Love?* And I suppose he *loves* you?"

"Y-yes," she said, swallowing hard.

"Is that why he's still sniffing after the Forsythe girl?"

"What?"

"Dutch, don't," Dominique said.

"She should know who she's dealing with. I've had one of my security men watching Harley Taggert because I suspected something like this might be coming down."

Miranda felt cold as death.

"That's right. And your precious Harley, the hypocrite who gave you that damned ring, has been two-timing you."

"No!"

Dutch shook his head at Claire's naïveté. "Of course it's true. But you're too much *in love* to see the writing on the wall. As for Weston," he said, eyeing his youngest daughter, "he's about as faithful as a mangy dog around a bitch in heat. That boy can't keep his pants up to save his life, so both of you, stay away from the Taggerts." Finally his gaze landed full force on Miranda. "You, at least, seem to have some sense when it comes to boys."

Miranda withered inside. *She* was the hypocrite. Her sisters didn't resort to sneaking around, but she was seeing Hunter on the sly, afraid of her father's reaction, tired of walking that thin good girl line.

"Girls. Shit." Shaking his head, Dutch held his tongue, but Miranda knew what was on his mind. She'd heard the argument that had simmered between their parents for years. Dominique had failed Dutch by bearing him only daughters. No sons. He'd begged her, pleaded, screamed, and demanded that she bear him another child—a boy child—but she'd refused, claiming the last pregnancy had nearly killed her. She'd risk no more of her health bearing Holland issue.

The fights had never been in front of the girls, and, Miranda supposed, as she pushed peas around on her plate, until tonight Tessa and Claire didn't know their father's deep disappointment at the sex of his children. Miranda had not had that luxury, as her room shared a wall with her parents' bedroom. There was no large bathroom or closet that muffled the sounds of their fighting, or their lovemaking. Fortunately the latter was infrequent because the thought of her mother and father rolling around on the bed and panting—actually *doing it*—especially after one of their fights, made Miranda sick. For years, she'd heard her father's complaints and Dominique's challenge that their family's sexual makeup was his fault. He obviously wasn't man enough to spawn sons in four tries. Even their first child, a baby miscarried early in the second trimester, had been a girl.

When she'd been younger, Miranda had felt guilty, as if the fact that she'd been born a woman was her fault, and she'd tried to please Dutch, to gain his favor, to be the son he'd never had. She was smart, excelled in school, was captain of the debate team, worked on the school paper, gained entrance to several elite colleges, but, damn it, she couldn't grow male parts of her anatomy, and for being a woman she would be forever punished.

At eighteen, she was just beginning to understand that she would never please her father. No accomplishment would make him proud of her, and so she'd quit trying to satisfy him and was now trying to please herself. With Hunter.

She watched as Dutch slammed one of the French doors behind him, rattling the glass panes and sending the chandelier swaying, so that the light from the hundred small candles swirled against the walls and reflected in teetering pinpoints in the windows.

Dominique cast a glance at her husband's silhouette and sighed with the patience born of years of living with a volatile man. Spooning a ladle of cheese sauce over her sliced potatoes, she said quietly, "Just let him blow off a little steam. It's his way, and there's nothing we can do to change it."

"He's a pig." Tessa, forever wearing her heart on her sleeve, couldn't control her rage.

Dominique raised both eyebrows. "He's your father. We have to deal with him."

Tessa glowered and fiddled with her water glass. "I don't see why. You could divorce him."

"Tessa!" Claire hissed. "You don't mean it."

"Sure I do. It's not a sin, you know."

Secretly Miranda wondered why her parents stayed together.

"I said 'until death do us part' and I meant it," Dominique said without a smile. "We're a family."

"So that means we do anything he wants? He tells us what to do and we just go along. Claire should give up Harley and I . . . I should give up my life?" Tessa ran angry fingers through her hair and glared at her father, who was leaning on the railing, staring out at the water, the tip of his cigar glowing an angry red in the darkness.

"I'll run away before he sends me to any school in Europe."

"That was just talk," Dominique said. "Let him cool off."

Claire scooted her chair back. "He can't stop me from marrying Harley."

"Of course he can, honey," Dominique said, her face suddenly appearing old.

"That's bullshit! He can't tell *me* what to do." Tessa shot her chair back and, half-running, took off for the front of the house.

"I worry about her," Dominique said. "Such a hothead, and you"—she reached out, touching Claire's hand with long, beringed fingers—"it's not wise to fall too deeply into love."

"Why not?" Claire said, but she looked nervous and drew her hand away from her mother's.

"You should always hold a little back. Just in case."

"In case what?"

"In case the man you love doesn't love you back."

"Harley does," Claire said swiftly as she shoved her chair away from the table. "Why doesn't anyone believe me?" She, too, walked out of the room, and, as she did, Miranda noticed the doubt in her eyes, the worry clouding Claire's gaze.

"Oh, Lord," Dominique said when she and Miranda were alone in the room. The sound of violins playing some soulful classical piece wafted softly through hidden speakers and filled the painful silence. "Take a lesson, Randa." She smiled sadly. "I guess I don't need to talk to you about this sort of thing."

"No, Mom, you don't," Miranda said, though she knew she was lying through her teeth.

"Well, someday a boy will touch you in a special way and then, for the love of God, watch out."

"Is that what happened with you and Dad?"

Dominique's face turned into a mask of sadness. She glanced out the window to the porch where her husband was sending clouds of smoke into the starless night. "No," she admitted. "The truth is that I grew up without any money, you know that. Your father was wealthy and I . . . I decided he was my only escape. I got pregnant."

"On purpose?" Miranda whispered, thinking about the baby who hadn't survived to be born. The older sister she'd never had.

Dominique lifted a silk-draped shoulder. "I did what I had to, and I've never regretted it. Well, except at times like this. I just don't understand why this family can't sit down and have a civil meal together."

Jack Songbird hiked the collar of his jean jacket closer around his neck. The wind was picking up, blowing in from the Pacific, a storm brewing. Good. He liked the fierce squalls. Bring it on! More than a little drunk, he glared at what remained of his campfire. Hot, red embers glowed in the night. He took a long pull from his fifth of whiskey and glanced upward, to the few stars visible through the clouds. Here on the ridge he felt above it all, the town of Chinook stretching along the inlet, lights sparkling as if to mimic the stars. Somewhere down there his father and mother were probably wondering where he was. Well, they could just damn wonder. He didn't care.

Slightly drunk, he pulled out his knife and smiled, remembering how it had felt to run the sharp blade along the car's sleek paint job. It had felt good. Right. No one would ever know. No one could ever prove he was the vandal.

His parents, if they ever found out, would be mortified. They seemed to accept their lot in life without any qualms. They had pride in themselves, in their heritage, but they didn't seem to accept the truth—Native Americans had gotten the shaft big-time. They seemed to give a little lip service to their ancestors and the "ways of the people" but they didn't do anything about it, they weren't angry that they were reduced to living near the poverty level, accepting wages from pricks like the Taggerts and the Hollands.

Shit.

It just wasn't fair.

And then Crystal. Jesus, what was she thinking? Running around with Weston Taggert while he treated her like dirt. Such a waste. Crystal was smart and beautiful. Too good for Taggert.

Jack glanced down at the blade of his knife and scowled. He marred the car, yeah, but gouging the paint had been the act of a coward. What he'd really needed to do was slit Weston Taggert's throat—show the bastard what it meant to treat a good woman like a whore. He slid the blade between his index finger and thumb, testing it, knowing that he would never have the guts to kill the bastard, even when he was balling Crystal and treating her like dirt.

You're just mad cuz he fired your ass.

Well, that was part of it. Jack dropped his knife onto his backpack then took a long swallow from his bottle. Maybe now he could blow this hick town. Take off in his pickup and head south. To California. Get away from Chinook for good. But first he needed to take a piss. Bad.

He heard a noise in the trees just out of the light of the fire. The hairs on the back of his neck rose. There had been sightings of puma and bobcat a little farther up in the hills and bears had been known to wander in these parts . . .

Jack cocked his head, his ears straining. Maybe it was nothing. A rabbit or possum or night bird . . . He heard nothing over the rush of wind, hiss of the fire and the dull roar of the ocean pounding the rocky shoreline a hundred feet below.

It was just his imagination, nothing more. The wind.

And yet . . . He felt the first few drops of rain and thought about leaving, going home, facing the wrath of his parents when they found out that he'd been canned. Jesus, Ruby would have herself a helluva hissy fit but the old man would be worse. From him, Jack would get the silent treatment. Yep, it was time to move on.

As he stood, he heard another sound. A footstep? Turning quickly, he thought he saw movement in the shadows. Jack froze. "Who's there?" he yelled, his eyes narrowing on the stand of fir just beyond the firelight.

No answer.

Hell, he was getting jumpy.

Too much booze, not enough food. He needed to go back into town. Walk off the alcohol. Face the goddamned music. Stumbling a bit he walked to the edge of the ridge where he'd imagined his ancestors had stood hundreds of years before, where he'd peed into the sea every time he'd come up here. He reached for his fly when he heard it again. The sound of footsteps rushing toward him. He whirled quickly. Saw a flash of movement. A jagged rock the size of a softball slammed into his forehead. Crack! Hot, white pain pounded through his head. He reeled backward, his boots slipping in the mud, his hands scrabbling in the air.

"Die bastard!" an evil voice hissed from the darkness.

Panicked, Jack pitched backward, his body slipping and bouncing off the rocky face of the cliff as he plummeted headfirst toward the rocks and angry black sea.

"You're out of your fuckin' mind!" Weston slammed his pool cue onto the table where he'd been practicing his bank shots before Harley had strolled down to the den and made his insane announcement. "You can't marry anyone."

"Why not?"

Weston leaned his butt against the edge of the billiard table and looked at his brother as if Harley were a bona fide certificate-bearing idiot. "Don't you have some unfinished business with Kendall?"

"It's over."

"Is it?" Weston glanced to the hallway, where he noticed a shadow sliding down the stairs. Paige. Hell, that kid was always sneaking around, listening for gossip. Not for the first time Weston wondered how he could be related to his spineless moron of a brother and nutcase of a sister. In Weston's estimation, Paige needed to see a shrink. *And what about you?* his mind teased, gnawing at him.

Harley picked up the eight ball and started tossing it nervously in the air. It was fitting somehow, the kid was always in trouble. He just didn't know how deep. It wouldn't be long before Kendall dumped the news on him that he was about to be a daddy—well, really an uncle—if things went as planned.

"Kendall seems to think that you two are still together."

"I don't know how."

"Maybe it's because you can't stay out of her pants."

Harley actually blushed. Jesus, he had no balls. "I'm not seeing her."

"Good. Then you can marry Claire Holland and life will be perfect, is that what you think? Even though Dad will cut you off and college will be out of the question. Don't you know you'll have to get work as a grease monkey or a waiter, or a factory worker if you can hold down that kind of a job? And you'll live in some crummy apartment in a bad part of Portland or Seattle or wherever it is that you finally find someone stupid enough to employ you. Dad won't give you a reference, you can bet on it, and you've never held down a job in your life. As for Claire, she'll have to work, too. As a secretary or receptionist . . . oh, no, she's not good at that kind of thing, is she? Maybe she'll train horses or give riding lessons or something. And everything will be just great. Perfect!"

"That's not how it's gonna be."

"Sure it is, Harley. She'll have no money and neither will you. Even your car is in Dad's name. I don't suppose you've broken the news to him yet, have you?"

"When he gets back into town—"

The phone rang shrilly and the shadow disappeared up the stairs. Good. Paige had a way of making Weston nervous. Why, he couldn't figure. She was just a gawky kid. "When Dad gets back from Louisiana, you think he'll embrace the fact that you're going to marry one of the daughters of his archenemy? Sure Harley, *that's* gonna happen. About the time I sprout horns."

"I've got news for you, Weston. You already have."

"Telephone for you, Weston!" Paige called down the stairs. "It's Crystal."

"Shit!"

Harley had the balls to grin. "At least I'm not banging some girl just for the hell of it. I'll bet her brother isn't too happy that you're using her as a squaw-fuck. Isn't that the term you use when you're talking about her? Maybe someone should tell Jack."

"Jack Songbird is an asshole."

"I wouldn't cross him."

"He doesn't scare me. No one does."

"I said Crystal's on the phone!" Paige's voice was shrill as a screaming saw.

"Tell her I'm out!" Weston yelled.

Paige's footsteps thundered down the stairs. "I already told her you were down here playing pool."

"Damn it all, Paige. Use your head." He crossed to the bar, wishing he had a good stiff drink, and picked up the phone. "Look, I'm busy right now. I'll call you back."

"Wait a minute. Did Jack show up at work today?"

Weston's gut clenched. "He was late."

"But he was there."

"Until I fired his ass."

"You . . . you what?"

"He's gone. History. Your brother was the worst worker on the green chain, Crystal. I let him go."

"But you couldn't." He heard the disappointment in her voice, and it got to him. There was something about her that got deep under his skin; that was why he doubted that he'd ever break it off with her, not completely. She'd be his mistress for life.

"I did. Ask him."

"I would, but he hasn't come home yet."

"I'd look down at the local watering hole. Sounds like your brother might just be drowning his troubles in firewater."

"You're a bastard," she said calmly.

"Always have been."

Before she hung up, she muttered something in Chinook, an irritating habit she had that bothered him. He didn't like not being able to understand what her gobbledygook language said, and though she probably just called him the Native American equivalent of an asshole, it worried him that she might have leveled a curse in his direction, not that he believed in all that tribal mumbo jumbo. Still, his skin crawled as he disconnected.

"Trouble with the little woman?" Harley taunted. Christ, his brother could be irritating.

"Not for me." Weston grabbed his cue, took the eight ball from Harley's weak fingers, and set up his shot again. He didn't have to worry about his brother's wisecracks, his sister's weird antics, or some whore and her curse. After all, he was Weston Taggert.

He could do whatever he damn well pleased.

CHAPTER 15

His old man was drunk.

Again.

And tonight it bothered the hell out of Kane. Why, he couldn't fathom, but ever since Jack's revelation that Claire Holland and Harley Taggert were engaged, Kane had been spoiling for a fight. He itched to slam his fist into a wall, a tree trunk, and/or Taggert's smug face, not necessarily in that order.

"Son of a bitch," he growled, reaching to the top of a battle-scarred chest of drawers where his keys rested in an ashtray. It was the middle of the month and Hampton had gone through his fifths of expensive booze. For the last week and a half all he'd been tossing back was cheap rotgut whiskey, while he groused about his ex-wife and what a conniving, self-centered bitch she'd been to leave him alone, crippled, and with a headstrong boy to raise.

"You don't know the half of it, Pop," Kane muttered under his breath as he slid open the window. He heard his father's wheelchair zip across the linoleum while the television blared, sounds of laughter for the late night's talk show host's monologue seeping through the thin plaster walls.

God, Kane hated it here. Trapped with a bitter cripple who spurned any help neighbors or relatives had extended. Kindhearted, churchgoing people in town had offered Hampton jobs—at the hardware store, the fish cannery, the feed store, and even an insurance company, but Hampton Moran, ex-tree-topper, wasn't about to take their charity. No, he was content to wallow in his misery and, when he did work, it was at his own form of chain saw art.

The front lawn and porch were littered with sawdust and Hampton's special kind of sculpture—unsold wooden sentinels that appeared to guard the place. Snarling bears, fierce-faced Native Americans, bowlegged cowboys with matches in the corners of their mouths, and rearing horses with wild eyes and curling manes were carved from the trunks of the kind of trees from which he'd fallen and lost the use of his legs. It was as if Hampton was engaged in a private war with the forests surrounding Chinook and Stone Illahee, and his enemies included every last stick of old growth timber as well as anyone with the last name of Holland.

People who stopped to look at his wares often thought the scarred chunks of fir were quaint, and that Hampton was an eccentric artist, a man whose dark disposition was the result of his inner need to express himself rather than because he held on to his hatred as if it were a gift from God or that he soaked his brain in cheap alcohol.

In Kane's estimation, it was all crap.

The front door banged shut and a minute later Pop's chain saw roared to life as yet another unsuspecting stump was about to become a wolf or salmon or some other Northwest icon. Kane wasn't about to stick around and find out. He lifted himself onto the window ledge, then slid to the edge of the roof and lowered himself to the ground. He wasn't sneaking out. No, his father wouldn't even miss him. He just didn't want to explain himself to the old man tonight.

And he wanted to see Claire. Badly. Even though he knew it was a mistake.

Firing up his motorcycle, he left the house of pain behind and flew down the night-dark strip of highway. He put the bike through its paces, needing to hear the whine of gears and feel the rush of salty air against his face as he huddled over the handlebars and leaned into a tight curve. The Harley shimmied for a second, caught hold, and skimmed over the highway again. Faster and faster, as if the devil himself were on his tail, Kane maneuvered the bike around the lake. Through the trees and across the moonlit water he caught glimpses of her house, the warm patches of the dozens of windows and, barely visible, smoke curling from the chimney. Just like some damned Currier and Ives painting.

The gate was open and he didn't hesitate, just boldly drove through, the headlight of his bike guiding him on. Sliding to a stop near the garage, he gritted his teeth as he marched up the stairs of the porch and nearly rang the bell. But she was there, curled into a corner of a porch swing, her long legs tucked beneath her, her eyes, luminous in the moonlight, staring up at him.

"What're you doing here?"

"Looking for you." He didn't move, just watched the play of starlight in her hair.

"For me?"

"I heard you're getting married."

Her smile was stiff and forced. "Don't tell me, you're going to try and talk me out of it."

"Not if it's what you want."

"It is." She tucked her knees under her chin.

He felt suddenly hot, and he imagined taking hold of her hand and running, as fast and as far as his legs would carry him, holding her close. If she couldn't keep up with him, then he'd carry her. But they couldn't stay here, not with the presence of doom huddling in the surrounding forest, glaring at them with hungry possessive eyes, as if there was no way out of this desperate, hateful situation. "Then I hope you're happy."

"You don't mean it." She unwrapped those long legs. "You didn't come here to wish me 'good luck' or 'congratulations.'" She crossed the short space that separated them, and he imagined she'd been crying, that there was just the hint of moisture in her eyes. Tilting her face to meet the questions in his gaze, she stood toe to toe with him. "What is it you want from me, Kane Moran?"

"More than I can have," he admitted, and he saw her lips twist downward a second. An owl hooted softly from a nearby tree, and farther away, from the other side of the lake, a dog, probably his dad's sorry old hound, gave a soulful bark.

"I'm in love with Harley Taggert."

"And that son of a bitch doesn't deserve you."

"Why not?" she asked, so close he felt her breath, saw the anger in the sudden spots of color in her cheeks. "Why does everyone in this damned town think he's no good?"

"He's weak, Claire. You need someone strong."

"Like you?" she challenged.

He eyed her for a second as a night bird let out a long, lonely cry and a faraway train rattled on its tracks. "Yep," he admitted. "Like me."

"You're leaving."

"Not quite yet."

Her sigh blew her bangs from her eyes, and it was all Kane could do to keep his hands where they were, plastered around his chest, holding on for dear life. He imagined taking her into his arms and kissing her, of cradling her so long and close that she couldn't move, of bending her back so that her hair brushed the floorboards as he kissed her, but he didn't move, didn't dare. Instead he sweated and closed his mind to each and every erotic image that burned through his brain.

"What do you want to do?" she asked suddenly, her voice softer.

He barked out a laugh. "You don't want to know."

"Sure I do."

"No—"

"You came here for a reason, Kane."

"I just wanted to see you again."

"And nothing more?"

He hesitated.

"What?"

His willpower fled on the salty wind blowing in from the ocean. "Christ, Claire, what do you think?"

"I don't know—"

"Sure you do."

"No, Kane—"

"Think about it." His gaze held hers, then flicked to her lips. Heat burned through his blood and desire, smoky with want, controlled his muscles. He reached forward and his hands surrounded the soft skin of her bare arms. Her lips parted and his cock sprang to attention. His thoughts raced like the swift current of the Chinook River through deep mountain chasms. "Whatever you think I want, you're probably right."

"Just say it," she said, her voice breathless.

He considered and decided what the hell. It didn't matter what she thought. "Okay, Claire," he said, fingers tightening over her arms. "The truth of the matter is I'd like to do anything and everything I could with you. I'd like to kiss you and touch you and sleep with you in my arms until morning. I'd like to run my tongue over your bare skin until you quiver with want, and, more than anything in the world, I'd like to bury myself in you and make love to you for the rest of my life!"

She tried to pull away, but he grinned and held fast.

"You wanted to know."

"Oh, God."

"And, believe me, I would never, *never* treat you like that bastard Taggert does." Then he let go. His own stupid words ringing through his ears, he walked back to his bike, hooked the heel of his boot over the kick-start, and jumped down hard. The machine roared to life, and Kane rode away, knowing she was standing just where he'd left her, on the edge of the porch, probably laughing at him and his sick romantic fantasies.

"Fool," he ground out as the bike whipped through the gates of her father's estate. "Goddamned idiot fool."

He roared toward town, hoping to outrun the feeling that he'd made the worst mistake of his life when he noticed the first cop car, coming up behind him fast. Lights—red, blue, and white—strafed the night, sirens screamed.

Glancing at his speedometer he knew the police had nailed him. At seventy-five he was twenty miles over the speed limit. He pulled off at a wide spot in the road and the police cruiser sped by, the officer never turning his head in Kane's direction. A second later an ambulance blew by and then another cop car appeared over the rise, bearing down on him with a fury, only to race past.

Heart hammering, Kane pulled onto the highway again and was relieved for a few minutes as he drove over the final hill into town. As bad as the night had been, at least he didn't have another ticket . . . then he saw them, the stream of cars turning off on Third Street near the old feed mill. Cop cars were parked at odd angles, policemen were guiding traffic and pedestrians past the fifth house on the left, the neat cottage owned by Ruby and Hank Songbird.

Kane's first thought was Jack. The law was always crawling up Jack's shorts. He was sure to be in the thick of it. What now? He'd already been arrested for a car theft when he was sixteen, minor in possession of alcohol at seventeen, shooting mailboxes and lampposts just before he turned eighteen, but now things would be worse. He would be looked upon as an adult—a serious criminal— rather than a juvenile delinquent who was just full of piss and vinegar.

Kane drove down the clogged street, over the railroad tracks that sliced through this part of town, and cut the engine of the bike while a policeman, Officer Tooley, whom Kane had the pleasure of knowing personally, waved him on. "Let's go, people, let's go. Nothin' to see here. Move along."

"What happened?" Kane demanded.

"It's the boy. He was hurt. Fell off the cliffs at Stone Illahee," one of the bystanders, a withered-looking man in a hooded sweatshirt and sweatpants said.

Kane didn't move. His heart stopped beating for a second. "Jack?" he hardly dared ask. For the love of God what had happened? Kane thought of him as he'd last seen his friend, cocky, half-drunk, and running off with a rifle strapped across his back.

"Come on, people, let's move," Tooley was intoning as he waved his flashlight and cars clogged the narrow street.

From in the house a keening wail, the kind of grief-stricken cry only a woman in the throes of deep despair could utter, erupted.

"Oh, dear God," a woman behind him whispered as she made the sign of the cross over her bosom with deft, well-practiced fingers. "Dear Lord in heaven, please listen to our prayers—"

Kane couldn't stand it a second longer, and, ignoring the cops, he ran to the front door just as it was thrown open and silhouetted by the dim light of the house, Crystal raced outside. Without a word she flung herself into Kane's arms and began sobbing hysterically. Deep, heart-rending gasps racked her small body and scraped his soul as rain began to fall.

"Jack!" she cried. "Jack! Oh, God, Jack!"

"Shh," Kane whispered, despair clawing at his soul. He was holding her, stroking her hair, trying to calm her when his own mind was screaming denials.

"For the love of God, no!" she cried.

"Crystal, please. Honey, it's gonna be all right."

"Never," she said with a finality that killed all his hope. "Oh, Jesus, Kane, he's gone."

"Gone?" But he knew before she said the damning words, he knew. Jack Songbird, cocky hellion, an arrogant son of a bitch whom Kane thought of as his only friend, was dead. Anger coursed through his blood, and his stomach clenched in disbelief. Tears burned the back of his eyes, and his fists curled. He wanted to hit, to scream, to flail at fate. But he couldn't. Not now, not with Crystal falling apart in his arms.

As gently as possible, he guided her back up the unpainted steps and through the front door. Jack's father Hank stood near the fireplace, dry-eyed, his face lined with an unspeakable sorrow, his fingers working nervously.

Ruby rocked in a chair near the cold grate, her eyes fixed on the braided carpet, staring, as she witnessed visions only she could see. She chanted softly under her breath in a smooth cadence and a language Kane couldn't understand. An aunt, Lucy Something-Or-Other, pried Crystal from his arms.

"The boy brought this on himself," his father said, stoical as ever.

"Jack wouldn't fall." Crystal's voice, though trembling, was filled with conviction. "He was as surefooted as an antelope. He'd been on that ridge a million times."

"He was drunk." Hank's tone brooked no argument.

"It doesn't matter."

Ruby closed her eyes, and she spoke sharply, the words that passed through her lips hard and foreign in the language of her elders. When her eyelids raised, she looked directly at Kane. "A curse," she explained dry-eyed, lips quivering, chin wobbling. "A curse upon the man who killed my boy."

Hank snorted. "Then you've cursed our own son's soul, Ruby." He stared at his wife with searching black eyes, but he didn't touch her, didn't offer her so much as a moment's consolation. These two people suffered alone. "Jack-the-fool killed Jack-our-boy. There is nothing more to it."

With a final grunt, Weston collapsed, sweating, the image of Miranda planted firmly in his mind as he placed a final wet kiss on Kendall's passionless lips. No wonder Harley hadn't been interested in her. She made love like a rag doll, just lying there, nearly frowning as he'd done all the work. But Weston didn't care. He needed time to clear his head, to think. His life, he felt, was slipping out of his control, and he'd begun to act rashly without thinking things through, and he couldn't afford to foul up now.

He was screwing Kendall, Tessa, and Crystal, a juggling act that was surprisingly less than satisfying, and he was still concerned that his old man had another family tucked away, or at least a son who was poised ready to come forward and demand part of the Taggert estate, and then there was the other thing . . . a darker, more sinister part of him that had come to the surface just last night . . . His blood ran alternately hot and cold thinking of it.

"Get off me." Kendall pushed on his shoulder.

"You know, you could help out with this," he teased, slapping her on her skinny rump as he rolled to the side of the bed.

She cringed. "It's so disgusting."

"What?" he said with a grin as he reached for his crumpled pack of cigarettes, "Oh, Kendall, I'm wounded." He spread one hand over his chest, above his heart as he shook out a Marlboro with the other. "Deeply wounded."

"Save it for someone who believes it." She snagged a beach cover-up from the chair near the bed and flung it over her head.

"You could have fun, if you let yourself." He reached for his lighter.

"Let's get this straight, Weston, this is *not* fun." She cinched the tie around her slim waist and walked to the windows, where the shades were drawn. "I just hope it works."

"It will. Given time."

She shuddered.

"Is it that bad?" Clicking the lighter, he watched the flame catch on the end of his cigarette.

"You don't get it, do you? I love Harley. He's the only boy I've ever made it with . . . well, until now, but this is different." Her chin quivered a little, but she had too much steel in her backbone to break down. "I'm just doing this for the baby."

Cigarette bobbing in the corner of his mouth, Weston reached for his slacks and slid his legs into the wrinkled khakis. "But you want to keep on, right?"

"Until I'm sure. Yes." Arms wrapped protectively around her middle, she added, "I thought you were seeing Tessa Holland."

"Bad news travels fast."

"So you really are," she said, disgust in her voice.

Slowly, he fastened his buckle. "Yeah, so what?"

"You really are an alley cat, aren't you?" she asked, peering through the blinds to the night outside. "If you're involved with Tessa, why did you call out Miranda's name when you were with me?"

"Did I?" He reached for his shirt. Of course he'd let his fantasies run wild while trying to get some kind of response from Kendall, whom he now considered queen of the tight, dry cunts.

"Yes."

"Well, to tell you the truth, it's always been a fantasy of mine."

"A fantasy?" She blanched.

"Yep, doing all three Holland sisters."

Her nose wrinkled in revulsion. "I don't want to hear this."

"Well, not all at the same time, of course—unless that's the way they'd want it."

"Weston, enough. God, how can you even think about that?"

His laugh was brittle. "Now, Kendall, what's this sense of latent virtue all about? You don't have much room to judge since you just fucked me so that you can pass off my kid as Harley's."

"Oh, God." She buried her face in her hands.

But he didn't stop. Who the hell did she think she was? "Just remember, Kendall, you're balling me so that you can trick Harley into marrying you."

"I know, but it's because I love him." She gave out a little sob and hiccup.

"Noble."

"You hate me."

"Of course I don't." Jeez, he hated it when females tried to pull the martyr bit on him. "Listen, just relax. Enjoy what we're doing." A cloud of smoke rolled up from his mouth. "It could be a lot more fun than you're making it, and you might just learn some tricks for when you're finally with my brother again."

She actually gagged. Christ, what a mental case she was.

Buttoning his shirt, he took a long drag on his Marlboro. "Tomorrow? Same time, same place?"

She sagged into a chair and hung her head, looking for all the world like the sacrificial lamb being led to the slaughter. "Yes," she said so softly he could barely hear her.

"I'll be ready," he promised as he opened the door and slunk into the night. The truth of the matter was, he wasn't enjoying their trysts any more than she was. Weston had always prided himself on his ability to please a woman, to make her come with just the right words or touch. But Kendall wasn't giving an inch. He'd tried everything short of rape to get her attention, and she was just going through the motions, lying on the bed, eyes closed, legs spread, nipples soft while he performed like a goddamned robot. It would serve her right if she didn't get pregnant.

But then that would foul things up. The thought that his seed was planted in Kendall's womb was comforting. Not only would Kendall get Harley to marry her, but the child would actually be Weston's descendant. He could use his paternity as a bargaining chip in making sure Kendall always came to heel, and if the truth came out, he'd claim the kid and whatever parcel of the Taggert inheritance—Harley's inheritance—the child would eventually end up with.

Yeah, screwing Kendall, though not physically charged, was worth the half hour of work.

He slid into his Porsche and tried not to notice the deep gash that ran from the front fender to the taillights—an ugly scar made by a coward. His jaw tightened in silent fury that anyone would have the nerve to maim the sleek machine. With an engine that hummed and paint that looked liquid in the right light, the Porsche was a classic. He felt the engine rumble to life as he switched on the ignition. This sleek baby was a woman you could count on.

He threw the racy machine into first and nosed out of the drive of Kendall's parents' beach house. He should have been sated; it had been a long hard day at the mill, starting with the fight. Jack Songbird had come in late, been stupid enough to try and alter his time card, and then mocked Weston, spitting at his feet. Weston had savored every minute of firing him while his coworkers looked on. Later they'd had it out and . . . poor Jack, a pathetic drunk, had fallen off the cliffs near Stone Illahee. Weston smiled to himself and felt the jackknife deep in his pants pocket—the knife with flecks of red paint on its ugly blade, a perfect match to the color of his car.

Yep, it had been a long emotionally charged day. Too bad that it had ended in Kendall's cold bed. What should have been a hot, satisfying fuck had been a disappointment. Screwing Kendall was as passionless as jacking off—coming dry. He was still keyed up and restless.

He needed a real woman with hot blood and wild imagination. He thought of Tessa; she was always ready, but deep in his heart he knew that she wouldn't cool the fire in his blood. Nope, the only woman guaranteed to satisfy him was her older sister. Miranda. *Just you wait, honey,* he thought with a low chuckle. *Someday soon I'm going to show you what love is all about.*

CHAPTER 16

Kendall dialed the phone reluctantly. What could she tell Harley? That she'd just started her period? That after three thrilling days of being late, she'd finally felt cramps and begun to bleed?

Could she put up with another month of doing it with Weston just so that she could trap his younger brother into a marriage Harley didn't want? A tear slid down her face and she wondered why she'd fallen in love with Harley. Why, when she could have dated anyone she wanted, had she set her sights on Harley? She couldn't explain to herself why she'd fallen for him, but she had, and the thought that Claire Holland, a tomboy without any figure to speak of, had stolen him away was a double punch to her already bruised ego.

Her parents didn't help. Her mother's constant questions—"What happened between you and that cute Taggert boy? Why don't you date someone else? Anna Prescott's son has been asking about you, he's awfully good-looking, and his family has money and—" It never ended.

"Taggert residence," a cool voice intoned.

"I'd like to speak with Harley," she said.

"Mr. Taggert's out right now."

She checked her watch, but it was past five, and she knew that Harley never stayed late. "When do you expect him?"

"Later. May I tell him you called?"

"No . . . I'll try again," she said, and hung up as tears filled her eyes. Harley was with Claire, she could feel it in her bones. Two-timing jerk, that's what he was.

She flung herself onto the bed in the beach house and stared up at the ceiling. Maybe she was going about this all wrong. Thinking she might be pregnant wasn't changing his mind, but if she did something drastic and landed in the hospital, maybe even claiming she'd lost the baby . . . but there were probably tests for that sort of thing. Someone at the hospital would figure it out . . . What was she going to do?

The thought of making it with Weston turned her stomach. She hated herself each time he came over. Her skin crawled at his touch. He'd tried, she'd give him that, touching her and kissing her and attempting to turn her on, but she'd resisted and now sometimes he didn't even take off his clothes, just tore down her panties, opened his fly, and pumped some Taggert sperm into her. When it was over, he always lit a cigarette and smiled down at her lying on the wrinkled sheets, offering her a smoke and making her feel dirtier than ever.

But it would be worth it. If only she'd get pregnant! Well, she'd just have to try harder. Make Weston do it more than once a day.

Bile rose in the back of her throat, but she told herself she could stomach making love with him a little longer. As soon as her period was over. She'd just pretend that he was Harley. And since she was going to make love to Harley, she'd take scented baths, put on her laciest teddy, and light candles in her room. When Weston came by in a few days, she'd kiss and touch him, slowly remove his clothes and seduce him just as she had his younger brother.

Romance was what she needed; not just sex.

But she had to have a backup plan. There was a chance that she couldn't get pregnant, so she had to think of another way for Harley to see the light, to realize that she was the woman for him and that Claire, the bitch, wasn't.

She would need help if she was going to make Claire look bad; otherwise, the plan might backfire. She would have to depend upon someone else to do her dirty work. Someone as dedicated to her cause as she. Someone who would do what she asked without questioning her judgment. Someone like Harley's twerp of a sister. Paige would do anything Kendall wanted.

The day of the funeral dawned hot and sticky. Storm clouds collected on the horizon, but there wasn't a breath of breeze. Jack's ashes were cast from the very cliffs from which he'd fallen, dusty cinders strewn over the rocky shoals far below.

Claire felt sick inside as she stood with her sisters and mother. Dutch was away on business, but had sent his condolences—a large horseshoe of lilies and a check made out to Ruby's family, to do with what they wanted. As if money would help.

Claire had hardly known Jack, but Ruby had worked for their family for years, and she'd been friends with Crystal, who sat, dry-eyed, staring out to sea, pale beneath her coppery skin. Without makeup she looked young and vulnerable as she twisted a red bandanna—the one Jack wore, Claire supposed—in her small hands.

Tessa rolled her eyes as a man from what had once been a thriving coastal tribe spoke. He looked no more Native American than anyone else, with his short-cropped gray hair and weathered skin, but apparently he had some authority and spoke in terms of the tribe and Jack's position and all young people today. Claire heard nothing but the thunder of the sea and the piercing cries of seagulls whirling and spinning overhead.

It was hard to believe that Jack was dead. Someone so young and vital suddenly gone. She heard the roar of a motorcycle and her pulse leapt. From the corner of her eye, she spied Kane as he parked the bike near a crooked pine tree and stood apart from the crowd, his hands pushed deep into the pockets of his leather jacket, his eyes hidden by sunglasses. His jaw was hard and square, his lips a thin determined line, his gaze focused on the horizon. How many days did he have left in Chinook?

I'd like to do anything and everything I could with you. I'd like to kiss you and touch you and sleep with you in my arms until morning. I'd like to run my tongue over your bare skin until you quiver with want, and, more than anything in the world, I'd like to bury myself in you and make love to you for the rest of my life.

She bit her lip and tried not to think about Kane and the last time she'd seen him, the night Jack Songbird's body had been found.

Believe me, I would never, never *treat you like that bastard Taggert does.*

Tessa, standing next to Claire, shifted from one foot to the other. "Where are the Taggerts?" she whispered.

"Don't know," Claire mouthed back, surprised that she hadn't missed Harley.

"You'd think they'd be here. Jack worked for their mill." Tessa's blue eyes scanned the small crowd gathered on the cliffs.

"Weston fired him that day."

"I know, I know," Tessa muttered, frowning and wishing she was anywhere else as her mother slanted her a warning glance and raised a finger to her lips. Tessa glowered back, but Dominique turned away, as if she had some interest in this morbid rite. Funerals were just so depressing. Such downers. Besides, Tessa wanted to see Weston again. She'd thought he would be here and had been disappointed when not one member of the Taggert clan had shown up.

"When's this gonna be over?" she whispered to Miranda, who, the last few days, had been more preoccupied than ever.

Miranda didn't answer, and Tessa itched to be anywhere else. Where was Weston? She felt a familiar gnawing in her guts lately and wished she hadn't started to care about him. Seeing him on the sly had been fun. Daring. She hadn't cried any tears over losing her virginity to him, but she hadn't expected to fall for him. He was too old, too worldly, too self-centered, and he didn't give a damn about her. That's what was so maddening.

Finally, the chieftain or whatever he was quit talking and the group started a soft chant. Tessa couldn't believe it. Jack Songbird might have been full-blooded Native American, but she doubted he gave two cents about his so-called tribe and whatever traditions they still embraced. It wasn't as if he'd run around in beads and feathers and rode a spotted pony.

As the foreign-sounding words faded, the group broke up, and Tessa didn't waste any time. She hurried along the path to the road where all the cars were parked. Trucks, Jeeps, a few sedans, and a couple of station wagons were wedged near Dominique's silver Mercedes. Tessa slid into the plush interior while the rest of the family made small talk with Ruby and Crystal.

Tessa wasn't interested in trying to be friendly. What could she say? Of course she was sorry Jack died. His death had to have been horrible. She shivered, imagining that terrifying tumble off the ridge. But there was nothing she could do, no words she could speak, that would change things. On top of all that, she didn't know what to say to Crystal. She slumped lower in the seat, hoping Jack's sister wouldn't see her. The interior of the car was muggy. Breathless. Tessa began to sweat as she stole a glance at Crystal. Jack's sister was staring at her—through her—with an intensity that was downright scary. Christ, Crystal could give a person the willies. Nervously, Tessa reached for the cigarettes she had hidden in her purse. No, that wouldn't do. Her mother didn't know she smoked.

Couldn't they just leave? Ever since Tessa had first started seeing Weston, she'd felt the daggers in Crystal's dark gaze slice into her heart as she'd glared at Tessa, knew the Native American girl despised her, but that was just too bad. Crystal didn't have any claim on Weston.

The trouble was, no one did.

The doors of the Mercedes opened again. Dominique slid behind the steering wheel next to Tessa. Miranda and Claire took their spots in the backseat. "I know this is a terrible loss for Ruby," Dominique said as she dabbed her eyes with a twisted handkerchief, then found her keys in her purse. "Losing a child . . . well, there's nothing worse." Engines started and cars rolled past as Dominique turned the key in the ignition. "But, even though you've suffered a great loss, this is no time to make changes you might regret." She nosed the Mercedes onto the narrow gravel road.

"What kind of changes?" Claire asked, and Tessa rolled her eyes. Who cared?

"Ruby quit," Miranda said, and Dominique's lips tightened.

"Quit?" Claire echoed.

"Well, I'm sure she'll change her mind." Dominique glanced in her rearview mirror. "She's just upset right now. In a few weeks, when she's dealt with her grief, she'll realize that she needs the stability of working for us." Sighing, Dominique adjusted the air-conditioning.

"I was going to offer her a raise anyway; maybe that'll change her mind."

"I don't think this is about money," Claire ventured.

"Of course it isn't. Not now, anyway, but once life settles down for the Songbirds, Ruby will have too much time on her hands. She's still got a daughter to think about, and Crystal wants to go to college. That's not cheap, you know." She flipped on a blinker as they approached the highway. "Ruby will be back."

Tessa didn't really give a rip. Ruby was a pain in the neck, always bossing everyone around. Even though it was her job, it bugged Tessa that one of their employees, a servant, thought she could tell her what to do. In Tessa's opinion, the family was better off without Ruby Songbird and her dark, condemning eyes. It was too bad about Jack, he seemed like an okay kind of guy, but Tessa's life wasn't going to alter just because he'd died.

"Oh, Lord. What now?" Dominique whispered, slamming on the brakes as a motorcycle whipped by. In a blur of black and silver, the bike and its rider sped onto the asphalt, ignoring the blast from a logging truck that was barreling south.

"Oh, God!" Claire cried, her hands flying to her face. "Kane—"

"Was that the Moran boy?" Dominique asked, a hand still over her heart. "I thought he had more sense than that, but then, why would he?"

"Meaning?" Claire asked, her eyes round.

Tessa watched their mother.

"No breeding in that hellion. His father's a drunk, and his mother left him." She checked the road again as she eased off the brake. "If he doesn't watch out, he won't live to see twenty."

"Don't even say that!" Claire stared after the disappearing motorcycle.

"Why do you care?" Tessa asked, her interest piqued.

"I don't. I just know that he was a good friend of Jack Songbird."

"Yeah? How do you know that?"

"I saw them hanging out together and . . ." Claire hesitated a second. "And he told me."

"When?"

"I don't remember."

"You *know* him?" Tessa asked, incredulous. She twisted around in the front seat to stare into Claire's pale face. What was going on here?

"Yeah."

"How well?"

Claire locked gazes with her younger sister. "Well enough," she said, and turned to look out the window again. "Well enough."

Three days after Jack's funeral, Miranda stared at the calendar. Something had to be wrong. She couldn't be late. Couldn't. She'd been careful. So had Hunter. Rarely had they made love without the use of a condom. But as she counted the days on the flat pages of the calendar and realized she wasn't three days late with her period, but ten, she felt the truth hit her square in the gut: She was pregnant.

On trembling legs she sat in her desk chair. This couldn't be happening, not to her, not to the girl who had her life planned so carefully. She clenched her fists and thought about a baby . . . *a baby,* for the love of God. It wasn't just the shame of being pregnant, it was the rest of it as well, that she would bear a child. Hunter's child. She rested her head in her hands and it felt incredibly heavy. "Help me," she whispered.

What would that mean for college? Graduate school? Her dreams of becoming a lawyer?

Tears burned in her eyes, but she refused to cry. This was a new person she was thinking about, a part of her and a part of Hunter. A tiny human being growing deep inside her. A baby! Unclenching her fists, she rubbed her flat abdomen, and, through the tears that she couldn't fight, she gave way to romantic fantasies of marrying Hunter, having the baby, and still going to school. So she'd have to work and Hunter, his dreams of owning his own ranch would be put on hold, but just because they were having a child, didn't mean it was the end of the world.

No, in fact, it might just be the beginning.

Still, she was scared to death. She would take an in-home pregnancy test, then if it showed positive, make an appointment at the local county hospital, find out for certain if this was a false alarm, then give the news to Hunter. How would he take it, she wondered, knowing how he felt about his own father—well, stepfather really.

Hunter Riley wasn't Dan's biological son as everyone seemed to think. No, Dan Riley had married Hunter's mother when Hunter was barely two years old. He remembered no other man in his life nor had Dan treated him any differently than if he'd been his own flesh and blood.

Hunter had confessed to Miranda that he didn't think he had another father, that no man could take the place of Dan Riley; therefore, he'd never try to find out who had sired him. That secret had been kept by his mother to her dying day, when Hunter was nearing his twelfth birthday and ovarian cancer had claimed her. At her funeral in the small Presbyterian church just outside of town, he'd half-expected some middle-aged guy to step up to him and claim that he was Hunter's natural father, but it hadn't happened, and, apparently, Hunter's biological dad didn't know he existed or just didn't give a damn. Either way, Hunter, didn't really care.

Miranda stood, walked to the window and opened it wide enough to let in the breeze. The smell of roses and honeysuckle mingled to drift up to her.

What if Hunter didn't want to marry her? What if his dreams were more important than she was, more important than having a child of his own? What if he insisted upon an abortion? Holding on to the window casing for support, she swallowed hard and realized that she knew so little about him, much too little to think of marriage.

And yet she loved him. Things would work out; they always did. She rubbed her belly and smiled. Corny as it sounded, maybe a baby was just what they needed.

"What's this?" Paige asked, her eyes bright as Kendall handed her a foil box with a big pink ribbon.

"A surprise."

"But it's not my birthday or Christmas or anything."

"I know," Kendall said, taking a seat on the desk chair and linking her fingers over one knee. "I just saw something I thought you'd like. Go ahead. Open it." Paige's smile was pathetic, just like this cloying room with its canopied bed and matching dresser, vanity, and desk. White with gold trim, pink rosebuds and gingham, lace trim on everything. For what? This oddball of a girl.

Smiling widely, Paige tore open the box, tossing aside the ribbon and tissue paper until she found the prize deep inside—a silver charm bracelet with a single charm—a cat with a curled tail—dangling from the tiny links. "Oh, my," she whispered, holding the damned thing to her eyes and watching as the kitten swayed rhythmically in front of her nose. For a second Kendall thought the pathetic girl might hypnotize herself. "It's beautiful."

"It's nothing."

"Oh, no, Kendall," Paige said, clutching the bracelet as if it were made of huge diamonds and holding it over her heart. "It's the nicest thing anyone's ever done for me."

"It's just a bracelet."

Paige shook her head and swallowed hard. She blinked as tears filled her eyes. "It's much more than that. Thank you."

"Don't thank me, just be happy with it," Kendall said, but she was really thinking the kid's reaction was all wrong. Hadn't anyone ever been kind to her? This rich child of Neal Taggert, the only daughter who wore gawd-awful braces and had endured rhinoplasty to ensure her beauty had to have been spoiled rotten. Surely Paige had received tons of gifts over the years.

"This is special because you gave it to me," Paige explained as she placed the links over her thick wrist and locked the clasp. "Not because you had to, but because you wanted to."

Kendall felt worse than ever. She had hoped to find a way to secure Paige's loyalty, of course, but she didn't want to be in a position of breaking the girl's heart. Guilt weighed heavily on her shoulders. "It's not that big a deal."

Paige's eyes were filled with adoration. "I wish you were going to be my sister-in-law instead of that stupid Holland girl," she said, as if she'd read Kendall's mind. Perhaps the kid was sharper than she looked.

"Me, too, but there's not much I can do. Harley wants her."

"Harley's stupid."

"You know I love him."

"Oh, I know." Paige nodded her head sagely, lank strands of hair moving against her shoulders. "And she doesn't. Not the way you love him."

"She couldn't." Kendall ran a finger over the edge of Paige's desk, along the gold trim. "If I could convince him, I would, but, believe me, I've tried everything."

"He just needs to spend more time with you and less with her." Paige walked over to the mirror and studied her wrist in the reflection, watching the silver cat dance in the sunlight. "I wish she would leave."

"That won't happen." Kendall sighed longingly.

"Then I wish she had the same kind of accident that Jack had."

"Jack Songbird?" A chill as cold as death itself climbed up Kendall's spine. Sometimes Harley's little sister was downright creepy.

"Yeah." Paige lifted her eyes to meet Kendall's horrified gaze in the mirror. "He died."

"I know."

"So he won't bother anybody anymore."

"I didn't think . . . I mean I don't think he bothered anyone."

"He stole from the mill."

"What?" Kendall's throat was suddenly tight. She had hoped to steer the conversation to Claire and suggest that Paige do a little spying on her or talking with that nitwit of a younger sister of Claire's to dig up some dirt. *No one* could be as lily-white as Claire Holland pretended to be, but somehow the discussion had taken a new and decidedly dangerous turn. Anxiously, she licked her lips and wondered how she could make a quick exit. Paige wasn't just weird, she was borderline psychotic.

"So God punished Jack for taking money from Daddy."

"Surely you don't believe that." Kendall was horrified.

"Why not? It's what they teach in Sunday school and everybody dies someday anyway." Paige tilted her head and studied the ceiling. "Yeah, I think it would be a good idea if Claire died."

"She's *not* going to die. She's seventeen, for crying out loud. People don't just keel over at that age."

"Jack did," Paige said philosophically as she stretched and reached for her favorite stuffed animal, a huge panda bear with sad eyes. "Well, he was a little older, but not much." She looked at the shiny cat with eyes that made Kendall shiver as Paige stroked the bear's wide head. "Claire could die, too, you know." She nodded to herself. "You just have to want it bad enough and pray real hard."

CHAPTER 17

With a click of his lighter, Weston lit a cigarette and wondered why he'd agreed to meet Tessa here, only a stone's throw away from her house, in the middle of the night. It was almost as if she loved tempting fate, becoming bolder with each of their clandestine meetings. He should break it off with her, she was a little too off-beat for him, but he liked the idea of screwing one of Dutch's daughters—even if it was the wrong one.

He paced along the shore of the lake, screened only by a hedge of arborvitae that ran from one end of the garage to the dock, and felt the hairs on the back of his neck rise, as if he was being watched by unseen eyes.

Gossamer clouds drifted over the moon, allowing only a weak light, but still he could see the outline of the lodge nestled in the trees, the garage, gardens, and stone paths and steps leading in different directions through the fir and pine. The lake was smooth, and mirror-dark. Overhead he heard the rustle of bats' wings. He checked his watch. She was late. Christ, this was a mistake.

Just then he heard light, hurried footsteps and squashed his cigarette. Peering through the lacy branches of the arborvitae, he watched as a woman ran toward him, her bare feet skimming the stones. He nearly called out, only to open his mouth and remain silent. It wasn't Tessa who was racing through the night but her older sister Miranda.

Long dark hair caught by a white ribbon streamed behind and she was breathing heavily.

Weston's heart pounded and his mouth felt as if it had turned to cotton. She was wearing a gauzy white dress, maybe her nightgown, that billowed and showed off her slim legs.

A low whistle caused her steps to falter, and then she sped down a path toward the lake.

Weston couldn't help himself. He followed. Darting between the trees, watching her gauzy dress flash in the darkness, he kept a short distance behind her and tried to quiet the desire that thudded in his temples. God, she was beautiful. She paused at the beach, moonlight playing upon her face.

Weston stopped behind a Douglas fir and swallowed hard as a man appeared—a tall muscular man, who, without a word, took Miranda into his arms and kissed her long and hard. She moaned, and Weston's blood thundered.

He recognized the guy. Hunter Riley. Son of the goddamned caretaker. Wearing only low-slung jeans, he kissed Miranda until her knees gave way and they tumbled into the sand. "Randa," Riley growled, his fingers plucking at the buttons on the front of her dress. "My beautiful Miranda." As the dress parted, exposing her lush, bare breasts, Weston felt his erection stiffen, and it was all he could do not to touch himself.

Like a sicko voyeur, he watched Hunter caress and kiss those breasts, sucking with deep, satisfied grunts.

Bastard! Who was he—a nobody, and yet he was touching the one woman Weston couldn't possess.

Riley yanked down the dress and Weston clamped hard on his teeth to suppress a groan. Her supple long legs were slowly exposed and that glorious nest of black curls at the juncture of her thighs caught in the moonlight. Riley buried his head in her abdomen and her fingers tangled in his hair as he moved ever lower, tasting and touching. Weston's breathing became shallow. He should look away, take his eyes off the erotic picture before him, but he couldn't, and his hands slipped the zipper of his fly downward to delve into his pants where he stroked his own throbbing erection, wishing he was riding that warm piece of flesh that was Miranda Holland.

Hunter kicked off his jeans and parted her legs. Weston bit down hard on his tongue to keep from crying out.

Her sounds were soft and eager, she was clinging to her lover, arching up against him, making love to him like the pure, sexual animal Weston had always thought her to be. His fingers moved ever faster as Hunter threw back his head and let out a long cry of triumph.

Weston cringed as Riley, sweating like a pig, fell upon her, holding her close, crushing those magnificent breasts. He whispered something into her ear then lifted his head for a second, and his eyes, dark in the night, seemed to stare straight at Weston. That was impossible, of course, he couldn't be seen in the shadows of the fir trees, and yet Hunter seemed to have Weston in his sights.

Weston's breath stilled in his lungs. Sweat trickled down his neck. He slid his hand out of his pants.

Miranda said something and Hunter turned his attention back to the long-legged, beautiful woman lying beneath him. Desire thudded through Weston's brain as he slowly picked his way back up the path. He stumbled once, his shoe crashing into a tangle of roots, his face slapped by fine-needled branches, but eventually he found his way to the dock.

His heart nearly stopped when he spied Tessa on the edge of the pier, her feet dragging through the water less than two hundred yards from where her sister was lying naked on the beach.

She turned as he approached and he noticed the tracks of tears drizzling from her eyes. "Enjoy the show?" she asked, her voice a harsh whisper that probably echoed over the lake.

"Let's get out of here."

"What is it with you?" she demanded. "Why do you keep seeing me when you really want her?"

"Who?"

She shoved her hair away from her face. "Don't be stupid. I have eyes, you know. I can tell that you want Miranda. I only wished I understood your fascination with her."

He didn't argue, and she didn't break down.

"She's in love with Hunter, you know." Struggling to her feet, Tessa dusted her hands and sniffed back any trace of tears. She had pride, if nothing else. "I don't know why, but Miranda thinks the earth, moon, and stars revolve around him." She wiped the back of her hand under her nose and squared her small shoulders. When Weston tried to touch her, she backed away quickly, nearly slipping off the pier. "Who would have thought? The ice princess—hot for the caretaker's son." Her smile was cold and direct as she stared into Weston's eyes. "Hurts, doesn't it?"

"Tessa," he said, reaching for her wrist.

She yanked her hand away. "Don't touch me," she snapped, drawing back and slapping him. Smack. The sound echoed over the water. "I won't be used like a two-dollar whore. Go back to Crystal if all you want is a quick fuck."

Weston's temper flared. "Hey—wait a minute," he ordered, grabbing her around her small waist. What was going on here? Tessa, who had always been so willing to please, was suddenly turning on him, showing him more fire than he'd seen in weeks. She was fighting him as he dragged her along the shore of the lake, down a path far from Miranda, away from the lodge.

"Let me go, you bastard!" Her heels dug into the dirt and caught on exposed roots. With a sickening rip, her blouse caught on a branch and tore.

"Why?"

"Because it's over!" She struggled and he held tighter, feeling a heat in his groin that was sparked by the fight.

"It's over when I say so."

"Leave me alone, Weston, or I swear—"

He clamped a hand over her mouth and felt her teeth sink into his palm. But he didn't so much as flinch. Let her struggle all she wanted. Right now she was his. Anger fueled his passion, fury caused his dick to rise and heat. She was scared now, he could feel the change in her body, the tension. The smell of fear reached his nostrils and he thought he could easily come in his jeans. "Don't you know that no one messes with me, Tessa? Haven't you figured that one out yet?"

Her body coiled and she struck out, twisting so that her knee connected with his groin. Pain exploded in his crotch. His breath expelled in a rush.

"You bitch," he wheezed, shaking her. "You goddamned bitch! Now you're going to pay!" Doubled over, he dragged her over stones, past berry vines that clung and clawed, over fallen logs to a clearing where his car was parked. He was sweating and breathing hard, but they were far enough away from Dutch's house that even if she was stupid enough to scream, no one would hear her. She wouldn't win. No matter what.

With one hand he reached into his pocket and found Jack Songbird's knife. With a click it was open, and he held it in front of her eyes. "Don't do something stupid and you won't get hurt."

He let go and she spit on him as she tried to stumble away. "You're asking for trouble," she hissed.

"Me? Looks like you're the one who needs help."

"I'm not afraid of you, Weston," she said with enough bravado to almost convince him. But her voice shook a bit and she couldn't take her eyes off his newfound weapon. "In fact I—I think you're pathetic!" She was sweating, and her perfume teased his nostrils. She turned as if to walk away, and he lunged. Her scream, before he held the knife to her throat, was a tiny squeak.

"Let me go, you cocksucker."

"No way, Tessa. We had a date, remember?" Holding her firmly against him with both arms, he felt her spine against his chest, her round butt wriggling against his fly as she struggled. Her breasts heaved against his arm, and her breath was hot as dragon's fire.

"Let me go, damn it."

He smelled her fear and it turned him on. She was a hellcat. He licked the skin at her hairline and she flung her head back, hoping to wound him. Silly bitch. "Careful, darling." He nipped at her salty skin.

Tessa cried out.

"That was for the slap." She trembled, and he loved the feeling of power it gave him, the feeling that he could control her, use her as his personal slave. "Now, you're going to do exactly what I want, bitch, and you're not going to stop until I say it's time. Get down on your knees."

He shoved her to the ground and held the knife up as if he could throw it at any second. "Now, beautiful, unzip my pants."

"No—"

He grabbed a handful of her hair and sliced it off.

"Ahhh!"

Yellow strands fell to the ground. "Now. Unzip my pants and go down on me like a good little girl."

"Go find Miranda. She's the one you want," she said bravely though her eyes were round with fear, her lips trembling.

"She's busy."

"What do you care? You like making it with more than one girl at a time."

"She'll have her turn."

Suddenly she leapt upward and swung at him, her fingernails raking down his cheek.

"Shit!" His entire face stung. He shoved her back to the ground. "No more games, bitch," he said, as blood dripped to his shoulder. "Open my pants and—"

"I loathe you."

"Do you? Too bad. Now, you've got no choice and if you so much as touch me with your teeth . . . I'll retaliate."

"No you won't," she said, with sudden insight as she stood in front of him. "You're not going to kill me, or even wound me," she said, "because you'd get caught. Even without a trace of evidence my father would hunt you down like a dog. People have seen us together and now—" she wiggled her fingers with their dirtied, bloodied nails in front of his eyes, "—there'll be traces of your blood on my hands."

His heart stopped for a second.

Tessa's smile was pure evil. "If you make me do anything I don't want to do, and I mean *anything,* I'll tell my father and swear out a complaint at the police department. You'll be arrested for . . . for trespassing, and . . . and assault and statutory rape."

He didn't believe her. "You wouldn't—"

"You bastard, I'd kill you before I ever let you touch me again."

He reached forward and she slapped his hand away. "You'll go to jail, Weston. My father will see to it." She looked at him with her jaw set and anger burning in her eyes. Her skin was smudged with dirt, her blouse torn, and she stared at him as if she'd like nothing better than to shred him to ribbons with her bare hands.

"Jesus, you wouldn't."

"Watch me," she warned, her eyes glinting like those of a wounded animal. Weston remembered a possum he'd trapped and how the beast had snarled, showing off razor-sharp teeth before Weston put him out of his misery.

"Leave," she ordered. She wasn't joking.

Every muscle in his body screamed to lunge at her, to throw her on the ground and tear off her clothes, but he wasn't stupid enough to make that kind of a mistake. Not now. She was, whether he liked it or not, jailbait.

Later, he told himself, he'd deal with her later. When it was safer, and she didn't have the upper hand. He clicked the knife shut and climbed into his car. In a squeal of wheels, he roared off, bouncing onto the old rutted road that led to this stretch of nowhere. He saw Tessa in his rearview mirror, her back rigid with pride, her torn clothes worn like a god-damned badge of honor.

His hands were sweaty on the wheel as he rounded the corner and shifted into second. His blood pounded in his veins, throbbing at his temples. If that little bitch thought she'd somehow gotten the upper hand, she was wrong. Dead wrong.

"I'm telling you, son, I'm counting on you." Neal poked a thick finger in Weston's direction as the ancient air conditioner in Weston's office at the sawmill rattled in the vents overhead. "Someone's got to talk some sense into your brother. No one, and I mean no one in this family, is going to hook up with a Holland! Jesus H. Christ, doesn't that boy see that she's only after his inheritance?" Pacing from one end of Weston's office to the other, he dabbed at his balding pate with a handkerchief. His ruddy face was more florid than usual, his nostrils flared in indignation, his gold tooth glinting as he talked. Sweat stood in small droplets on his forehead and stained his sleeves. "What the hell happened to your face?"

Weston managed a smile, though the thought of Tessa's fingernails made him see red. "A local whore and I got into a disagreement." Not exactly a lie.

"Hell, it wasn't that Songbird girl, was it?"

"Crystal? No."

"Good. We can't afford to rile anyone associated with the local tribe, you know. They own some valuable land around here, land we might want to buy for another resort, one to rival old Dutch's. Even though you and I know that Jack Songbird was a screw-off, his parents might start yammering about discrimination and such. The whole damned tribe could get involved."

"I don't think they're putting together a war party," Weston sneered. "Relax."

Neal let out his breath in a world-weary sigh. "Maybe you're right. But we still have problems, starting with your brother and his stupid-ass plan to marry one of the Holland girls. Shit, what a mess."

"Don't you think Claire Holland will inherit enough money from her father? Do you really think she's after ours, too?"

"Of course she is. They all are. Greedy, like their son of a bitch of a father. He's never forgiven me for outbidding him for that piece of land just north of Seaside."

"And building Sea Breeze."

"Yep. That was a real bug up old Dutch's butt." Neal chuckled, his gold tooth flashing as he smiled. "Makes Stone Illahee look cheap. The bastard had it coming."

"But that was years ago."

"Well, the old fart knows how to hold a grudge."

"Maybe it's time to get over this."

"No way. Not until Dutch makes the first move."

"Why?"

Neal's eyes flashed darkly. "This goes beyond business, son. It's personal."

You bet it is, Weston thought, and wondered if the old man knew that his wife had been bedded by his worst enemy. In his mind's eye, Weston saw Dutch's freckled back and the shattered mirror in the guest house. Since that fateful day, he and his mother hadn't gotten along. The lies had simmered between them. Always.

Neal loosened his tie. "So, don't play devil's advocate with me. I told Harley I'd cut him off rather than let any Holland bitch get her grubby fingers on my money, and I meant it. Same goes for you." He dabbed at his face with the handkerchief. "Christ, it's hot."

"I'm not the one planning on marrying into the Holland family," Weston pointed out, still in a foul mood from the other night, when he'd caught Miranda with Riley. And Tessa. Just wait until he got her alone. She'd be sorry she'd ever pushed him so far.

"I know, but Harley . . . oh, he never did have a lick of sense. Always a whining crybaby. When I first heard that he was dating one of Dutch's daughters, I figured it was just a fling, kind of a rebellion thing, nothing to worry about, but, then he didn't stop, just kept seeing her." Neal pinched the bridge of his nose as if he could forestall a headache. "What was wrong with Kendall, that's what I'd like to know. She's a damned sight prettier than all three of those Holland girls put together, and her father and I get along, do business together. Why the hell doesn't Harley want to marry her?"

"Don't ask me." Weston played the innocent to the hilt and his old man was so intent on his own need to vent his anger that he didn't notice.

"We'll find out how our boy likes it without a dime. I'm giving him one more chance to see things clearly, and then, if this whole Claire Holland thing hasn't blown over within the week, I'm going to yank his job out from under him, repo that damned Jag, and kick him out of the house. Then we'll discover just what the Holland girl's made of. Ten to one, she runs in the other direction."

Weston wasn't about to take that bet, though he thought Claire had more grit than his old man gave her credit for.

"Maybe she's a great lay," Weston offered, his thoughts again wandering to Miranda.

"Fine. So he can fuck her from here to kingdom come, but he can't marry her!"

"What's the difference?"

Neal stared at his son as if Weston had just announced he wanted to build their newest resort on Jupiter. "The difference is that if he just sleeps with her and uses her as a whore, he's the victor. If, however, she manages to get her claws into him and he marries her, then she wins. Christ, I shouldn't have to explain this to you."

"So it's a matter of respect."

"Bingo." Neal rubbed his face, grumbled under his breath, then waved in the air, as if to shoo away a bothersome fly. "Just make sure he understands what's at stake. Now, there's a couple of other things we need to discuss. I want an internal audit of the books, a meeting with Jerry Best of Best Lumber to see why he pulled his account and . . . some kind of payment to the Songbird family—you know, because of the death of their son."

Weston's head snapped up. His muscles froze. "Jack had insurance through the company. I think it was still in effect even though he was fired that same day he died."

"I know, I know, I doubt the insurance company will balk. We throw too much money their way, but it's not enough. I want Taggert Milling to do something more for the family, you know, kind of a PR thing."

"It's not as if he was killed in an on-the-job accident," Weston argued, galled that his father would stoop to such theatrics. "Jack Songbird was a less than stellar employee—check his personnel records. Every supervisor he ever had gave him low marks. He was always late, never wore the safety equipment, took long breaks, flirted with the secretaries, even broke into the Coke machine, I think. You name it; Songbird did it."

"Doesn't matter."

"But—"

"Look, I know you fired the stupid son of a bitch, but for Christ's sake, Weston, think for a minute about the good press we can get out of this. The company will donate five thousand dollars, which I'll match personally, and we'll start a trust fund for his family and the tribe—wasn't he a Chinook?"

"Clatskanie or some damned thing," Weston muttered, galled. Who the hell gave a rat's ass about Jack Songbird? The kid was a punk, penny-ante thief, and vandal. The world, especially Chinook, Oregon, was better off without him. Weston laced his fingers together, popping his knuckles. "If you were so worried about appearances, you should have gone to his funeral."

"No, *you* should have. I was at the convention in Baton Rouge."

"With Dutch Holland."

Neal grimaced. "Yeah, the old fart was there, still trying to steal my accounts. It makes me sick to think that one of his daughters has her hooks in my boy." Sighing loudly, his eyes met those of his oldest son. "Harley's always been a problem."

"Dad—"

"Can it, Weston. I'm not telling you anything you don't already know. I was hoping that he'd grow up and become stronger—but I guess it's not going to happen." Disappointment clouded his father's gaze. "You know, you were a hard act to follow. I keep trying to remind myself of that. I suppose I should have had more."

"With Mom?"

Neal's eyes thinned a fraction. "Of course with your mother. Who else?"

"You tell me."

"You're still buying into the gossip that I've got me a passel of bastards running around somewhere, don't you?"

"Just one."

"Forget it, Weston. You're my favorite. Firstborn. That's special, you know." Rapping his knuckles on Weston's desk, he headed for the door and appeared suddenly old. "Don't forget to give Harley my message. Maybe if it comes from you, he'll believe it."

"And maybe he won't."

"Then he doesn't have the brains I think he has." Neal hesitated a second. "You know, when you have a son—a newborn son—you have all this hope and pride bubbling up inside. You know that he's gonna be the best damned man to ever walk this earth and then, as the years tick by, and the disappointments and worries pile up, you just hope that he'll get by. With Harley . . ." He shrugged. "I don't know. I just don't know." Neal swung the door shut behind him, and Weston, smiling inwardly, leaned back in his chair until the old springs creaked. He'd been going about this all wrong, he realized, and cursed himself for being such a fool. He'd been actually trying to help Harley when, in truth, the kid was his biggest rival.

True, Weston was set to inherit the lion's share of his father's wealth, but there were provisions in the will for Mikki, Harley, Paige, and any other children sired by Neal Taggert, whether they were legitimate or not.

If Harley married Claire, then he'd give up his share of the fortune, most of which would fall to Weston. Neal had already made it clear that his sons were to run the company and inherit the business. If Harley conveniently cut himself out of the picture, then Weston would be in charge of everything—the resorts, lumber mill, logging operation. An eager smile tugged at the corners of his mouth. Why the hell was he trying so hard to help his brother out by getting Kendall pregnant? It would be better if Harley did marry Claire. When his old man kicked off, he'd be left with everything other than the house and monthly pittance for his mother and Paige. He cringed a little as he thought about his little sister. Paige the ugly. Paige the weird. Paige, who was just odd enough to end up in some friendly mental institution painted with serene pastel walls. All Weston had to do was to find some enterprising psychologist who needed a little extra cash, and then Paige would spend her days wandering down well-worn paths that wound through stately trees and past calming ponds filled with lily pads. She would be locked away forever behind steel gates.

Of course his father had to die first, but that was just a matter of time. Neal Taggert was a walking heart attack; his doctor had warned him time and time again. All Weston had to do was be patient. And quit seeing Kendall. That part wouldn't be difficult.

Avoiding the Holland girls wouldn't be quite so easy. Though Tessa had thrown him over and wouldn't return his calls, he didn't much care. But the more he saw of Miranda, the more he wanted her, which was just plain stupid. She was trouble, a woman to avoid at all costs, and she'd never hidden the fact that she loathed him. Even Tessa had admitted that Miranda had gone off the deep end when she'd figured out that her kid sister was seeing him.

What did she care? Had she really objected to Tessa being with him, or was she, at some level she didn't even consciously recognize, jealous? His blood heated just a bit. Perhaps Miranda had a wanton streak that she couldn't control, a lust for that which was forbidden. God, the way she ground her hips into the sand that night! He clenched his fists until his knuckles turned white.

But why Riley? He was a nobody, a bum, the stepson of their goddamned caretaker. For some reason she enjoyed slumming and wasn't afraid to take a walk on the wild side.

Then there was Tessa. He still had to figure out how to handle her. If she began mouthing off—making good on any of her threats, his life, as he knew it, would be over.

If he was smart, he'd forget all the Holland girls and go back to college before he made any mistakes. His violence was escalating. He felt the adrenaline rush, the anticipation of his next encounter and he knew he was walking a dangerous line. He should stop. Now. But the thought of giving up on Miranda was too much. Just one night—that's all he wanted, one night to show her what it was like to have passionate, animal, hedonistic sex—the kind that numbed the mind for hours and lingered on the wrinkled sheets for days.

Clicking his pen nervously as the air-conditioning gave up with a final wheeze, Weston considered Riley, a man who, whether he knew it or not, was his rival, a man who'd better watch his step. Ten to one, Riley's motives weren't all that pure. The guy had a checkered past—he wasn't even the caretaker's real son. Who had fathered the bastard, Weston wondered as he swiveled in his chair and stared through the blinds. A thought as cold as death entered his heart and he wondered if Hunter could be his father's long-lost bastard. But that was crazy, wasn't it? His old paranoia crept through his blood.

It wouldn't take long to uncover the truth because, for the past few weeks, ever since his fascination with Miranda had developed into a more than passing interest, Weston had done some digging on his own and discovered that Riley had more than his share of skeletons in his closet. It was only a matter of time before he was able to expose the son of a bitch as a fraud.

Weston was content to be patient. He believed in the old adage that good things come to those who wait. Well, he was willing to wait for a long, long time, as long as he knew that, in the end, he'd get his own little taste of Miranda Holland.

"Mr. Taggert?" His secretary's voice broke into his thoughts.

"Yes?"

"Miss Forsythe on line two."

Weston felt a warm sense of satisfaction. Time to break it off with Kendall. What a shame. "I'll be right with her," he said, then set the alarm on his watch for two minutes. Kendall, that cold, lifeless bitch, could damn well wait.

CHAPTER 18

Miranda's fingers closed around the bottle of prenatal vitamins she'd gotten at the clinic. She was pregnant, there was no doubt, the doctor and a pregnancy test confirming what she'd already suspected. Now she had to tell Hunter. Oh, God. What if he didn't want the baby? Tears threatened her vision as she climbed into her car. What would she say to him? To her parents? Claire and Tessa?

She, who had always been in control.

She, who had mapped her life out at the age of twelve.

She, who had tried so hard to be a source of pride to her family.

Pregnant.

"Remember: It's not the end of the world, but the beginning," she told herself again as she flipped on the radio and rolled down the window. Pushing on buttons until she found a station that was playing a bluesy Bonnie Raitt tune, she drove toward Stone Illahee. Warm air blew through her hair and on impulse, she pulled off the road near a beach turnout, kicked off her shoes, left the vitamins in the car and walked barefoot onto the sand. The dunes gave way to flat, deserted beach, and soon she was near the ocean, feeling the icy water of the tide wash over her feet as she stepped around clear pieces of jellyfish and the jagged edges of eviscerated crabs and clams. Marauding gray seagulls kept watch, hoping for another scrap of food, and on the horizon a few fishing boats drifted on the sea.

She found a log wedged into the dry beach. One side was blackened from campfires, the other nearly buried from the drifting sand. Would she come here with her son or daughter, build sand castles, chase the waves, throw a Frisbee for a rambunctious pup?

Would she marry Hunter?

Sitting on the log, she clasped her hands together and was so lost in her own thoughts, she didn't realize she wasn't alone until a shadow fell over her shoulders.

Startled, she turned quickly and nearly died.

"Thought that was your car," Weston Taggert said, squatting so that he was on eye level with her.

"What do you want?" The last person she needed to deal with was Taggert.

"Company."

"Buy a dog."

Weston's eyebrows quirked up. "Bad day?"

"That just got worse." She started to rise, but he caught her hand. "What's got into you?"

"Common sense." Yanking her hand away, she picked up her sandals and let them swing from her fingers as she walked to her car.

"What have I ever done to you?"

Her back stiffened, and though she knew she shouldn't be baited by him, she whirled, sand fleas skipping out of her path. "I've seen the way you look at me and I think it's disgusting," she said, remembering the leers he'd cast in her direction while they were both still in high school. "I heard some jokes you started at my expense, and, worst of all, you've been two-timing my sister as well as my friend."

"Friend?"

"Crystal. You remember her?"

"Vaguely."

Miranda saw red. "Leave them both alone."

"Is that a threat?" he asked, as if he couldn't believe his ears.

"Take it any way you want, Weston, but why don't you do everyone a favor and go back to college early?"

"Why?"

"I don't like the way you treat Tessa, okay?"

"Maybe I'd treat you better."

Stunned, she lost her voice for a second, then, when she realized what he was suggesting, she felt sick inside. "Go to hell."

"You'd rather I'd continue seeing Tessa."

"I'd rather you drop dead." She started for the car again, hot sand squishing through her bare toes. The nerve of that guy! He had the morals of a street dog.

"Miranda?"

She didn't turn, wouldn't give him the time of day.

"I think these are yours."

"What?" She glanced over her shoulder and he tossed a bottle into the air. With a sickening feeling she realized before she whirled around and her fingers curled over the plastic that he'd found her vitamins, that he knew she was pregnant.

"Congratulations."

Bile rose in her throat.

"You know, if Riley doesn't take the news well, you can always come and see me." His smile was pure evil. "I'd make an honest woman out of you."

"I'd die first." She reached the car, threw the bottle of pills through the open window and onto the driver's seat, then scooted behind the wheel. Her stomach was in knots, her mouth filled with saliva, but she wouldn't give him the satisfaction of watching her vomit. No way. She took off with a squeal of tires, turned onto the highway while gunning the engine, and didn't stop until she rounded the corner and turned into a private lane where she threw open the car door and lost the contents of her stomach in a dry ditch filled with bleached weeds and empty beer bottles.

"You're sure?" Hunter's voice was quiet, barely audible over the crackle of the fire. They lay together after making love, and Miranda's announcement that she was pregnant hung between them in the rustic cottage.

"I went to the doctor today."

"Jesus," he whispered, staring at the ceiling where the golden shadows of the flames played upon the old plaster. "A baby."

Miranda's chest constricted. "Yes. In March."

He rolled off the bed stark naked and shoved both hands through his hair. "A baby."

Refusing to let the tears clogging her throat free, Miranda sat up and drew the old sheet over her breasts. "I know it's unexpected . . . and inconvenient."

"Unexpected?" he repeated. "Inconvenient?" His shoulders sagged, and with the fire as his backdrop, his body, tall and lean, was silhouetted against the shifting flames. "It's a damned sight more than that."

"Oh, God, you don't want it."

"No . . . Yes . . . Hell, I don't know." Letting out a long breath, he walked back to the bed and stared down at her with eyes that were dark with concern. "I can't think straight. A baby?"

She nodded, her throat so thick she could barely breathe.

"And I take it from your reaction that you want to have it."

"Oh, God, yes."

"You won't consider an—"

"Don't even say it." She grabbed his forearms, her fingers tightening in desperation. "Please, Hunter, I always thought I could make that kind of decision easily, but I can't. Not when it's my baby. Not when it's yours."

His lower lip rolled over his teeth, and he shook his head slowly from side to side. "This is gonna be tough."

"Everything worth having is."

"So now you're a philosopher."

"No," she said, lifting up her chin. "What I am—or will be—is a mother." She took his big hand in hers and said, her voice shaking, "Like it or not, Hunter Riley, you're going to be a father."

"Christ."

"In my opinion, you'll be the best."

His fingers, callused and strong, tightened over hers. "What I am, Miranda, is a nobody. I haven't had time to be somebody yet."

"You're somebody to me and to this little person." Slowly she tugged and placed his hand over her flat abdomen. His face was so close to hers, she kissed his cheek. "I believe that you and I can take on the world, Hunter."

"I believe *you* can. I'm not so sure about me."

"Have faith." She kissed his cheek again. "Together, Riley, we're a terrific team."

"You think so?" One side of his mouth lifted and his hand flattened possessively over her belly. His ring rubbed against her bare skin.

"I know it."

"Okay." His voice cracked as he slid beneath the sheet and took her into his arms as he settled next to her. "Let's . . . Let's think this through. You know that I would like nothing more than to spend the rest of my life with you."

Her heart soared. "Would you?"

"And I'd always hoped that someday, if I could finish school, buy a place and, you know, establish myself, that there was a chance for us."

"There is."

He looked into her eyes and sighed. "This—the baby— wasn't part of my plan."

"Nor mine."

"What about your career?"

"A baby won't stop it. Just put it on hold."

He thought a minute. "It would be hard."

"I know, but it's not like I don't have some money—"

"Forget it. If we're going to make this work—I mean get married and start a family, we have to do it on our own. No help from your father. No tapping into money you've saved for college."

"It's my trust fund," she said, "and it's not that much."

"We're not using it." He kissed her forehead. "I'm enough of a chauvinist to want to support my own wife and children. Oh, God, would you listen to that? My children!" He laughed and squeezed her, one strong leg pinning hers against the mattress. "This is insane."

"I know."

"But I love you."

"And I love you." She blinked back those damned tears that kept threatening her eyes.

"That does it," he said with a half smile. "I guess there's no getting around it now." Sliding out of the bed, he bent one knee and, while the firelight played upon his nude body, asked her the question she'd hoped she'd hear. "Miranda Holland, will you be my wife?"

* * *

So it was true.

In the privacy of the sauna off the recreation room in his parents' house, Weston read the private investigator's report for the third time. His fingers shook and he wanted to scream. The old man had another kid—a bastard son. One who, if and when he found out the truth, would claim his inheritance.

Sweat dripped down Weston's body and he closed his eyes as he sat on the bench and added water to the coals. More steam clouded the room. Breathing was difficult. His heart was pumping wildly, and he wadded the documents, a computer printout and a copy of a birth certificate, in his fists.

"Shit. Shit. Shit. You dumb old bastard."

This wasn't a complete disaster. Not yet. No one but his father, Weston, and the slimy private investigator he'd hired knew the truth.

So there was time to make adjustments. Nothing he couldn't handle. He just had to think. He considered burning the papers here, in the sauna, but decided someone might notice the ash, so he found his lighter in the pair of shorts he'd draped on a hanger near the door and strode through the rec room with a towel slung low on his hips. He lit the damning papers, tossed them into the brick fireplace, and decided he needed a smoke, a drink, and a woman, not necessarily in that order.

Why the hell was everyone, including his old man, always fucking up? He walked back to the sauna and found his cigarettes. By the time he'd slid into his shorts and T-shirt and returned to the rec room, his little fire had extinguished itself, leaving no evidence in the sooty grate that it had ever existed.

He'd pay off the PI which was no problem; the guy was a greedy snake who could keep his mouth shut. Then, he'd take care of his half brother. His pulse quickened at the thought, and he hated himself for the excitement he felt charging through his blood.

He had to be careful, but a plan was forming in his head as he climbed the stairs and rubbed vaguely at a powdery black smudge on the wall, the only mar on the otherwise freshly painted surface, but he couldn't think about anything other than the problem at hand. Once that was handled, he'd find an expensive bottle of booze and a woman—the only woman he really wanted.

*　*　*

Bitch!

Randa was such a snotty, holier-than-thou bitch.

Tessa, hiding in her mother's forgotten studio, sat on the window ledge and watched sunlight play on the water of the swimming pool. A half dozen partially finished canvases were scattered around the room, and a potter's wheel was silently collecting dust as she picked at a tune on her guitar and tried to quiet the rage that had eaten at her insides ever since she'd seen Weston watching Miranda and Hunter go at it by the lake.

"Damn it all to hell." What was it that Miranda had that Tessa didn't? So she was taller, more sophisticated, older and . . . oh, what did it matter? Weston was a sicko—the way he had held that knife to her throat, the cool blade pressed against her skin, as if he'd wanted, really wanted to draw blood. She'd never been so scared in her life.

"I hope you rot in hell," she said, her fingers shaking a little at the horrid memory. She was glad to be done with him. Glad. Glad. Glad. Let him take out his perverted fantasies on someone else.

Like Miranda?

She hit the wrong chord. "Shit!" Tessa had never liked losing, especially not to one of her sisters, and for Randa not only to have been right about Weston, but to also be the object of his obsession, galled Tessa and fed the rage that burned deep in her gut.

If she had the nerve, she should stick it to Weston, the way he did to her. Hold a knife or gun on him and make him sweat, watch while he stripped himself bare and was forced into some humiliation, maybe to jack off in front of her.

"Forget it," she told herself. "Forget him." But the beast of fury within her continued to grow. She wasn't satisfied letting things sit as they were. Weston would have to pay.

She didn't hear the sound of footsteps on the stairs and was surprised by a quiet tap on the door before it was pushed open, and Miranda stepped inside.

Great! The last person she wanted to see.

"I'm practicing," she said, barely looking up.

"I know. I heard you."

"I like to do it alone."

Randa didn't take the hint, just walked barefooted and long-legged into the middle of the room. Beautiful as their mother, but more statuesque, Miranda had spent years down-playing her looks and avoiding boys, but, as Tessa so painfully knew, in Weston's eyes she was a goddess.

"I think we should talk." Miranda folded her legs beneath her as she sat on the edge of an old ottoman.

"What about?" She continued picking out a tune on her guitar, slowly plucking the strings, ignoring the fact that her oldest sister was obviously worried. Who cared? Miranda was a sanctimonious bitch most of the time and a worrywart the rest.

"Weston."

Tessa hit the strings so hard, she felt the taut metal cut into her fingertips. "Jesus," she swore. "Now look what you made me do." Resentment burned bright in her heart. Compressing her lips, she tossed her hair over her shoulder and sucked on her bleeding fingers. "For the record, I don't give a shit about Weston. Now, is there something else you wanted?"

"Yeah. I'd like to know that you're okay," Randa shot back.

"As you can see I'm just fine."

"As I can see you're up here with these dusty relics hiding."

"Hiding? That's a laugh."

"As well as probably licking your wounds—and I'm not talking about your fingers."

Tessa's muscles coiled. It was all she could do not to lunge at Miranda's throat and inform Her Highness that it was her fault that Tessa's life was screwed up. "I don't know where you get off." She turned her attention back to the song she was attempting to write.

"Weston's face looks like someone took a steel rake to it."

Tessa hit a sour note. "You saw him?"

"Yeah, today. He was at a stoplight in town and I had to walk across the street on my way to the library and . . . well, I know this sounds crazy, but the top of his car was down and, even though he was wearing sunglasses, I had a good look at his face. One side looks like a cat clawed it to ribbons. I thought he might have been in an accident . . . or maybe a fight."

"Bingo. The brilliant one deduces the truth yet again. You know, Miranda you should be on some game show—what's the one where you figure out the clues?—'Concentration'? That would be right up your alley."

"You scratched him?" Miranda asked.

"Yeah, Sherlock, I scratched him," Tessa admitted with a careless lift of her shoulder. "As hard as I could. And if I had the chance now, I'd do it again, only this time I'd scrape his friggin' eyes out of their sockets."

"Why?"

"I was mad, okay?"

"Because—"

"It's none of your business."

"Did he hurt you?" Miranda asked, and Tessa's hard heart cracked a little at the concern in her sister's voice. Yeah, she'd been wounded. She hadn't slept all night, just stared out the window to the breathless darkness, plotting ways of winning him back only to spurn him, or thinking of satisfying ways to kill him.

"We broke up," she admitted, bending her head over the guitar again. "You were right about him and I was wrong. Satisfied?"

"Only if you're okay."

"I'm fine. I'm always fine," Tessa said, hooking a thumb at her chest. "I'm a survivor."

"He's not worth feeling bad about."

"Don't start with a lecture. I've heard it all before, and I've already got a mother. Remember?"

"But you're only—"

"Yeah, yeah. Fifteen. I know." She gave up on the song and slid the guitar onto a table cluttered with old palettes and a dead geranium. Anger pulsed through her blood and she wanted to strike back. This time she had ammunition. "So . . . did you say good-bye to Hunter last night?"

"Good-bye?" Miranda's eyes were suddenly in sharp focus. "Why?"

"He didn't tell you?" Tessa scowled, but felt an inward sense of satisfaction that she was finally giving a little heartache back to Miranda, who, whether she knew it or not, was always shoveling some in Tessa's direction.

"Tell me what?" Miranda's voice was low, as if she expected the worst. Well, good.

"That he was leaving." Tessa reached into her purse for her cigarettes.

"Leaving? Hunter Riley? Going where?"

"Hell if I know."

"No, I don't think he's taking off—"

"Dan said he's already gone. Left sometime in the middle of the night." She found a new pack and opened the cellophane with her teeth.

"For where?" Even though she didn't trust Tessa, Miranda felt as if the earth had buckled beneath the garage. No way would Hunter have left her—not alone and pregnant. This was all a mistake, malicious gossip or Tessa's cruel idea of a joke.

"I don't know," Tessa said, and seemed to enjoy giving Miranda the bad news. "I heard Dan tell Mom this morning that Hunter had taken off, without so much as a good-bye or a note. His car was left at the train station in Portland late last night or early morning. You—you didn't know?" She finally managed to get the pack open and plucked out a long Virginia Slim.

"I don't believe you." Miranda shook her head. This was just another one of Tessa's fantasies, her lies. The girl was always making up stories, and for some reason Tessa was angry with her; she'd felt that tension, the unspoken accusations in Tessa's eyes the minute she'd stepped into the old studio.

"Fine, don't believe me, but it's true. He's gone. At least for a little while. I couldn't hear all of the discussion, but . . ." She paused as she jabbed the cigarette into her mouth and struck a match. ". . . he's definitely out of here. I, um, thought you knew." She lit up and waved out the match. "Don't give me any lectures about lung cancer."

"It's your body," Miranda said, but her thoughts were a million miles away. *Gone? Hunter was gone? Don't believe her. She's lying. She has to be. But why?* Uncertainty, like a clenched fist, pummeled her. *Trust Hunter. You love him. You can't doubt him.* There had to be some mistake. "Either you're lying or your information is wrong."

"I don't think so. What's wrong, Miranda? Are you so perfect no man would ever dump you?"

"No, but—"

"If you don't believe me, ask Dan," Tessa said, though some of the snarl had left her words. She looked away, refusing to meet Miranda's eyes, and ran her fingers over a table, disturbing the thin layer of dust that had accumulated ever since their mother had given up her art a year before. "The reason I believe it, is that I just got the feeling that Dan was upset. Really upset. He tried to hide it, for Mom's sake, but there's something going on, Miranda, and whatever it is, it's not good."

The baby. This was all about the baby. Hunter was probably going to look for work or something . . . maybe even sort things out in his mind. But he'd call, and he'd be back, and everything would work out. Unless he was running away. Oh, Lord, no. He wouldn't leave her alone and pregnant. He couldn't. And yet as she left Tessa sitting on the window ledge, Miranda noticed the storm clouds rolling in from the Pacific, and she felt a shiver of doom, as if the devil himself had taken his finger and run it down her spine.

CHAPTER 19

"That's right. He left. Without so much as sayin' good-bye." Dan Riley leaned on his rake and avoided Miranda's gaze. A wiry man with thinning gray hair cropped into a crew cut and teeth yellowed by years of cigarettes and coffee, he lifted a baseball cap from his head and rubbed the back of his wrinkled neck in frustration. "Always knew the day would come when he'd move out. Didn't expect it to come like it did." His tired eyes found Miranda's, then moved swiftly away, as if he was embarrassed, as if he knew or suspected something more. "I just wish I knew why. Why wouldn't he talk it over with me first?"

Because he was scared—afraid of the responsibility of becoming a father, Miranda thought uneasily, but managed a thin smile. It had been three days since Tessa had told her that Hunter had left, but she hadn't believed her younger sister, waiting to hear from him, keeping faith that he hadn't run out on her.

Finally, this morning, she'd decided to speak with his father. "I don't know why he wouldn't talk to you," she said, though it was a lie. Of course he wouldn't confide in his father about this.

"No trouble is that bad."

"Trouble?" Miranda repeated. "What trouble?"

Dan considered his answer and squeezed air through his teeth as he stared at the inside rim of his grimy cap. "That boy found trouble like a hound finds a dead rabbit. For years he . . . well, he and the police got to know each other real well. I always blamed it on him losing his ma at such a tender age. Anyway, in the past half a year he straightened out, paid his debt to society so to speak, managed to get his equivalency degree for high school and started taking classes down at the community college. I had a mind that he'd finally started walkin' the straight and narrow."

"He had," she said, and Dan elevated a graying eyebrow, noiselessly challenging her defense of a boy that, to Dan's knowledge, she barely knew.

"Hunt had changed a mite lately, was sneakin' around, doin' God only knows what." Frowning, he replaced his tattered Dodgers baseball cap and dragged the rake over the ground around a mossy oak tree that had grown near the north side of the house. "Things've been different around here." He looked up sharply. "Your ma— she find anyone to replace Ruby?"

Miranda shook her head. "Not yet; I think she's still hoping Ruby will change her mind and come back to work for us."

"I doubt it; that woman's stubborn as they come when she has a mind to be. Besides, losin' a child, well, there's just no gittin' over it. She won't be back. Too many memories here— memories of the time that Jack was alive." He raked a clump of old twigs and leaves into a small, decaying pile. "Kee-rist A'mighty, I just hope I hear from Hunt soon."

Me too, Miranda thought, as a dark, foreboding sense of doom pounded in her heart. "You will."

Scowling, he scratched at the ground again. "If I do, I'll let you know, and if you hear . . . well, why would you?" But his eyes had sharpened when he looked up from his task and Miranda suspected for the first time since the start of her relationship with Hunter, his father was beginning to get the picture.

"I . . . I will," she promised, crossing her fingers and silently praying that Hunter would call.

"And if he don't, well . . . maybe he's not worth the bother." Scratching his neck until his whiskers rustled, he said, "There's a lot you don't know about that kid, Miss Holland. A lot he wouldn't want anyone to know. But he was his mama's boy and good to me."

Miranda's throat turned to cotton. "What don't I know?"

"Nothin' good." He swiped at the ground again. "He had a side to him that was . . ." He frowned slightly. ". . . well, the Reverend Thatcher once called him evil."

"Oh, no—"

"The Reverend, he went too far, was too judgmental, but Hunt has a streak in him that's wild and will never be tamed."

"I don't believe it," she said, and turned, her feet feeling sluggish, her heart pounding. As she left she thought he whispered, "Be careful, Missy," but she wasn't sure, and it could have been the sound of the wind hissing through dry leaves as it moved ever inland.

"The story I heard is that he was fooling around with a fourteen-year-old girl in Seaside."

"Fourteen?" Miranda repeated, staring at Crystal as if she were out of her mind. When she hadn't heard from Hunter for nearly four days, Miranda had driven into town, circling the streets restlessly until she'd finally stopped for a Coke at the Dairy Freeze. She'd spotted Crystal, who had visibly started at the sight of her, but Miranda hadn't been deterred by Crystal's grief over her brother or her jealousy of a Holland for snagging Weston Taggert's attention. Crystal and her mother both had ears for gossip, so with Dan's mention of Hunter and trouble in mind, Miranda had slid onto the empty bench at Crystal's table then asked about Hunter and any gossip surrounding him.

Now, as oil sizzled in deep fryers behind the counter, the cash register dinged and the blender whirred before spitting out the next milk shake, Miranda sat across the yellow plastic table from Crystal and waited as she sipped her drink.

"The way I heard it is that Hunter got this girl pregnant, then he wanted her to get an abortion, but she's underage."

Miranda felt the color drain from her face and nearly dropped her soda.

"Her mother's some kind of religious nut—real right-wing, Born-Again Christian who doesn't believe in abortion in any circumstance. Anyway, the girl, she spills the beans that she's gonna have a baby, and the woman nearly has a heart attack."

"No way." Miranda swirled the crushed ice in her cup of Coke and shook her head. But doubt, like an ever-faster flowing whirlpool, surrounded her, threatening to drown her last shred of faith in the boy she loved. "I—I can't believe that he . . ." She swallowed hard to fight off a brutal attack of nausea.

"Hey," Crystal said, dunking a french fry into a pool of catsup. "I'm only telling you what's going around. I don't know if it's true."

"Hunter wouldn't . . ." Or would he? Her throat closed, and she fought a rising sense of panic. "Who's the girl? What's her name?"

Crystal lifted a shoulder. "No one seems to know."

Miranda was determined to find out. "I think it's a lie."

"Maybe." Crystal frowned. "Who knows?"

"Someone knows."

"Yeah, Hunt."

"And the girl. If she exists. Who told you this story?"

"My mom. She heard it from some of the women she plays pinochle with, and that lady said her husband told her the story because it was going around the Westwind Bar late last night."

"But—" But she'd been with Hunter only a few nights ago. How would anyone have known? Miranda would make it her personal mission to find out. She finished her drink and stood. "Look, thanks. You know how bad I feel about Jack."

Crystal's gaze slid past Miranda's shoulder, to a middle distance only she could see. "He didn't just slip off the ridge that day, you know," she said, her voice flat. "He'd been on that path a million times." Shoving her fries aside, she chewed thoughtfully on her lower lip. "And he didn't fall because he was drunk."

Miranda had heard the stories that Jack, after being fired from Taggert Industries, had drunk his fill of hard liquor, driven up the ridge, and then, while walking along an old Indian trail, fallen from the cliff to his death.

"He was pushed." Crystal sounded certain.

Miranda's stomach clutched. "Pushed?" Again, her queasy stomach revolted, and she had to swallow back the bile that rose in the back of her throat. "As in murdered?"

Crystal brushed a tear from the corner of her eye. "There's no doubt in my mind or my mother's. We just can't prove it yet. But we will."

"Good luck, I guess." Miranda felt suddenly awkward. "We miss Ruby, you know."

"Do you?" Crystal gave out a heartless laugh and pinned Miranda with sharp, black eyes. "Or do you miss having an Indian squaw for a slave?"

"You know that's not true! We think of Ruby as one of the family," Miranda said, rising. "We always have."

"Then why doesn't your dad use some of his stinking money and hire a first-class private investigator to find out what happened to Jack?"

"I thought the police ruled it was—"

"An accident, right. And they thought they were saving us some embarrassment by not suggesting that it could have been a suicide. *Suicide!* Can you believe it? No one loved life more than Jack."

"I'm sorry—"

"Then do something. Aren't you planning to be some kind of hot shit lawyer?"

"Someday."

Crystal's lower lip quivered, and she buried her face in her hands. "Damn it all." Too proud to cry in public, she scrambled out of the booth and hurried outside. Miranda, feeling worse than ever, followed her and walked, head bent against the wind, to her car. Crystal had been right about one thing; she was going to be a lawyer, the best damned attorney this town had ever seen, and she'd have to use her wits to outsmart opposing counsel. So trying to find out what really happened to Jack Songbird and Hunter shouldn't be so hard.

Except that she was an emotional wreck. Crystal's story about Hunt, coupled with Dan's warning, chipped away at her trust, her faith in love. "Don't," she told herself. She needed to talk to Hunt, to sort the truth from the lies. So she had to find him. That was all. How hard could it be?

Taking Crystal's suggestion to heart, she stopped at a phone booth, flipped through the tattered Yellow Pages, and stopped at the page where private investigators were listed. Running her finger down the column, she found the name of a man in Manzanita and reached into her purse for her coins.

She'd find Hunter, one way or the other, and then she'd face the truth—however grim it might be. She owed it to her baby.

The ceiling fans were keeping time to Madonna while silverware rattled on the business side of the counter, where the cash register rang up the latest order of burgers and fries.

Paige licked the last bit of whipped cream from her sundae and swung her legs from the booth at the local Dairy Freeze. She'd seen Miranda Holland and Crystal Songbird sitting in a booth near the corner, and she'd hidden behind a fake wood trellis that partitioned one section of the Dairy Freeze from the other. The older girls were in some kind of grim conversation, and Paige would have given two months' allowance to find out what they were talking about, but she'd slunk down in her booth until they'd left and wondered if Weston was any part of the conversation. Probably. Crystal was such a pathetic creature.

But Paige didn't want to think about Crystal or Weston or anyone but herself right now. Her charm bracelet hung from her wrist and she liked the way it jangled when she moved. It reminded her that Kendall still liked her, and that gave her a sense of peace, as did the gun in her purse. She swallowed a smile. Wouldn't everyone in the place flip if they knew she was carrying the pistol?

Ever since Kendall had hinted that she wished Claire would drop dead, Paige had considered it her personal mission to find a way to eliminate her. But she couldn't be stupid, like shooting one of Dutch Holland's daughters; no, the police would figure it out, and she wasn't really sure that she could shoot anyone anyway. There was a big step between killing someone and thinking about it, and the truth of the matter was, Paige was a little on the squeamish side. No, just because she had the gun didn't mean she could actually pull the trigger, but maybe she could scare Claire a little, make her back off. Or, better yet, maybe she could scare Harley. *That* shouldn't be too hard.

She left some change on the table and sauntered out of the cool interior to the street, where sunlight glinted off the sidewalk and the brisk scents of salt and seaweed covered up exhaust fumes from the highway running through town. She didn't know what had possessed her to carry the gun today, but she didn't want to take a chance on leaving it at home, where it might be found. Any day now she was sure her mother would miss it, and then Paige would have to lie, or own up to having taken it. She winced inside at the thought of explaining why she'd borrowed the thing in the first place. Mikki Taggert had strict rules about her things. Once she'd caught Paige playing dress-up in her old slip and high heels, and Mikki hadn't missed a beat. She'd slapped her daughter across the face, told Paige never to touch her things again, then stripped her of the clothes and shoes and left her naked in the attic. She'd had to find an old sheet that smelled musty to wrap around her as she'd run, crying, to her room. The incident was never mentioned again, but Paige had felt the welt on her cheek for hours.

So, she'd have to make up a story about the gun or replace it. She walked past a bookshop, an antiques dealer, and an artist's gallery before seeing Claire standing on the promenade that flanked the beach. The prom was a wide cement walkway with an intricate, but short, stone wall separating the beach from the town. Every three blocks there was a gap in the wall which allowed pedestrians access to trails leading over short grassy dunes to the sea, and there, at one of the openings, was Claire Holland, dressed in jeans and T-shirt, looking nervous and trying not to appear interested in the scruffy-looking boy straddling a huge black-and-chrome motorcycle. She couldn't think of his name, but Paige had seen him before. He was a troublemaker, she thought, a kid whose dad had some kind of problem, and he was staring at Claire as if she were the only girl in the universe.

Paige smothered a pang of jealousy and swallowed hard. She slipped over the wall, ducked through the dunes, and edged closer, hoping to hear some of their conversation. Oh, what she would do if only some boy, *any* boy, looked at her the way this guy was staring at Claire.

The wind kicked sand into her eyes and mouth. She spit and wiped her tongue with her sleeve as tears took care of the particles behind her eyelids. She was close enough that she heard their voices, but the words were muffled by the roar of the wind and surf. Unless they came closer, walked down the path near the dune behind which she was hiding, she'd probably never hear what they were talking about.

Blinking, Paige glanced down at her bracelet. What did it matter what Claire said to the guy? The fact that she was talking to him might be ammunition enough for Kendall. Now, if she could just remember his name . . .

Claire clutched her keys until the metal cut into her palm. Of all the luck! She'd hoped to run into Harley, and she'd ended up seeing Kane. As she'd come out of the sporting goods shop, he'd spied her and turned a quick U-turn in the middle of the street to brazenly drive his bike onto the promenade, in front of God and everyone, disregarding the signs announcing that there were no motorized vehicles allowed on the wide pedestrian walkway.

Her heart was thumping a quick double time, as she hadn't seen him since Jack Songbird's funeral, hadn't spoken to him since the night when he'd bared his soul. She'd dreamt about him, always in sexual, wanton ways that caused her, upon awaking, to find it hard to catch her breath, and continuously made her feel ashamed, as if she were somehow cheating on Harley.

And here he was again, seated on his bike, reflective sunglasses shading his eyes, black leather covering his body.

"So, Princess," he drawled in that suggestive and irritating way of his. "How's the world treating you?"

"Just fine." It was a lie. Why did she feel she always had to side-step the truth around him?

"Is it?" A wayward eyebrow arched over one of his shaded lenses. "No complaints?"

"None," she lied easily again, and wondered if he had the ability to read her mind.

"Lucky you." His voice mocked her, silently accused her of a thousand untruths.

"That's right."

"Good. Then I can leave with a clean conscience."

"Leave?" *Oh, no!*

"Day after tomorrow."

"For the army." She felt a sinking, lost feeling tunnel through her body, a sensation that something vital and strong was about to become missing from her life.

"Basic training in Fort Lewis."

"Oh." It wasn't the end of the world. Fort Lewis was in Washington, 150 miles away. "And then?"

"And then the world." His smile was tight, and his fingers, curled around the handlebars, moved restlessly.

A gust of wind blew a clump of hair over Claire's eyes, and she tossed her head in order to see him more clearly. "So this is goodbye?" An ache deep in her soul began to throb.

"Yep."

Forcing a smile she didn't feel, she said, "Good luck."

"I don't depend on luck."

Her heart kicked, and though she knew she was making a stupid mistake that she'd regret later, she crossed the short distance separating them, leaned over, and brushed her lips across his cheek. "Take a little with you anyway."

She straightened and he swallowed hard. Behind the reflective lenses of his sunglasses, his eyes bored into hers. The world, for one short second, seemed to stop, and the sounds of the ocean pounding the shore, car engines thrumming, seagulls screaming, and the wind rushing, muted for the span of one life-altering heartbeat. She tried to smile, failed, and felt a tear slide from the corner of her eye.

"I'll miss you," he said, and for a second she was certain he'd wrap his long fingers around her nape and draw her head down to his so that his lips would melt against hers.

"I—I'll miss you, too."

A muscle worked overtime in the corner of his jaw as he stared at her. "Take care of yourself, and if Taggert ever so much as lifts one finger . . . oh, hell." He twisted his wrist, the bike revved, and he popped the clutch, roaring down the promenade before jumping the curb and spinning around a corner.

"Oh, God," she whispered and sank onto the rock wall. What was she doing? Did she really love Harley Taggert? Then why, oh, why, did her pulse leap every time she heard Kane Moran's name? Why did he, dressed in black leather and riding a huge motorcycle, invade her dreams and touch her as intimately as any lover? Why, when she'd professed to love Harley with all her heart and soul until her dying day, did a pain rip through her at the thought that she'd never see Kane again.

Pounding her fist against her thigh, she saw the diamond on her ring finger, a diamond that was supposed to mean forever, and she felt sick inside. The horrible truth of the matter was that she couldn't marry Harley, not when she was so confused, not when she had any doubts. She bit her lip so hard she tasted blood and slowly, knowing she was about to make the single most important decision of her life, she removed her engagement ring. From the corner of her eye, she thought she saw a movement near the dunes, the flutter of stringy brown hair, but when she looked the image had disappeared, and she decided her mind was playing tricks on her, that she'd seen a sandpiper, or seagull, nothing more.

Fighting tears, and silently cursing herself for her wayward thoughts, she tucked the ring into the pocket of her jeans and told herself that she would meet Harley to break the engagement.

Though she hated the thought of facing him, she had no choice. Tonight, she thought, as storm clouds gathered over the Pacific. She'd tell him tonight.

CHAPTER 20

The letter was waiting for her when Miranda walked into the house. In the stack of junk mail, magazines, and bills strewn on the table in the foyer, there was a plain white envelope, the address typed as if on an old standard typewriter, the postmark Vancouver, British Columbia. "Hunter," she said softly, feeling a mix of fear and elation as she tore open the envelope and extracted the single white page. It, too, had been typed with only Hunter's signature at the bottom to indicate that it was personal.

With trembling fingers and a thumping heart she leaned against the wall for support. He was in British Columbia working for Taggert Logging. Weston had given him a job out of the country when things got a little tense. He felt like a heel for walking out on her and the baby, but honestly believed she would be better off with someone who was from her station in life, someone who could give her and her child everything they wanted; everything they deserved. He loved her and she would always hold a special place in his heart, but he couldn't face the responsibilities of being a husband and father.

She crumpled the note in her hands and clenched her lips together so that she wouldn't cry out loud. How could this have happened? Didn't he love her? He'd said they'd get married, that they would work things out.

You know that I would like nothing more than to spend the rest of my life with you . . . I'd always hoped that there was a chance for us . . . Miranda Holland, will you be my wife?"

He'd wanted to marry her, hadn't he? Or had he felt cornered—trapped? He'd never said he loved her and had only proposed when she'd told him about her pregnancy.

This—the baby—wasn't part of my plan.

She squeezed her eyes shut but still the tears drizzled down her face. Was it possible that she'd been so blind, so caught up in her own dreams that she'd ignored his? She swiped at her face, sniffling loudly and thinking of the rumors racing through town like a wildfire, that he'd gotten some girl—some fourteen-year-old girl pregnant. Could that have been true as well? Wrapping her arms around her belly, she rocked, as if to comfort her unborn child as well as herself. "It'll be all right," she said, not believing a word of the lie. Even Hunter's own stepfather didn't trust him, not really . . . but, oh, how she loved him, and this painful ache in her heart felt as if it would tear her apart.

Stretched across her bed, Paige touched the charred scrap of paper with gentle fingers. As near as she could tell the legal document was the remains of a birth certificate, but the curled, blackened edges made it hard to piece together. Weston, in a fit of fury, had tried to burn it, as if it were threatening or vile. But why? Who were the people listed and what did they have to do with her older brother?

A boy had been born in August twenty years earlier to Margaret Potter. Who was she? Everything else, other than the name of the hospital where the birth took place, had burned away.

Paige had spent hours trying to puzzle it out, but couldn't figure why Weston cared. It had to be important, so Paige tucked the little scrap of paper back where it belonged in the slit of her panda bear, near her other prized and secret possessions.

The phone rang and Paige picked up just as someone else in the house took the call. She listened to find out who it was and she heard Weston's curt, "Hello."

"Hi." A woman's voice—soft, as if she'd been crying. For a second

Paige thought it might be Kendall, but that was crazy. Why would Kendall be calling Weston?

"What do you want?"

"To see you."

A pause.

"Why?"

"Because we have unfinished business."

"Oh, Christ, I don't think . . . Sure, what the hell? I'll meet you tonight. At the boat. Around midnight."

Click.

The line went dead and Paige just stared at the receiver. Was the woman Kendall, or someone else. But who? Crystal? Or someone else he'd been seeing—Paige had seen him in town with Tessa Holland . . . or was it someone she didn't know about.

What, she wondered, was Weston up to?

As Tessa stripped off her cover-up and tossed the terry cloth onto a lounge chair, she wished to God she could scream or hit or do some kind of damage. To someone. Anyone. No, that wasn't quite right. She only wanted to hurt Weston and Miranda because she knew, could sense instinctively, that they were attracted to each other. Now that Hunter was out of the picture, Weston would make his move, and Miranda, despite her protests to the contrary, would fall for him. Everyone did. Damn but it was hot and sticky. Not a breath of air. A few sinister-looking clouds hovered on the horizon, as if waiting for a Pacific squall to blow them inland.

She held her hair off the back of her neck and snapped a rubber band around the clump. She had to do something to shake this feeling that she wanted to climb out of her skin.

She stepped onto the diving board and slowly counted, trying to calm herself by concentrating on nothing but swimming, as if she were in competition. With lithe footsteps she ran the length of the board, sprang into the air, and knifed into the cool water. Surfacing, she started swimming laps, one at a time over and over, trying not to feel dirty and used, attempting to ignore the need for revenge that burned through her blood and crept into her dreams.

Stroke. One. Two. Breathe.

Who did Weston think she was to treat her like a common

whore? Ever since that last night, when he'd threatened to cut her if she didn't do what he wanted, she'd been seething and scared to death.

Stroke. One. Two. One. No! Breathe. Stroke. One. Two. Breathe. That's it.

Never before had she thought anyone would hurt her.

Never before had she been unable to sleep even with the door to her bedroom locked and her windows closed tight.

Never before had she looked over her shoulder at every turn and jumped at shadows. Even now, when she remembered the blade of his knife pressed cold and deadly against her skin and the look in his eyes, as if he'd love to slit her throat, she wanted to propel herself from the pool and scream bloody murder.

Or get even. What was the old saying? *Don't get mad, get even.* How could she ever possibly even the score? Weston had taken away her pride, her self-worth, her joy in being a woman.

Bastard. Shitty cock-sucking bastard!

Stroke. One. Two. Turn at the end of the pool and stroke again. Over and over. Beat this need to slice out Weston's faithless heart. *Three. Four.*

Oh, God, he had no right, *no damned right* to make her feel this way. No one did.

Don't get mad. Get even.

Tonight.

Stroke. One. Two.

"All I want to know is if you hired Hunter Riley." Miranda's voice was firm as she sat in the single chair in Weston's office. The windows were closed, and the temperature was hovering near ninety despite the irregular hum of what she assumed was an overloaded and dysfunctional air-conditioning unit.

Most of the office staff had already gone home for the evening, but through the window she saw the yard of the sawmill. The lights were coming up and beneath their eerie glow, timber was still being stripped of bark, loaded into sheds, and sliced into lumber. Stiff as a board, she held her purse in clammy fingers and wished she was anywhere else on earth. But she had to uncover the truth about Hunter no matter what.

Weston leaned back in his desk chair, his hands tented in front of him, his eyes a hot, appraising blue, the scratches on his cheek nearly healed but still visible—a reminder of his affair with Tessa. "And I thought you came to see me."

"Guess again."

Screwing up one side of his face, he yanked on his tie, loosening the once-crisp knot, then reached for a tumbler of liquor that was sweating on a corner of his otherwise tidy desk. "Hunter was in a jam. Needed to get out of town. Out of the country and fast. Our operation in B.C. needs people, so I talked to Dad and we relocated him." He reached for his drink and took a long swallow.

"Just like that? And he came to you rather than his father or me?" She didn't bother softening the skeptical edge to her voice.

"Yeah."

"Why?"

"I imagine because he thought I wouldn't be as judgmental as his father or as wounded as you might be . . . considering your condition and all." He finished his drink and reached into his bottom desk drawer, from which he drew out a half-empty fifth of Dewar's Scotch.

"Leave my 'condition' out of it."

He shrugged and lifted the bottle. "Have one?"

"No—"

"Because of the baby?"

"Because I don't usually drink with jackasses."

He smiled. "You don't like me much, do you?"

"Not at all."

"But you want information from me."

"As I said," she said with surprising calm, "it's the only reason I'm here."

"A woman with a purpose."

"And not a lot of time," she said, wanting to get this conversation over with as soon as possible. But Weston might have information about Hunter—information no one, not even the police—had discovered.

He tapped his front teeth with the end of his finger as if he were lost in thought, but his gaze hadn't changed. There was still the promise of passion lurking in his eyes, and she wondered just how full the bottle hidden in his drawer had been at the beginning of the day.

Inwardly she shivered. She shouldn't have come here. But she had to.

"Hunter figured that I—well, Dad, really—could give him what he wanted."

"And that was—?" She heard a secretary's voice calling 'good night' through the pebbled-glass door, and every muscle in her body tensed, ready to spring as she realized she was alone with him. There was no one else in the building, and the men working across the street in the mill might as well have been a hundred miles away. If anything should happen, they could never hear her screams over the whir of saws, smack of lumber being tossed on the green chain, and the rumble of trucks. But nothing was going to happen. Her imagination was running wild because she didn't trust Weston, and Tessa had clawed him.

"Hunter needed sanctuary."

"No way."

One brown brow rose over pitying blue eyes, as if he understood what she was going through and felt sorry for her. He sipped at his drink, then cradled it. "I know this is hard for you, especially since—" His eyes slid to her abdomen and she held her purse over it, as if to protect the baby. It was insanity to be here alone with him and yet she couldn't budge. He was the only person in Chinook who seemed to have any kind of information about Hunter—be it truth or lies—and was willing to share it. She gritted her teeth and stayed planted in the uncomfortable chair.

"I know you don't want to hear this, but it looks like Hunter got himself into trouble down here. Something about a fourteen-year-old girl."

"The one without a name."

"Oh, she's got one. Cindy Edwards. Lives near Arch Cape. If she files charges, he'll have to come back to the States and face them." Absently he touched the wounds on his face.

"I don't believe you." But Miranda made a mental note of the girl's name.

Outside a shrill whistle announced a change of shift or dinner break.

Weston shook his head and ran stiff fingers through his hair. "When are you going to figure out that Hunter isn't a saint?"

"You don't know anything about him," she countered, but felt as if she'd stepped square into the middle of a well-set trap.

"No?" Another swallow from his glass, and when he set it back on the desk, some of the scotch splashed onto the desk. "He worked for the company already, you know. Had a decent enough job history. I read his personnel file along with his new résumé, and I talked to him. Believe me, Miranda, I know more about Hunter Riley than you do." Weston's smile was cold as ice. "He got involved with Cindy about six months ago, when he was still doing community service for some little disagreement over a car he claimed was borrowed, though the woman who owned it said it was stolen. Anyway, the community service and probation were part of his sentence."

"I know that much," she admitted, as sweat collected under her arms and around her hairline.

"I think this all happened before he got involved with you, or so he said."

"He *told* you about us?" This wasn't ringing true at all. Hunter had been adamant that no one should know of their affair. No one. Not even his father.

"He didn't want to, but I admitted that I knew about you and the baby and—"

"Oh, God." *No way!* Her brain screamed denials. This couldn't be happening. "He would never have said a word."

Weston sighed patiently, as if willing to let her anger run its course, but his eyes moved from her eyes to her lips and lower still before returning, bright and eager to hers. "You're right, he wouldn't have. Seemed embarrassed about it, but his back was to the wall, and so he asked for a job out of the country and we provided one. He even took out a life insurance policy through the company naming you as primary beneficiary. The original documents are at the company headquarters in Portland, but I think we have copies here . . ."

He rolled to his feet, nearly stumbled, then caught himself and was out the door of his office, leaving Miranda and her doubts to face each other. How much of the truth was he telling? How much fiction was woven into the facts?

She was relieved that he was gone for a few minutes. She had to pull herself together, find a way to prove that he was lying, and yet the feeling of doom, that what Weston and Dan Riley were telling her was true, clasped around her throat as cold and hard as a steel chain.

Could it possibly be true? Every instinct told her that Weston was lying through his straight, white teeth, but she had no way of proving it. The private investigator she'd hired a few days before had turned up nothing.

"Here ya go," Weston said, his speech slightly off, as he reentered the room and dropped an employment folder onto the desk in front of her.

Miranda scanned the documents. Health history, life insurance policy application, old job employment reviews. All signed by Hunter Riley. Her heart dropped. Some of what Weston was telling her had to be true; there was no other explanation. A buzz, like the singing of heavy electrical wires, started in a distant part of her brain.

Weston didn't take his chair again. Instead he stood behind her, close enough that, as she looked over the documents, trying to concentrate, fighting against an overwhelming sense of defeat, she sensed him; felt his heat. So close. Too close.

He leaned nearer, his breath hot and smelling of scotch. "Whether you want to face the truth or not, Miranda, the fact of the matter is that Hunter Riley is a snaky son of a bitch. He stole cars and knocked up underage girls. Fourteen, for crying out loud. How old is he? Nineteen?"

"Twenty."

Her head was pounding. This was wrong—so wrong, but the pages of black and white that blurred in her vision were evidence, hard, solid testimony that Hunter had left her. Her insides squeezed painfully.

"But he does have some redeeming qualities, I suppose," Weston went on, whether to make her feel better or to give credence to Taggert Industries' decision to hire him. "Riley's a hard worker, when he stays out of trouble. He does right by his old man, and he wants to provide for you and the baby— at least when he dies."

"No," she whispered, shaking her head.

"Face it."

"He wouldn't leave me."

"Sure he would. He had no choice." Rounding her chair, he faced her and dropped a hand to her shoulder. His fingers were hot. Tense. "I'd like to take care of you, Miranda," he said.

"Don't touch me," she warned as she tried to scoot away.

"Can't help myself."

The buzz in her mind cleared and she realized he was more drunk than she'd first suspected. "Don't even think about it," she cautioned, but he was already closing in on her. "Weston, for the love of God, don't—"

Both his arms surrounded her, and he hauled her effortlessly from the chair. "I care about you, Randa. Always have."

"You've got me mixed up with Tessa."

His laugh was short and brutal. "Don't think so."

"But—"

"Didn't she tell you? She quit seeing me because every time I'd touch her, or kiss her, or make love to her, I was thinking about you."

"I don't want to hear this," she said, trying to scramble away, the room spinning as he grabbed her and pulled her close.

"Don't you know how hard this is for me?"

"Then stop." Dear God, what was happening?

"I can't, Randa girl, and you know it. You've felt it, too, the heat between us. I never wanted Tessa. Never. She was just someone to fill a void."

She hit at him, tried to scramble away, but he was strong, his body hard from years of athletics, and the more she fought him and struggled, the more insistent he became. "Let go of me, you bastard, don't—"

But his lips crashed over hers. Hard. Hot. Anxious. Tasting of scotch.

Nausea roiled in her stomach as she fought, her hands scratching and clawing even though her arms were pinned and she couldn't strike him with any force. She kicked, but he shifted and as she opened her mouth to scream his tongue darted between her teeth. Quick and slick it delved. Possessive and vile. She bit down, but he was quick, the tongue withdrawn as he twisted her around so that her rump butted up against the edge of the desk.

"You little bitch, admit it, you want it. You're as hot for me as I am for you."

"No—"

His crotch was pressed against her abdomen, his erection rigid and straining against his fly. The room spun. He kissed her again and lust—raw animal lust and hunger—pulsed in the air.

She realized then that there was no stopping him. She didn't know what had set him off, but sensed he wouldn't be satisfied until he'd forced his body into hers.

Sick and reeling, she struggled, but by sheer strength he pushed her ever back, his weight bearing down on her, the desk hard and flat beneath her back. "Let go of me!" she yelled when he lifted his head.

"I'll take care of you."

"Bull! Let go of me, Weston, or I'll scream."

"No one will hear you. The doors are locked, babe, and no one else is here."

"Go to hell!" She let out a scream to wake the dead, but it only echoed back to her in the small room. Then he was upon her.

His breath was hot, his body heavy, his purpose singular. "Come on, Miranda. Don't fight it."

Wrenching her body, she managed to get one hand free and slapped him. Smack! Her palm collided with his cheek. He yelped in pain. "You bitch! You stinking bitch! You're as bad as your sister!"

"Keep Tessa out of this."

"I should do to you what I did to her."

"Wh-what?"

His face, looming over her, was menacing, his skin flushed, his eyes burning with lust. She struggled, but he was strong, his muscles young, firmed and honed by years on the gridiron. He managed to grab both her wrists and haul them over her head to clasp them in the steely fingers of one hand.

"I knew you'd be a fighter."

"Get off me!"

"What'd you say? Get off on me?" His leer was obscene. "I intend to, baby. Over and over again. If you can give it to that lowlife Riley, then you can damn well spread your legs for me." With his free hand he unzipped his fly, and Miranda realized that he wouldn't stop.

"Don't do this, Weston," she said, sick at the pleading sound of her voice. He yanked down her skirt. A seam gave way. Miranda thrashed violently as her panties ripped.

She started to scream again, but he placed his mouth over hers, her breasts crushed, his body beginning to move. With his free hand he found the buckle of his pants. They slid to the floor.

Triumph gleamed in his eyes as he poised above her on the desk. "Now, baby," he growled, breathing heavily and sweating like the animal he was, "let's see what you've got."

Claire's heart was a drum, her hands cold as ice as she tugged on her engagement ring. Biting her lip, she waited on the pier near the Taggert sailboat and watched the diamond wink mockingly in the starlight. What was she doing? Breaking up with Harley, wonderful Harley, because of some stupid chemical attraction she felt to Kane Moran. *What about all those promises you made, those vows to yourself and to Harley, those indignant protestations you made to every member in your family?*

Closing her eyes, she leaned against the rail and heard the gentle clang of a buoy rolling on the tide. Kane was leaving, joining the army, taking off to places unknown, and she'd probably never see him again. Yet she was convinced that she would never be happy with a boy only a month ago she swore she'd love forever.

Tramp!

But then Harley hadn't been true, either. Whether she wanted to face it or not, he'd kept seeing Kendall, never completely severing their relationship even though he was supposed to be engaged to Claire.

Sighing, she took in a deep breath of salty air and stared at the heavens, where storm clouds were moving restlessly in the dark sky.

She wasn't alone. The same shadow-thin wharf cat she'd seen during earlier visits to the sailboat slunk past her and hopped lithely into a small fishing boat moored nearby. In another slip, on a sleek yacht, a party was in full swing, voices loud and boisterous, laughter and the sound of the Eagles' "Hotel California" drifting over the still waters of the bay.

"Come on, come on," Claire muttered under her breath, check-ing her watch and willing Harley to appear. Now that she'd made her decision, she wanted to get it over with, was eager to make a clean break and end the sham of an engagement.

"Welcome to the Hotel California . . ."

She heard his car before she saw it, then caught the gleam of flashy wheels and emerald green paint as the car sped under a secu-rity lamp. *Give me strength,* she silently prayed while wondering if breaking off with him would hurt him at all. Maybe he'd be as re-lieved as she to be unshackled from a burdensome relationship.

". . . pink champagne on ice . . ."

Throat dry she watched him walking rapidly along the weath-ered pier. "Claire." Raising a hand, he smiled and jogged the short distance separating them.

". . . we are all just prisoners here, of our own device . . ."

"God, I've missed you," Harley said, spinning her off her feet and holding her close. Her heart began to shred as he buried his face in her neck and kissed her with a pent-up passion she could feel in the heat of his skin.

And yet she didn't respond. Couldn't. He tried to kiss her lips, but she pulled her head back and disentangled herself.

"Don't." Her voice was husky with unshed tears. Suddenly this wasn't as easy as she'd hoped it would be.

"What?" he asked, his handsome face perplexed as he lowered his face close to hers.

". . . you can check out any time you like, but you can never leave . . ."

"Just stop."

"Are you serious?" He smiled, that shy, unsteady smile that had once melted her heart.

"Very. Look, Harley, we need to talk," she said, and cringed when she saw his expression turn guarded. He glanced at her ring-less hand and slowly let out his breath.

"This is about Kendall, isn't it?"

Her heart sank. Even though she'd planned to break it off with him, she didn't want to think that he'd really been unfaithful. But he had. The truth was evident in the newfound defiant tilt of his jaw. "No, not really," she choked out, surprised that his quick confession stung so deeply. She'd assumed the rumors to be true, but to hear it from his own lips . . . "This is about us. It's . . . it's not working."

"Oh, God." He paled, his face blue-white in the glow from the bulbs strung along the pier.

"I think we both know it." She took his hand, turned it palm up, and dropped the ring that had been cutting into her skin into his open fingers.

"No," he whispered. "Claire, no."

"It's for the best."

Tears sprouted in his eyes. "But I love you. You know I do."

"No, Harley, I don't think—"

He reached forward and she shrank away from him. "Don't." But his fingers were already digging into the muscles of her shoulders, fastening her to him.

"I can't lose you."

"It's over."

"I'll tell Kendall we're through. For good. I swear. I'll find a way to make her see that I love you. Only you."

"No, Harley—"

He kissed her. Crushing her against him, tears sliding down his cheeks, he kissed her, and she tasted the bitter salt on his lips as well as more than a trace of alcohol. "I'd give up everything for you," he swore. "Everything." He clutched her hair and sobbed brokenly against her neck.

"No, Harley, please, don't . . ." Her own eyes burned as he clung to her.

"I'll make it up to you, I promise. You'll never regret this, but, please, Claire, don't . . . don't say it's over."

Heart breaking, she held him. "I can't help it, Harley."

"You don't love me," he accused, and she felt as vile as the most wicked creature in the universe.

"I can't change how I feel."

"But I can!" He took her hand and started leading her to the sailboat.

"No—"

"There's wine on board. Champagne."

"I don't want a drink—"

"Hey!" a man's sharp voice rose over the din on the nearby vessel. "Is there a problem down there? Is that guy bothering you?" A gray-haired guy with a sailor's cap stepped under the security lamp, his glasses reflecting the illumination from the bulbs strung overhead.

"No—no problem," Claire said, and followed Harley on board. She owed him that much, she supposed, as she settled into one of the seats, and he found a bottle of Dom Pérignon in the small bar.

"You can't break up with me," he said, as he worked the cork free and it popped loudly. Champagne bubbled over the bottle's neck. Quickly, desperately, he poured them each a long-stemmed glass.

"Harley, don't—"

"It's an unwritten law." Walking back to the cushion where she sat, and, looming over her, he held out a glass.

"A law?" Tentatively she took the drink. This was wrong. Not going well.

"Yeah. No one *ever* breaks up with a Taggert." He tossed back his drink in one long swallow and promptly poured another.

"That's not a law, it's a pipe dream. Look, I've got to go." She set her untouched glass on the bar.

"Not yet."

"Good-bye, Harley," she said as she stood. "I hope we can still be—"

"Don't even say it. We'll never be friends, Claire," he said, his eyes brimming with tears again. He finished his drink, dropped the glass on the carpet, and took a swig from the bottle. "Lovers can never be friends."

"I'll see you."

"No you won't, Claire. If you leave this boat tonight, I swear, I'll get so drunk I can't see straight, then I'll haul my ass over the rail and jump into the bay."

"No—"

"You think I'm lying?" He sighed. "Christ, Claire, if I don't have you, I don't have anything."

"That's not true," she said, but saw the conviction in his gaze. "Come on, I'll drive you home."

He stretched out on the bench and began drinking from the bottle. "Stay."

"I can't."

"Because of Kendall? Or Kane?"

She jumped, and he smiled crookedly, his hair falling over his forehead. "Didn't think I knew, did you?"

"There's nothing to know."

"Ha!" Another long swig as the sailboat gently rocked in the water.

"I've met Kane—"

"*Met* him. Just met him? Come on, Claire, you can do better than that. You've not only met him, you've spent time with him and gone"—he waved wildly in the air—"riding with him on his damned motorcycle in the middle of the night."

Her cheeks burned in silent testimony as she stood in the doorway. Guilt tore a jagged crater in her soul. "I would never have met him if you'd been faithful," she said, though she wondered just how true that statement was. "I haven't cheated on you, Harley. Not ever."

"Not yet, maybe," he said, resting the butt of the near-empty bottle on his chest, "but you're itching to. I can see it in your eyes. Jesus! And to think I loved you."

"Harley—"

"Go on, get out of here," he growled, then promptly drained any remaining liquid from the bottle.

"I can't, not if you're going to—"

"Ah, hell, leave me alone," he said, as if the mention of Kane had changed everything. "I'll be fine." His gaze was abruptly harsh and for half a second he looked like his brother. "Leave, you two-timing whore, or come back here and remind me why it is that I want you."

Heart in her throat, she climbed up the ladder to the deck and half ran off the boat. He was drunk and angry and hateful, but she didn't believe he meant anything he said. When he was sober . . . what? What would happen? Nothing would change. She stopped at the gate where the security guard was sitting, eyes closed, on his stool. "Would you check on berth C-13?" she asked.

"The Taggert slip?"

"Yes, Harley Taggert's inside and . . . I think he needs a ride home."

He looked her up and down and, jangling his keys, started down the ramp. "I'll see to him, Missy. Mr. Taggert, he would want to know that his son's okay."

"Yes . . . yes, he would," she said, and walked briskly to the Jeep she'd taken from her father's fleet. Sounds of the party still drifted up to her, and somewhere not far away a dog was barking his fool head off.

She reached into her pocket for her keys and realized that the course of her life had taken a quick, unexpected turn. For better or worse, she couldn't say, but for the first time in months she was unfettered and free.

"Things will be fine," she told herself as she cranked the steering wheel of the Jeep and drove under the arched neon sign of the marina. They had to be.

So what about Kane?

Her hands perspired on the wheel. He wasn't the kind of boy a girl could depend upon. He was leaving for the army.

She couldn't fall in love with him. Wouldn't.

But as she drove through the forested hills leading back to her house, she knew she was lying to herself. Like it or not, she was half in love with him already.

CHAPTER 21

Claire stepped on the brakes, and the Jeep slid to a stop near the garage. Still shaking inside, she stared at her ringless left hand and fought tears. She'd spent the past three hours driving around in circles, avoiding the hangouts where Harley might look for her, not bothering to go home for fear he might call. He needed time to think things through and sober up. She needed space so that she could consider the new course of her life.

Since she'd left the marina, the storm that had been threatening all day had broken. Wind rushed through the branches of the trees overhead, making them pitch and dance. Rain poured from the sky, drizzling down the windshield and peppering the ground. Puddles had begun to form on the low spots in the asphalt, and the old lodge, the home she'd cherished, looked bleak and forbidding.

No one was home. Randa's car wasn't parked in its usual spot and Dutch was spending most of his nights in Portland, meeting with architects, lawyers, and accountants about the next phase of Stone Illahee. Dominique had gone with him this time, though Claire didn't know why. It seemed as if her parents had less and less in common as the summer edged toward fall.

Dominique had never been one to suffer in silence. She'd complained for as long as Claire could remember about hating this "godforsaken place in the middle of nowhere."

Tessa was probably out as well. Where or with whom, Claire couldn't guess. She and her younger sister had never been particularly close, but this summer their relationship had become more strained. Tessa was a powder keg ready to explode. Claire was prickly, defensive of her relationship with Harley.

Except it was over. Maybe now she and Tessa would see eye to eye.

Miranda was the only person in the family who was rock-steady, the one Claire could count on.

Yanking her keys from the ignition, she pulled her collar around her neck, climbed out of the Jeep, and heard, over the gurgle of rainwater in the gutters and downspouts, the smooth hum of a powerful engine. Headlights flashed through the trees. Her heart clutched. *Harley.* He'd sobered up and now he was coming after her!

She couldn't face him again.

Yet she stood transfixed, like an animal caught in headlights as the car rounded a final bend. Claire steeled herself, ready to stand firm with him and insist that their breakup was for the best. Somehow, some way she'd convince him.

Miranda's Camaro squealed into the parking area. Claire let out her breath. The car skidded to a stop just ten feet from her.

"Get in!" Miranda yelled through the open window. Her voice was desperate. "Now!"

"Wha—?"

"Don't argue, Claire. I don't have time for it. Just get the hell into the damned car." There was a frantic edge to Randa's words, and Claire didn't dare argue, just opened the passenger door and found Tessa slumped and shell-shocked in the front seat. She looked white as death, her eyes vacant, her teeth chattering. Miranda was just as bad. Her dark hair was mussed and wild, her clothes torn, her expression hard. Something akin to fear pulled at the corners of her mouth. She looked as if she knew someone or something evil was chasing her, and she was running for her life. For Tessa's life.

"Randa—?"

"Get in, damn it!"

Heart pounding with an unknown dread, Claire squeezed into the back. "What's going on?"

"Close the door!" Randa ordered, and Tessa, as if she didn't have a mind of her own, did as she was told.

Cranking the steering wheel, Miranda stepped on the gas and peeled out of the driveway. Trees, black sentinels guarding the silvery waters of the lake, sped by in a rush.

Claire's heart hammered; her palms began to sweat. "Would someone please tell me what happened?"

"Did you see Harley tonight?" Miranda asked as the car slid around a corner and a back tire hit mud. The wheel spun crazily before gaining purchase on the slick asphalt again.

"Yes."

"At the marina?"

"Yes, yes. What is this? Twenty questions?"

Barely slowing, Miranda turned north onto the county road that rimmed the lake. Unwittingly, she was taking Claire closer to Kane's house, and Claire tried to quell the sense of panic that was crushing the air from her lungs. What had happened? Why did Miranda and Tessa look as if they'd just seen the apocalypse? Tessa began to sob quietly in the passenger seat.

"When did you see him?" Miranda demanded.

"Harley?" She shifted mental gears again. "I, uh, met him at ten-thirty. Why? For God's sake, Randa, will you tell me—?"

A police car, lights flashing red, white, and blue, sped in the opposite direction. "Shit!" Miranda said and made the next turn onto a gravel side road filled with potholes.

"Miranda—"

"In a minute, okay? I just want to get us out of this mess."

"What mess?" Claire nearly screamed, and Miranda stamped hard on the brakes. The Camaro skidded to a stop, barely missing a telephone pole. Berry vines scraped the passenger side.

"Get out of the car." Miranda left the engine running, but killed the lights.

"What? I just got in."

Miranda was already opening the car door, stepping into the muck, and Claire, heart thudding, followed. For the few seconds that the interior light blinked on she noticed the bloodred stains on Miranda's skirt.

Blood? Claire's stomach curdled. *Blood?* But how? Why? Her throat closed. She didn't dare breathe. Suddenly she didn't want to know what had happened. In an instant of clairvoyance she knew that her life and the lives of those she loved were about to be irrevocably altered. For the worse. She glanced at Tessa huddled near the door, tears running down her cheeks, streaking her mascara, her arms cradled around her knees, and realized that something evil had captured them all in its vile net.

"We don't have a lot of time, so just listen," Miranda said as Claire stumbled out of the car. She grabbed Claire's shoulders in her tense fingers, gripping so tightly Claire nearly cried out. Miranda's gaze was fierce, her jaw set, her eyes wilder than Claire had ever seen. Rain slashed from the sky, drenching Randa's hair, dripping from her nose, running down the back of Claire's neck. "Harley's dead."

"Wha—" Claire's voice died in her throat and her knees threatened to give way, but Miranda held her fast against the fender, forcing her to stand. "What? No!"

"He died tonight at the marina."

"Randa—"

"It's true, Claire."

"But—but—"

"He's dead!"

"No—" Again her legs wobbled, and this time she slid to the ground, Miranda still holding on to her.

Miranda's voice cracked. "I—I don't know all the details, but he was found floating in the bay an hour or so ago."

"No. Oh, God, no!" Claire was shaking, her insides quivering and she told herself this was all a dream—a horrid nightmare. She'd wake up soon and none of this would have happened.

"It's true."

"But I just saw him—" Denial was her crutch, and Claire leaned on it heavily. Miranda was lying. She had to be. But why? Maybe she just heard the facts wrong. That was it; this was a mistake, a horrible, ugly mistake. "You're . . . you're making this up."

"Oh, Claire, why?"

"I don't know, but it's not true! It can't be! You heard the story wrong, that's it!"

Miranda let out a pained little cry. "I'm so sorry; I know how much you loved him."

The words didn't sink in, just bounced off her brain like a stone skimming across water. She shook her head. "You're wrong, Randa. Harley's fine. He's just drunk."

"He's dead, Claire. Dead. He died a couple of hours ago, drowned in the bay."

"No—"

Miranda shook her hard enough to rattle her teeth. "Listen to me, damn it!"

And then it hit her. With the force of the ocean crashing over her, pinning her underwater, making breathing impossible. She gasped, shaking her head, until Randa grabbed both sides of her face and forced her to stare into her older sister's agonized gaze. Mary, Joseph, and Jesus, it was true!

With a keening wail to rival the wind, Claire clenched her fist and pounded it into the mud, splashing dirt and muck onto her clothes, spattering dirt onto her face. "But I was just with him less than three hours ago."

"I know, the security guard saw you."

"Harley, oh, please, no—" Grief and guilt clawed at her soul. If only she hadn't agreed to meet him, or hadn't agreed to go onto the boat with him, or left him, he might still be alive. It was her fault that he was dead. Her damned fault!

"They don't know if it was an accident, murder, or suicide," Randa was saying, her voice sounding distant, though she was close enough that Claire felt the warmth of her breath. "The thing is we're all going to be questioned, especially you, since you were involved with him and were one of the last people to see him alive."

Still wallowing in the mud, Claire was barely listening. All she knew was that Harley, precious Harley, was dead. Her spirit broke and left her. "It's my fault," she said.

"No, don't even say it." Randa, back braced against a rear tire, was holding her, cradling her in the mud, stroking her cheek as if she were a tiny child who had bumped her head.

"I broke up with him and—"

"You what?"

"I broke off the engagement. Oh, God, it's my fault."

"No!"

"But I . . . oh, Harley." Claire felt as if her body had been ripped in half. She had loved Harley once, believed in him. Deep, soul-jarring sobs convulsed within her. Tears drizzled from her eyes. Guilt for somehow harming him gnawed at the corners of her conscience as Miranda held her fast, gently rocking her. "How . . . how do you know? How did you find out?" she asked, not really caring.

"I was in town and heard the news," Miranda said, obviously avoiding the details. Claire didn't care, was suddenly too tired to question her. "I knew you'd gone to see him but were probably back at the house, so I headed there. I found Tessa hitchhiking on one-oh-one. I picked her up and drove home to find you."

"But why? What happened to you?" Claire asked, touching Miranda's ripped blouse and refusing to look at the stain on her skirt. Blood. Whose? Randa's? Harley's? Sweet Jesus, had Randa been with Harley, had she come looking for her sister and found him dead drunk and . . . what then? No! No! No! Nothing was making any sense. If only she could turn the clock back a few hours and alter the events of the night . . .

"It's a long story. We don't have time," Miranda said, and Claire's head thudded dully. "What have you been doing since you left Harley?"

"Driving around." Why was she so cold?

"Who saw you?"

"I don't know. No one, probably." Bile climbed up her throat. She was going to be sick, right here.

"You're sure?"

"I—I don't know." Her teeth were chattering, her skin alive with goose bumps.

"We can't worry about it now, Claire, but you have to pull yourself together. Claire—?" Again Miranda shook her, but Claire threw her off and crawled to the side of the road, where water was running in a ditch and weeds slapped her in the face. Her stomach contracted, and she retched violently, over and over again until there was nothing left.

She felt Randa's hand on her shoulder. "Are you okay?"

"No!"

"But are you with me? Can you get back into the car? We have to leave now. Claire?"

"I—I don't know if I can." She wiped her mouth with the back of her hand, but the vile taste lingered in her mouth as a sense of doom captured her soul.

"Try. Now, the three of us, we're going to make up a story very quickly. Are you with me? We have to come up with alibis—where we were when Harley died."

"I don't understand—"

"We all need to be able to explain where we were."

"Why?" she asked before staring into Miranda's eyes and suddenly understanding that not only was Harley dead, but Miranda was in trouble. Big trouble. Somehow she was involved. A hand with fingers cold as death seemed to reach for her throat and close off her windpipe.

"So this is it. We went to the drive-in up the coast and we were watching that special run they've got—a trio of old Clint Eastwood flicks: *Hang 'Em High, Play Misty for Me,* and *Dirty Harry.* During the second one we decided to go home and left before we saw the last. I fell asleep at the wheel and we drove off the road and into the lake."

"What—? That's crazy. Why?"

Miranda didn't answer, just stared hard into her sister's eyes. A current of understanding passed between them. "Trust me, Claire. We don't have any choice. If Harley was murdered, and I think he was, then you'll be a primary suspect. I was at the marina tonight, too."

"What?"

"And Tessa."

Miranda's voice sounded as if it came from the far end of a tunnel, echoing and unclear, and yet enough of what she was saying was piercing Claire's foggy brain.

"All our names will come up, and none of us has an alibi."

"But I didn't kill Harley. Neither did you or Tessa. Can't we just tell the truth?"

"Not this time," Miranda said with a heart-rending sigh. "This time the truth will damn at least one of us and, believe me, the Taggerts won't stop at anything to see us hang."

Claire blinked against the rain. "I don't see how . . ." she started to argue, but stopped herself short. Miranda was involved to her eyeteeth. Whatever had happened looked bad for her . . . *She* needed an alibi. Swallowing with difficulty, Claire nodded. "Okay."

"Good." Miranda helped her to her feet, then opened the door of the car, where Tessa sat, unmoving, staring sightlessly out of the window. "Sit on the gearshift. I don't want you to be trapped in the back." As Claire squeezed against Tessa, Miranda started the car and drove toward the far side of the lake. "None of us is ever going to tell anyone, not each other, not Mom and Dad, not our best friends, *no* one, what really happened tonight. From now on our story is and always will be that we were at the drive-in. Claire—you're going to have to help me with Tessa when we drive into the lake."

"You're not really going to do it!" Claire said, suddenly terrified. "You're just going to say that—"

"I have to! This has got to look authentic, okay? The lake's not that deep at the north end. We'll be fine." She turned onto the county road.

"This is crazy. People drown in bathtubs. And Tessa—she's not really conscious." The car picked up speed as Miranda shifted. "Randa—"

"Just promise that you'll stick to the story."

"You've lost your mind—"

The road turned and Lake Arrowhead came into view through the trees. The water was dark and turbulent, the wind creating whitecaps on the surface.

"Randa—no!"

Faster and faster the Camaro tore over the road, windshield wipers slapping away the rain, tires singing on the pavement.

"Come on, Claire, you're with me on this, aren't you?" Miranda trod hard on the accelerator as the trees gave way to a grassy stretch of beach.

"What about Tessa?" Claire asked, panicking.

"She's agreed."

"She hasn't said a damned word."

"She's in!"

"Okay, okay!"

"Hang on!" Miranda cranked on the wheel.

The Camaro jerked. Tires slid as they hit the gravel of the shoulder.

"For the love of God—"

The car bounced over stones, grass and boulders, driving faster and faster as the lake, a yawning black hole rushed at them.

"God help me." Miranda stood on the brakes, causing deep ruts in the sand where the tires tried to grab hold. The car hit the water. Hard. Claire hit her head on the roof. Her scream nearly shattered her eardrums as water swirled up to the windows and the engine died.

"Okay, now! Help Tessa!"

Miranda pried her door open and Claire, reaching over her sister, managed the same. Water poured inside. Claire scrambled, coughing, dragging Tessa to the surface, then realized she could stand. She sank past her ankles in the muddy bottom, but her head was still above water.

Harley. Oh, God, Harley, I'm sorry. Heartache pounded through her soul.

"Come on, come on." Miranda placed a shoulder under Tessa's limp arm and started back toward the road, trudging through the dark water. "Now what movies did we see?"

"Hang 'Em High."

"And?"

"Play Misty for Me. Come on, Randa, how's Tessa going to do this?"

"Tess?" Miranda prodded. No response as they waded knee deep. "Tessa?"

"Dirty Harry," she whispered.

"But we didn't see that one, left before it came onto the screen. Remember that. And stick with me; don't let them split us up."

Voices seemed to come from nowhere and a pickup, the beams of its headlights glowing in the rain, was idling on the shoulder of the road. A man in a yellow slicker was running toward them.

"Hey!" he yelled, his voice rough and frightened. "Are you all right? For the love of Christ, what the hell happened here? First the Taggert kid and now this!"

So it was true. Claire's legs felt like lead.

Other cars stopped as the first man reached them and gathered Tessa into his strong arms. "You girls okay? Is there anybody else in the car?"

"Just us," Randa said. "We . . . we're all right."

"You sure?" He swiveled his head in Tessa's direction, and Tessa smelled the stale odor of beer. "How 'bout you?"

"Fine. I—I'm fine."

"What happened?" a woman asked, as cars pulled at odd angles around the pickup. "Christ A'mighty, did someone drive into the lake?"

"I—I must've fallen asleep at the wheel," Miranda said, her teeth chattering. *The lie was just beginning.* Claire shuddered. "One minute I was on the road, and the next—"

"Dear God," a woman said. "Well, let's warm you up. George, George, get the blanket out of the trunk; these girls are going to catch their death."

Numb, Claire let herself be guided into the small group of vehicles scattered helter-skelter at the edge of the road.

"Would you look at that?" an old man said.

"They're lucky to be alive." A woman this time, a dark silhouette in a raincoat cast in sharp relief by the groups of headlights.

"Not like the Taggert kid."

Claire's knees buckled, but someone held her up, propped her on her feet, and kept her walking. Grief cut through her, as surely as any knife, and she began shaking violently.

"Did anyone call an ambulance?"

"Hang in there, girls," a smooth male voice intoned. "You're gonna be all right."

Claire recognized the voice—didn't remember his name—but knew that he worked at the gas station where she filled up. "Are any of you hurt seriously?"

She couldn't find her voice.

"I don't think so." Miranda again. In charge.

Claire managed to nod to Tessa, who only whispered, *"Dirty Harry."*

This was wrong. So wrong.

"What did she say?" a woman asked.

"Sounded like dirty something or other."

"They're probably all in shock."

Claire blinked in the rain, shuddered from the cold, felt her wet, dirty clothes cling to her just as pain wrapped over her heart.

"George, for God's sake, didn't I tell you to give them the blanket that's in the back of the car?"

Somewhere nearby, probably from one of the vehicles scattered on the shoulder of the road, a baby cried so hard he was beginning to hiccup. From the back of a pickup a big dog barked wildly.

"Shut up, Roscoe!"

The dog was silent.

"Say—" a woman whispered loud enough for everyone to hear. "Aren't they Dutch Holland's girls?"

"Someone should call their parents."

"Deputies are on their way."

"How the hell did they end up in the lake? Jesus H. Christ, they're lucky it was in this spot, anywhere else along this stretch, they would've crashed into a tree."

One of the women guided Claire toward her Oldsmobile sedan. "You girls get inside—don't worry about getting the interior dirty; it's plastic. Can always be washed. I haul my dogs around all the time. But you need to keep warm."

She opened the door, and Claire slid inside. Tessa and Miranda followed until they were huddled together, blankets wrapped around them. The owner of the car, a woman with a craggy face and gapped teeth, offered Claire a cup of coffee from a thermos. Other Good Samaritans gave Tessa and Miranda cups that they cradled, steam rising, in their cold hands.

Flashlights cast long beams in the rain as the women huddled and men started to look for the car.

"Did anyone call a tow truck?"

"The cops will."

From the coffee and their breath, the windows of the sedan misted up and Claire was grateful for the privacy it offered, a fragile, dripping screen that protected them from curious eyes.

A siren screamed through the night. Red, white, and blue lights strobed the area. Claire jumped, sloshing her coffee on the Indian blanket that surrounded her.

She glanced at Miranda, and Claire's heart sank, because Miranda, for all her planning, was scared. Her face was the color of chalk and streaked with mud, her hair hung lankly and dripped and as she met her middle sister's eyes, she swallowed hard. "Remember," she said, as a cruiser from the sheriff's department arrived.

Two deputies emerged from the car. Shadowy figures through the foggy windows. One of the officers stayed near the road, using his flashlight to direct traffic and keep it moving as the other approached the car.

He paused and talked with some of the crowd for just a few seconds, asking questions that Claire could only partially hear, then he opened the door of the backseat and the interior light flickered on. Tall and bulky, he wore some kind of waterproof gear and rain dripped from the broad brim of his hat. "Hi, girls, I'm Deputy Hancock. First I want to find out if any of you are hurt and how seriously. Paramedics are on their way to help out. Next, we'll have to sort out what happened for my report." He offered a reassuring smile that scared Claire to her bones. She braced herself for her first confrontation with the law.

"It's my fault," Miranda said, meeting Hancock's eyes. "I— I lost control of my car. I guess I must've fallen asleep at the wheel."

"Anybody hurt?"

Claire shook her head.

"I don't think so," Miranda said.

"What about you, honey?" The deputy stared at Tessa. She lifted her eyes and shuddered.

"Dirty Harry."

"Pardon?" he asked, his eyebrows pulling together.

"We were at the drive-in," Miranda cut in. *"Dirty Harry,* that's the movie we missed because we decided to come home early once the storm broke."

"Oh." He rubbed his jaw and eyed the sky. "Bad night for a drive-in."

"Yes . . . it . . . it was a mistake."

He tapped his flashlight on the side of the car. "Well, you can tell me all about it once we find out that you don't need medical attention. I've called for an ambulance and a tow truck."

"We don't need to go to the hospital," Miranda protested. "We're fine."

"We'll let the paramedics determine that." Another siren cut through the night, and the cup of coffee Claire had been holding slipped through her fingers. It didn't matter. Nothing did. Harley was dead, and she was sitting in a pool of lake water in the back of a stranger's car. She was too tired to think, too sick to her stomach to try and figure out the truth— why Miranda had insisted they lie, but as she looked at the fear etched on her older sister's face and the shock registered on Tessa's features, Claire told herself that she'd lie through her teeth for them. Her sisters were all she had left in the world.

What about Kane?

He was leaving.

Joining the army tomorrow.

She heard the sound of booted feet approach. The footsteps crunching on gravel echoed through her brain. *If only she could see Kane right now, talk to him, hold him* . . . Tears began to flow from her eyes as she and her sisters were helped from the car, while a dozen pair of eyes stared at them. Shepherded through the crowd, they were examined by paramedics as more deputies arrived.

Claire was vaguely aware of someone stretching yellow tape around the area, saw, as if from a distance, a huge tow truck appear, but above the noise, she heard the steady drone of a motorcycle.

She turned toward the road, but the solitary rider sped by, the huge machine barely slowing as a deputy waved him on.

Was it Kane? Claire's hands twisted in the wet blanket.

"What a night," one of the deputies said to the other. "First the Taggert kid, and now this!"

Claire jolted inwardly as she was jerked back to the here and now, away from her fantasies about Kane Moran.

Harley was dead and, somehow, she was responsible. Whatever had happened after she'd left the sailboat was because she broke up with him. She knew it. Harley, sweet, sweet Harley, might not have been the love of her life she'd once thought him to be, but he certainly didn't deserve to die.

CHAPTER 22

Claire couldn't sleep. She tossed and turned in her bed, while images of Harley and Kane blazed through her mind. Alternately crying to herself or lying dry-eyed and numb, she watched the clock and listened to the house creak in the storm. Somewhere a limb battered a window, and rain splashed noisily in the gutters until, right before dawn, the rain stopped suddenly.

Still she couldn't sleep. The past few hours replayed themselves in her mind, like a record that skips to the same few notes over and over again.

After being examined by a physician and questioned by several deputies and detectives, the Holland girls had been released to their parents, who had been called back to Chinook from Portland. Dominique, in tears, had fussed over her daughters and Dutch had promised them the best legal counsel on the West Coast. No one, not even Neal Goddamned Taggert, was going to win this one. He told the girls that he believed them, that of course none of them had killed the Taggert boy, but his words lacked conviction or empathy. Harley's death was just one more obstacle in Dutch's cluttered life.

As Claire had huddled in the backseat of her father's Lincoln, she'd caught his harsh, uncompromising gaze in the rearview mirror and suddenly realized that his concern wasn't grief over the loss of a young man's life but worry about a scandal surrounding his daughters. He was only worried what stockholders in Stone Illahee and his other holdings might think.

Now, Harley's handsome face slid through her mind, and his desperate pleas for her not to break the engagement rang in her ears.

I can't lose you. I'd give up everything for you. Everything. Please, Claire, don't . . . don't say it's over.

Tears rained from her eyes. "Harley," she mouthed. She'd never intended to hurt him. And now he was dead, found, according to what she'd overheard at the sheriff's office, facedown in the bay, maybe the victim of an accident, or suicide, or murder.

Suicide? Dear Lord, she prayed not. *Murder?* Who would hate him enough to kill him?

Miranda's skirt was stained with blood; Tessa was nearly catatonic. They'd both been to the marina and needed alibis. *Oh, Harley, what have I done?*

Squeezing her eyes shut, she willed his image away. She couldn't spend the rest of her life feeling guilty because he'd died on the night she'd broken their engagement, but, deep in her heart, she knew that a cloud of dark uncertainty would follow her for the rest of her days.

She pulled herself into a sitting position and buried her face in her hands. But it didn't help. In her mind's eye, she spied Kane, tall and rawboned, dressed in faded denim and black leather. His rugged face, intense gold eyes, and smoky voice commanded her attention.

I'd like to do anything and everything I could with you. I'd like to kiss you and touch you and sleep with you in my arms until morning. I'd like to run my tongue over your bare skin until you quiver with want, and, more than anything in the world, I'd like to bury myself in you and make love to you for the rest of my life . . . And, believe me, I would never, never treat you like that bastard Taggert does.

She couldn't take it another minute. She threw off the covers and tossed off her nightgown. Silently she grabbed a pair of jeans she'd flung over the end of her bed and grabbed a sweatshirt that was lying wrinkled on the floor. She struggled into a clean pair of socks and carried her boots in sweaty hands as she passed by

Tessa's room with the door firmly closed and Miranda's room where light from the bedside lamp sliced through the crack in the doorway to fall upon the worn rug in the hallway. Slowing, Claire peeked into the room. Miranda sat on her window ledge, her knees tucked up inside her nightgown, her arms wrapped around her legs as she stared vacantly out at the lake. There was a soul-rending sadness in her eyes that Claire had never seen before.

Quietly, she stepped into the room.

Miranda slid a glance her way. "What are you doing?"

"Going for a ride."

"It's not light yet."

"I know, but it will be soon," Claire whispered. "I can't sleep. Can't stand another minute in bed." Suddenly she felt awkward and out of place in this sad, somber room with its pine-paneled walls and bookcases filled to overflowing. "What happened to you last night?" she finally blurted as she crossed the room and rested the edge of her rump on the other end of the window ledge.

Miranda's smile was brittle, her skin pale. Blue smudges made her eyes appear sunken. "I grew up."

"What's that mean?"

"You don't want to know." She looked out the window again. "And I don't want to tell anyone."

"There . . . there was blood on your skirt."

Randa nodded and ran her fingers on the edge of the open window frame. "I know."

"Was it yours?"

"Mine?" She shuddered. "Some of it."

"Oh, God, Randa. Aren't you going to tell me what happened?"

Miranda's eyes focused sharply on her middle sister and she looked older than she ever had. "No, Claire," she said firmly. "I'm not going to tell anyone. I'm eighteen, remember. An adult. I can make my own decisions."

And you're considered an adult in a court of Oregon law. Anything illegal you did, could send you to prison rather than juvenile hall. Claire didn't say it. Didn't have to.

"Just remember our pact. Stick with our story. Everything will work out."

The words sounded hollow, but Claire didn't argue as she passed her parents' room, where the rumble of heavy snoring and the ticking of Dominique's antique crystal clock could be heard.

Stealthy as a cat sneaking up on an unwitting bird, Claire slipped down the stairs and through the kitchen. For the first time since Jack's death she was grateful that Ruby, who sometimes had appeared at five in the morning, wasn't around.

Outside the sun was just beginning to chase away the night. The new dawn was fresh, evidence of the storm visible in the puddles and litter of branches in the yard, but the air smelled clean, and the mist that had settled over the lake began to rise.

Claire entered the stables, threw a bridle over a surprised Marty's head, and led him through a series of paddocks before opening a final gate and, with a running start, hopped onto his bare back.

He sidestepped just a bit, then once she was astride and pressing her knees into his ribs, the horse responded, loping up the familiar trail, splashing through puddles, jumping over a few fallen logs.

Towering stands of old growth timber spread lacy needled branches overhead, allowing little of the gray light of dawn to pierce the forest floor.

"Come on, come on," she urged, as the little paint edged ever upward, past an outcropping of clay-colored rock to the crest of the ridge, the sacred, haunted spot of the Native Americans—the place where Kane had camped before.

She licked her lips nervously as the horse rounded a bend in the trail, her eyes scanning the still-dark timbers.

Her heart beat a sharp cadence of anticipation as she reached the clearing and spied him leaning against the moss-and fungi-covered bark of a tree. A shadow of a beard darkened his chin, his hair was wild and uncombed, his leather jacket battered, his Levi's threadbare and sun-bleached. A cigarette burned slowly between his fingers.

Tears of relief burned in her eyes as she slowed her mount.

A dying campfire sent up a smoldering curl of smoke, and a tarp had been strung between two trees to protect his motorcycle and bedroll.

"Lookin' for me?" he drawled. His blade-thin lips barely moved, and his eyes were the intense shade of aged whiskey she remembered. Her heart cracked. "Yes."

"Thought you might be, so I waited." He tossed his cigarette into the fire and started toward her. She was off the horse in an instant as she raced over the uneven ground and flung herself into his arms. Tears rolled down her cheeks, and all she wanted to do was hold on to him. To cling to him forever and never let go.

His arms surrounded her, giving her a warm haven, silently promising her that everything would be all right. "I heard about Taggert."

She let out a long, pained cry and felt the world tilt all over again. "Oh, God, Kane, it's my fault."

He stiffened. "Yours?"

"I broke off the engagement. Gave him back his ring." She was sobbing now, the words rushing out of her like water spilling through a broken dam. "Down at the marina. He was drinking on the sailboat and . . . and I left him."

"Shh." He kissed her crown and the scents of smoke, leather, and musk surrounded her in a comforting mist. "It's not your fault."

"But he was upset and . . . and . . . I had the night watchman look in on him . . . but . . ."

"But nothing." Taking her hand, he led her to the tent and sat beneath the sodden tarp on the dry ground. Still he held her, his arms offering support as she leaned against him. "It's gonna be all right."

"How? He's dead, Kane. *Dead!*" Broken sobs escaped from her throat as she pounded feebly on his chest.

"And you're alive. Don't beat yourself up over it, Princess."

"Don't call me—"

"All right. Hang in there. I'm here, Claire. You knew I'd be here waiting for you, didn't you?"

Of course she did. That's why she'd come. Guilt trod eagerly over her bare soul. "I—just—didn't love him enough." Sniffing loudly, she pulled back to look into Kane's eyes. "Because of you."

"It's *not* your fault." He shifted his gaze to her lips, and she knew they had to be swollen, her eyes were red and wet, her skin mottled. "You did nothing wrong, Claire. Nothing." Staring at her, he pulled her close again and his lips found hers. No longer gentle, he kissed her with a pent-up passion and heat she'd never felt before. Hard, eager lips demanded more. He wrapped those strong arms around her until she couldn't breathe, couldn't think, and the pain slowly faded away to be replaced by desire, a slow deep throb that pulsed deep within her. His tongue rimmed her lips, and she opened to him, body and soul, knowing that he would soon be gone, and throwing caution to the wind.

Somewhere in the back of her mind Claire knew that kissing him was wrong, that she was too emotionally drained to make the right kind of decisions, but she didn't care. He was warm and comforting, his hands, as they touched her, hard and callused, the heat uncoiling deep within her, moist and wanting.

His fingers found the hem of her sweatshirt and touched her back, tracing the curve of her spine, sending desire racing through her blood, numbing the sorrow and guilt that were just beneath the surface of her consciousness.

With a groan, he discovered she wore no bra, and his hands moved forward to caress both her breasts as his legs wound through hers and they were lying together on the bedroll. She felt the hardness straining against his fly, the pressure of his erection against the V of her legs through denim and cotton.

Lifting the sweatshirt over her head, he stared at her breasts and then moved his gaze upward, his eyes dark with desire, a muscle jumping near his temple.

"You're more beautiful than . . . than . . ." He pulled her breasts together and rubbed her nipples with his thumbs. Passion glided through her blood. Hot. Wild. Uncaring. She moaned as he kissed her on the lips, then moved downward, his tongue circling the hollow of her throat and the tight skin over her sternum before finding one of her breasts and nipping gently.

"Kane," she cried, bucking upward, and his hands cupped her buttocks, fingers hard and eager. "Kane . . ."

The trees overhead began to spin and damp heat swirled in counterpoint deep in her most feminine of places. His beard was rough, his tongue wet, his hands firm. Fingers dug into the muscles of her rear as he straddled her, his erection solid beneath his jeans, the ache between her legs pulsing with want.

This is wrong! You don't love him. You don't even know him. Think, Claire, he's using you! a voice deep in the back of her mind screamed, but she didn't care. Wouldn't listen. Swept on a current of passion, she reached up and skimmed his jacket from his shoulders, then worked at his T-shirt.

He yanked the worn cotton over his head, and, as the sunlight blazed over the eastern ridge of mountains, she watched the sinewy muscles of his chest flex as she touched him. "You're playin' with fire, darlin'," he warned, but she didn't stop and watched in fascination as he trembled when the tip of her fingertip caressed his flat nipple. "Claire . . . don't stop . . . I can't—" His voice was rough. "Do you know what you do to me?"

"What?"

"Everything," he admitted, and found the waistband of her jeans. With one quick jerk the waistband and buttons of her fly opened in a series of sharp pops. Practiced hands skimmed the denim over her hips.

"Claire," he said, kissing her abdomen, his warm moist breath circling her navel. "Claire . . . tell me . . . if this isn't what you want."

"I want you."

"You'll regret it later."

"No—" Was he going to reject her? "I need you."

His groan was as primal as the forest. "Are you sure?"

"Yes . . . oh, God, yes."

Urgent fingers delved inside her panties, pushing aside the soft cotton to touch her intimately, to probe that dark, feminine region now dewy with need.

She whispered his name over and over again as he lowered himself, sliding the underpants down her legs, kissing her thighs, licking her knees, opening her legs so slowly that she thought she would die with the want of him.

His breath fanned her curls and desire like a wisp of smoke curled deep inside her. Raw female need, a fire out of control, burned through her blood, and sweat drenched her body.

"Please," she cried, as he touched her gently at first, then opening her like a special gift and kissing her so intimately tears burned behind her eyes.

"I've wanted you forever," he vowed, the words muffled by the sound of the sea crashing on the rocks below and her own thudding heart.

He kicked off his jeans as he caressed her and she writhed, wanting more, needing all of him. Eagerly she lifted her hips from the ground. "Kane . . . I . . . oh . . . Oooooh . . ." He placed her knees on his shoulders and delved more deeply. The earth cracked—the trees overhead careened—her soul was flung to the heavens, and she shuddered against him as she convulsed.

"That's a girl," he whispered, his face taunt with slipping self-control. "Lose yourself." And she did. As if she were riding a spirited rodeo bronco, she gasped and twisted while he pleasured her with his hands and tongue. When at last she was panting, her naked body soaked in sweat, he slid upward and spread her legs with his knees.

"Wh-what do you want?" she asked, gasping.

"Just you, Claire. That's all I've always wanted." And he took her. With a strong thrust and a primal cry, he drove deep between her legs, and though she was certain she was spent, her heart quickened, her breasts filled, and she moved with him easily, catching his rhythm, her fingers digging into his shoulders, her legs wrapped around his hips.

"Claire, Claire, Claire—" he cried, as he stared down at her and stiffened.

Her body clenched around him, and she was certain heaven and earth collided as their bodies joined, and he spilled himself into her. "Love me," he whispered, collapsing against her and crushing her breasts with his weight. "Just love me today."

"Because you'll be gone by tonight."

He didn't answer, just rolled onto his back, so that she was above him as he buried his face between her breasts.

She stayed with him until nearly noon, making love beneath the sun, whispering together in the sacred forest, forgetting the pain of Harley's death and knowing with an aching certainty that as the sun set this evening, they would never see each other again.

PART 3

THE PRESENT

CHAPTER 23

Claire, Claire, Claire.

Kane gritted his teeth as he sat at his desk, forcing himself to concentrate, but the words on the monitor blurred and Claire's face, haunted and beautiful, burned into his brain. No matter what he did or how he tried to occupy his mind, she was always there, just beneath the surface of his consciousness, ready to appear to him at any given moment.

It was a damned curse.

"You stupid son of a bitch," he muttered under his breath as he snapped the lid to his computer shut and reached for his bottle of whiskey. His investigation into the night that Harley Taggert had died was stalled, his interest sidetracked. All because of Claire. That same white-hot desire that had gotten into his blood sixteen years ago had been dormant for years, but now was heating up again, distracting him, causing his mind to slip from its single-minded purpose of revenge against Dutch Holland.

There were reasons Kane hated Dutch, reasons that ran true and deep. Benedict Holland had single-handedly ruined his life. Now the tables were turned. Kane had a chance to give Dutch a taste of his own medicine.

Except seeing Claire again muddied the waters a bit, clouded his purpose. Christ, he was pathetic. How could one woman turn around his thinking?

Holding the neck of the bottle with two fingers, he walked through the cabin, now clean and painted, a few pieces of new furniture scattered around to take the place of the broken-down rose-colored sofa and scarred metal table. Frustration gnawed at him. Never before had he not been able to concentrate, to focus on a project. His best traits were his clarity and dogged determination. He'd always known what he wanted, went for it, and, like a dog at a bone, wouldn't let up until he won the prize.

Until now.

Shit!

With difficulty, he forced his thoughts back to the stormy night sixteen years ago, the night Harley Taggert had lost his life, the night when so many questions had been left unanswered.

Not that he'd found out much. Kane had spent the past week spinning his wheels. He'd tried to talk to the deputies and witnesses who had seen Harley in his last few hours or been on the scene when Miranda's car plunged into the inky waters of the lake. But a lot of years had passed, and in that time memories had been lost, perceptions altered, the incident a closed police file collecting dust in some locked cabinet somewhere.

Sheriff McBain, the officer in charge of the investigation was dead of liver cancer, and the other deputies, none of whom were still with the force, were tight-lipped, their memories fuzzy. They seemed sincere enough, just older and tired, and not much interested in reopening a case that had been ruled an accident. There had been rumors to the effect that the entire investigation had been hushed up, either by Neal Taggert or Dutch Holland and their ability to pay.

Kane was betting on Dutch.

He walked back to the old wooden desk he'd bought at a used furniture store. Glancing at his notes, he scowled and cracked his knuckles. Not only had Harley died under suspicious circumstances that night, but Jack Songbird had fallen to his death off the Illahee Cliffs only days before. Hunter Riley, apparently involved with Miranda Holland, had up and disappeared while rumors swirled through town about him knocking up some younger girl and stealing a car. Riley had blown the country, worked for Taggert Logging in Canada somewhere, then disappeared from the face of the earth. Kendall Forsythe, distraught over Harley's death, had ended up marrying Weston Taggert.

"Think!" he ordered himself, and flipped through copies of the original police reports. Harley Taggert's official cause of death was drowning, but he'd either bashed his head on a rock or some other sharp, jagged object after falling off the boat, or someone had clobbered him before pushing his unconscious body overboard.

When the police had dragged the bay, searching for clues or perhaps a murder weapon, all that had been discovered in the refuse and sludge was a small pistol.

Was the pistol related to the crime? Or was it just a coincidence that the gun was near his body?

Kane found a glass on the desk, wiped out the dust with the edge of his shirt, and poured himself a stiff shot. The key to finding out the truth was talking to as many people as possible and checking their stories, playing one against the other.

He wanted to start with Claire. Not because she was the logical choice, but because he wanted—needed—to see her again. Christ, she was becoming an obsession. *Think, Moran, think! Use that blasted brain of yours!*

So much had happened in sixteen years. He'd spent the past few months chasing down leads, trying to find all of the people—or were they suspects?—who were involved.

Sitting on the edge of his chair, he opened a spiral notebook filled with the names of all the players in the tragedy.

Neal Taggert, after suffering a near-fatal stroke, had stepped down as the president and CEO of Taggert Industries. Weston was now filling those executive slippers. Daughter Paige took care of her ailing father most of the time.

As for the elder Taggert son, Weston was married to Kendall Forsythe and had one child, a daughter, Stephanie, who was fifteen. They had married soon after Harley's death, had no other children, and from all accounts their marriage was as rocky as the Illahee Cliffs. Neither Weston nor Kendall had alibis for the night Harley drowned, but the sheriff's department had dismissed them as possible suspects. Just as they'd dismissed everyone. As far as the official records were concerned Harley Taggert's death had been an accident. Nothing more.

Hank and Ruby Songbird were retired and still living in Chinook, where they ran a mobile home park. They'd moved from their house shortly after Jack's death, and Ruby had never gotten over her only son's demise. She'd become a grim, thoughtful woman, who was known to talk in her native tongue at a moment's notice and who forever gazed out her window to the cliffs where Jack had lost his life.

Crystal had left Chinook after that summer, finished high school and college, and was now married to a doctor in Seattle. She rarely visited her parents and seemed to have no happy memories of this tiny town on the coast.

As for the Hollands, they were an interesting lot. Miranda had never married, rarely dated as far as Kane could tell, and was totally devoted to her career, a career that could well be derailed if it were proved that she was somehow involved in Harley's death.

Tessa flitted from one apartment in Southern California to the next. She'd supported herself by painting, as her mother had before marrying Dutch, or playing guitar and singing in some less-than-five-star establishments in L.A. A party girl by nature, she'd been picked up for speeding, driving under the influence of intoxicants, and possession of a controlled substance, that substance being cocaine once and marijuana twice. She'd lived with several men who were on the outer fringes of the entertainment business, but, like Miranda, she'd never walked down the aisle and said, "I do."

And then there was Claire. Beautiful, lively, enigmatic Claire who had run away from Chinook, married an older man and had two children only to find out that her husband was involved in an affair with his son's girlfriend. "Bastard," Kane muttered, tossing back another swallow of whiskey.

Claire deserved better. Any woman did. He hoped he never laid eyes on Paul St. John.

Checking his watch, he scowled at the time and wished to God he could avoid the next appointment. But it was necessary if he was ever going to finish his book.

Morning rain had given way to high clouds that were pierced by rays of sunlight and created a warm mist in the forest. Puddles had collected in the low points of the driveway but were already drying as Kane climbed into his Jeep and felt his old war wound act up again. The last person he wanted to talk to today was Weston Taggert, but he needed Harley's older brother's take on the events of sixteen years before.

In Chinook he parked in the lot across the street from the newest building in town, a two-story office complex with a view of the bay. Ensconced within were the new headquarters of Taggert Industries. Kane passed through a reception area and took the elevator to the second floor, where a desk was positioned in front of double oak doors.

"Kane Moran," he told the petite woman with short red hair and matching lips. Wearing a phone headset, she looked up at him through oversize lashes. "I've got a meeting with Mr. Taggert."

Scanning the appointment book, she found his name, punched a button on the telephone to announce him, and within seconds he was seated in a huge corner office with floor-to-ceiling windows. Live trees in enormous clay pots were spaced upon a bronze-colored carpet. A bar was situated against one wall, two couches were tucked into another corner, and in front of the wall of glass stood a massive rosewood desk where Weston was waiting for him.

Wearing a thousand-dollar-plus suit, he was leaning back in his chair, fingers tented under his chin, eyes narrowed thoughtfully. Aside from a few lines around the corners of his eyes, he hadn't aged at all. His jaw was still hard, his body trim, his hair showing no sign of thinning or turning gray. He'd called Kane for a meeting rather than the other way around.

"Moran." He rose and shook Kane's hand over the desk. "Have a seat." Motioning toward the chairs positioned in front of his desk, he asked, "Can I get you something? Coffee or a drink?"

"Don't bother." Kane lowered himself into one of the matching oxblood leather club chairs and waited. This was, after all, Weston's idea.

The CEO of Taggert Industries got straight to the point. "I've heard that you're writing a book about my brother's death."

"That's right."

"Why?"

Kane shifted in the chair and smiled inwardly. So Weston couldn't wait to find out what was going on. Good. What secrets did Harley's older brother know? "Too many unanswered questions."

"It's been sixteen years."

Kane felt one side of his mouth twist upward. "Well, I've been busy. Just got back to it."

"You seem to think that writing the book now will serve some purpose," Weston said, leading him by the nose. Kane didn't like the feeling, but played along.

"I think Dutch Holland knows more about your brother's death than he's saying and I suspect that he—or maybe your father—bought off the local authorities to hush the whole thing up."

"Why would they do that?"

"An interesting question. Why don't you take a stab at it?"

"I don't know."

"Think, Weston."

"You mean if someone had something to hide. A cover-up?" Weston sounded incredulous. Kane didn't buy the act.

"Just a theory, but one worth checking out."

"Why stir up the muck? This thing's been laid to rest for a long time. Everyone's gotten over it." He smiled widely, a grin that was meant to encourage camaraderie yet was as cool as the darkest depths of the sea.

"I haven't. And I think that since Dutch Holland has decided to run for governor, all his dirty little secrets should come to light."

"What's it to you, Moran? You didn't give a damn about my brother."

"It's personal," Kane said, countering Weston's icy grin with one of his own. "Between Dutch and me." He settled onto the small of his back. "Besides, I'm not just interested in Harley's death, but the events leading up to it," Kane admitted, willing to give out a little information in order to retrieve some.

"Such as?"

"What really happened to Jack Songbird."

Weston shifted, then reached into the inside pocket of his suit coat for a pack of Marlboros. "Jack got drunk and fell off the cliffs." With a flick of a gold lighter, he lit up, drawing hard on the cigarette and sending a plume of smoke to the ceiling.

"Maybe. Some people think he jumped. Others suspect he was murdered."

"Let me guess—Crystal Songbird, her folks, and some of the elders from the tribe are pushing the murder theory. Hell, they've been whining about it for years, but the fact of the matter was Jack was just another screwed-up Indian who drank too much firewater and paid the price."

The muscles of Kane's back tightened, and it was all he could do not to clench his fists and pound Weston's perfect face. But there was no reason to let Weston know what he was thinking.

Weston studied the tip of his cigarette. "You know, Moran, if you write anything that libels my family, I'll sue your ass up one side and down the other."

"I'd think you'd want the truth to come out and have a chance to get a little back at Dutch Holland at the same time."

"The truth doesn't interest me. As I said, it's water under the bridge—ancient history. As for Dutch; he'll get his. One way or another. He doesn't need any help from you."

"Mr. Taggert?" The receptionist's voice broke into the room. "It's your wife on line one. I told her you were busy but—"

Irritation yanked Weston's brows together as he punched a button for the intercom. "I'll take the call." Then, to Kane, "If you'll excuse me."

Kane didn't need an excuse to leave. He'd gotten what he'd come for—a little insight into the Taggert family and Weston in particular. He would have thought the entire clan would have been jumping for joy at the thought of an exposé written about the family's old nemesis, but no, Weston had an aversion to his project. As if he were guilty. But of what?

As he jaywalked across the street to his car, Kane felt a little thrill of victory. Already he was stepping on toes, important toes. Surely something would break.

He jumped into his Jeep and threw it into gear. He was feeling better by the minute. Yep, old Wes was jumpy, but why? Kane had a couple of more interviews this afternoon. He wanted to talk with reporters who had covered Harley Taggert's and Jack Songbird's deaths. He'd read their articles, of course, had most of them memorized, but he hoped that picking the reporters' brains would give him more clues. Next, he wanted to talk to the first people on the scene of Miranda Holland's accident—the Good Samaritans who had seen firsthand how the girls had reacted. Maybe they could give him a little insight, a new angle on the tragedy. Only then would he visit Claire again.

"I want you to find out everything you can about a guy named Denver Styles." Miranda faced Frank Petrillo across the scarred Formica table of Francone's, the only Italian restaurant in town that Petrillo thought was worth the price of a slice of pizza.

"He givin' you a rough time?" Frank asked, wadding a stick of gum into his mouth despite the fact that he'd just ordered a pint of beer. "He the guy who's been hangin' around?"

"Not a rough time. He's on my dad's payroll."

One graying eyebrow lifted as a buxom waitress left their drinks on the table. Petrillo took a sip and squinted over the top of the glass. "What's the problem?"

"Dutch hired him to snoop into our—my sisters' and my— lives, and I don't trust him." She gave Frank an abbreviated version of her meeting with Styles, careful not to mention too much about the night Harley Taggert died. "He's supposed to be a private investigator, some guy from out of town, I think, but I get the feeling I've met him before." She took a sip of her chardonnay and turned the wineglass in her fingers. "I'd just like to know who he really is."

Petrillo rubbed his jaw and the stubble scraped as he thought. "Styles, eh?"

"Denver Styles. Other than his name, I don't know anything about him."

"You will." Petrillo snapped his Juicy Fruit and took another long swallow of beer. His dark eyes twinkled at the prospect of a new challenge, and Miranda felt a little better. Frank would dig until his fingers bled, but he'd find out what there was to know about Dutch's newest employee.

She only hoped it was in time. Before Denver Styles or Kane Moran found out the truth. She sipped her wine as the pizza, some concoction of shrimp, green pepper, and olives that Petrillo favored, was deposited on the table.

Frank joked with her as he pulled out a stringy slice and tried to put her at ease, but she couldn't shake the feeling that she was being backed into a corner, a dank, black corner that had been always one step away and was now looming closer.

She sensed that she was being watched, but a quick glance around the restaurant convinced her that her imagination was running away with her. Denver Styles wasn't lurking near the video machines or seated in a smoky corner of the bar. No, it was just her mind toying with her again, her guilt rising from the watery grave in which she'd buried it years before. *Hold on,* she silently told herself as she reached for a slice of pizza that she didn't want. Forcing a smile, she took a bite.

"Relax, kid," Petrillo said. "Everything's gonna be all right."

"You're sure?"

Petrillo's brown eyes twinkled. "Abso-fucking-lutely."

Miranda smiled and wished to heaven that she could believe him. But, damn it, she couldn't. Even in this cozy little pizza parlor with people laughing and talking, the bartender wiping down the brass on the bar, and Frank Petrillo winking at her from across the table, she felt the cold breath of doom against the back of her neck. And she was scared. More scared than she'd been in sixteen years.

"Tell me about Dad." Samantha hopped onto the counter in the kitchen where Claire was unpacking the last of the moving cartons. They'd been in Chinook nearly a week, and yet they hadn't completely settled in.

"What do you want to know?" Claire asked.

"Is he as bad as Sean says?"

Claire gritted her teeth. The ache in her heart had ceased long ago, when she'd first learned that Paul was having an affair. It probably hadn't been his first as he was forever attracted to younger women. Now all she felt was shame and remorse. "Your father isn't bad," she said, wondering if she were lying. "He's just weak."

"Weak?"

"Yes. He, uh, likes women."

"Girls," Sam corrected.

Anything in a skirt. "Yes, sometimes girls, too."

"Then he is bad."

"I don't want you to think of him that way."

"But *you* do," Samantha charged, her eyes showing only a little of the pain that had to be echoing through her young body. She drew her legs up, balancing the arches of her feet on the edge of the counter and resting her chin on her knees. There was dust caked on Samantha's long legs, dirt in the cracks of her bare toes, but Claire didn't say anything. This wasn't the time to turn the subject to matters of cleanliness or germs.

"I just don't want to think about him period." Claire decided to be honest. Kids could see through lies too easily.

Sam wrinkled her nose. "Yeah. Me neither." She gnawed on the corner of her lip. "Will he go to prison?"

Shame burned up Claire's neck. "I don't know. Maybe—or he could get a reduced sentence and be on probation, I suppose, but we'll just have to wait and see."

"Well, if he's a jailbird, I don't want to see him," Samantha decided, tossing her head. "Even if he isn't. What he did was wrong." Her chin trembled. "Dads aren't supposed to do anything wrong."

"No, honey, they're not," Claire said, walking to the counter and wrapping her arms around her daughter's slim shoulders. "But they're just human and sometimes . . . sometimes they make mistakes."

"He should never have done it."

"I know." Claire felt Sam's tears, hot and wet, drip onto her blouse.

"We didn't deserve it."

"No, baby, we didn't," she agreed, as Samantha coughed loudly. "But we have to face it. Like it or not."

Samantha shuddered, then lifted her tear-streaked face. "Sean says this sucks."

Claire nodded even though she hated the crudity of Sean's language. "This time, he's right. Come on, I'll make you a cup of cocoa, and we'll try and find a movie to watch."

"A happy one," Samantha said, sliding down from her perch.

"Yeah, a happy one."

CHAPTER 24

It was nearly midnight when Claire, restless, threw off the thin covers of the bed. Without snapping on the lights, she slid her arms through her robe and padded barefoot down the hallway past the open doors of her sleeping children's rooms before heading downstairs. Her mind was spinning, images of Kane and Harley and Paul all racing through her brain as if they were in a tornado, whirling ever faster, confusing her.

She stopped in the kitchen for a book of matches, then hurried out the French doors of the dining room and down the weed-choked path to the lake. She stopped only to light the citronella torches planted every ten feet on the dock, and hoped to keep the marauding mosquitoes at bay.

Her match sizzled in the night and soon six torches glowed, giving off their sweet-acrid scent and allowing her to sit on the last board of the pier, her bare legs swinging out over the water, her face uplifted to the heavens. Thousands of stars twinkled brightly and a slice of gleaming moon hung low in the sky, giving a silvery sheen to the dark waters. Fish jumped, splashing in the lake, crickets chirped, and, not far away, an owl hooted softly.

Claire had always loved it here. Despite all the heartache and pain of her childhood and the tragedy of Harley Taggert's death, she felt a great peace in the house and on the shores of Lake Arrowhead. Her gaze drifted across the glassy waters to the Moran cottage, its windows bright squares of light in the darkness, and she wondered about Kane. What was he doing? Working on that damned book? Digging deep into the past? Discovering secret truths that were better left hidden? Her heart ached a bit and she realized that years before she'd loved him with a passion that was as foolish as it was fierce. There was something about him that could turn her inside out, cause her to give up reason for desire, seduce her to sacrifice everything—even her stubborn pride—to be close to him.

"Idiot," she muttered under her breath. No man was worth a woman's dignity. No man. But, oh, even now, if she had the chance to kiss Kane, to touch him, to feel his hard, naked body straining over hers . . .

"Stop it," she hissed, angry with the wayward turn of her thoughts. "You're not a teenager anymore. For heaven's sake, you're over thirty! A mother! You've been hurt so many times before!" If she were only more like Miranda. Strong. Independent. Courageous.

Instead, sometimes she felt like a frightened little girl. "For the love of God, Claire, pull yourself together." Sighing, she ran her toes through the cool water and tightened the belt of her robe.

Years before, Claire had buried her love for Kane deep in her heart, turned her back on the primal, raw emotions he'd stirred in her because they'd had no future together. Fate, it seemed, had intervened. After Harley's death, Kane had gone into the army and she had left Chinook as well, running away from all the heartache and pain and meeting Paul St. John, a man she'd never really loved, but one who had promised to take care of her. She'd been seventeen when she'd met him at a local community college, where he'd taught English and she was studying for her GED. He'd found her crying on a bench in the quad and had offered her his handkerchief for her eyes and a steady shoulder to cry on. Claire wasn't used to the kindness of strangers and wouldn't have turned to him, but she'd just visited the local clinic and been told that she was pregnant. And alone. Miranda was already in college; Dominique, finally unable to deal with her husband's lust for other women had threatened divorce, then taken Tessa and flown to Europe. Dutch had never been close to Claire. Harley was dead; Kane in the army.

She and her baby were utterly alone in the world. Except for the kindness of Paul St. John.

Stupidly she'd poured her heart out to him. Her meager savings were dwindling and her part-time job waitressing at a restaurant where she'd lied about her age barely paid the rent. Her only hope was to face a formidable father who would probably toss her out and call her a whore for conceiving a Taggert.

Paul, for some unfathomable reason, had been intrigued with her and her plight. Maybe it was her utter helplessness that had appealed to him, or maybe she'd been just the right age, not yet even eighteen, to interest him, or perhaps he thought that she might inherit some of the Holland wealth. Whatever the reason, he'd courted her, offered to marry her, and helped her finish high school and college. At thirty he'd been older and wise to the ways of the world, and she'd needed desperately to trust someone. Anyone. Even a stranger she barely knew. She had thought him to be a rock and didn't realize for years how wrong she was about him.

When Sean had been born, Paul had pretended to be the baby's natural father, and Claire, in order to make everything appear normal, had lied about the date of Sean's birth, pushing it back three months so that no one, not even her sisters, would suspect that the baby was really Harley Taggert's son—or so she'd thought. Since no one in her family saw the baby until he was past one, there had been no questions asked. Sean had just appeared bigger, smarter, and a little more coordinated than the other children his age.

Claire had lost her heart to the darling baby and knowing he was a living, breathing part of Harley made him all the more precious. But as he grew, it became obvious that he didn't have a drop of Taggert blood in his veins.

With a heart-slamming jolt, she realized that her toddler was the spitting image of Kane Moran. If possible, she loved her son all the more. Now she'd always have a part of the hellion she'd come to love and as such was more precious than ever. She would always be close to Kane and someday . . . well maybe someday she'd track him down and tell him about his wonderful, handsome son.

Within three years the lie of Sean's parentage rolled easily off her tongue and Claire became pregnant with Samantha. If her life wasn't perfect, at least it was fulfilling and if Paul wasn't as attentive as he'd once been, Claire decided it was because of the pressures of work. But she'd been wrong. Bitterly so.

During the second trimester of her pregnancy with Samantha Claire first learned of her husband's infidelities. One of Paul's colleagues had let it slip that he'd been seeing another woman on the staff. From that point on, the marriage had gone downhill and eventually foundered.

Claire and Paul had split up years before but the divorce hadn't been final until this past year when Paul, visiting Sean, had met Jessica Stewart, Sean's girlfriend and had promptly seduced her.

That same sick feeling rolled over Claire again, the nausea that accompanied thoughts of her husband and a girl too young to have been involved in consensual sex.

"Don't think of it," she told herself as she turned her attention back to the Moran cottage and wondered again about Kane. Was he there? Her heart skipped a beat, and she closed her eyes. It was useless to think of him. Whatever innocent love or lust they had shared was over a long, long time ago.

He'd quit six years before, but now, staring at the torchlights burning across the lake, Kane wanted a cigarette. And he wanted one badly. Like runway beacons showing a pilot the correct path, those golden torches lured him into unknown and dangerous waters.

Knowing full well that he was making a mistake of the highest order, he unleashed the old motorboat at his dock, shoved off and primed the engine. Grabbing hold of the handle he jerked hard on the pull start. With a crack and a sputter, the twelve-horse Evinrude caught fire and Kane opened her up. The little boat flew across the water, prow slicing the surface, white wake churning behind, wind whistling through his hair as his fingers sweated over the handle.

After interviewing witnesses all afternoon and learning less than he'd hoped, he'd given up his idea of seeing Claire again. He wasn't ready; there was just too much about her that he found intriguing. He lost his objectivity when he was near her, and instead of the hard-edged, pushy, news-or-nothing reporter he'd always prided himself on being, he reverted back to those hellish teenage years when he was randy as a wild stallion and wanted to make love to Claire Holland every way up from sideways. As a horny kid, he'd spent nights touching himself, imagining his tongue running up and down her body, between her breasts, and down her spine. In his mind's eye he'd seen himself kiss the dewy thatch of red-brown curls sprouting between her legs before touching her wildly with his tongue as he explored the dark and moist secrets of her womanhood. He imagined stripping her of clothes, of kissing her breasts until they blushed and filled in his hands, of sucking like a newborn babe until she was trembling and filled with the same heart-pounding, hot-blooded lust that coursed through his veins.

Those same old fantasies had reawakened lately and he, always in control, the cool journalist who never let a woman get too close to his heart, was a frustrated, horny teenager again.

"Shit," he growled. A smoke wouldn't solve the problem. Neither would a pint of whiskey or another woman. Nothing but bedding Claire Holland St. John would.

The torchlights grew brighter and the scent of citronella wafted in the hazy smoke that curled heavenward from the torches. Claire was seated on the dock, her slim legs dangling into the water, a shiny white wrap surrounding her body.

He cut the engine and the boat drifted slowly to the pier. She was watching him, her eyes luminous in the moonlight, her face scrubbed free of makeup.

He flung the anchor line around a rotting post and hopped onto the dock.

"You're trespassing," she said, as she had in the past.

God, she was gorgeous. "Good to see you, too."

"It seems to be a habit with you."

He grinned and sat next to her, stretching his legs on the dock, facing away from the water and staring at her face. "One I haven't been able to break."

"It'll get you into trouble."

"Already has." Just looking at her heated his blood, and the beginnings of an erection stirred deep in his loins.

"So why're you here?" Her gaze, silver in the moonlight, drilled into his.

"Couldn't sleep. Saw the lights."

Her jaw slid to one side, and her fingers brushed at the deck. "So it's not because you're trying to dig up some dirt on my father for your book?"

"I'm just looking for the truth."

"Are you?" She shook her head and sighed. "No way, Kane. This is some kind of vendetta with you."

He wanted to argue, but bit his tongue. No more lies. There could be no more lies.

"What is it? Why do you hate us so much?"

"I don't hate you."

"Don't you?" She whirled, dragging her feet out of the water, sending a spray of drops over the dock and his shoulders so that she, too, was facing away from the lake, her shoulder brushing against his. "Then why don't you just leave us all alone?"

"I have a deal—"

"You said yourself this isn't about money, so what is it?" she demanded, her teeth flashing as brightly as the fire in her eyes.

"Something that needs to be done."

"Just to derail my father from his bid for the governorship?" she asked, frowning into the darkness. "I don't think so. Why would you care?"

"We go way back, me and your dad."

"To your father's accident?" she asked, and when he didn't answer immediately, she looked over her shoulder to the lake. "I'm not standing up for Dutch," she admitted. "He . . . he's never been perfect, and what happened to your father was unforgivable."

"You don't know the half of it."

"Don't I?" She glanced at him with her wide, furious eyes, and he was undone. Her cheekbones, more pronounced as she turned, her lips, moist and shining, her eyebrows lifted in skeptical disbelief, all worked against his hard-fought promise to himself that he wouldn't touch her again, would never step across that painful barrier. But as he watched her, his determination began to crumble, and the images that had kept him awake at nights, of her lying naked in his arms, became more real, more attainable. He smelled her skin, freshened by the scent of perfume, and the fire between his legs became a furnace. "I know that your father paid an ex-con to haul him over here years ago. The man helped Hampton break into the house, and then the two of them took chain saws to the stairs, decapitating the posts of their art."

Stunned, Kane didn't move. "What?"

"That's right, Moran. Your old man came into the house and trashed the place. The only reason Dutch didn't press charges is because he was afraid of the bad press. It would've made your father, a poor unfortunate cripple, the underdog. A victim. So it was all hushed up and forgotten." She sighed and blew her bangs from her eyes. "Not that it matters now," she said. "Dad's fixing the railing now that we're here and . . . well, I guess I understand why your father was angry. Why he hated us."

"Not you. Just Dutch."

"As you do."

A muscle leapt in Kane's jaw, but it relaxed when Claire placed her hand over his.

"Look, I didn't mean to jump down your throat. I know your father died, and I'm sorry."

"He's better off," Kane said, as the softness of her fingers stroked the back of his hand.

As if she realized what she was doing, she pulled away. "Sorry."

"Don't be. He was a miserable son of a bitch while he was alive. Maybe he's found some peace now." But he didn't believe it. Hampton Moran's soul would be as tormented and angry in the afterlife as it was when he'd walked this earth. He'd been a furious man with a chip on his shoulder before the accident that had crippled him, and afterward he'd let his dissatisfaction and jealousy eat a hole in his heart and poison his system so that his wife had left him and his son slowly lost all respect and love for the shell of a man he'd become.

"I won't be used, you know," she said softly.

"Used?"

"By you. For your book. I know you've been snooping around, poking your nose into the past, but if you came here because you thought I'd tell you some great secrets about the night Harley died, then you're wrong."

"I came here because I wanted to see you," he said, surprised at his own honesty. "I was going to come by earlier, try and talk to you about the past, but I was too tired, then I saw the torchlights and—" he caught himself before he said too much, but then he looked into her eyes and his soul clutched. Before he could stop himself, he reached upward and cupped the back of her head, drawing her face to his.

"Kane—no—" she said breathlessly, his tongue brushing those perfect lips. "I can't—"

But it was too late. His mouth claimed hers and memories of what it felt like to be with her, to touch her, to take her supple body with his own, washed over him. He wrapped his arms around her and pulled her close. Her breathing was as erratic as his own, he could feel the flutter of her heartbeat against his chest. "Claire," he whispered. "Claire—"

She moaned, opening her mouth, offering him access to the inside of her. His tongue touched her teeth and the ridges of the roof of her mouth before finding its mate and dancing in a sensual and moist intimacy that caused his erection to grow and ache.

He felt her shudder and he reached upward, scaling her ribs with his thumbs, reaching inside the shiny wrap with his fingers, unfastening the tiny buttons of her nightgown.

"Kane—oooh." His fingers delved beneath the soft layers and found her breast, full and hot, the nipple erect and waiting. "Please—" With one hand he clutched her hair, with the other he stroked her breast and opened her robe, exposing more of her white skin to the night, watching in fascination as one glorious globe spilled out of the fabric and the slit opened farther, giving him a glimpse of the firm tight muscles of her abdomen, the erotic impression of her navel, and a glimpse of her reddish curls where her legs joined.

With a groan, he lowered himself until he could kiss her breast. She arched upward and he licked at the nipple, feeling her heat, knowing she was as eager as he.

Encircling his head with her arms, she held him close, writhing against him as he opened his mouth and sucked hungrily. She began to pant, to breathe in short sharp breaths, and she didn't fight him, but moved closer, as if she, too, couldn't resist. Her hips ground against his, and he slid one hand through the fabric of her robe, touching her abdomen and reaching farther downward until he grazed the juncture of her legs with his fingers. She cried out as his hand cupped her thigh before touching that warm soft haven deep within her. She shuddered and moved with him, tossing her head back, losing herself. "Kane," she cried, as he delved deeper still and then, as if realizing she was at the point of no return, she grabbed his arm with her hands. "Oh, no," she whispered, as if suddenly realizing where she was and with whom. "No, no, no!"

He froze, his fingers still deep in that sacred warm center of her.

"Oh, God. Oh, no." She moved away from him and then moaned as if in agony. "Kane, please—we can't just . . . Oh, God, I'm a mother . . . I'm too old to—"

"Shh." He hushed her by gathering her close, wrapping both arms around her and fastening his lips over hers. His crotch was on fire, his manhood throbbing to join with her, but he forced himself to slow down, to quiet his breathing, to realize that she was right. They couldn't finish this act. Not now. Not ever. "I'm sorry," he said when at last he could speak.

She trembled in his arms. "Don't be."

"But—"

"Please." She kissed him lightly on the lips and cradled his head between her hands. "I know what you're feeling. God, do I, but . . . there's too much between us. Too much time. Too many memories. Too many mistakes." She blinked rapidly as if fighting tears and then, as he held her, she slipped out of his grasp. "I . . . I just can't do this . . . not yet. I don't even know you."

"You know me," he said. "You remember."

"Yes." Tears tracked down her cheeks. "I do." She licked her lips nervously, as if there was something she wanted to tell him, some dark and painful secret, but she suddenly shook her head, and then she was on her feet, running away from him as fast as her bare feet would carry her.

CHAPTER 25

"I'm tellin' ya, the man's got no past," Petrillo said as he plopped himself into the one chair pushed up against Miranda's desk. After more than a week off, she was back on the job, determined to keep her equilibrium, refusing to let her father or one of his henchmen, particularly Styles, run her life. "It's as if Denver Styles doesn't exist. No police records, nothing through the computers or Social Security or the IRS or the DMV." He reached into the pocket of his too-tight sport coat and found a pack of Juicy Fruit. "My guess is his name is a phony; he's got an alias."

Miranda, seated behind neat stacks of mail and files on current cases the department was prosecuting, shuddered. She touched the scar on her neck, and refused to let her mind wander toward the murky depths of that time in her life. Instead she wondered about her father's latest employee.

"How did your old man get in touch with him?"

"He wouldn't say."

"Humph. Probably didn't go through the Yellow Pages." Petrillo unwrapped a stick of gum, then folded it neatly before plopping the wad into his mouth. His pager went off and he glanced at the read-out, then scowled as he turned it off.

"No, I don't think so."

"Styles could be connected to the underworld."

"I don't think he's a mobster, if that's what you're getting at," Miranda said, conjuring up a picture of Denver Styles in her mind. Handsome, cold, arrogant, and something else, yes, persistent. She didn't doubt that once Styles set his mind to do something, it was done. No pussyfooting around. She bit her lip nervously. He bothered her. He bothered her a lot.

"Well, if he ain't connected with the Mafia, then he's connected to somethin' else, and I'll bet ya dollars to doughnuts that it ain't on the up and up, if ya know what I mean. Upstandin' citizens have addresses, phone numbers, licenses for their cars and dogs, and are registered with the military and the government. This guy— Styles—it's like he's a ghost." He snapped his gum and rubbed one jowl. "But I ain't givin' up," Petrillo promised. "I'll find out who he is and what he's doin' connected with your old man one way or another."

"How do you propose to do that?"

"Tail him, if I have to." His brown eyes twinkled at the prospect of a challenge. "I want to find out just what this guy's story is."

"So do I," Miranda thought aloud. She picked up a pencil and tapped it lightly on the blotter covering the middle of her desk. Just who was Denver Styles? How had he linked up with her father? Was he a political ally or some kind of shady private investigator, kind of a soldier of fortune, a man who would do anything for the right amount of cash? Her pencil tapped out a rhythm as she glanced up at Frank and saw him staring at her. "I don't mean to take up a lot of your time on this guy. You've got to have other work for the department."

"I'll squeeze Styles in," Petrillo said, turning on his pager again. "It could be fun."

And it could be dangerous, Miranda thought as she remembered Denver Styles's intense gray eyes, determined set of chin, and general aura that when he set out to do something, it got done.

Well, not this time.

Claire's hands shook as she poured herself a cup of coffee. What had she been thinking? Kissing Kane Moran. Touching him. Letting him touch her. Even now, in the kitchen, with the morning sunlight streaming through the windows, she tingled between her legs when she thought of his hands, mouth, and tongue and the wonderful ministrations that had turned her inside out. She'd nearly made love to him. As if all the years, all the lies, all the pain didn't exist.

As if he wasn't Sean's father.

For the love of God, what was she going to do?

"You're a fool," she muttered under her breath as she poured pancake flour into a mixing bowl. Cracking two eggs with a vengeance and adding milk, she tried to concentrate on the task at hand rather than the wickedly delicious sensations Kane had created in her body.

It had been a long time since she'd been with a man. Years. She'd probably just reacted out of desperation, nothing more. As she stirred the pancake batter, she stared out the window and across the lake to Kane's cabin. She had to forget what they had once shared—because he was a changed man, a man with a vendetta against her family.

Don't trust him. He's only using you to get information for his damned book. Remember that.

And yet her body still tingled at the memories.

Pouring batter onto the hot griddle, she heard Samantha's light tread on the stairs. If Paul hadn't done anything else right in his miserable life, at least he'd blessed her with their daughter.

Sam burst into the room. Already dressed in her swimsuit and slathered with tanning oil, she carried a beach basket which she plopped onto the counter. "Where's Sean?"

"Asleep, I think. Why don't you wake him up and tell him breakfast's about ready?"

"He's not in his bed. I already checked."

"No?" That was odd. Sean was known to sleep until two in the afternoon. "Maybe he went horseback riding," she said, though her heart was suddenly heavy.

Sam pulled a face. "He hates horses. He's into computer games and skateboarding."

That much was true, and through the French doors Claire saw all three horses, heads lowered to the ground as they plucked at a few blades of grass and switched their ears and tails against bothersome flies.

"Then a hike."

"Early in the morning? With who?"

"Whom," Claire responded out of habit.

"Okay, whom? He doesn't have any friends up here. He's always e-mailing or instant-messaging kids back in Colorado."

"He'll make some new friends when school starts."

Sam rolled her eyes. "Sure—oh, Mom, the pancakes?"

Smoke was rolling from the griddle, and Claire tossed the first batch of burned hotcakes into the disposal. "Why don't you take over for a second?" she asked her daughter. "I'll track down Sean."

"Sure."

She had already opened the door when she saw a Jeep wheel into the drive. Her heart sank. Kane was driving and Sean, jaw jutted forward rebelliously, eyes downcast, sat in the passenger seat. She could barely move for a second. Couldn't Kane see it—how much Sean resembled him? Straight nose, blade-thin lips, broad shoulders, and bad attitude, all rolled up into a hellion of a boy. Though Sean had yet to develop into the lawless, arrogant son of a gun Kane had been, he was on the right track. Her fingers were suddenly sweaty and she felt as if the earth was shifting beneath her feet. How could she tell either of them? Sean would condemn her for her loose morals. Not only had she sheltered him from the truth, but she'd lied as well. He'd never forgive her.

Nor would Kane. When he discovered that Sean was his natural son, what would he do? Demand custody? Call her a cheap tramp? Or open his arms and heart to his son? She cleared her throat of all emotion and tried to concentrate on the problem at hand. "What in the world—?"

Before the Jeep had come to a full stop, Sean bolted from the vehicle and strode toward the front door. He wore black jeans and a ripped black T-shirt along with a pair of dilapidated running shoes. Claire met him on the porch. "What's going on?" she asked. "Where've you been?"

"In town." He tried to brush past her, but she caught hold of his arm. His nostrils flared and he jerked away.

"What happened?" From the corner of her eye she saw Kane approach at a leisurely pace, as if willing to let her grill her son before being part of the argument that was brewing in Sean's stormy eyes. Battered leather jacket, white T-shirt, disreputable jeans and boots in sore need of polish were his companions and only served to remind Claire of the boy he'd once been, the hoodlum to whom she'd lost her heart sixteen years before. She'd been such a simpleton, such a stupid romantic.

Right now she had to deal with her boy. "Sean?"

"I got in trouble, okay?" Sean started for the door again, but Claire planted herself in his path.

"What kind of trouble?" she asked, her heart pounding. Sean was so volatile these days, always on the edge, ready to explode. "And no, it's definitely not okay."

"It's no big deal." He shot a look at Kane, then rolled his eyes and swore under his breath. "Oh, hell, I got caught shoplifting."

"Shoplifting." She froze. Stealing? This was worse than anything he'd done in Colorado—well, worse than anything she knew about. She turned to Kane and hoped she'd get the straight story. "What happened?"

Sean shifted from one foot to the other and chewed on a thumbnail that hardly existed as it was.

Leaning against one of the rough-finished posts supporting the roof, Kane crossed his arms on his chest. With a nod to Sean, he said, "I think you'd better fill your mother in on all the details."

"Who cares what you think?" Sean shot back, his words spiced with hate.

"Sean!" Claire pointed a finger at her son's chest, and one of the horses nickered softly. "Don't be rude. Let's just get to the bottom of this."

"I tried to jack a pack of smokes."

"Cigarettes? You were shoplifting cigarettes?" Her heart sank. They'd been in town less than two weeks, and already Sean was looking for and finding trouble. Big trouble.

"Yeah and a bottle of Thunderbird."

"Thunderbird?"

"Wine," Kane supplied and received a "drop dead" stare from Sean.

"Oh, God, now what?"

Sean nodded toward Kane. "He caught me. Made me put everything back and apologize to the store owner." Sean's face was a deep shade of purple, his gaze still stonily rebellious, cast to the floor-boards.

"Chinook's a small town," Kane explained. "Everybody's got his nose in everybody else's business. You don't want to get yourself a reputation, 'cause it's hell to live down. Trust me, I know."

"What? You were some kind of crook or somethin'?" Sean asked.

"Or somethin'." Kane's eyes found Claire's, and in the short span of a heartbeat she remembered him as he was, the roughneck of a boy with a crippled father. Always in trouble. Always outrunning the law. Smoking cigarettes, drinking beer, and riding his motorcycle hell-bent for leather. And she'd loved him. With all her fickle heart. Now, as she looked into his golden eyes, she experienced the same rush of adrenaline that she'd always felt around him, the acceleration of her heartbeat, the sudden shortness of her breath. All the might-have-beens chased through her mind.

"I can't believe you did this," she said to her son.

"I didn't take anything!"

"Because you got caught."

"So?"

"So you're grounded. For two weeks."

"Big effin' deal," he muttered. "There's nothin' to do in this place anyway. Who gives a shit?"

"Don't—"

Angry and embarrassed, he flung open the door and strode inside. Claire wanted to collapse on the front steps. At times like this one, she regretted not having a husband to count on, a man to back her up in her decisions.

"He's angry," Kane observed, his eyes finding hers.

She swallowed hard. "About a lot of things."

"Including his father?"

She nearly stopped breathing. Seconds slipped by, counted by the rapid beat of her heart. Why hadn't Kane seen the similarities—the resemblance to his own features? "Paul let us all down."

"He was a shit."

She wanted to argue, to tell him it was none of his business, but she couldn't. "He's . . . he's still the kids' father. I don't think it's necessary to put him down."

"Just callin' 'em as I see 'em." Kane's smile, enigmatic and crooked, touched her heart. "Tell me about Sean."

She licked her lips. *He's asking, so tell him the truth. Tell him he's a father!*

"You've got your hands full with that one," he observed, his eyebrows slamming together as he glanced at the screen door, where Sean had made his gruff exit.

"He'll be all right."

"Not unless you sit on him hard."

"So now you're Dear Abby?" she asked, slightly irritated and fighting all the conflicting emotions running through her veins. *Tell him,* her mind screamed. *Tell him that he's Sean's father!* And what then? How would he react? And what about Sean? How would her son feel to know that his mother had lied to him for all these years? Her stomach twisted into a raw knot of anxiety and she avoided Kane's eyes, focusing instead upon a bumblebee as it flitted from one rosebush to the next.

"You don't want any advice about your kid?"

"No." She reached for the door handle. "Sean's having a tough time, not only dealing with all he knows about his father, but also about the move here. He left a lot of friends and . . ." Her heart squeezed as she thought that she might be messing with her son's life. ". . . and living here is an adjustment."

"It's not so bad, though," he said softly, and, for a second, as he gazed into her eyes, she expected him to reach forward and touch the side of her face with those callused fingers. "You and I made it."

"Did we?" she wondered aloud, then cleared her throat. Every time she was around this man the clarity in her mind suddenly clouded, and the atmosphere seemed to change, to become more dense and sticky. She licked her lips.

"Yes."

Swallowing hard, she yanked on the screen door. "Thanks for saving Sean's skin," she said. "I appreciate—oh!"

The flat of his hand slapped the door shut. Bam! In a second he stepped closer, so that his body nearly touched hers. The toes of his boots were a hairbreadth from her own sandals, his chest was only inches from hers and his face was close enough that she could see the striations of color in his eyes, feel the heat and hostility radiating from his body. "I came by for another reason."

"And . . . and that is?" she whispered, her skin alive at his nearness, her pulse leaping in her throat.

"To apologize for last night."

"You don't have to."

"You took off like a scared rabbit."

"I—I didn't know what to think . . . to do," she admitted even though her blood was already racing, her throat tight, her breathing shallow.

"Sure you did," he cajoled and he placed his other hand on the door as well, trapping her head between his arms, keeping her pressed against the door by the nearness of his body. He was lean and muscular and tough. No longer was there a trace of any boyhood in his features, no longer was there any part of him that was soft with youth. His lips curved down and he sighed as if about to admit his darkest secrets. "I can't stay away from you, Claire," he said. "I told myself when I took on this project that I'd keep my distance, reminded myself that what we had a long time ago was gone, but I just can't seem to convince myself."

She swallowed hard, and he watched the movement of her throat.

"Christ, you're beautiful." With a finger he captured a curl that had fallen over her face. Her skin, when his fingertip touched it, nearly sizzled. "Too damned beautiful."

She wanted to melt into his arms. Over the thudding of her heart and the rush of blood in her ears, she heard her daughter, yelling from the kitchen.

"Mom! Mom! The pancakes are done."

She shoved one of his hands away. "Look, I've got to go . . . but . . ." *Don't say it, Claire. Don't invite him in. For all you know he could be using you, trying to weasel information out of you for his damned book. He's dangerous!* ". . . if you haven't had breakfast yet . . ."

"Is this an invitation?" His smile was so sincere it nearly broke her heart.

"Yes."

He glanced into the interior of the house, to the foyer where the mutilated railing of the stairs was still visible. "I think I'd better pass this time. You've got a lot to work out with your kids."

Disappointment shrouded her insides, but she forced a smile. "Another time."

"I'd like that." He shoved away from the door and turned away quickly, as if afraid to second-guess himself. Claire sagged against the exterior wall and caught her breath. What was wrong with her? Certainly he was a lover from her past, one she'd buried deep in her heart, but that was years ago. A lifetime.

"He's a prick!" Sean's voice filtered through the screen as he bounded down the stairs.

"Wait a minute. Don't talk like that."

"He is. I saw the way he looked at you. He just wants . . . well, you know."

She opened the screen door and found her son, freshly scrubbed from a shower, hair wet, clean shorts and T-shirt, standing on the bottom step of the staircase and towering over her. He'd grown so fast and he looked so much like Kane. Why neither one had noticed, she couldn't fathom. But, for the time being, it was a blessing.

"I don't trust him," Sean said, glaring through the mesh of the screen. "Not half as far as I could throw him."

He was waiting for her. The minute Miranda drove into the garage of her row house in Lake Oswego, Denver Styles climbed out of a rental car he'd parked across the street.

Great, Miranda thought, *just what I need.* Grabbing her briefcase and purse, she locked her car and pressed a button to close the garage door. Not that it mattered. By the time she walked up the five steps to the living room level, he was at the front door, leaning on the bell.

"Determined son of a gun," she said, tossing her briefcase and purse onto a chair in the kitchen before walking to the foyer and opening the door. "What is it?"

"We need to talk."

"There's nothing to discuss."

He arched a serious black eyebrow. "I think so."

"I said everything to you I needed to when we met with my father. I don't know why he's obsessed with the idea that any one of my sisters or I had anything to do with Harley Taggert's death."

"Because he halted the investigation himself and he knows that Kane Moran won't give up until he finds out the truth."

"The truth is that we were at the drive-in and—"

"And I would think you'd want to know what happened to Hunter Riley."

Her knees nearly gave way. "Hunter?"

"You were involved with him."

Sixteen years were suddenly stripped away and she was eighteen again, running along the beach, holding Hunter's hand, meeting him at the cottage, making love to him until the wee hours of the night. Her heart nearly collapsed on itself. "Hunter . . . Hunter was my friend."

"Who left you."

"He took a job in Canada."

"Did he?" Styles's eyes, gray and harsh, didn't flinch. His lips compressed. "He never made it to the logging camp."

She held on to the wall for support. "But Weston Taggert told me—he showed me employment records."

"And you believed him?" Styles shoved his hands into the back pocket of his jeans. "From what I understand there was no love lost between your family and the Taggerts."

"Can't argue with that," she admitted, hardly finding her voice. What was he suggesting? That Hunter had lied to her? To everyone? That he skipped out because she was pregnant? An old pain, raw as if it were brand new, sliced through her heart and nearly drove her to her knees.

"Except for your sister Claire. She was engaged to Harley."

"But she broke it off that night," Miranda said, scrabbling to grab onto the rags of her composure. She couldn't slip, couldn't allow Denver Styles to find a chink in the armor that was her alibi.

"That's right." He looked past her into the house. "Why don't you invite me in?" he suggested. "I think we have a lot to discuss."

Tessa was back. And looking better than she had the last time he'd seen her. With shaking hands, Weston lit a cigarette and walked out to the back deck, where Kendall insisted he smoke. Why he put up with his wife, he didn't know. Maybe because she had a certain class to her, maybe because he knew she'd take him to the cleaners if he ever made noise about divorce, or maybe because she turned her head and allowed him his little dalliances. She was nothing if not loyal, his wife.

He leaned against the rail and looked out to sea. A fishing trawler was moving slowly along the horizon, and a few hazy clouds deigned to hide the sun. From this monstrosity of a house on the hill, he could look over the town of Chinook and feel as if he were the king.

The house was Kendall's idea. Glass, cedar, brick, and tile, it curved along the face of the cliff and glinted in the reflection of the sunset. The largest and most ostentatious house on the northern coast, it fit him and his passion for building his own empire. He hadn't been content to run his father's businesses. No, when he took over, he'd pushed for expansion and now there were three more resorts on the coast, an interest in a casino on tribal lands to the south, and two more sawmills in western Washington. And each time he outbid Dutch Holland for another scrap of land, each time he raised a bronze sign for Taggert Industries over another development or building, each time he heard that Dutch's interests were dwindling, he felt a moment's satisfaction. *Take that you old bastard. That's what you get for fucking my mother.*

"You're home early." Kendall's voice surprised him, and he turned to find her, as was her custom, balancing a pitcher of martinis and two glasses on a slim tray. She placed the tray on the table under the oversize umbrella and poured them each a glass.

"I'm meeting someone tonight."

"Here?" Kendall was surprised.

"No." He never discussed business with her, and she never asked. It was their own unwritten agreement.

"Paige was going to stop by."

The thought of his sister turned his stomach. She was still a pathetic, overweight, sneaky bitch. And she hated him. She'd never even tried to hide her animosity. Weston's back teeth clenched as he took the drink from Kendall's slim fingers. She was a beautiful woman with her pale hair and big blue eyes. She kept herself in shape, hadn't gained a pound in all the years that they'd been married, and dressed with flair. Even after Stephanie had been born, Kendall had been careful, losing the few pounds she'd gained, refusing to breast-feed as she was concerned that her breasts would flatten, and exercising with a personal trainer until she was her usual size four. He couldn't complain. Except that she was boring as hell.

Not like the Holland women.

"Isn't Paige taking care of Dad?"

"Not tonight. The caregiver's there. So, I thought we could barbecue and watch a movie." Kendall's slim fingers wrapped over his wrist. "Come on, Weston, you haven't seen much of Stephanie lately."

He felt a tiny prick of guilt. His daughter was special, no doubt about it. Regardless of the fact that his plan for Kendall to trap Harley had worked all too well and she'd ended up pregnant, and that had Harley lived, she would have passed the kid off as his, Weston loved Stephanie. More than he loved anything on the earth. He should have slapped Kendall around when she told him she was pregnant and that since Harley was dead, he would have to step up to the plate and claim his child. He should have insisted that she get an abortion. He should have told her to fuck off. But he hadn't. And the one thing in his life he didn't regret was his kid. The trouble was, Kendall knew it and used it to her advantage.

"I'll see Steph tomorrow. We'll go looking for a car for her," Weston offered.

Kendall laughed. "She's only fifteen."

"Sixteen soon enough." He ground out his cigarette and took a long sip from his martini glass. The drink was always just right. Kendall took special care. He should love her, he supposed, but decided he was incapable. Besides, love and all romantic notions were for idealists and had nothing to do with reality. Weston's feet were firmly planted on the ground.

"But—"

"Don't argue, dear," he warned, and she closed her mouth immediately. Over the course of their marriage there had been a few times when he'd had to get a little rough with her, just a couple of slaps across the buttocks or face when she'd opposed him. Afterward, when she was contrite and willing to prove her love for him, he had come up with intricate sexual maneuvers for her to perform to show just how much she appreciated being Mrs. Weston Taggert.

She'd always been so willing to please. It was strange really. He'd once thought her cold as ice, her pussy tight and impenetrable. He'd learned differently. When she realized that he was her meal ticket, her entrance into the royalty that was the family Taggert, she'd become a hot little love machine, giving eagerly of her favors. No wonder Harley, that wimp, had never been able to break it off with her. But outside the bedroom, she bored him.

"Just don't disappoint Stephanie tomorrow," she said and Weston clinked his glass to hers.

"I won't. Promise." But that was tomorrow. First he had to get through the rest of the evening. Tonight he was going to meet with Denver Styles and offer Dutch Holland's newest employee a deal too sweet to pass up.

He sipped his martini slowly and grinned.

CHAPTER 26

"So you didn't get any correspondence from Riley at all. No phone calls. Nothing?" Denver, seated in one of the cane-backed chairs that surrounded Miranda's small kitchen table, was settled low on his back, the heel of one boot hooked over the base of another chair. Throughout their conversation, he regarded her with eyes as sharp as an eagle's, eyes that missed nothing, eyes that made her want to squirm away. But she wouldn't. She'd faced murderers, rapists, wife beaters, and worked hard to put them behind bars. She'd been cool against big-league defense lawyers and even survived Ronnie Klug's knife attack. She'd even managed to lie and put that God-awful night sixteen years ago to rest. As intimidating as Styles was, he still couldn't get to her.

"I didn't hear from Hunter. No letters, no phone calls. Nothing." Sunlight streamed through the bay windows, warming Miranda's back. The Metro section of this morning's copy of *The Oregonian* was lying open by a basket of fruit. Styles's beat-up jacket was tossed carelessly over the back of another chair and looked as if it belonged there.

Coffee, unwanted by either of them, cooled in ceramic mugs and scented the air. Styles's cell phone chirped. He ignored it.

"Didn't you think that was odd?"

"Yes, but . . . I assumed it was because of the charges that were going to be brought against him."

"Statutory rape and grand theft auto?" he asked, obviously having done his homework.

"Yeah."

"No charges were ever filed."

"I know, but I thought it was because he left the country."

"There are extradition proceedings, you know."

Of course she knew. Now. But at the time she'd been much younger, less knowledgeable about the law, and hurt, wounded that Hunter had betrayed her and been involved with someone else. When he'd never contacted her it had been easier to close her eyes and turn her head, believe the worst. Besides, by that time, it didn't matter. Not really. The baby was already gone. And somehow she'd survived those dark, debilitating nights.

That old pain, the one she'd tried so desperately to lock away, stole past her defenses to grab hold of her heart and twist mightily, squeezing until she could barely breathe. Dear God in heaven how she'd wanted that child, needed that special part of Hunter he'd left with her.

"I was young," she admitted, fiddling with her coffee mug. "And scared."

"And pregnant."

The word seemed to echo through the room like the reverberations of a chapel bell, resounding through her heart.

"Yes." There was no reason to lie; he knew too much already. Dry-eyed, she stared him down and refused to let him see the pain that was still with her after all these years. "Not that it's anyone's business."

A flicker of tenderness and understanding passed through his harsh eyes, but it quickly vanished, and she wondered if she'd imagined it. Styles wasn't the empathetic type. "Just doing my job."

"Digging up the dirt on people. Great job."

One dark brow quirked upward. "Not unlike yours, counselor."

"I'm always looking for the truth."

"So am I." He took a swallow of tepid coffee and set the mug onto the table again. His voice softened when he asked, "So what happened to the baby?"

Closing her eyes, she said, "It's not something I want to discuss." Oh God, the pain. Losing the child, losing a part of Hunter. And because . . . because . . . She felt as if she might be sick.

"I know."

"You couldn't," she whispered. "No one could."

"All right, no more platitudes." He looked so deeply into her eyes she was certain he could see past her pain, past her lies, to the truth. The seconds ticked by in silence and finally Miranda opened her eyes. What did it matter what he knew? "I lost it."

"When?"

"The night that I lost control of the car and it ended up in Lake Arrowhead. I'm sure you've seen the hospital reports. There must've been some mention of a miscarriage." Not many people had known. She'd been eighteen at the time, and so her parents were never told that she'd been pregnant and was suffering the loss of her baby. Miranda had been well enough versed in the law to know that she had rights and that patient-doctor confidentiality wasn't to be compromised.

If her father had ever found out, he'd never mentioned it, and so the subject had been avoided. But somehow Denver Styles had come up with the information. How? She rubbed her arms against a sudden chill.

"How did you link up with Dad?" she asked, wondering about him. An interesting, but threatening man, one who had no past. If Petrillo couldn't find anything on him, no one could.

"He came looking for me."

"And how did he find you?" she asked. "Somehow I don't think you're listed on the Internet."

The ghost of a smile touched his lips and his gray eyes sparked for a heartbeat. "Through a mutual acquaintance." He finished his coffee and reached for his jacket. "But we're not here to talk about me, remember?"

"How could I forget?"

He leaned closer to her. "You know, Miranda, you're a smart woman. Clever. But not quite as clever sixteen years ago. Personally, I think the story you've peddled to the sheriff's department about the night that Taggert was killed is bullshit. I think you and your sisters made some sort of pact that you'd be each other's alibis, and I think, whether you want to face the truth or not, the whole damned thing is going to blow up in your face. Now you could tell me the truth, and I could keep it between me, you, and your old man. Or else Kane Moran or your father's political enemies will grab hold of it and it'll be the biggest scandal that's ever hit good old Chinook, Oregon. Your job will be on the line. Tessa could end up needing more than a personal shrink, and Claire will think that little scandal with her husband in Colorado was just a teeny ripple in her life compared to the waterfall that's going to sweep over her when all this comes out."

"You're wrong," she insisted, anger surging through her, but his words scared her spitless. "And if you're finished, I don't think we have anything else to discuss."

He scraped his chair back. "You'll change your mind."

"Nothing to change it to."

"We'll see." He snagged his jacket from the back of the nearby chair, reached into the pocket, and dropped a business card for a motel in Chinook, the Tradewinds, onto the table. "Room twenty-five if you want to talk to me. My cell phone number is—"

"Don't hold your breath." She didn't bother picking up the white card. The less she knew of him, the better. For the first time in her life, she wasn't eager for the truth, didn't know how she could face it.

He slung his jacket over one shoulder, and touched her lightly on the back of the neck with his free hand. "Think about it, Miranda," he said softly as her skin heated beneath his fingertips. "I'll show myself out."

As she heard his footsteps retreat, her skin still was warm where he'd touched her. A second later the latch of the front door opened, then softly closed again. He was gone. She let out her breath and sighed. It was all falling apart. All the lies that she'd so carefully fabricated. Biting her lower lip, she dropped her forehead into her hands. "God help me," she whispered because she knew the end was near. Come hell or high water, Denver Styles wouldn't rest until his job was done.

Tessa felt the breath of salty breeze against her face and wished she could find some peace of mind, the kind that was supposed to come when a person stared out at the vastness of the ocean, the serenity that people felt just walking on the sand, but as she ambled along the edge of the sea, feeling the frothy tide nibbling at her toes only to ebb away again, she only felt restless and distracted.

She should never have come back to Oregon, should have stayed away, but one of her shrinks, the bald one with the red beard—Doctor Terry, was his name—had told her she would have to face her demons someday. She'd have to return to this hellhole of a spot in Oregon and confront those who had used and abused her.

The sand was squishy under her feet, and here and there she spied round razor clam holes or the soft spoonlike impressions indicating a crab was just below the surface. Kelp and broken sand dollars, the shells of eviscerated crabs and clams and pieces of clear jellyfish littered the white sand of the beach that curved close to Stone Illahee, where Tessa was now living in a private suite. Complete with Jacuzzi, sauna, two king-size beds and a spectacular view of the ocean, the suite was hers for as long as she needed it. Dutch wanted her to be comfortable.

"Thanks a lot, Dad," she said, picking up her pace to a slow jog. She'd come back to Oregon with a single purpose in mind and now as she splashed along the edge of the sand, she couldn't help but savor her own sweet revenge. She'd waited sixteen years, hoping that the need to get back at those who had wronged her would disappear with years of counseling. But she'd been wrong. As long as she was in California, away from her sisters and the memories of that one hellish, pain-riddled night, she'd been able to push all thoughts of vengeance aside, but now that she was back in Oregon, faced with all the torments of her youth, she could only think of one thing. She needed to get a little of hers back, and those who had hurt her would pay. Big-time.

From the attic over the garage where she and Samantha were refurbishing the studio, Claire heard the sound of a motorcycle engine. She poked her head out the window and her heart clutched.

Astride a huge black Harley-Davidson, Kane Moran wheeled down the drive. Reflective aviator glasses shaded his eyes, dusty jeans and his battle-scarred leather jacket covered his body. Old memories of riding with the wind racing through her hair, her arms wrapped around Kane's leather-draped torso, the smell of leather and smoke drifting to her nostrils assailed her. She thought of the days of longing for him and the nights wanting nothing more than to hold him close.

His hair was burnished by the sun's final rays this late afternoon, and she couldn't help but remember how much she'd loved him, how much she'd cared. "Oh, God," she whispered.

"What? What is it?" Samantha demanded while standing on her tiptoes and peering over her mother's shoulder. "Oh, wow!" she said on the heels of a gasp.

Sean had been shooting hoops at the old backboard he'd mounted over the third bay of the garage, but at the sound and sight of the motorcycle, he'd stopped, tucked his basketball between his wrist and hip, and stared in awe as Kane slowed the bike to park not five feet from him.

"Is this yours?" Sean asked as Kane climbed off the bike.

"As of today."

Unaware his mother was watching, Sean let out a long, low whistle of appreciation. "Holy shit."

"Sean!" Claire said from the window.

"But Mom, look, a Harley!"

Harley. This was all about him.

"Big deal," Samantha muttered under her breath.

Kane wiped his face with the back of his hand. "Like it?"

"Like it?" Sean repeated. "What's not to like?"

"Want a ride?"

"You mean like I get to drive it?"

"Wait a minute!" Claire dashed across the room and hurried down the stairs. She was through the garage and outside within seconds. Samantha was right on her heels. "Sean doesn't have a driver's license or even a permit in Oregon."

"Aw, Mom, come on." Sean dribbled the ball, but his eyes never left the big shiny bike.

"No way. Don't you have to have a special license to drive one of these?"

"Legally," Kane agreed, balancing the machine between his legs.

"I'm only interested in legally."

"But, Mom—"

"Sean, please." She shot Kane a look that could cut through steel and saw again the resemblance between father and son. The square jaw, thick eyebrows, long straight nose. How could they not?

"I'll tell you what, hop on and I'll give you a ride," Kane said to the boy he didn't know was his son. He reached behind him to find a helmet and tossed it to Sean, who caught the headgear and let his basketball drop. The neglected orange ball bounced toward the garage.

"What about me?" Samantha asked.

"You're next," Kane promised, and Claire had the distinct feeling that she was being manipulated.

Sean walked around the machine, his eyes taking in every detail of the shiny bike. "This is really kickin'!"

"Come on." Kane cocked his head toward the boy, and Sean needed no more encouragement. Despite his earlier vows to hate "the prick," he climbed on the bike behind Kane, strapped the helmet in place, then, rather than circle Kane's waist with his arms, grabbed hold of the belt that wrapped around the long seat.

Kane revved the engine, and the bike flew forward.

"Be careful," Claire called, but it was only to the wind as the motorcycle raced forward, winding through three gears before they hit the first corner and disappeared through the trees.

"I thought Sean hated that guy," Samantha observed as she tossed her hair off her shoulders.

"So did I."

"One look at the motorcycle and he changed his mind." Sam shook her head. "Men," she muttered under her breath.

"Amen," her mother agreed. Far in the distance they heard the motorcycle whining through the gears again, and Claire felt the weight of the moment. Father and son were together alone. Though neither understood the heart-wrenching significance of their solitary ride, Claire felt the sting of tears behind her eyes. Her throat clogged, and she blinked rather than break down in front of Samantha. Somehow, some way, she had to find the words to tell Kane the truth, that he was a father, but she couldn't bear to ruin everything just yet. Too many emotions, too many hearts were at stake. When he found out, Kane would surely hate her for her lies, for passing off his son as another man's child, for never mentioning to anyone, including Sean, that his real father had left her for the army and gone on to become a semifamous journalist turned writer determined to ruin Sean's grandfather's life. *God help us,* she silently prayed as the sound of the big bike's engine approached. Her hands clenched into fists of frustration as the motorcycle, catching a few last rays of sunlight, rounded the bend to slide to a stop near the garage.

"Your turn," Kane said to Samantha as Sean reluctantly dragged himself from the bike. Though she feigned coolness and seemed unaffected by riding the Harley, Sam couldn't hide the twinkle in her eyes as she strapped on the helmet and they took off.

"Don't know why she needs a ride," Sean grumbled. "She likes horses and dogs and junk."

"Maybe, this'll change her mind."

"Nah!" But he seemed worried and shot free throws until the motorcycle and Sam were back.

"*Awe*some," she said, as she climbed off and dusted her hands.

"That it is."

"We went up to the Illahee Cliffs!"

"Did you?" Claire asked.

Kane twisted his head to the side and his eyes, shaded though they were, found Claire's in a look that caused her breath to stop somewhere in her throat. She had to look away, to distract herself, because his gaze was filled with a sexual promise she couldn't ignore. "How about you?" Kane asked in a husky voice that caused goose bumps to rise on her skin.

She hesitated a second before Sam said, "Go on, Mom. Have a little fun."

"I don't know—"

"I'm next," Sean insisted.

"Next time," Kane told him.

Claire, knowing she was flirting with emotional danger, couldn't resist. Though she realized she was making a big mistake and remembered her response when they were alone on the dock in the middle of the night, she felt compelled to be with him again. Alone with him as the wind raced past and the coming night flew by. She swung a leg over the back of the cycle, wrapped her arms around

Kane's waist, and felt a surge of power as the bike took off down the driveway.

In the paddock the painted gelding let out a high-pitched whistle and, tail aloft, ran to the far gate. Fir trees covered with moss and ivy sped by in a blur, and Claire rested her head between Kane's shoulders as she had as a teenager. *Be careful,* an annoying inner voice warned, but she lost herself in the feel of his muscles moving as he shifted through the gears. Her heart thudded deep in her chest, and she sensed the tension in his body as she clung to him.

God, it was good to hold him and for a few glorious minutes she forgot the past, ignored the fact that they could never be lovers again. As the sun hovered just above the horizon, she let her fertile mind conjure scenes of kissing him and touching him, and making love to him over and over again.

A wet breeze rolled in off the ocean, mussing Weston's hair as he waited on the deck of his pride and joy, the *Stephanie,* a racing yacht he'd bought for himself just this past year. He glanced at his watch. Eight-fifteen and no sign of Denver Styles. Shit, the guy was probably going to stand him up. Who was the bastard, and why had Dutch Holland hired him? For what purpose? Dutch always had a reason. But what was it?

Reaching into the pocket of his jacket, Weston found his pack of Marlboros and lit up.

Who the hell was Styles, a man on whom there seemed to be no record whatsoever? It was as if the guy had appeared out of thin air. And to do what? Christ, it was maddening.

He flicked ash into the water and watched the sun inch its way into the Pacific. For the past few years Weston had enjoyed hiring Dutch's key employees away from him. Better yet, a few of Dutch's men were still employed with Holland International, still kissing up to old Dutch, but were secretly on the take and reporting everything that went on at the company headquarters in Portland to Weston. No one knew a thing about Denver Styles, so Weston decided it had something to do with Dutch's bid for the governorship. Or maybe that nasty little book Kane Moran was writing. The book bothered Weston. Though he liked the idea of an exposé of sorts, spilling all the dirty little Holland secrets, this one might just backfire. Too many of the Taggert skeletons were locked in the same closets as those belonging to the Hollands. Too many of Weston's own personal evils might be unearthed.

"Son of a bitch," he muttered, glancing up the dock to the parking lot of the marina. Where the hell was Styles?

His cell phone rang, and he flicked the butt of his cigarette over the side of the railing before walking back to the main cabin.

"Weston Taggert," he said curtly, checking his watch again. Was this Styles giving him the brush-off?

"Well, Weston, how're you doing?" a sexy female voice asked. Weston's heart nearly stopped. He should recognize the woman, but there had been so many over the years. From the sultry tone of his caller, though, he should be able to conjure up her face.

"Who's calling?"

"Don't you remember me?"

"Should I?" Anxiety began to nip at his brain.

"Mmmm. I think so."

Christ, who was it? The bitch was getting to him. "I'm not into playing games."

"Aren't you? That's not the way I remember it. Oh, Weston, don't tell me you've changed now that you've become an honest, upstanding family man."

Who? Who? Who? A dozen faces flashed before his eyes and were quickly discarded. "Who is this?" he demanded.

"You don't remember?" she asked as if disappointed. Weston sensed she was only toying with him. "I'm sooo hurt." A breathy sigh rushed over the wires, and then she hung up.

"Wait!"

But she was gone. He stared at the phone for more than a minute, willing for her to call back, but she didn't, and as he thought about the conversation he began to put two and two together. It was someone from his past, someone he'd been involved with before he'd taken a wife and started a family. Shit, the list was still long.

He heard the sound of footsteps on the dock and looked out a porthole to spy Denver Styles walking toward the *Stephanie*. Though unnerved by the caller, he managed to drag his thoughts back to the present problem with Dutch Holland.

Holland. That was it! His lips curved into a hard grin. The woman on the phone had been involved with him before, involved to her pretty eyes. "Just you wait," he said under his breath and started planning a way to see Tessa Holland again. She'd been a hot little virgin sixteen years ago. Now, with a little age and maturity, she was probably even more of a hot-blooded woman. He grinned. She had nerve, to call him up and tease him like some twenty-dollar whore. Well, he'd play her little game, whatever it was. His groin tightened at the thought.

So she thought she had him at a disadvantage, did she? Wouldn't she be surprised? The tables were about to turn on Dutch's youngest daughter. Weston couldn't wait.

CHAPTER 27

The sun was setting in a blaze of peach and amber, high clouds reflecting the brilliant colors and tossing them back to the sea. Claire told herself that he was using her, getting close to her because of his damned book, but she couldn't resist the feeling that she was falling in love with him all over again. That notion was silly, she knew, but it was a quiet little fantasy that was hers alone—one she didn't dare examine too closely.

On the far side of Chinook, past the Taggert sawmill, Kane angled the bike inland, driving north along the county road that led back to Lake Arrowhead. Instead of turning back toward the lodge, he pushed the bike onward, ever faster, the asphalt beneath the Harley's tires slipping away.

"Where are we going?" she called loudly, but her words were stripped away by the wind.

"You'll see."

She laughed for a second, lighthearted, before she realized what was happening. Dear God, no! Her heart sank and she shuddered slightly when she felt the bike slow and saw the stand of oak and fir give way. He turned off the road, onto the sandy banks of Lake Arrowhead, the beam of the cycle's headlight bobbing through the long grass to land upon the still waters of the lake, dark and glassy and forbidding.

A shudder slid down her spine. She couldn't be here, not in the very spot where Miranda had driven off the road and into the lake sixteen years ago. Claire's arms slackened around him. Her stomach kicked over, and she didn't know how she could find the strength to face the questions he was sure to ask her.

The bike flew over a final short dune before skidding to a stop, throwing sand in its wake. Kane cut the engine. His voice was still low, but instead of teasing, it was deadly serious. "I think we need to talk."

"You tricked me," she said, releasing him and sliding off the motorcycle. In her mind's eye she saw herself and her sisters in the interior of Miranda's Camaro, black, frigid water swirling around them, panic banging through her body. She couldn't breathe, couldn't think. She rubbed her arms as if cold to the marrow of her bones when the summer night was still warm. "You brought me here on purpose," she said, all her dreams crumbling before her eyes.

He didn't bother denying it. "Guilty as charged." He slid his sunglasses off his nose and she was staring into gold eyes that didn't look away—just stared at her as if he could see into her soul.

She was having none of it. "Why?"

"I think it's time for everyone to come clean about that night." He got off the bike and walked toward her, but she backed up to the far side of the dune and an outcropping of rocks and brush.

She didn't want to be close to him. She was afraid of how she would respond if he touched her. "If you think I'm going to come up with some confession, or some kind of alternative story to what I've told the police, you've got another think coming."

"Claire—" He was so close. Too close.

"For the love of God, Kane, I've told you and the whole world over and over again what happened that night! Check the police reports." She stumbled on a rock and nearly fell to her knees, but he caught her, one large hand around her arm and holding her upright.

"I have."

"And the newspaper accounts."

"Them, too." He didn't let go of her, and his hand where he touched her burned through her sleeve.

She stood stock still. "Then ask anyone who was here or was with Harley that night."

"I'm asking you." His fingers tightened possessively. An unwanted thrill skittered down her spine.

"So that I'll tell you something else that you can use to print and destroy my family?"

"Harley Taggert died. We owe it to him to—"

"You didn't care about him at all. That's what's so crazy about all this," she said, her heart pumping wildly, her flesh suddenly on fire as his fingers rubbed the inside of her arm. Why wouldn't he let her be, accept her lies, drop his warm hand, and take her home? Before she said something that would hurt her family. Before she blurted out that Sean was his son.

"I cared about *you*."

"Oh, God." His confession seemed to fill the evening. As the first stars began to blink and twilight swirled around them, she fought the urge to tilt her face up and kiss him, to tell him that she'd never stopped loving him, that if not for fate, she would have waited for him forever.

"You're carrying around a burden that you shouldn't."

"I—I think we should let Harley rest in peace."

"Is that what you want, Claire? For me to back off?"

"Yes," she said, but her throat closed.

"Liar."

"No, I—"

"That's the problem, don't you know? You've always been a lousy liar."

If you only knew. Oh, Kane we have a son. A wonderful boy, one to be proud of and . . .

He tugged on her arm, dragging her closer to him, and as she felt heat spread through her limbs, his strong arms surrounded her, wrapping around her body as if she were the only woman on earth and he the only man.

"Kane, I don't think—oh."

His lips found hers in a kiss that was hot and fierce and hungry.

Her knees threatened to give way.

"Claire," he whispered, his voice cracking over her name. "Sweet, sweet Claire."

She closed her eyes and told herself to fight him, to push him away, that getting close to him was playing with fire, but as his kiss deepened and his tongue forced its way past her teeth, she melted inside, and all the reasons to deny him fled. She opened to him, like a flower to the sun, wanting more, feeling her breasts fill with a need to be touched and stroked and loved. Desire curled lazily inside her, stretching and moving, heating her blood and causing a moist warmth to form deep in the center of her womanhood—a warm ache that she hadn't felt in years. She wanted him. How she wanted him. She wrapped her arms around his neck and let his weight push them to the ground.

He buried his face between her breasts, his mouth open, his tongue stroking her blouse, the fabric wet as he reached behind her and pulled her buttocks closer so that she fit against him, felt the firm rod of his erection through his jeans press against her, knew he wanted her as much as she wanted him.

His fingers were at the buttons of her blouse, opening it quickly while she breathed in shallow gasps against his neck. He skimmed her bra, brushing the lace with his fingertips before yanking hard on the cup so that one breast, nipple erect, was free. His breath was warm and moist, and she curved against him, cradling his head, allowing him to kiss and tease the hard little bud, his teeth and tongue exploring and causing wanton ripples of need to whisper through her body.

He sucked noisily, hungrily, and he rolled her atop him so that she was lying on his erection, her mound, though covered by denim, pressed intimately to his arousal. His hands were on her buttocks, curling inward so that the tips of his fingers brushed against the juncture of her legs. She writhed and moaned, he held her fast, stripping her of her blouse and bra, kissing and sucking at her nipples, the stubble of his beard rough against her skin.

Desire raced like wildfire through her veins. The ache within her grew. She rubbed against him, wanting more, knowing somewhere deep in the back of her mind that she was begging for trouble. But she couldn't stop herself. It had been so long . . . so very long. His fingers delved into the waistband of her jeans and slowly undid the zipper. Her breathing was shallow and needy, and he skimmed the jeans away from her body with ease.

Don't, Claire. Don't make this same mistake again.

With a groan he pressed his face into the front of her panties, his breath fanning through the sheer lace to her skin.

"Claire," he murmured into her abdomen. "Are you sure?"

She wasn't sure about anything except that she wanted him. As the blood swirled through her veins, she wanted all of him. "Y-yes. Yes, Kane, yes," she said, as he flicked the panties off her legs, lifted her hips to his shoulders, and buried his face in her most intimate of places.

Her body turned to jelly. She squirmed, feeling his lips and tongue, his hot, sweet breath. She arched against him, her back bowed, his hands caressing her flesh.

"Kane," she cried, her voice unrecognizable.

Stroking her legs with his hands, he kissed her and loved her, his tongue working magic as she moved against him, wanting more, needing so much more.

"That's it, darlin', let yourself go. That's iiiit," he said, the sound muffled, the words dear. She moved against him, unable to stop. The stars and moon swirled overhead, and she felt the earth shift as the first convulsion rocked her. She cried out, her fingers tangling in his hair, her body slick with sweat as spasm after delicious spasm rocked her.

"Kane—Kane!"

"I'm here, Princess," he said, moving upward between her legs, kissing her abdomen and neck before pressing his lips to hers. Tears filled her eyes and he kissed them away. "It's all right, Claire."

"No, I shouldn't—"

"Shh. Just feel good." He nuzzled her neck and fondled her breasts, offering comfort and yet asking for more. She couldn't stop, and though a thousand denials flitted through her brain, and she was still breathing wildly, she slid her fingers beneath his jacket and shirt, peeling off his clothes and feeling him suck in his breath as she touched his nipples and abdomen, tracing the ridges of his muscles. She reached for his fly.

His hand surrounded her wrist. "You don't have to—"

"Shh." She lowered his zipper, pushed the Levi's down his legs, touched him intimately, and felt him groan as she found his thick erection. "I want to," she said, throwing caution to the wind and breathing against him. "I want to."

He groaned and she kissed him, then he was as lost as she, desire mounting as he bucked against her, holding her fast, moving intimately.

"Be careful, Claire, don't—oooh," He shifted suddenly, pushing her onto her back and sliding down so that he was lying atop her, his pulsing arousal pressed deep into her abdomen. "Tell me 'no.'"

"I—I can't."

"This is a mistake."

"Is it?" she asked, looking up at him, seeing the strain on his face, the tension from holding back.

"Oh, God, forgive me." He cupped one cheek with his hand and then swiftly parted her legs with his knees. "I didn't mean for this to happen," he said.

"Of course you did. So . . . so did I."

"Yes." His mouth claimed hers again as he plunged into her with an unleashed and primal lust that caused her bones to melt.

She gasped as he thrust into her. Her stupid heart soared as he withdrew only to thrust again, hard and slow. She couldn't breathe, couldn't think as he kissed her eyes and throat. The stars blurred in her eyes and she caught his tempo. Faster. Faster. Faster. Slick, hot, and wet. Until she knew she'd explode.

"Kane," she cried as she convulsed around him. The moon and earth collided and her soul was flung to the stars as he kissed her hard. "Oh, God, Kane."

With a triumphant yell, he fell upon her, spilling his seed, crushing her breasts, holding her with a desperation that tore at her heart. "Forgive me," he whispered against her skin. "Forgive me."

"For what?"

"Wanting you so much."

"It's not a sin," she said, tears filling her eyes.

"Isn't it?" He rolled off her, but pulled her close, cradling her in his arms, kissing her neck, sighing into her hair.

She froze as his words sank in. Was he using her? Is that what he was trying to say? Her throat was suddenly thick and she wondered what had possessed her, what had caused her to let down her guard and let him get so close to her? "I—I should be going."

"Not yet." Strong arms pinned her to his side.

"But, the kids—"

"—will be fine. Stay just a minute, Claire. Let me hold you."

"Why? So that I'll tell you something about the past that you don't already know? So that I'll change my story?"

"No. Just because I want a little peace in my life." He levered up on one elbow, his naked body stretched close to hers. "Is that so hard to understand?" His gaze, dark with the night, delved deep into hers.

"I—I want to trust you."

"Do."

"But you're trying to ruin my father, my family, everything that I believe in."

"No, darlin'," he drawled, stroking her hair. "I'm just looking for the truth."

"And you believe that the truth can never hurt a person."

"Nope. The truth stings like a bitch sometimes, but it's better than living a lie."

She wondered. But she had lived a lie for so long, she probably wouldn't know the difference. "Really, I've got to get back." She reached for her clothes, but he stopped her, grabbing her wrist with one big hand.

"Just believe that whatever happens, I don't want to hurt you."

"But you will," she said, finally understanding and feeling the cold breath of doom whisper through her heart. This man was driven by unknown forces, and he wouldn't rest, wouldn't give up, until he knew the truth. "You will," she said, reaching for her clothes. "Because you think you have no choice."

"I don't."

"Wrong, Kane. We all have choices." *Yes, and you choose not to tell him the truth about Sean. Now, you've made love to Sean's father again. Oh, Claire. Will you never learn?*

CHAPTER 28

"Looks like your kids are surviving," Kane observed as he watched Claire in the kitchen, where she was pouring them each a caffeine boost. He'd had to pry Sean off the Harley. The kid couldn't stop asking questions about the machine, wanted to ride it over and over, and had only agreed to go upstairs to bed when Kane had promised to bring the motorcycle over at another time and teach him how to ride. At least the boy was warming to him, though there was still distrust in Sean's eyes whenever Kane touched Claire. So the kid was protective of his mother.

"Promoting Sean's riding your bike isn't a good idea," Claire had warned at the time, but Sean was in seventh heaven, and, the way Kane saw it, the kid needed something to look forward to in his life. He obviously missed his friends back in Colorado. The few kids he'd picked up with here in Chinook were borderline punks and hoods. *Like you were.*

"Here," Claire said, handing him a cup of coffee, liquor, and whipped cream. "Let's have these outside."

Together they walked to the porch and sat on the old swing. The sounds of the night closed in on them—a moth flitting against the windows, cars whizzing by on the highway, fish leaping in the lake, a train rattling on far-off tracks, and the muffled throb of a heavy metal CD pounding through Sean's open bedroom window on the second floor.

"You're right. Sean and Sam are surviving here—Sam better than Sean, but he's older, had more friends."

"He'll find his niche here."

"Mmm. Kids are resilient," she said, though, from her expression, he assumed it killed her to think of the pain her children had borne.

"More resilient than you?" He had one arm slung around her shoulders and he rubbed the back of her neck.

She sighed and leaned her head back, exposing the white length of her throat, causing him to get hard all over again. What was it about this woman? One look and he was lost, his blood on fire. It had always been this way, probably always would be.

"More resilient than me? Maybe." She blew across her cup, and he tried not to stare at the way her lips puckered suggestively.

"Tell me about him."

"Who? Oh, Paul?" She wrinkled her nose, then lifted a shoulder. "What do you want to know?"

"How'd you meet him?"

Scowling slightly, she glanced away from him and into the woods. "He was a professor at a community college where I was working on my GED. Divorced from wife number two. I should have been smarter about him, but unfortunately I wasn't." She took a sip from her cup and wondered just how much she could confide. It was time to tell him the truth, that the boy with whom he'd spent the better part of the day was his son, but she couldn't. Not yet. Once he found out that Sean was his child, her life would be thrown into worse turmoil than it already was. So she told him only a few of the essentials, leaving out a lot of the story.

She explained that after Harley's death and Kane's induction into the army, she'd left Chinook and moved to Portland, where she finished high school at the community college. She didn't mention that she was pregnant or that she planned on having the baby alone. If her parents had found out, they would've screamed bloody murder, but she was quiet and neither Dutch, nor Dominique before she divorced Dutch and moved to Paris, had guessed the truth. If they had figured out that she was carrying a child, Claire wouldn't have cared. This child, who she first believed was fathered by Harley, was special to her. The fact that he was so obviously Kane's child, only endeared Sean all the more to her.

"Paul liked being married—liked having a wife cook, clean, take care of his house, and look good when he went to business affairs. He liked the idea of being married to a young girl, especially since my name was Holland and he probably thought I'd inherit a lot of money someday. What he didn't tell me was that his divorces were based on his affairs with young girls, some barely sixteen."

"Great guy," Kane muttered, and took a gulp of his drink.

"Remember, I was just seventeen myself. Marrying him was such an irrational thing to do." But she'd been adrift and frightened. Paul had been an anchor. At least at first. And he pretended her baby was his. They even lied to everyone about Sean's birth date, saying that he was born in July, rather than the end of April. Since Harley had died the previous August, and because Claire was somewhat estranged from her family at the time, no one knew the truth. Her parents hadn't met Sean until he was over a year old, and even he didn't know his true birth date as Claire doctored the birth certificate he used to get into school. "What can I say? It was a mistake."

"And you're finally rid of him."

"Except that he is the kids' father." Well, at least he was Samantha's.

"But you named Sean after Taggert. Sean *Harlan* St. John."

"Another error," she said. Originally, Claire had thought the baby should be named Taggert, but decided that it would be best for her child to have a clean slate in life, and then, as it became clear that the baby was fathered by Kane, she'd been at her wits' end. She'd decided to concentrate on her marriage and try to make it work. Claire did everything Paul asked, though her second pregnancy was unplanned and Paul wasn't thrilled about the thought of having another child to support, even if this one was his. The baby came—a daughter—and he accepted her. Meanwhile Claire managed to juggle her life, going to school, running the kids around and keeping the house clean enough for Paul's white glove inspection. Later, Claire started working as a teacher. She spent more and more hours away from the house and, over time, the marriage crumbled. Claire had grown up, became more independent, and developed a mind of her own. Paul disapproved.

As Sean reached adolescence, Paul became inflexible—he couldn't stand the fact that Sean was in trouble with the law, picked up for vandalism and petty theft. Then there were the girls. Pretty high school girls were throwing themselves at the handsome boy. Eventually Paul's old character flaw, his desire for young girls, raised its ugly head, and he ended up seducing Jessica Stewart, one of Sean's girlfriends. But his liaison blew up in his face when Jessica not only told her parents but the police as well; other girls came forward and Paul was indicted.

"—I didn't divorce him until the charges were filed, even though we'd been separated for a long time, because I thought it was better to stay married. For the kids' sake."

"And now?" Kane prodded, drawing her closer still.

Sighing, she rested her head on his shoulder. "And now I think I would have been smarter to leave him the first time I learned that he was fooling around, about the time Samantha was two. But I was young and utterly dependent upon him. My only other option was to crawl back to my father and beg him to help me out." She looked into the darkening woods and shook her head. "I didn't want to do that. Not ever."

"So you stayed with a man who treated you like dirt."

"No, we separated. I just never found the courage to divorce him until I realized there was absolutely no future with him. Even though I wasn't in love with him, I believed in marriage and that it should last forever." Her smile was bitter. "A romantic fantasy left over from my youth, I guess. Randa always said my romantic streak would be my undoing. Seems like she was right." Troubled, she sipped from her cup, but the coffee had grown cold, the alcohol strong.

"So you didn't love him."

Never. Not like I loved you! "It wasn't about love, Kane. It was about commitment. To him. To the kids. To the family." She let out a brittle little laugh. "He just didn't feel the same. I finally figured that out, and so here I am, divorced, unemployed, trying to raise two headstrong kids." *And lying through my teeth to you. Oh, God,*

Kane if you only knew. If you could guess that Sean is your son, not Paul's. Not Harley's. Yours!

Claire shuddered. All of her secrets were unraveling, as surely as if Kane had found the broken thread of her life and began tugging, her lies were about to be exposed. Either by Kane or Denver Styles. And what then? She couldn't think of the consequences, was grateful that she didn't have a crystal ball to see into the future.

Kane kissed her temple and she bit back a sob. It wasn't fair to fall in love with him again. Not when she was sure that when the truth came to light, he'd hate her for the rest of his days.

"So you're working for Dutch Holland," Weston said, handing Denver Styles a drink, shutting the teak cabinet, then taking a seat on the opposite side of the cabin of the sailboat. He didn't like being alone with Styles and felt restless as a dog one pen away from a bitch in heat. But, unfortunately, right now Weston needed this man.

"That's right."

"Special project?"

"You might say that." Styles sat low on his back in one of the chairs. One booted ankle rested on his opposite knee, his expression bordering on insolence.

Weston tried to shake the feeling that he was being manipulated. First by Tessa on the phone and now by this silent man with his eagle-sharp eyes, black jeans, faded T-shirt, and lightweight jacket that had seen better days. He wore cowboy boots with worn heels and an attitude of arrogance that rankled Weston, rankled him to the marrow of his bones. The guy's nose had been busted more than once from the looks of it, and there were white scars on the tanned skin of his hands, probably from fistfights or knife fights in his younger years. Styles was tough, lean, and, if the confidence that surrounded him was to be believed, knew his own strengths and weaknesses.

A man Weston didn't want against him, at least not until he found out more about the quiet stranger. Somehow he had to figure out Styles's flaws, so that they could be used against him. But the guy didn't seem to have a past; it was as if Denver Styles had landed on Dutch Holland's doorstep by an act of magic.

But Weston wasn't about to be derailed. He'd find out the truth about Styles even if the guy had come straight from the portals of Hades. Everyone had a past, and those who hid theirs so well probably had some ugly little secrets they didn't want exposed. Perfect. Come hell or high water, Weston was determined to find out just what it was that made Styles tick, and what skeletons were hidden in his closets. Weston didn't like being at a disadvantage. Ever.

"What is it you're doing for Dutch?"

Styles tossed back half his glass of scotch as his gaze flicked around the polished wood of the cabin. As if he were assessing every tiny detail. "Is it any of your business?"

"Could be." Weston grinned in a way that usually put people at ease. Styles obviously wasn't buying it. "I think you're here for damage control."

One dark eyebrow rose, encouraging him.

"The way I figure it, Dutch is planning to announce his candidacy for the governorship, but he wants to clean house a little before he meets the press. He doesn't want any surprises, no scandals or skeletons jumping out of closets that he doesn't know about. He's having enough trouble with Moran and his book. He doesn't need anything else to sidetrack him or derail the campaign."

No comment from Styles. Just those intense eyes, unblinking and silently charging him with any number of crimes. The guy gave Weston the creeps. No doubt he was good at his job, whatever the hell it really was.

"What is it you want, Taggert?"

The question surprised Weston. He didn't expect Styles to be so direct.

"Well, you know that the Hollands and my family aren't exactly buddy-buddies."

Styles swirled his drink slowly as the sailboat gently swayed against its mooring. Outside the sound of a muted foghorn bellowed in the distance.

"In fact there's been this feud going on for years, and, believe it or not, I think it's good for the company," Weston added. "You know I believe that a little honest competition stimulates the economy."

"*Honest* competition?" Styles's expression was mocking, as if

Weston was wasting his breath because he didn't believe a word of Weston's speech. "Don't bullshit me."

"Well, honest for the most part."

"You've stolen most of Holland's key employees."

"Hey, they were unhappy. Wanted more money."

"And you probably have a few spies over at Dutch's place." Styles's eyes narrowed thoughtfully. "Don't try to snow me, okay? This isn't about competition, this is some kind of vendetta, and it works two ways."

Christ, the guy had more information than he should have. Weston started to sweat. Styles would be a much better ally than enemy. "I was thinking you might want to cut yourself a better deal than the one you've got with Dutch."

"With you?"

Weston nodded thoughtfully, his gaze centered on Styles, searching for any sort of reaction. There was none.

"Doing what?"

"Nothing more than you are now."

Slowly Styles sipped from his glass. He didn't flinch, didn't show any sign of emotion. As if he had nerves of steel. Hell, Weston would never want to come up against him in a poker game.

"All I want is for you to do whatever it is you're doing for Dutch and report back to me."

The hint of a smile—hard-edged and sardonic—twisted Styles's thin lips. Outside a buoy clanged. "So now we're finally down to it."

"It could be worth your while."

"What makes you think I can be bought?"

"Everyone's got a price." Weston was getting a little more comfortable. The liquor was warming his blood, making him bolder, and now he was on solid turf, dickering about money for favors, an area he'd traveled many times before. Styles wasn't bolting for the door, wasn't even spitting out righteously indignant epithets against him for suggesting that he could be bought. Oh, no. The man was still sitting, sipping his damned scotch and *contemplating* his options. Good.

"I'll pay you whatever it is you're getting from Dutch, so you'll be making double the money, but you'll have to report it to two people."

"And that's it?"

"Well, I might ask you to keep some information from good ol' Benedict."

"No deal."

Weston's head snapped up. He'd been so certain Styles would swallow the bait.

"I'm not interested in pissing off 'good ol' Benedict.'"

"He won't find out."

"No?" Styles's grin grew sterner and his fingers tightened around his glass, showing white knuckles under his tanned skin. "Why should I trust you?"

"Why not?"

"If I sign on with you and you make it known, I'm out of a job."

"I won't breathe a word. This is just between you and me."

"Is it?" Styles's eyes sparked with an intensity that scared Weston. Who was this guy? Lucifer incarnate? "As I asked before, why should I trust you?"

"Because I wouldn't pay you a shitload of money just to blow your cover."

"And what's a shitload?"

So he was listening. Weston felt an evil bit of glee. Denver Styles was out for number one. Just like everyone in this whole damned world. "I said I'd—"

"Not interested."

"So what if I double it—no, triple it?" Weston was anxious to get down to serious business. Any amount of money was insignificant. "Whatever Dutch is paying you, I'll pay three times."

"Up front?" Those intense eyes didn't leave Weston's face. "Three hundred grand."

"A hundred grand to begin with. The rest later."

Styles's jaw worked as he thought.

"And for that I'd want to know whatever it is you're checking into for Dutch, and I'll want information about his new project— the next phase of Stone Illahee."

"That's pretty much common knowledge—just check the county records. He's adding on to the original tract, going to build another smaller lodge with a golf course, tennis courts, the whole ball of wax."

"Where?"

"About half a mile inland from the main building."

Weston felt a tremor of dread. He'd been expecting this, but had hoped his information was wrong, that Dutch had found a safer, more scenic spot for his newest construction project. Hell, even the best-laid plans . . .

"The county's already approved the site. Excavation starts this week." Styles was staring at him again, as if he were trying to read Weston's mind.

"So soon. Jesus." He reached for his cigarettes and felt sweat collect on his forehead. *Be cool,* he told himself. *There wasn't a problem yet.* But he had trouble flicking his lighter to the tip of his Marlboro. All his perfectly laid plans could be destroyed with one swipe of the bulldozer's scoop. *Stay calm. You're borrowing trouble.* "Well, do we have a deal?"

Styles paused, his jaw hard, his muscles tense, as if he thought he was actually bargaining with the devil instead of the other way around.

"You could be a rich man when this is over," Weston prodded.

"Or a dead man."

We both could be, Weston thought, but didn't say it. Instead he offered Styles his hand.

Denver nearly sneered, but he wasn't man enough to walk away. Excellent. "All right, Taggert," he finally said, standing but refusing Weston's handshake. "You've got yourself a deal. But if word of this leaks out, you'll be sorry."

"Will I?"

"I'll rake up enough muck on your family to drown you in it. From what I've uncovered already, it looks like the Taggerts aren't any purer than the Hollands. In fact, I'm not sure the reverse isn't true." His eyes narrowed, and his lips flattened in some kind of superior attitude. "You're dirty, Taggert, and we both know it, so don't double-cross me."

"Is that a threat?" Weston couldn't believe his ears. This lowlife thug was actually trying to scare him?

"I'm just advising you. Take it anyway you want." He walked to the door and didn't turn around. "I'll expect cash. One hundred thousand. In three days."

Weston watched him leave and tried to convince himself that the guy was all talk and no action. Another blowhard. But Styles did walk with authority, could stare down a jaguar, and had a few scars to prove that he'd spent some time on the streets. Weston wiped suddenly sweaty palms on his slacks. He only hoped that his gut instincts were right, and that he hadn't just made the worst mistake of his life.

CHAPTER 29

The gun bothered him. As Kane reread all the information concerning Harley Taggert's death, he kept coming back to the gun—a small caliber pistol without a registration. At the time the detectives had dismissed the weapon, even though it had been found in the silt of the bay not twenty feet from where Harley Taggert's body had been floating. It had prints on it, but none that matched anyone's.

So why was it there? Could it have been used in another crime and just tossed into the bay, turning up coincidentally at the same time as Harley's body? Or could someone have thrown it into the dark waters just to complicate the investigation and send the cops looking in the wrong direction? Was it a fluke or important evidence? Did it have anything to do with Claire? His heart jolted as he thought of her again, of making love to her. Visions of her naked body drenched in moonlight bombarded his brain, caught him off guard, and made him horny as hell. Remembering the touch and feel of her skin against his brought him to arousal and he found himself plotting ways to be with her, to touch her, kiss her, and feel her heartbeat as she trembled in his arms. He wanted nothing more than to get her alone, to make love to her over and over again, exploring every part of her body with his tongue and lips.

Hell, he was turning himself on just thinking of her, and he didn't have time to fantasize. Not now. Not when he felt he was close to piecing together what had happened that night.

Of course the sisters had lied. They were either in it together or protecting each other, but he didn't know which. He couldn't picture Claire as being a cold-blooded killer, but maybe there had been an accident. Maybe after she told Harley she was breaking up with him, he'd gotten violent, yelled and screamed and told her he wouldn't let her leave. Perhaps they'd struggled and in the ensuing fight, in self-defense, she'd hit him hard with a rock or other odd-shaped object, and he'd fallen overboard.

No. That couldn't be right. If Harley was killed accidentally, why not call the police? Why run? Why come up with some cockamamie story about being at the drive-in and convince your sister to drive her car into the middle of Lake Arrowhead? No, it didn't make sense. But nothing did.

As he stared at the picture of the small pistol, he doubted that he'd ever know the truth. And then Dutch Holland wouldn't have to pay for all his sins. Kane walked to the front porch, where his father in the years before his death had sculpted so many stumps into bears and such. There had been no love lost between himself and Hampton Moran, and Kane had felt only mild sympathy for a man who had made the least of an unfortunate accident, continually blaming the owner of the company for his misery.

But Kane hadn't known the whole truth way back then. He hadn't realized that his mother had become Dutch's mistress, that she'd moved to Portland, lived in a condominium and been supported by Benedict Holland, that the checks for three hundred dollars each month had really come from Dutch. Claire's father.

"Bastard," Kane muttered under his breath. His mother had died from heart failure just this past winter and Kane had learned the painful truth that Alice Moran had left her husband and only son to become Dutch Holland's mistress.

Kane's stomach turned over at the thought of his mother and Dutch and he remembered the nights he'd been alone in his room, waiting for her to return, fighting back tears, refusing to believe that she'd really abandoned him. He'd always held out hope that she'd return. Even his father's harsh words, reminding him that she was just "a rich man's whore," or that "she didn't care nothin' for you or me boy. Nope. All she wanted was money and she finally found it by laying on her back and spreadin' her legs. Remember that about women, son. They'll do anything for a buck. Even your own mother."

His jaw tightened and his fists clenched. Benedict Holland had single-handedly turned his mother away from her family. No wonder Hampton had taken a chain saw to Dutch's precious lodge. The man deserved everything he got, and, if Kane had his way, Dutch Holland was going down in flames.

So what about Claire? What will happen to her? When you bring down her father and her sisters and perhaps implicate her in Harley Taggert's death, what will happen to her and her kids?

He stared at the picture of the gun and told himself it wasn't his problem, but he knew he was only lying to himself because, damn it all to hell, he was beginning to fall in love with Claire Holland St. John all over again. It seemed to be his personal curse.

"Denver Styles is a pain in the butt." Tessa, dressed in a black bikini and white lace cover-up that slid suggestively over one shoulder, looked up from her guitar as Miranda entered the suite where Tessa had taken up residence. Her belly-button ring was visible beneath the lace and her tattoo bound her upper arm like a slave bracelet.

"He's been bothering you?" Miranda didn't want to think about Styles. He was too complicated, too dangerous. She felt as if he were breathing down her back, watching her every move and waiting for her to make some kind of mistake. Then, like a patient hunter, he'd pounce.

"Yeah, he's been here a couple of times."

"What'd you tell him?"

Tessa smiled, and her blond eyebrows elevated. "Specifically?" She strummed a single note. "I told him to fuck off."

"Nice, Tessa."

"The man's bad news," she said, setting her six-string on the carpet near a potted plant.

Miranda walked to the fireplace and sat on the raised hearth though no flames flickered in the grate. "I called Dad and told him that hiring Styles was a mistake, that dredging up the past wasn't in his best interests, but it was the same as before. He didn't listen."

"Never does. Haven't you learned that yet?" Tessa asked. "Hey, how about a drink? I've got wine coolers in the fridge." She was on her feet in an instant, padding barefoot to the kitchen and the tiny refrigerator tucked around the corner.

"None for me."

"Oh, Randa, lighten up!" Tessa returned with two opened bottles of some kind of peach and wine concoction. She handed Miranda one of the bottles. "Cheers." Clinking the necks of the bottles together, she winked at her sister, then took a long swallow.

"Look, Tessa, I'm afraid Styles is going to find out the truth," Miranda admitted, then took a swallow of the god-awful drink.

"Let him."

"No way."

"Maybe it's time." Tessa's face clouded, and she gnawed on her lower lip, the way she had whenever she'd been uncertain or confused as a little girl. "I'm tired of lying, Randa. This was a mistake."

"No! It's too late to change anything." Miranda shook her head vehemently. "We've got to stick to the story."

"I don't know."

"It's worked so far." Restless, Miranda walked to the sliding glass door and leaned against it.

"Has it?"

"Just hang in there." Miranda stared at the vista that was the Pacific Ocean. Green and murky, stretching to the horizon, the sea shifted restlessly, as if it, too, had secrets too deep and tragic to reveal.

"You don't have to worry about me," Tessa said. "It's Claire who's going to be the problem."

"Claire?" Miranda repeated. Claire didn't even know the real story. "Why?"

"Because she's getting herself involved with Kane Moran."

"No." Miranda hoped that Tessa was making this up. Sometimes Dutch's youngest daughter fantasized, other times she was just plain confused.

"I've seen them together."

"Is she out of her mind?" Fear caused Miranda's heart to pound a quick, irregular cadence.

"You know what a romantic she is. Always has been. A fool for men. She was involved with Harley and he died and within months she married that jerk Paul. I only met him once—around the time of the wedding, but he was already looking at other women. Including me!" She sighed and flopped back on the couch. "Claire's an idiot. Always has been."

"Moran's just using her."

"Probably."

"I'll talk to her."

"A lot of good that will do. No one could talk her out of seeing Harley Taggert, could they? And then Paul—Jesus, I told her he'd been coming on to me and she wouldn't believe me. You can talk to her until you're blue in the face, Randa, but, trust me, it won't do a bit of good."

For once, Tessa was right. Claire had never listened to anyone when her heart was involved. This was worse than Miranda had thought. She felt as if she'd just stepped into the quicksand of the past and there was no escape. Sooner or later she, her sisters, her father, and her damned career would be dragged under.

God help them all.

He had to forget about her. That was all there was to it. But Weston never was one to let a willing woman pass him by, and from the breathy telephone calls he'd been getting from Tessa Holland, she was more than willing to pick up where they'd left off so long ago.

Shit. What was he going to do? He floored the Mercedes and the convertible sped down the highway, tires singing, engine purring, wind whipping by. An expanse of gray-blue ocean stretched to the west, breakers rolling inland in frothy waves, and to the east a bank of forested hills rose high enough to brush the sky. But Tessa was on his mind, and he couldn't shake her image.

He'd seen her in town, walking into the liquor store, her round rump swaying beneath a short, tight, red skirt, her luscious breasts straining against a white shirt tied just beneath her bra. She hadn't aged much, though her hair was a little shorter and more spiked than he remembered and her cheekbones were more defined with the added years. Her eyes were still round and blue and he imagined her tongue could still work its special kind of magic.

Christ, what was he thinking? If he got involved with Tessa, or any of the Holland girls again, Kendall would kill him. Besides, each of the Holland sisters had her own ax to grind with him and would be the worst possible candidate for a quick affair. And yet, he couldn't stop thinking of the possibilities. Miranda had always gotten under his skin. More so than Tessa, but then Tessa was available, or so she'd led him to believe when he'd answered his cell phone last night.

"Guess what I'm doing?" she'd cooed, and he hadn't been able to speak as he had been with his wife and daughter in the family room watching television.

"I'm touching myself. Do you want to know where?" Her voice had been low and smoky.

"I don't think so."

"I've licked my finger until it was wet and then touched my nipples. They're wet now, too. Hard. And now I'm going to go down a little farther and—"

"I'll talk to you later. I never discuss business at home," he'd said, loud enough for his wife to hear, though he'd turned his back on her to hide the evidence of his erection straining against the fly of the slacks she'd bought for him just last week.

"I'll be here. At Stone Illahee. Waiting."

He'd hung up and nearly come in his pants. What kind of game was she playing with him? The last time he'd seen her, she'd wanted to scratch his eyes out and now . . . now, she was acting like she couldn't wait to get him into bed. He was long through with her, he reminded himself, but his hands began to sweat on the steering wheel. He was an upstanding citizen now, had a reputation to protect, but he couldn't help remembering how it felt to ride her. A sensation of pure, raw power had surged through him. The knowledge that he was humping a Holland girl, making her beg for mercy— or more—was heady, a rush he'd never had before or since. Even the kinky sex of his youth or the string of mistresses he'd bedded hadn't given him that savage adrenaline high that Tessa had so willingly lured from him.

And was willing to provide again.

Christ, he was hard.

He braked for a corner, skidded a bit, then the car took hold again and he tried to push Tessa out of his mind. Now wasn't the time to be distracted by a woman. He had other more important situations that demanded his attention. He topped a hill and caught a glimpse of Stone Illahee. His stomach tightened, and he spied the bulldozers hard at work at the next stage of development of the resort. Scraping topsoil, debris, brush, and small trees, the machines rolled over the ground on their huge cat tracks. Ever digging. Finding things that were better left buried. His cell phone rang and he answered it, eager for a distraction, forcing Tessa and the excavation at Stone Illahee from his mind.

"You know, I think our family's kind of a sideshow," Tessa said as she plucked a grape from the fruit bowl on the kitchen counter in the house where she'd grown up. Claire poured them each a glass of iced tea. Sam was outside splashing in the pool, and Sean had taken the boat into the lake. It was a lazy afternoon, and Claire had finished filling out some applications for the local school district in the hope of being able to substitute teach in the fall.

"A sideshow?"

"Yep. Dad into his own personal power trip. Governor, for God's sake. Can you imagine?" She tossed the grape into the air and caught it deftly in her mouth. "Dutch Holland with that much power is a pretty scary thought."

"He hasn't been elected yet. Not even by his own party."

"Good point." Tessa sat on a bar stool near the counter and twirled on her rear. "You know, I've been calling Weston again."

Claire froze. "Calling him? Why?"

"Oh, you know, just teasing him. Talking dirty, that kind of thing."

"Are you out of your mind? He's not the kind of guy you tease and get away with it."

"Why not? I think he should sweat a little."

"Sweat a little? For what? I don't understand." Blind panic took hold of Claire, though she didn't really understand why. Weston couldn't hurt any of them. Or could he?

"Trust me, you don't need to. But I think Weston needs to be put in his place. He's had things his way for too long."

"And you're going to straighten him out?" Claire laughed, but she felt uneasy, the same kind of sensation that swept over her just before an electrical storm broke and lightning ripped through the sky.

"Weston's beyond being straightened out. What I'm going to do is bother him."

Claire shook her head. "Leave him alone. He's not worth the trouble."

Tessa's eyes narrowed, and she looked over Claire's shoulder to a middle distance that only she could see. Her face twisted in pain and tears, real and fresh, filled her eyes. "Yeah, well, what did he ever do to deserve his perfect little family, huh? He's not exactly a paragon of virtue."

"Life's generally not fair."

"I know, I know, but it galls me that he's got this . . . fake side . . . you know the epitome of the American dream— faithful, loving husband to Kendall Forsythe, spoiled-rotten daughter, even one of those yappy purebred toy poodles." She sniffed and cleared her throat. "It's enough to make me sick."

"It's nothing to you."

Tessa blinked rapidly, fought the damned tears that came at her in uneven rushes when she least expected them. She drummed her fingers on the counter and decided against arguing with Claire any further. What good would it do? "I suppose you're right, but it bugs the hell out of me."

"Let it alone."

She should. Claire was making sense, but Tessa wanted to throw up to think that Weston was on the city council, that he was considered a pillar of the community, that he was a fucking icon to the men and women who were employed by Taggert Industries. The man was pure evil. Lower than a rattlesnake's belly. How she'd love to expose that ugly side of Weston Taggert to the world. Besides, though no one but she knew it, Weston Taggert had single-handedly devastated her life.

Maybe now it was time to ruin his.

* * *

Claire was lying. Kane could sense it. As he lay with her in the pool house, one hand caressing the cleft of her bare buttocks, the other stroking her spine, he tried to figure out what it was that she was keeping from him.

He knew that her story about the night that Harley Taggert died didn't hold water, and that scared the living hell out of him. What if she'd accidentally killed Harley? Was he, with his exposé, going to send her to jail? His guts twisted as she sighed sleepily on the old bed where they'd made love. The smell of chlorine from the pool seeped through the open windows, and a breeze sighed through the trees, rustling the fir needles and oak leaves.

Claire wouldn't allow him in her bedroom, not with the kids in the house, so they met here, like teenagers sneaking to a private lovers' tryst, in the pool house, where she was close enough to know that her children were safe, but private enough that they could lose themselves in each other.

And lose himself he had. No other woman had ever touched him like Claire Holland St. John. She had a way of turning him inside out and upside down. His feelings for her, so close to love it scared the hell out of him, made him question everything he believed in, everything he'd planned for all his life. He'd been so hell-bent on baring all of Dutch Holland's sins to the world that he'd lost sight of anything other than his own personal need for revenge.

She moaned in her sleep, and he kissed the skin between her shoulder blades.

"Kane," she whispered, still not awake, but reaching for him. His heart swelled in his chest. God she was beautiful. Moonlight filtered through the blinds to stripe her white skin in silvery bars. Her waist was small, her ribs visible, and as she rolled over and he saw her breasts, he began to get hard again. With her he couldn't get enough, with her he was never sated for long. Her nipples were soft and round, but as he breathed across them they tightened, and even in sleep she responded.

"Beautiful, beautiful Princess," he said, wishing things were different between them, that he wasn't going to use her for his own private revenge, that he could come to her with his conscience clear and his heart pure. Instead he had an ulterior motive for getting closer to her.

Guilt gnawed at his pride, but he took her into his arms and kissed her. She sighed, her eyes fluttered open, and she smiled, that sexy naive little grin that was always his undoing. "Again?" she asked, yawning, her tousled hair spilling over his arm.

He kissed her and her lips fit perfectly to his. Her tongue slid into his mouth, her nipples hardened, and within seconds her drowsy body was awake and alive, her blood as hot as his own.

Her arms wrapped around his neck and he buried his face in the hollow of her breasts before he swept her legs apart with his knees and drove into her as hot and randy as any nineteen-year-old.

"Kane," she whispered into his ear as he began to pant. Perspiration broke out on her skin, and she arched up to meet each of his thrusts with her own hungry desire. Faster and faster he moved, holding her close, his eyes squeezed shut as his guilt pounded through his brain. He couldn't do this, couldn't betray her, couldn't love her so much it hurt, only to devastate her and her family.

And then he came. With a lusty cry and a final thrust, he fell against her, his body melding to hers in a union that was meant to be and cursed by all the demons of hell.

Tortured, he kissed her forehead, tasting the salt of her sweat, feeling her shudder as her own climax slowed. "I never want to hurt you," he said, brushing her hair off her face with his lips.

"You won't," she replied, smiling and trusting as she gazed up at him.

He kissed her again, long and hard, and knew that he had no choice. Despite all his vows to himself, he was destined to betray her, and then, no matter what else happened, she would hate him for the rest of her life.

CHAPTER 30

"Stop it, you're making me crazy. What's the matter with you anyway?" Paige asked, glaring up at Weston from her game of bridge. She grabbed a handful of mixed nuts and plopped an almond into her mouth.

"Nothing's wrong," Weston lied and gave himself a mental shake for allowing his emotions to show. He'd been pacing again, back and forth through the kitchen and den where Paige, Stephanie, Kendall, and his father were playing cards. Neal's wheelchair was pushed into position, and though he couldn't walk and had little use of his right side since the stroke, he was able to talk and use his left hand effectively enough to handle a weekly game of bridge.

"Something's up," Neal said, one eye narrowing on his son. "You're always restless when something's bothering you."

"Daddy's fine," Stephanie interrupted, and Weston felt a warmth inside him. She was always in his corner, defending him against the world. With her wheat blond hair and sparkling blue eyes, she'd inherited the right combination of genes to make her drop-dead gorgeous. "Leave him alone. Mom, it's your bid." Daddy's little girl. But the others were right. He was going out of his fucking mind.

Paige, still overweight and forever jangling that irritating bracelet, could see straight to his soul, and it scared the living shit out of him. Sometimes she smiled at him in an eerie way that suggested she had something on him—something life-threatening, something that kept him from crossing her. She'd made hints about it as well. "I'd better never end up dead from an 'accident' or something, Wes, because it won't work. If I have an unexpected early death, the police will come looking for you." He'd laughed and asked her to explain herself, but she'd only smiled that creepy little grin and said, "I'm not bluffing."

"You're making it hard to concentrate." Paige sent him a drop-dead look and turned her attention back to the cards. "Either sit down or leave."

"You don't have to go anywhere, Daddy." Good girl, Stephanie. You tell 'em.

"You *are* fidgety," Kendall said, disapproval edging the corners of her mouth as the dog trotted through the kitchen and stopped at his water bowl.

Weston couldn't stand to be cooped up another minute. "I've got to run to the office," he said, and Kendall's eyes followed him. She'd never trusted him, believed that he chased anything in a skirt. Not completely true, but he had fallen into his share of relationships, bad and good.

"New business?" Neal asked, always interested in what was happening at Taggert Industries.

"No, just tying up a few loose ends." Weston grabbed his keys and walked out the back door. The wind had picked up, tossing the branches of the trees near the garage, and the scent of smoke, riding on the back of a salt-laden breeze, drifted up from a few campfires on the beach.

He drove away from the house and tried to calm down. His sister was right. He was in knots. For several reasons. First and foremost, Denver Styles had been on his payroll for nearly a week, and so far he'd come up with nothing new on Dutch or any of the other Hollands.

Nothing. Nada. Zilch. The man just wasn't doing his job or he was holding out on Weston, probably for more money, which would be a mistake. A big mistake.

Second, there was the excavation at the most recent phase of Stone Illahee. His stomach cramped and bile rose in his throat. To top things off, Dutch was going to officially announce his candi-

dacy for next year's governor's race at a party the following weekend, and the thought of Benedict Holland even having a shot at a
position of power anywhere in the state made him physically ill.
No, it couldn't happen.

He drove like a madman, pushing the speed limit, squirreling
around corners until his office came into view. He was supposed to
meet with Styles tonight, and he couldn't wait. Somehow he had to
get his money's worth from the man. In the back of his mind he
wondered if he'd been conned. What was preventing Denver Styles
from pocketing the cash Weston had given him and reporting nothing? Weston was ready. Either Styles came up with some information, important information, or there would be hell to pay.

His jaw tightened and his lips flattened hard against his teeth.
Weston had never liked being bested, and he'd worked long and
hard to prevent just that. So if Styles was going to double-cross
him, he'd pay. He'd pay with his goddamned life. Just like those
who'd tried to cheat him before.

At the office building, he unlocked the back door, as he'd told
Styles he would, then took the elevator to his private office. He'd
just poured himself a stiff shot of brandy and loosened his tie when
Denver Styles, dressed in black, strode in.

Weston motioned to the bar, but Styles shook his head and declined. Instead he leaned against the wall of glass and stared outside.

"What have you found out?"

Styles lifted a shoulder. "Not much."

Anger spurted through Weston's veins. "Surely in a week,
you've dug up something."

Styles turned to face him. "A few things. Nothing substantial.
Nothing about the night your brother was killed, even though
that's what Dutch is most concerned about."

Weston tried to be patient, he knew that it was in his best interest to let Styles give him the information in his own way and time,
yet he wanted to strangle the man and shake answers from him.
"You think one of his girls killed Harley?"

"Don't know." He paused. "Yet."

"What do you know?" Weston asked, and couldn't hide the
nasty little tone in his words.

"That Dutch is nervous, that he's worried someone will find out that one of his kids is a murderer, though he's got no evidence to support his theory, and that when Claire Holland left Chinook sixteen years ago, she was pregnant."

Weston was stunned. "Pregnant? Claire?" *But Miranda had been the sister who was knocked up.* He did a few quick mental calculations. "You mean with her son?"

"Yes. Sean Harlan St. John. He wasn't born in July as she claimed but in April, which meant she was pregnant *before* she met her husband."

"The baby was Harley's?" Weston's legs were suddenly unable to hold him, and he had to sit down. This was impossible. There couldn't be another Taggert . . . Harley couldn't have fathered a boy and yet . . . His mind turned back to another birth certificate, one he'd burned years before, proof that his father hadn't been faithful to Mikki. Bile rose in his throat, and his gut squeezed painfully. There was another heir to the Taggert fortune? His fists clenched. He'd worked so hard to inherit everything and now this kid, this interloper . . . oh shit!

He felt the nervous beads of sweat form on his upper lip and his ribs seemed suddenly to crush the air out of his lungs. *No! No! No!* Not now. Not when he'd been certain to inherit everything but a small percentage of his father's estate. It was already mapped out in the will. Even Paige knew that as a daughter and one who didn't work at the company, she would only inherit the old house where they'd grown up, but now . . . with Harley's son . . . no, it couldn't happen. "Who knows about this?"

"Just Claire St. John, although Moran's sure to pick up on it."

"Damn it all to hell!"

"The boy has no idea, and the kid's supposed father, Paul St. John, has enough problems of his own that he won't give a plugged nickel about the fact when the truth comes out."

"You think Moran will publish this?" The wheels in Weston's mind were turning, faster and faster, to the inevitable ending, that Sean St. John would be proven to be a Taggert. His father would be thrilled, even though the kid's mother was a Holland. One of Neal's biggest disappointments in life was that he had no male heirs to carry on the Taggert name. Kendall had refused to have more children, had gone so far as to have surgery to ensure that she was sterile. Her pregnancy with Stephanie had been miserable, and she wasn't about to go through the pain, bloat, or emotional roller coaster ride that carrying a baby for nine months had given her. Stephanie had been worth it, but Kendall wasn't interested in another child.

So now this problem.

"I assume Moran will publish anything to smear Dutch," Styles said. "He hates the guy and with good reason. His father was crippled in a logging accident, never completely compensated for his injuries and the father was abusive, if not physically, then emotionally. Moran's mother, Alice, left him and the dad at an early age. As it turns out, she ended up living in Portland as Dutch's mistress, and never had any contact with the kid all the time he was growing up with a drunk bully of a dad."

"Son of a bitch," Weston muttered and thought about his own experience with Dutch Holland. In his mind's eye he could still see Dutch's freckled back as he humped on the antique quilt, Mikki's legs wrapped around him while they fucked like two damned animals. The image had haunted him and he'd had dreams about it . . . disturbing dreams where he'd killed Dutch, then mounted his whore of a mother, but when he'd looked down it wasn't Mikki Taggert he was screwing but one of the Holland daughters, Miranda or Claire or Tessa.

"Other than that, I don't have anything," Styles was saying, snapping Weston from his hideous reverie.

"Keep looking," Weston said, still reeling from the information. At least Styles didn't appear to be holding out on him.

"I will. Especially into the night Harley died." He turned and faced Weston for the first time, and those harsh flinty eyes thinned with a personal vengeance. Weston's heart nearly stopped. "I'm with Moran. Something about that night doesn't add up."

This was dangerous turf. As far as Weston was concerned, the less anyone cared about the night Harley bought it, the better. Styles reached into his jacket pocket and pulled out a piece of paper— a copy of a report and a picture of a gun. "Moran seems obsessed with this bit of evidence," he said, holding out the pages for Weston to take. "What do you make of it?"

Weston stared down at the copies. "Couldn't guess."

"The gun was found not far from the body."

"I know, but the police didn't connect it to the crime."

"But it's odd, don't you think?"

Not so peculiar, Weston thought, as he snatched the paper from Styles's hand and folded it neatly. He didn't want to be reminded that his mother's gun had been found at the scene. No one claimed the little pistol, and it hadn't been registered, of course, but everyone in the Taggert family knew that the gun was the one that had been missing from Mikki Taggert's dresser drawer for weeks. "Yep," he said, shaking his head and meeting the questions in Styles's eyes. "Very odd."

"You're telling me that Sean was fathered by Harley Taggert?" Dutch demanded, his face ruddy, a cigar clamped between his teeth as he glared at Denver. They sat facing each other in the bar of the Hotel Danvers, a Portland landmark.

"Could be. I have to check on blood types yet."

"Jesus H. Christ! How long does that take?"

"Not long. A few days. I might even know by tomorrow."

"Why would Claire lie?"

"You'll have to ask her that," Styles replied. He hadn't touched his coffee laced with brandy, while Dutch was on his second drink.

"What about the night Taggert died? Did he know about the kid?"

Styles shrugged. "The only one who knows the answer to that one is Claire."

Dutch drained his drink and scowled. "I guess this isn't the worst news I could get, but it's not great."

"Tell your campaign manager—Murdock—and he can do some damage control."

Dutch rubbed his face and sighed. "People are counting on me to run. I can't afford to be hit in the face with some old scandal. You've got to get to the bottom of this Taggert mess, Styles, before my opponent or Moran does. If we know what we're up against, we have a chance and if not . . . oh, Christ, let's not think about that. Just find out what happened that night."

"I will," Denver promised, and he meant to do just that, even though his agenda was far removed from Benedict Holland's.

* * *

After work on Friday, Miranda drove straight to the construction site where the next elaborate lodge, an extension of Stone Illahee, was to be built. According to her father's secretary in Portland, Dutch was going to be overseeing the site preparation all weekend, and Miranda needed to talk to him before he announced his candidacy at a party on Sunday night. Only Dutch could tell Denver Styles to back off.

The man was getting to her, no doubt about it. He'd stopped by the office and her house four different times, and all the while she was with him, she was in knots. It wasn't so much the questions he asked, but Styles himself. Brooding, thoughtful, with features that could change from pleasant to harsh in a heartbeat, he unnerved her. She, who had prided herself on her cool appraisal of any situation, she, who no defense attorney, hostile witness, or volatile suspect, could rattle. This one man had her second-guessing herself, tripping over her own stories, and ready to jump out of her own skin.

"Take it easy," she said, driving through the open gate of the chain-link fence surrounding the excavation site. Dust blew across the Volvo's windshield, and the air smelled dry, without the usual dampness from the ocean. Several pickups were parked haphazardly around the area where trees, grass, and boulders had been scraped from the ground. Dutch's Cadillac was wedged between a half-ton pickup in primer gray and a station wagon that was a patchwork of colors because of dented and replaced fenders. Dutch wasn't inside his car, but Miranda spotted him easily.

Chomping on the butt of a cigar, he stood with a group of workmen, staring at a spot in front of an idling bulldozer that was belching black smoke into the hot summer air.

The men were grim, talking in low voices, and Miranda, as she slid out of her car, felt her stomach clench with the premonition that something was wrong—very wrong. Far in the distance she heard the first wail of a siren, and, in an instant, as the sound drew nearer, she realized that for some reason the police were on their way. Her steps quickened across the dirt as dread stole through her. What was it? Had someone been hurt on the job? As she approached, she heard scraps and bits of the conversation.

". . . been there for years," a big bear of a man wearing a hard hat and bib overalls mumbled.

"Holy shit, who?" Another worker, skinny with short-cropped hair and rimless glasses.

"No one missin' that I know of." The bear again.

What were they talking about? Who?

"Never seen the likes of it."

"Me neither," Dutch said, puffing on his short cigar and staring at his feet where the ground dropped off as the bulldozer had taken a huge bite of earth from the spot.

"Wonder if there's any ID?"

Behind Miranda, a siren screamed as a cruiser for the county shot through the gates. Still walking, she glanced over her shoulder as the car slid to a stop near her Volvo. Two all-business deputies climbed out and hurried toward the men just as Miranda reached her father's side. She looked down the embankment at her feet, to the gaping hole in the earth, where the dirt was wet and fresh, and tangled in the debris of leaves, rocks, and litter was a body—little more than a skeleton with a few rags still clinging to its bones.

The contents of her stomach rose, threatening her throat. "Oh, God," she said, as her father finally noticed her.

"Randa, what're you doing here? You should be—"

"I've seen bodies before," she snapped back, but something about this decomposed body bothered her, and as the first drip of premonition slid into her brain, the deputies approached.

"Okay, what've we got here? Jesus! Would you look at that?"

"Let's rope it off," the second deputy said. "Don't disturb anything else." He eyed the bulldozer as if it were a tool of the devil, then swept his gaze over the small crowd. "Forensics and the ME will need to see this. No one's to disturb anything."

But Miranda barely heard the command. Her eyes were drawn to the right hand of the corpse and the ring that hung loosely around one skeletal finger. *No! It couldn't be!* Her heart dropped. A small cry escaped her lips. "No!" she cried. "No! No! No!"

"What the hell—?"

Her knees gave way, and her father caught her by the arms. Pain screamed through her brain. It couldn't be . . . oh God, please, no. Not Hunter. Not her beloved . . .

"Miranda, for the love of St. Peter, what—?"

"Hunter," she whispered, tears falling like rain from her eyes. "Oh, no, Hunter!" She tried to deny what her eyes saw, but she couldn't, for there, on that lifeless hand, was the ring that Hunter Riley had worn just before he disappeared. He hadn't run away to Canada she realized, trembling and fighting the urge to wretch. Somehow, some way, by someone, he'd been killed.

Seated at his worktable, Kane gritted his teeth as he stared at the evidence of Claire's lies. The state of Oregon's records of Sean Harlan St. John's birth were different from the story Claire had told him. She'd said that Sean had been born in July when in actuality he'd entered the world at the end of April, just about nine months after Harley had died. So Sean wasn't a St. John at all, but a Taggert.

Or was he?

Another thought, more damning than the first, raced through his brain. At first he discarded it as wishful thinking, but the longer he turned the idea through his mind, the more convinced he was that it was a concrete possibility.

Why couldn't Sean be his son? Hadn't he made love to Claire over and over again before he left for the army, the morning after the night that Harley Taggert had died? The timing was right. Perfect, in fact. Was it possible? Could he have a boy? A strange, unwanted feeling crept through him. A son. He could be a father!

"Shit." He walked through the house to the front porch. The night had darkened the waters of the lake, and a few stars had begun to wink in the purple heavens. The kid looked like him. More than like a Taggert, but maybe that was just foolish male pride talking. He'd like to think that he was the father of Claire's boy rather than Harley Taggert, but he couldn't. Hadn't she named the kid after Taggert? Sean *Harlan* St. John.

His fist clenched around the condemning paper. What was Claire thinking, passing off her kid as belonging to one man when in reality, in truth . . . who the hell knew the truth?

Only Claire. Who had lied to him, to the world, for sixteen long years.

Cramming the copy of the certificate into the front pocket of his jeans, he strode down the overgrown path to the dock, climbed in the old boat, and revved the motor—only to have it die twice before he realized he was out of gas. He could drive around the lake, but decided he needed time to think things through, to cool off. So he took off at a slow jog, around the perimeter of Lake Arrowhead. It would take him nearly an hour to walk or jog to the other side, but by that time, his head might be clearer, his anger might wane.

With only faint light from the moon as his guide, he kept moving, over rocks and sandy beaches, through thickets of trees and undergrowth, ever steady, intent on his purpose. The time for lies was over. From here on in, he was only interested in the truth, no matter how painful or disgusting it might be.

Soon, no matter what, Claire was going to come clean with him.

He was sweating by the time he saw the patches of light coming from the first floor of the old lodge. He walked past the stables and fields where the horses, sensing him, snorted before turning back to grazing. The birth certificate burning a hole in his pocket, he strode across the lawn and up the path to the front door, but as he approached, voices caught his attention and he walked around the side of the lodge toward the back porch, where he saw the sisters, all three of them, seated around a table with a single flickering candle giving off meager light.

He was about to shout a greeting when he realized that one of the women was crying softly. He stopped dead in his tracks. No one had seen him yet, as the night was dark and a hedge of arborvitae offered some concealment. The kids weren't around and he assumed they were already in bed, asleep in their rooms, as it was well after midnight.

"You're sure it was Hunter?" Claire asked, her voice touching Kane as no other could.

"Yes, yes." Miranda sniffed. "His clothes, his ring . . ." She sobbed, then caught herself, and Kane's mind was whirling. Hunter? As in Hunter Riley?

"So he never went to Canada?" Tessa this time.

"I don't think so. I don't know." Miranda was in more control, and a dozen questions raced through Kane's brain.

Was Hunter back in town?

"Whoever killed him wanted him never found."

Killed? Riley was dead?

Kane didn't move a muscle, and though he felt guilty about eavesdropping, he couldn't barge in on their private conversation, nor could he tear himself away.

"You think he was murdered?" Claire asked, disbelieving.

"Of course. He was healthy, and though the police don't know how . . . how he died, he was buried in the woods and no one knew about it for God, what? Fifteen, no, sixteen years."

"Jesus," Tessa said.

Claire sighed. "Oh, Randa, I'm so sorry."

"One person knows what happened." Miranda's voice was stronger, filled with a new conviction. "Weston Taggert lied to me. The day that I went to see him, to ask about Hunter, he said Hunter was on the payroll in Canada, working for Taggert Industries. That was a lie."

"You think Weston killed him?" Tessa asked as she lit a cigarette, and the flame from her lighter illuminated her face. Tears were filling her eyes as well.

"Or knows who did."

"This is all such a mess." Tessa blew smoke toward the roof of the porch and the scent of burning tobacco reached Kane's nostrils. "What can we do?"

"Go to the police." Claire was convinced, and through the branches of the arborvitae he saw her face, shadowy in the candlelight but still beautiful.

"I don't know if we can."

"Why not? Look, Randa, we're talking about murder. For all we know, Weston did it."

"There's more," she said, and Kane, silently cursing himself, strained to listen. "I saw an object not far from the body."

"What?" Tessa asked.

"A knife. I'd seen it before."

"Like the murder weapon?" Tessa drew hard on her cigarette, and the tip glowed deep red in the night.

"I don't know. But it was Jack Songbird's knife. The one no one could find after he died."

"So you think Jack killed Hunter?" Tessa's fertile mind was already jumping to conclusions.

"No, no. Hunter was still alive when Jack was buried, but . . . but whoever killed Hunter probably killed Jack."

And Harley Taggert? Kane's jaw was so tight it ached. What the hell was happening here? He should burst in on the sisters, demand the truth, but he couldn't break in on their privacy and grief just yet.

Claire reached over and touched Miranda on the shoulder, and Randa, always the tough one of the group, slumped a little lower. A soft wail of deep mourning escaping her throat. "I loved him." Randa shook her head and wrapped her arms around her middle, as if in self-protection. The tough as nails prosecutor was gone, an anguished, grieving woman in her place. "I loved him more than I thought was possible," she whispered.

"I know," Claire whispered.

"Love sucks." Tessa shot a stream of smoke into the air, then crushed the butt in a tray on the table.

"Sometimes," Claire agreed, and took in a shuddering breath. "This investigation is bound to open up everything again—you know, about Harley Taggert and Jack and Hunter."

Tessa snorted. "Kane Moran and Denver Styles have already taken care of that. God, that Moran can be such a pain in the ass and Styles—that guy gives me the creeps. You *never* know what he's thinking."

"Weston Taggert gives me the creeps," Claire said.

"Amen." Miranda closed her eyes and rocked slightly, as if trying to comfort herself.

"Okay, but listen. Everything that happened that night is going to come out. Kane and Denver Styles and Dad won't be the only ones interested," Claire said.

"She's right," Miranda said, her voice cloaked in doom. "People will start to wonder."

"And Ruby and Hank Songbird will make a stink about Jack's knife. Reporters from all over the country and Dad's opponents in the race and even just the townspeople that remember what happened that night are going to start asking questions, nosing around. They're going to find out the truth."

"Oh, God," Tessa whispered and started to shake.

"We'll stick to our story." Miranda's voice was calmer again. She was in control.

"It doesn't hold water." Claire was on her feet, pacing the length of the porch, her silhouette dark against the light glowing from the windows as she walked back and forth. "And I don't know the truth about that night."

Kane felt a wash of relief. Claire hadn't been a part of it— whatever it was. *But she lied to you, didn't she? About your son!*

Claire touched Miranda's shoulder again. "You never told me what really happened."

"It was better if you didn't know," Miranda said, as Claire kept up her pacing.

"Are you kidding? I've been going out of my mind for years wondering why we were lying, trying to figure out what happened." She stopped suddenly and wrapped her arms around herself as if to shield her heart from the truth.

Kane let out his breath. She hadn't killed Harley, not that he'd ever thought she was involved, but he'd known she'd lied to him. To the world. And she didn't even know why.

"It's . . . it's my fault," Tessa said, her voice weak.

"No, Tessa, don't—"

"Shut up, Randa, you've been taking the fall for this for years and protecting me."

Tessa? The killer?

Tessa rammed both hands through her short blond hair. "I was drunk and with Weston that night. We were in the pool house when Randa walked in on us and went ballistic."

"I should have killed him," Randa said.

"Randa tried to break us up, to tell me what a loser he was, but I'd had a lot to drink and he'd come to me and . . . and . . . oh, shit, I was always a fool around him, you know that."

Claire didn't comment, just stared at her youngest sister.

"I couldn't take it," Miranda said. "Weston had already nearly raped me in his office. I got out by kicking him in the crotch, so when I found him with Tessa, I saw red. I tried to break them up and Weston . . . he decided to teach me a lesson, so . . . oh, God . . ." Her voice trembled. ". . . so when I attacked him, he came undone and he . . . he . . . Claire, he raped me so brutally that I . . . ."

"She miscarried," Tessa whispered.

Kane's hand curled into fists. His stomach knotted.

Claire didn't move. "Miscarried?"

"I was pregnant with Hunter's baby."

"Oh, Randa!" Claire walked behind Randa's chair, fell to her knees, and hugged her sister fiercely. "I'm . . . I'm so sorry."

"That's not all," Tessa added. "I just watched him do it to her. I was too drunk, too stunned to do anything but watch as he hit her and kicked her, tore her clothes off her, threw her across the sofa, and dropped his pants and . . . and . . . Oh Randa, I'm so sorry, so damned sorry."

"Shhh."

Bile rose in Kane's throat, and he thought he'd be sick. If he ever saw Weston Taggert again, he'd personally coldcock the bastard, then choke the life from him. And that was just the warm-up.

"I—I was so upset that when I could get my legs to work, I chased Weston down," Tessa said. "Only when I got to the Taggert estate, I saw him leave again." She took in a deep, shuddering breath. "I followed him to the marina."

"Oh, God."

"Tessa, don't," Miranda said, her eyes flying open. "This isn't smart."

"But it's the truth, damn it. I thought I was following Weston onto the boat, but it was dark and I was drunk and . . . and he was looking the other way, and I guess I thought Harley was Weston, so I hit him, with a rock I'd picked up and he turned . . . and it was Harley and . . . and he fell over the railing. I didn't mean . . . I wouldn't . . ." She started crying and coughing. "I saw him struggling, flailing but . . . but he couldn't swim. It was like he was trapped and . . . and . . . Oh God . . . I ran. I left him there. I . . . I . . ."

"No," Claire whispered, pain cracking her voice. "No. No. No."

"I found her walking home, dazed, still holding the rock," Miranda cut in, her voice surprisingly steady. "She told me what happened, I called nine-one-one anonymously from a phone booth, but the police were already there because someone on another boat saw his body. Anyway, I drove home and we found you."

"And the blood on your skirt was from the baby?"

"Yes," Miranda whispered. "Hunter's baby."

"What . . . what about the rock that Tessa used to hit Harley?"

"I don't know. I threw it away when we stopped the car and told you that Harley was dead. Remember that stretch of road?"

Claire nodded. Her face was white as death, her expression twisted in horror. She hadn't known.

"I pitched it into the woods."

Claire was on her feet in an instant, racing to the far end of the porch, where she fell against the railing and threw up over and over again. She was crying and retching so painfully that it was all Kane could do to stay hidden in the shadows. He wanted to run to her, to wrap his arms around her, to comfort her. Despite her lies. Despite the years and circumstance separating them. But he couldn't.

Nor could he write the story of Harley Taggert's death. Not now. Not knowing the truth. Too many innocent lives would be ruined. As of this night, Kane's personal vendetta against Dutch Holland was over. It had to be. Dutch, the bastard, was Claire's father and his own son's grandfather. Kane stood in the shadows of the hedge and knew that he'd destroy everything he had on file. If the sisters wanted to spill their guts, so be it. But he wouldn't bring them down or haul Tessa in to face justice. Weston Taggert, if he was indeed Hunter and Jack's killer, would be found out soon enough.

As for Claire and her lies about Sean, he'd talk to her later. He watched as Miranda scooted back her chair and walked toward Claire. "It'll be all right," she whispered, and the two sisters clung to each other.

"But what about Weston?" Tessa said. "We can't just let him go free."

Miranda's face was grim. "The police will figure out that he lied about Hunter's employment records. They'll put two and two together and besides, I've done some investigating on my own with the help of a friend, Frank Petrillo, in the department. Some of Weston's business dealings, especially that one he's trying to put together with one of the tribes for a casino, aren't on the up and up. He's going to have more legal trouble than he ever dreamt. Not that it matters."

"Of course it matters," Tessa said, her voice a monotone. "He's got to pay."

"Shh. Don't talk like that," Miranda commanded. "And have some faith. I know it's hard, but things will turn out all right."

"They'll never be all right," Tessa said, as Kane, guilt heavy on his shoulders for eavesdropping like a common snoop, slipped away and headed back to the path that rimmed the lake. But Tessa's voice chased after him. "I think we're doomed," she said in a monotone. "Every last one of us."

CHAPTER 31

Claire couldn't eat or sleep. After last night's revelations she'd spent the remaining hours tossing and turning, staring at the clock and remembering Harley, sweet, sweet Harley. She'd loved him with that silly naive love of youth, and until she'd met Kane she hadn't questioned her feelings for him. Whatever Harley's faults, whatever his shortcomings, he hadn't deserved to die, nor had Tessa deserved to become a killer.

Claire dressed and showered, took the kids over to Stone Illahee for tennis lessons and a day at the pool, then returned home and wondered how she could ever put her life together. She considered calling the police, reached for the phone several times, then decided to let Miranda handle it. She was with the District Attorney's office for Multnomah County, which was basically the greater Portland metropolitan area, but as an officer of the court had some responsibilities to truth, justice, and the letter of the law. The authorities in Chinook would become informed.

And what about you? Don't you care about right and wrong? Harley's death? Weston's rape of Miranda? The loss of Miranda and Hunter's baby?

Pain ripped through her. There was so much agony. Too much.

As she had as a child, she felt the need for escape, and, ignoring the list of things she was to do today, she walked to the barn and noticed clouds sliding across the sky. Who cared? Within minutes she'd saddled a little bay mare and headed up the familiar and overgrown trail to the sacred grounds of the local Native American tribe, the clearing on the cliffs that Ruby had warned her of all those years ago, that special place where she and Kane had found love.

Kane. Her heart ached at the thought of him. Surely he would uncover the truth, discover her lies. He'd somehow divine that Sean was his boy. And what then? Would he hate her forever, abandon her, try to gain custody? Her thoughts spun out before her in worried circles. Oh, God, she had to tell him and soon.

A flock of seagulls rose above the trees and spiderwebs, sparkling with dew were flung between the branches. A few leaves slapped at her face as the mare loped steadily upward toward the clouds.

At the top of the cliffs, she slowed and reined her mount toward the campsite where she'd found Kane so often. But today it was vacant and aside from cold ashes from a long-ago fire, it showed no hint that anyone had ever been there. A chill crawled up her spine, causing her flesh to rise in little bumps, and she wondered if Ruby was right, that the spirits of the dead inhabited this stretch of land.

Disappointed, she let the mare graze as she sat in the saddle and stared over the ridge to the ocean, dark and brooding, the clouds above rolling ominously. She hadn't wanted to ride, she realized, but was hoping to see Kane again. It wasn't this gloomy little rendezvous spot she'd needed to visit again, but Kane.

And so she would.

"Hiya!" She yanked on the reins. Turning the horse toward the lodge, she pressed hard with her knees and urged the mare into a gallop. For some reason she felt as if she was running out of time, that if she didn't reach Kane soon and tell him the truth, all hell would break loose.

The last person Weston expected to find at his office was Tessa Holland, but here she was, seated on the couch, her shapely legs crossed, a cigarette burning in one hand. Somehow she'd sneaked by his Nazi of a receptionist, but Weston didn't mind. She was still as sexy as ever in her tight white sweater and short black skirt. He felt his cock quiver and silently damned his overactive sex drive, which forever got him into trouble. Serious trouble.

"Tessa," he said, hoping to sound casual as he propped his butt against the corner of his desk and clasped his hands over one knee. "To what do I owe the honor?"

"I thought it was time to come clean."

"You?"

"No. You." She took a puff from her cigarette and let a cloud of smoke rise from her mouth. "You've heard they found Hunter Riley's body at the excavation site for the next phase of Stone Illahee?"

He had to be careful here. Obviously she knew more than he thought. "I heard they found *a* body, one assumed to be Riley because of some ring he wore, but that there wouldn't be a positive ID until dental records were examined and reviewed."

"Just a matter of time." She cocked her head to one side and eyed him in a way that made him want to squirm. "You did it, Weston," she said. "We all know it, because you lied about having him on the payroll in Canada." She clucked her tongue. "You know, I thought you were smarter than that."

"So you came here to what—? Accuse me of being a murderer?" He laughed. "Come on, Tessa. Lighten up. The way I remember it, we had some good times together. Isn't that really why you're here, why you came over?"

"In your dreams. I just wanted to play with you."

"Tessa, baby—"

"The way I remember it, we had some bad times," she said, her blue eyes widening a bit. "Like the time you beat me and forced me to go down on you."

"Now, I don't—"

"And then there was the time that you raped Miranda. Remember that? She miscarried. Did you know?" Tessa rose to her feet and strode close enough to Weston that she could poke him in the chest with the two fingers holding her Virginia Slim. She seemed empowered and hell-bent for vengeance, no longer a scared little girl. "You were so brutal with her that she lost the baby. And I was so weak, so damned worthless, that I couldn't even get up and help her. I should have killed you then, Weston, and saved the state the trouble when they find you guilty of Hunter Riley's death."

"I didn't—"

"Then you know who did." She let ash drop onto his carpet. "You'd better get yourself a damned good lawyer, Taggert, because you're going to need it."

"You have no proof of anything you're saying," he replied, cool on the outside while his guts turned to water. "And who would believe you? How many shrinks have you seen in the last fifteen years? Five? Ten? And wasn't there some rumor about you having sex with one of your therapists? Christ, Tessa, I don't know what you're talking about. You're just another deluded psycho."

She didn't back down an inch. "And what about Jack Songbird? You know they found his knife by Hunter's body." She smiled strangely, her lush lips stretching under a sheen of red lipstick. Tapping her head as if she just came upon a thought, she asked, "Didn't I see you with that knife—you remember, right after your car was vandalized?"

Weston was starting to sweat, but he was too used to this game to break down. "You *are* deluded, aren't you?"

"You're going down, Taggert, and it's about time. I just wanted you to know that I can't wait to testify, not only about the knife, but about everything else as well. I've got nothing to lose and you know what, it feels good."

Weston laughed even though he felt like strangling her. "Go ahead. I have nothing to hide. Why would I want to kill Riley or Songbird?"

"Good question, but you know," she said, grinding out her cigarette in a brass tray on the table near the couch. "The cops are good at finding motives. Oh," she stopped as if she'd just had another thought, though her timing was so impeccable he was certain this was all a show. "I suppose you know that your business is being investigated as well."

His stomach knotted. "Investigated?"

"Yeah, I'm not sure which branch of the government is checking you out—the IRS or the state department of revenue or whatever, but you'd better hope your records are all in order." Clutching her purse in one hand, she walked to the door. "I came by with the good news because I figured I owed you one for everything you've done to me and my family." She blew him a kiss and reached for the doorknob. "See you in court."

Then she was gone, breezing out of the room and leaving the scents of smoke and expensive perfume. She was bluffing; she had to be. Or did she hate him so much that she'd humiliate herself by testifying? Wasn't there a statute of limitations on rape and assault or . . . had that changed? As for murder . . . *Think, Taggert. Think. You've been in tighter spots than this; there's got to be a way out of this!*

He rounded the desk and sat in his chair. His heart was hammering and sweat stood out all over his body. He thought he might lose control of his bowels for a second, but the feeling passed as he realized he had an ace up his sleeve. All he needed to do was get rid of Tessa. And Sean as well. The kid was Harley's son, a threat to the inheritance, and so he'd have to be taken care of. Weston had worked too long and hard and taken more than one life in his pursuit of more and more of the Taggert fortune. Only Paige was left to rival him for her share of the wealth, but he'd never been able to get rid of her. He needed her to take care of the old man, and there was something about Paige, an edge to her that he saw in the superior lift of her chin or the glint in her eye, that warned him she could be very dangerous. Though she'd never said as much, he was certain she knew everything vile he'd ever done, cataloged the act, and waited to use it against him.

He reached for the desk phone, thought better of it and found his cell in his briefcase. He snapped the phone open. With practiced fingers he dialed Denver Styles, reached an answering machine, and left a message for Styles to meet him later that evening.

Never in her life had Claire been to the little cabin across the lake. She'd known Kane had lived there, even roared by the place while boating, but she'd never stopped, and her relationship with Kane had been so short and fierce before he'd joined the army that there hadn't been time. Besides, in those days, Kane was always looking for excuses to leave the house and his drunk of a father rather than stay in.

Now, as she drove to the parking area next to the house, she felt her heart pound. Kane's Jeep was in the drive and she'd have to face him and tell him he was a father. No more lies. Her fingers were wet with sweat, and she found a thousand excuses to put the inevitable off, but she couldn't. It was time.

She walked up the front steps as Kane opened the screen door. "Looking for me?" he asked, and he seemed more distant than he ever had. He didn't hold her or kiss her or even offer her much of a smile, but he was still as handsome as ever, as virile, and a part of her wanted to throw her arms around his neck, kiss him and never let go.

"We need to talk."

A gold eyebrow lifted in interest. "About?" he asked casually, but she noticed an undertone of something . . . condemnation? . . . in his voice.

"A lot of things."

His mouth was a hard line, his eyes guarded as he held the door open for her and she ventured inside. The place was clean, aside from his work area that was strewn with papers, pens, files, and paper clips, as well as his computer. She felt him standing behind her, waiting, and she tried to find the words to make him understand. "There's . . . something you need to know." She was shaking inside. How long had she waited for this moment? Dreamed of it? Feared it? And now the words stuck in her throat. Sixteen years of lies. Sixteen. Until she sometimes doubted the truth.

"Turn around, Claire," he said, touching her on the shoulders, gently rotating her so that she was forced to look into his eyes.

"This is hard." She cleared her throat. "It's . . . it's about Sean."

Kane's lips tightened a fraction. "He's not Paul's son."

"What? No, but—" Oh God, he knew!

"He's mine."

The words seemed to echo through her brain, and yet there was nothing but silence in the room. Was it condemnation she saw in his eyes or just plain anger? "Yes."

"Why didn't you tell me?"

"I—I couldn't. By the time I knew, I was married, Paul had agreed to claim the baby as his own and I thought . . . I mean, until Sean was three or four months, I believed . . ." Tears filled her eyes, shame colored her cheeks.

"You thought he was Taggert's."

"Yes." Her voice shook. "I—I—oh, Kane, I'm so sorry." Never had truer words been spoken. How she rued all the deception, all the time that had been lost.

She stepped into his arms and felt him stiffen.

"I thought the baby was Harley's. All through my pregnancy and during the first few months of his life, I believed that Sean's father was dead, that there could never be any kind of reconciliation and then . . . as the months and years went by it was obvious that he was your boy, but I got pregnant with Sam and it was just easier to pretend that we were a happy, normal family." She blinked against the hot tears invading her eyes. "Of course we weren't."

A shudder ran through his body and something inside him seemed to crack. His arms, so distant a second before, wrapped tightly around her body, holding her close, as if possessing her, body and soul. "It's all right," he said against her hair, and her knees sagged. What had she done to deserve his understanding? He kissed her crown, and she let out a cracked little sob.

"I love you," she said, and he held her even more fiercely.

"I love you." His hands reached up and turned her face up to meet his. "I knew about Sean."

She froze. "You did?"

"I found out yesterday."

"What?" Dear God, he'd known and he'd let her humiliate herself, grovel at his feet? She tried to pull away, but he held her close, forcing her head against his shoulder.

"I got a copy of his birth certificate."

"Oh, no—" She wanted to die a thousand deaths.

"At first I thought he was Taggert's boy, and then, as I thought about it, he looked too much like my family. The blood type matches. I checked."

"I didn't know until it was too late, and then I thought it would be best for him to think that Paul was his natural father since we were married." She sniffed. "Another mistake."

"It's gonna be fine," he said, surprising her. How she wanted to believe him, to trust him.

"I don't see how."

"I want you to marry me, Claire," he said, looking down at her and offering just the hint of a smile. "We've lost a lot of time, but I think it could still be good. For all of us."

Stunned, she stared up at him. *Marriage?* He wanted marriage? "But Sean and Samantha—"

"Will both be my children."

"I don't think . . . I mean . . . Kane, you're writing a book about Harley." This was all happening too fast. Or was it? Sixteen years was a long time to right a wrong.

"It's over. I have a confession to make." He led her to the sofa, and they sank upon it together. Once seated, he placed an arm around her shoulders and told her about the night before, how he'd jogged around the lake intending to confront her about Sean and then, when he'd overheard the sisters' conversation, been unable to tear himself away from it.

"I shouldn't have stuck around and eavesdropped," he said, guilt obviously still eating at him. She was rocked again to think he'd overheard her private conversation, Miranda's grief and Tessa's chilling confession. "But I couldn't leave. Believe me, your secret is safe with me."

"Nothing's safe anymore." That was the one certainty in life.

"Shh."

He kissed her and tasted the salt of her tears. "Just trust me, Claire."

"I do." She shuddered against him and gave out a tiny sigh of surrender. How long had she waited to hear him utter those words? There had been a time when she would never have thought they could ever be together.

"Be my wife."

"I—I will," she promised through her tears. "I will."

Weston adjusted the jib and the sail snapped in the breeze. He'd put in a call to Denver Styles, requested a private meeting, and now they were alone on the *Stephanie,* tacking toward shore. As he guided the sleek boat, Weston wondered just how far Styles could be trusted. The greedy son of a bitch would do just about anything for the right amount of money, Weston was sure of it, and as far as he could discern, Styles had no scruples whatsoever. Styles was a rogue private investigator of sorts with possible ties to the under-world.

"I've got a problem," Weston admitted, steering into the wind.

"What kind?" Styles flicked his damned gaze in Weston's direction.

"One I'm hoping you'll help me solve."

"Maybe."

"I need some people to . . . disappear."

The wind kicked Styles's hair across his face, but he didn't change expression, just stared at Weston with those gunmetal gray eyes.

"What do you mean 'disappear'?"

"As in leave permanently."

Styles rubbed his jaw. "You want them killed."

Lifting a shoulder, Weston said, "That would be the easiest, I think. An accident up on 101 where the road curves high above the sea—the guardrail could be weakened and the car could be forced off the road. It would plunge off the cliffs and end up in the ocean."

Styles's jaw tightened nearly imperceptibly. "And who would be in the car?"

"Tessa Holland and her nephew, Sean St. John."

"What if I say 'no'?"

"There's a lot of money involved."

Styles hesitated, and Weston knew right then and there that he had him. The bastard was certainly money-motivated. "How much?"

"Half a million. All you have to do is find a way to abduct them, pour a little liquor down Tessa's throat, maybe the boy's as well, he's a troublemaker, and I'll bet has already emptied his share of beer bottles. After they're inebriated put them both in Tessa's car, and while everyone else is at the party tomorrow night, the one where Dutch is going to announce his candidacy for the governor-ship, they have an accident."

"So you'll have an alibi." There wasn't a trace of inflection in Denver's voice.

"Bingo." Weston turned the sailboat into the channel leading to the bay. "What d'ya say?"

"Five hundred thousand?"

"That's right. A hundred up front."

The flinty eyes sparked and there was only the slightest hint of hesitation, or twinge of conscience. Then the hard-edged smile that stretched from one side of his mouth to the other. "It's a deal, Taggert," he said. "But I'll want to be paid tomorrow night as soon as the party's over. Then I'm outta here. You'll never hear from me again."

"All the better," Weston said, deciding that he liked the man's style. "All the better."

CHAPTER 32

"There's something I want to talk to you about," Claire said when Sean stormed into the house. He'd been gone a lot lately, still angry about moving to Oregon. Though he hadn't been caught stealing again, he'd been hanging around some kids she didn't trust, coming in late, and mouthing off. Oftentimes he smelled of cigarettes and beer, though she'd never caught him red-handed or drunk.

He was heading up the stairs to his room.

"What?" Belligerent, he turned on her, then noticed her cream-colored dress. "Oh, shit. You think I'm going to that damned party, don't you?"

"It's Grandpa's big night."

"Grandpa can go suck pondwater for all I care. He's a manipulative bastard."

"Sean!"

"Well, he is. Besides, I've got plans."

"With whom?"

"Does it matter?"

"Of course. But this party isn't something you can ditch out of."

"Sure I can. Grandpa doesn't care if I'm there. He doesn't like me anyway."

"Why would you say that?"

"I can tell by the way he looks at me."

"You're paranoid," Samantha said as she skipped down the stairs in her new dress. Made of rose-colored silk, it swished as she passed.

"Yeah and you're a—"

"Let's not get into this now, okay? We don't have time. Come into the kitchen, Sean, there's something we've got to talk about." *It's now or never,* she told herself. Too many people knew that Sean wasn't Paul's son. It was time for him to know the truth.

"If anyone says I've been swiping things, it's a big lie—"

"Samantha, we need to be alone for a few minutes," Claire said, and Sam nodded as she flitted outside to the front porch. "Don't get dirty."

"I won't. Don't worry." The screen door slammed behind her.

Claire followed her son into the kitchen and watched as he rummaged in the refrigerator before plopping onto a stool at the counter with a can of Coke and a piece of cold chicken. His eyes were distrustful, his hair hung in his face, his expression was one of irritation, and yet she loved this boy with all her heart. "There's something I want you to know. Something I should have told you a long time ago."

"Yeah?" He popped the tab of his soda. "What?"

"It's about your father."

"He's a pervert." He took a long swallow of Coke.

"No, Sean, I'm not talking about Paul."

"Shit, then what—?" He looked up sharply.

She laid her fingers across his forearm and felt his muscles tense. "Paul St. John isn't your biological father."

"What the fu—?" He drew away from her as if he'd been burned. "What do you mean—not my biological father?"

"Just that. Listen to me. I wasn't married when I conceived you. I was involved with someone, and he went into the army and didn't know about you."

"What?" He jumped off his stool and it scooted across the floor to bang into the wall. *"What?* For Christ's sake, Mom, is this some kind of sick joke?"

"No joke."

"But . . ." He shook his head in disbelief.

"Kane Moran's your father."

Sean's mouth went slack. "The guy with the motorcycle?"

"Who got you out of the shoplifting charge."

"He's my father?" Sean's voice cracked. "This is just another lie, isn't it?"

"No." She eyed him in dead seriousness and his color changed from ruddy rebellion to ghost white.

"No way."

"Yes, Sean, I should have told you sooner."

"Damn straight you should have! What is this, Mom? Are you gonna tell me that my whole life is a lie?"

"No, but—"

"Jesus, I can't believe this!" Tears sprang to his eyes. "You were screwing him and then passing me off as that pervert St. John's. For the love of God. What about Sam?" His voice cracked again and his eyes filled with unwanted tears.

"Paul's her father."

"Holy shit, Mom."

"Sean, just listen—"

"No way!" Backing up, tripping over the stool, he made his way to the door. "No fucking way!" He barreled out of the door, running as fast as his legs would carry him. Claire chased after him, through the French doors and down the porch, but her heels caught in the floorboards and she couldn't catch him as he ran down past the garage, past the dock, and into the woods. "Sean!" she yelled. "Sean!"

"What happened?" Samantha, who had been sitting on the porch swing, asked.

"I gave him some news he didn't want to hear."

"What?"

"I'll tell you about it later. Right now I've got to find him."

"Just let him cool off," Sam advised. "He doesn't really have to go to the party, does he?"

"He should."

"He'd just be a pain if he went," Samantha said sagely.

Claire stared into the woods and felt powerless. Maybe Sam was right. Then again, she felt that she should follow her boy, hold him and tell him everything would be all right, that she was sorry she lied, but life would go on. Dear God, she prayed that he was okay and she was doing the right thing.

"Okay, let's let him have a little time to himself," she said to Samantha, and turned toward the house. They walked into the kitchen as the phone rang. Claire snagged the receiver on the third ring.

"Claire?" Miranda's voice was shaking. "Have you seen Tessa?"

"No? Should I have?"

"She and I were going to the party together, but she's not in her suite or anywhere else around Stone Illahee."

This wasn't a surprise. "You know how she is."

"I know she didn't want to go, but last night she told me she would."

"She's changed her mind before."

"This is different," Miranda said, and a new uneasiness slithered down Claire's spine. "I talked to her two hours ago, and she said she'd be ready but the trouble was I think she'd already been drinking."

"Sometimes, when she needs a little confidence—"

"I know, I know, she takes a drink. But . . . oh, well, there's nothing I can do. I'll see you at the party. Maybe Tessa will show up."

"Maybe," Claire said, but stared out the window to the woods where her son had disappeared. He'd come home. He always did, but not until he was damned well good and ready.

She glanced at the evening sky and couldn't shake a premonition of certain doom.

CHAPTER 33

Weston's hand trembled as he poured liquor into a glass. He was losing it. Big time. And it bugged the hell out of him. Tonight Dutch Holland was making his official bid to run for governor. And while the bastard was at it, wining and dining Oregon's elite, dancing the night away, laughing, drinking, getting ready for a late-in-life thrill ride, the police would begin piecing together what had happened to Hunter Riley.

Not to mention what Kane Moran with all of his damned research had uncovered. Hell.

Weston lifted the glass of whiskey to his lips and stared out the windows of his office, a panoramic view of the town of Chinook and further, beyond the rooftops, the vast Pacific Ocean, dark and brooding, a mirror of his own fathomless thoughts. His office was dark except for light spilling in from the hallway and he caught sight of his reflection in the glass, a ghostly figure, drinking alone, beyond which the lights of the town glowed fiercely. It was as if he was super-imposed over the rest of Chinook and that was as it should be, a Taggert always in the shadows, always above, always making an impression over the town.

But there was another image as well, one he saw only in his mind's eye, a small boy locked in a dark basement, threatened with losing his home, his inheritance, his parents' love.

"Don't you ever talk back to me again, boy," Neal Taggert had yelled, cuffing Weston alongside his head as he pushed him toward the basement door. "Nor your mother either. If you do, I swear, I'll beat you to within an inch of your miserable hide and you can forget living here with me, with your ma. I'll make sure everything goes to Harley and Paige." His fingers had dug into Weston's arm and he'd leaned over, closer to his son's ear. "And I'll even make sure any bastards I sire get more than you do." He hadn't laughed or smiled. Neal Taggert's expression had been hard as stone, his eyes dark with disappointment and rage as he'd told Weston to walk into the cellar alone. Trembling, Weston had done as ordered and visibly started when the door had slammed shut behind him and he'd heard the lock slide into place.

There had been no light in that tomb, the switch had been placed at the bottom of the stairs on the other side of the door. Neal Taggert had sworn under his breath as he'd mounted the stairs and Weston had been left alone, the barest hint of light under the door his only source of illumination. He'd waited for hours, each minute seeming an eternity, fear crawling steadily up his spine, his imagination running wild with the thought of rats and spiders and bats. He'd sat at the door, his arms over his knees, his bladder so full he'd nearly passed out before he'd finally stumbled to a far corner and relieved himself against the wall. Later, the stain discovered by a maid, he'd been beaten again, his father assuming that he'd pissed just to show even more rebellion.

God, the old man was a bastard, mellowed now only because age and infirmity had bowed his back and taken away his legs. At least he was no longer capable of spawning more children. And so far, no more bastards had appeared. There had been one . . . Hunter Riley . . . but he was now dead. As was Songbird. Weston hadn't been sure about the Indian. There had been rumors about Neal and Ruby Songbird, never really proven, but the kid had been such a prick, showing up to work late, getting into Weston's face, vandalizing cars. . . and Neal never had wanted to fire the son of a bitch . . . so Weston had put one and one together and come up with two. Even if Jack hadn't been Neal's son, he was a thorn in Weston's side, always getting on him about the way he'd treated

Crystal and then the car . . . one way or another the sorry son of a bitch deserved to die.

The lights of town were fading a bit as the first wisps of fog rolled in from the sea.

Weston swirled his drink, then swallowed it as he noticed a police car, lights flashing, racing through town, disappearing around a corner as the fog thickened. He checked his watch. It was time . . .

Another tragedy was about to take place.

Weston had already set the wheels in motion. He walked to his computer and sent a couple of e-mail messages, one to his accountant, another to a foreman at the mill, knowing that they would be dated and timed. Then he made two quick calls from the office phone, just in case the police checked any phone records. His car was parked in its usual space, guarded by a night watchman, and he wouldn't move it—he had another at his disposal, a truck once used for deliveries, one that had been used by Kendall's father years ago, nondescript, dark blue, a Ford like a dozen others in town, nearly identical to the one driven by Jack Songbird's father, Ruby's husband . . . yes, it would do nicely. Especially since the license plates had been switched with two that didn't match, the front plate Weston had taken from a Dodge parked at a local bar, the back one had been removed discreetly from Songbird's truck just last night as it had been parked in front of the Songbird double-wide. Everything was set for this night when Dutch Holland intended to announce his bid to run for governor; there were just a few loose ends to take care of.

Pulling on a pair of tight black gloves, Weston locked the door to his office and stole down the back stairs.

Noiselessly opening the back door, he slipped unnoticed into the mist-shrouded night.

Sean kicked at a rock and scowled as it skipped across the street, hit a pothole and ricocheted into the fender of a shiny new Toyota. Great. Just what he needed. More trouble. As if he wasn't in enough. He kicked his skateboard into place and quickly rolled through the streets of this dumb little town. God, he hated it here in loserville. Why his mom didn't move back to Colorado, he didn't understand.

Sure you do. It's because of the prick. Your real father.

That thought stuck in his craw and he spit as he wheeled around the corner and felt the moist air on his face. Luckily it was getting foggy so he could cut through parking lots, yards and alleys at will, with no one spying on him. The thought of his mother and that guy. Kane Moran. "More like moron," he muttered, hiking up the collar of his army jacket and refusing to think about his mom—shit, she hadn't been a whole lot older than he was now and she'd been doin' it with that creep. He didn't like the guy. Just because Moran liked motorcycles didn't change things. The guy was a creep, always hanging around and . . . and . . . Sean would never, *never* call the jerk "Dad." Oh, hell, no.

He saw a cop car, lights flashing, heading north through town and he quickly turned south, away from the wailing siren. He didn't need that kind of trouble tonight. His mom had probably already called the police because he'd been gone so long. Sean felt a niggle of guilt; he didn't want to worry anyone, he just needed some space, time to think about how to deal with all of this. He knew there was no way his mom was moving back to Colorado, but it bugged him. Maybe he could work a deal with Jeff and his parents—maybe they would take him in.

Like Claire would ever allow that.

He heard a car behind him and he shifted his weight so he could turn into the parking lot of the grade school. Expecting the car to drive on, he thought about heading back toward the old lodge, but the headlights, unclear in the mist, turned into the lot.

Crap!

Sean headed for the exit.

The car followed. Twin beams caught him in their diffused light as he skirted a pothole.

Great. Just effin' great.

He pushed off harder, picking up speed and hazarded a glance over his shoulder. No hood rack. Not a cop. In fact . . . the car looked like his aunt Tessa's Mustang. He felt better. He liked Tessa. His mother's older sister, Miranda, an assistant DA for crying out loud, struck him as a city bitch. She was way too serious and she worked for the damned cops, but the younger one with her bleached hair, navel ring, tattoo and guitar was cool. He started to slow down as Tessa rolled down her window. "Sean?"

Busted.

She'd seen him. No matter what happened, she was bound to tell his mom. Unless he talked her out of it. He slowed and turned. Tessa's face, illuminated by one street lamp was drawn and white, fear showing in her eyes. "I think you should get in the car."

"Nah—I—" Then he noticed the guy. Sitting in the passenger seat. The guy's face was in shadow, hidden by the darkness and the fog, but the vibes Sean picked up weren't good, not good at all and then there was the strain in his aunt's face.

"Your Mom is worried."

Too bad. "She'll get over it."

"Sean, please." God, she sounded desperate, her voice tight.

"No." He turned as if to take off when he saw the man move, get out of the car.

Adrenaline surged through Sean's veins. Fear catapulted him onto his board, but the man was around the car in an instant. "You'd better get in the car now," he said in a voice that scared the living piss out of Sean. He jumped on his board, but the man caught hold of his arm in a punishing grip. "Let's go, Sean," he said as his jacket opened to give Sean a glimpse of a gun tucked in a shoulder holster. "Now."

Kane tapped his pencil on the table and glared at his notes. Included was the autopsy reports for Hunter Riley and Jack Songbird, two people who died mysteriously, along with Harlan Taggert sixteen years ago. Three men, who, from outward appearances, had little in common other than they all lived in Chinook and worked for Neal Taggert. Harlan, Claire's lover, had been a spoiled rich kid not fit for his job, Jack, a Native American, had been a rebel with a bad-ass attitude, and Hunter had been a kid from the wrong side of the tracks who was trying to better himself. He'd also been in love with Miranda Holland, had gotten her pregnant.

Two of the men had been involved with Holland women. Two of them were from the poorer part of town. All three were dead before their time.

Why?

Who would benefit from their deaths?

If Tessa had killed Harley, then had she killed the other two? To what end? She didn't appear a psychotic and she'd killed Harley thinking he was Weston . . . Kane grimaced as he thought of the eldest son of Neal Taggert. Self-important. Manipulative. Just plain evil. The pistol that had been in the water was still unclaimed, but Kane had dug up some information that Mikki Taggert had purchased a small caliber handgun years before, at a gun show. The only reason he knew this is he'd interviewed a former maid who had worked in the Taggert home. She'd sworn she'd seen the gun in Mikki's dresser drawer and though it looked like the pistol found in the bay near Harley's body, she couldn't swear to it. Besides, she'd confided, the gun had been stolen or misplaced months before Harley had died. The staff had been interrogated several times about missing items, the pistol being one.

But Harley wasn't killed by a gun. No bullet wound. The gun that had been found by his body had been loaded, but every bullet had been tucked neatly in its chamber.

Tessa killed Harley.

Tessa couldn't have killed Jack or Hunter.

Kane had mapped out where everyone had been when Jack was assaulted—assuming that he hadn't just slipped off the cliff face, which, because of the other murders, Kane discounted. It was just too coincidental. Nah. Kane didn't put too much stock in coincidence.

He turned to his laptop where an image of a map of Chinook and the surrounding area was glowing. He was missing something. He clicked to another screen, checking a list he'd made of all the primary players in the mystery—the Hollands, Taggerts, Songbirds, Rileys, and wondered at the connection.

There had been widespread rumors that both Neal Taggert and Dutch Holland were far from monogamous. Hell, his own mother had succumbed to the charms of good ol' Benedict. Kane's jaw tightened as he considered his own role in this drama—more like a soap opera when he considered his old man's accident, his mother's betrayal, and Kane's infatuation with Claire Holland. It seemed that everyone in Chinook was tangled with everyone else.

There had been talk of illegitimate children fathered by Neal Taggert. The old guy had been romantically linked with several local women.

Years ago DNA testing hadn't been available, or so widespread, but now it was possible. Paternity could be proven. Where once there was only a rumor, or a blood test that might prove a man a father, now it was certain. So Kane had checked. The blood tests taken years before proved that Hunter Riley could have been Neal Taggert's son. But Jack Songbird wasn't, despite the rumors that had passed through the alleys, taverns, churches and coffee shops of Chinook.

Kane had tried time and time again to talk to Neal Taggert, but the old man had refused to see him. Tonight, on the night his old rival was going to announce his bid to run for governor, seemed a fitting time for Neal Taggert to come clean. What was the old saying, If Mohamed won't come to the mountain, the mountain would come to him? Something like that. Well, the mountain was definitely going to Mohamed.

Leaving his notes on the table, Kane found his keys and walked out of the tired old cabin where he'd grown up.

Outside the fog was thick and damp, brushing against his collar and flattening his hair. Kane barely noticed as he slid behind the wheel of his Jeep, flipped on the ignition and put the rig into gear. Tonight, come hell or high water, he was going to get the truth.

Headlights cut through the night, two beams that refracted in the rolling fog as a car—no, some type of SUV pulled into the circular drive. As Paige peered through the blinds, she felt a premonition of bad things to come. No one visited her and her father at night. No, this wasn't going to be good. She licked her lips nervously as she spied a man climb from behind the wheel. As he opened the door of the rig, the interior light switched on. Paige's heart clutched as she recognized Kane Moran. His features were blurry in the gloom, but she recognized Kane Moran just the same. Damn, the guy was a pain in the rear, as sticky as gum on a shoe on a hot day.

She didn't wait for him to ring the bell, but opened the door as he climbed the two steps to the deck that circled this house set on the cliffs, the same house she'd lived in all her life. "What are you doing here?" she asked and slipped onto the front porch so that her father wouldn't hear the conversation.

"I need to see your father."

"He's resting," she said quickly. "He's an invalid. He goes to bed early."

"He's been ducking me."

"Do you blame him?" Jesus, the guy wasn't taking a hint and Paige was nervous. She glanced over her shoulder to the windows of the den where her father had been watching television. "You're dredging up a lot of pain for him. I would think you would have the decency to let everything be."

"I just want the truth."

"So you can profit from it," she said, raising a disdainful eyebrow. "Don't try to elevate this from anything more than what it is, one person making money off another person's tragedy."

"You think that's what I'm doing?" One side of his mouth lifted into a sexy smile, the same kind of grin she remembered from her youth, before she'd lost twenty pounds, before the braces had come off, before she'd learned how to color her hair and have it layered into a flattering style, before she'd discovered the magic of makeup. It was the same knowing grin that Weston's friends had bestowed upon her as they'd teased her so mercilessly.

"I know what you're doing."

"What are you afraid of?"

"Me?" she asked, breaking out into a nervous sweat. "Nothing."

"Then let me see Neal. Hear what he has to say."

"No, not now, you'll only upset him."

"Would he prefer to be served with a summons?" Kane asked, his smile disappearing, the glint in his eyes hard determination. "Because that's my next step. I think I have enough evidence to prove that your brother was murdered and that it was done by someone who knew him. I'd think you, and your father, would want that information. I'm sure the police will. There's no statute of limitations on murder, you know, and if you'll recall, three men died that summer. Three young men. Harley was just one of them. I think they're all connected and the most common thread is that they all worked for dear old dad. Now either I talk to him right here, right now, or I show the DA what I've found and Neal can talk to a homicide detective."

"He already has, dozens of times." She sounded forceful, but her palms were damp and it was all she could do not to rub them down the front of her khakis.

"Well, that was just a warm-up for the main event," Kane said and, from the corner of her eye, she saw the blinds of the den move, fingertips pushing the slats down, old eyes behind glasses peering through. Oh, God, it was all unraveling.

"Just go home and leave us alone."

"Can't do it."

Tap. Tap. Tap. She and Moran turned toward the window. Her father drew the blinds open and waved them both inside. Paige's heart dropped like a stone. She shook her head but Neal scowled and motioned more violently.

"Looks like he wants to chat," Kane observed and walked past her toward the door. She grabbed hold of his arm.

"I don't know what you found, but I think I should talk with you first."

"Something you want to get off your chest?"

She licked her lips. Her head was pounding with the truth. Images of the night Harley had died. Brutal pictures. Dark memories. It had been so dark aside from the lights of the marina. The sailboat had been rocking on its moorings, its masts jutting upward, lights glowing from inside. In the distance Paige heard a party going on and some music drifting over the water. There were people on the deck of the sailboat, a tall man she recognized as Harley and a woman with blond hair and something in her hand. A weapon.

Paige shivered now. Even though she'd been far away and it had been dark, Paige remembered how the woman had struck Harley from behind. Fiercely. Angrily. Hard enough that the sound, the sickening crush of bones had echoed over the water. Paige, standing in the shadows had gasped and dropped her gun, the gun she'd intended to use to scare Harley into wising up, into realizing that Kendall was the woman he loved, but now . . . now some blond—Kendall?—was in a rage, intent on bashing Harley's face in. Paige had dropped her mother's gun. It had slid across the deck and into the water with a loud plop. Paige didn't wait to be discovered.

She'd turned and run as fast as her legs could carry her to her bike, hidden between the parked cars. And then she pedaled away as fast as she could before Kendall saw her, before Kendall, sweet, beautiful Kendall had realized that Paige had witnessed her crime.

You should have stayed. You should have called for help. You should have done something to save your brother's life, even if it meant incriminating the only girl who had treated you with any grain of dignity, but instead you ran, refusing to let anyone see you, leaving the gun, leaving Harley to drown. There was a chance you could have saved him. He didn't die from the blow, but because he drowned and you knew how to swim, had been on the swim team . . . Guilt tore through her and she realized that she was crying, tears drizzling down her cheeks as Kane Moran stared at her. It was over. All the lies were at last being uncovered.

"Yeah," she finally said, swiping at her face with the back of her hand. There was no reason to try and protect Kendall any longer. And some of Paige's infatuation with her friend had worn thin over the years . . . how could Kendall have ever married Weston? Harley had been weak, but Weston . . . he was just plain cruel. "Maybe you're right," she admitted. "But there are some things I want to tell you without my father hearing." She opened the door and led him into the den where her father was about to learn that his daughter-in-law, the mother of his grandchild, had killed his son.

She walked him into the den where her father sat in his motorized wheelchair. He looked Kane up one side and down the other, then motioned Paige to the bar. "Get our guest something to drink."

"I'm fine," Kane said, shaking his head.

"Well, I'm not. I'll have a scotch and soda"

Paige hesitated. "But the doctor said—"

"To hell with that old sawbones. Get me a drink. What more damage can it do? Put me in a damned wheelchair?" he demanded. Paige knew there was no talking to him. He was in one of his moods. Fine. Then she'd pour him a double—no, maybe a triple. He didn't seem to mind as she handed him the glass and he took a long swallow. "Now why the hell are you here? For that damned book you're writing."

"That's the main reason."

"So tell me, who killed my son?"

"I'm still working on that." Kane glanced at Paige and she looked pointedly at the television where an old rerun of a comedy her father had enjoyed years ago was playing. "I thought you two could help me."

"Bah. I've already said what I had to say a long time ago. You think my story has changed?"

"No, but I thought you might shed some light on who would want him killed." Kane had a theory, one that he'd been working on. He knew that Tessa had hit Harley over the head, that she in essence had delivered the blow that had taken his life, but there were still some pieces to the puzzle that were missing. The gun in the water didn't make sense. Harley drowned, the blow to his head hard, but not severe enough to have necessarily caused him to black out. So why hadn't he tried to save himself?

"Who?"

"That's what I'm asking you."

Paige could barely breathe. This was getting too close.

"He had women trouble. Worse than Weston did. Couldn't choose between Claire Holland and Kendall Forsythe, who's now Weston's wife." He snorted as if there were no choice involved. Kane visibly bristled, but Neal didn't seem to notice. "Kendall came from a good family, loved that boy, she did, but he was all twisted up over the Holland girl, the middle one. She had him twisted around her finger so bad that Harley thought he was going to marry her." He snorted, then tossed back his drink. "If you ask me, she probably did it. Harley must've called off the engagement . . . and she freaked out."

All the muscles in Kane's shoulders bunched. His smile had long ago disappeared. "I don't think so. According to Claire, *she* broke off the engagement."

"Yeah, right." He acted as if no one would be that stupid. "I always told the police she was the one. Harley didn't just fall over the side of the boat and hit his head and drown."

"Not like Jack Songbird?" Kane threw out.

"What're you saying, that the same person killed them both?"

"And Hunter Riley."

"For the love of Christ, you *are* writing fiction, aren't you?"

"All I want to know is who would most benefit from Harley's death."

Paige swallowed hard as her father glared at Kane over the rim of his glass. "Well, that's pretty simple to figure out, isn't it? But believe me, Weston didn't kill his brother."

Kane's eyes narrowed and Paige saw a spark in his eyes. As if he'd been waiting for Neal to say just those words. "Why didn't he?"

"Because he was far away from there. Not even in town."

"You're certain?"

There was a moment's hesitation and in that split second Paige knew her father was lying. Had been for sixteen years. Just as she had been. "I said he was with me, didn't I?"

"For most of the night. Some of the rest he was with Kendall, but there are still some holes."

Kendall? Had she and Weston lied to protect each other? That didn't make any sense.

"You're fishin', Moran. Without any bait." The old man laughed as if he'd pulled one over on Moran, but Paige knew differently and she realized that tonight, she'd have to tell the truth. She'd borne the lies long enough. Been loyal to Kendall for all the wrong reasons. She'd tried to protect the only friend she'd thought she'd had and to what end? It was all unraveling anyway and Weston was losing it. It was only a matter of time before he would completely snap and then everyone, she herself and Kendall included would be in danger.

"I don't like it . . ." Claire rubbed her arms and stared into the damp, foggy night. Sean had been missing for four hours, not long enough to file a missing person's report but enough hours had passed to move her from worried, past edgy, and into frantic. For the first time since he'd first brought it up, she wished she'd broken down and bought him a cell phone or a pager so that there was some way to communicate with him. Already she'd waited, then gone looking and now, like it or not, she reached for the telephone and dialed Kane on his cell.

He picked up on the second ring. "Moran."

She sagged against the edge of the kitchen counter. Just the sound of his voice was steadying, yet made her want to cry. "It's Claire." Her voice caught.

"You okay?"

"No . . . not really. It's Sean. He's missing."

A swift intake of breath. "How long?"

"Over four hours."

"Where'd he go?"

"I don't know. We had an argument and . . . and . . ." *Pull yourself together, Claire!* "And he took off. I thought he'd go somewhere and cool off, you know, once he'd sorted things out, he'd be back. That's the way it usually works."

But nothing's been usual since you came back to Oregon. She glanced out the window, couldn't see past the murky fog.

"What was the argument about?"

She hesitated. Gathered herself. "I told him the truth about you. That you're his father."

"And I take it he wasn't thrilled at the prospect."

She snorted. "Not thrilled at all."

"Where would he go?"

"I don't know. I waited a couple of hours and then drove around." She bit her lip and moved her finger along the edge of the counter. "I went to a couple of places where kids hang out and then called three boys he's mentioned since we moved here, but I couldn't find him and if the boys know where he is, they're not saying."

"It hasn't been that long." But there was something in his voice, something he wasn't saying.

"I know," she said as she heard a beep stutter on the handset. "Another call is coming in. I'd better take it. It might be Sean."

"I'm on the road, only twenty minutes away. I'll be right over. Stay put," Kane said and hung up.

Claire took the call that was waiting. "Hello?"

"Claire?" Tessa's voice sounded far away and frightened.

"Where are you?"

"Sean's with me."

"You found him? Good. Bring him home." She glanced at the clock. "We can still make the party if we push it—"

"I'm not going."

"Why not?" Dread skittered through Claire's heart. "Wait a minute. Let me talk to Sean."

"I can't." Was Tessa's voice slurred?

"Why not?" she asked.

"Because it's too late, Claire. It's too late for us all."

"Wait a minute, Tessa. Where are you? Tell me where you are and I'll come to you."

Click. The line went dead.

Claire was left standing in the kitchen, staring out the window at the shifting shadows. Tessa had Sean, they were together. Tessa had killed Harley. Tessa sounded desperate on the phone—different. Dear God, what was she planning to do?

Quickly she picked up the phone again and dialed Kane's cell. One ring. Two. Three. "Come on, come on," but his voice mail picked up and she hung up in frustration. He was on his way, hadn't he said so? Give him time to get here. She needed to calm down, to think clearly. What could she do? Call Miranda. As an assistant DA she had enough connections in the police department to get the help they needed to find Tessa and Sean. Tessa's Mustang wouldn't be hard to spot.

Claire punched in the numbers of Miranda's cell and waited as the phone rang. God, wasn't anyone answering tonight? One ring. Two. Three. Finally she heard her sister's voice.

"Hello?"

"Miranda, it's Claire. You have to help me. Tessa has Sean and—"

"Hello? Hello?" Miranda's voice crackled over the phone.

"Miranda, it's me! Tessa's got—"

"Claire is that you? I . . . breaking up . . . call back . . . minutes."

"Miranda! Please, you have to listen to me!" But the static on the phone got more intense and suddenly the phone went silent.

"Damn it!" She started to dial Kane's number again.

"Mom?" She whirled, hadn't expected to see her daughter standing in the doorway to the kitchen. Samantha's face was pulled into a knot of worry as she stood wearing a yellow two piece dress that showed off part of her flat little abdomen. Her hair was piled onto her head and she was wearing too much eye makeup, lip gloss and something that made her skin shimmer. "Is something wrong?"

Everything. "I'm just worried about Sean," she said, trying to stay calm. No reason to panic Samantha.

"He'll be back."

Oh, God, I hope so.

"He's just being a prick—a jerk."

If only I could believe that.

"You're not dressed . . . Hey, is something wrong?"

"I said I'm worried. I, um, might not be going to the party after all. Kane's on his way over and we're going to look for Sean."

Samantha's face fell. "This means we're not going to Grandpa's party, right?"

"We'll go later. When we find your brother."

"That's what he wants, you know. To mess things up." She rolled her overly shadowed eyes and crossed her arms under her chest. Her dress rode up, exposing more of her stomach.

"Why don't you change into something more appropriate?" Claire suggested, though her mind was screaming with fear for her son. Where the devil was Kane? True it had been only a few minutes since she'd talked to him, but it felt like an eternity.

"I like this."

"It's fine. You look good in it, but you need something a bit more conservative." She was marching her daughter upstairs and into her room. Once there she rifled through the closet, but anything she pulled out, Samantha vetoed.

"You want me to look like a nerd."

"No, I want you to look like a geek," Claire shot back, forcing a humor she didn't feel. She didn't have time for this kind of argument. She didn't have time for anything other than finding her son. *Where the hell were Tessa and Sean? Why was her sister pulling this stunt? And Kane, why the hell hadn't he—* She heard the sound of an engine roaring toward the house. "Look, Sam, I was just kidding. Why not wear this?" she asked, and pulled out a navy blue sheath with beading at the neck and hem.

"Bor-ing. Aunt Tessa wouldn't be caught dead in something like this."

"I wouldn't call Aunt Tessa a fashion maven. Let's not put what you're wearing up to her . . . or even down to her standards." She dropped the dress over the back of Samantha's desk chair. "Just find something sedate and tasteful, okay? Kane's here."

"And you're really worried about Sean."

"Yeah," Claire admitted, "I am." She was already racing out of the room but caught her daughter rolling her eyes and muttering under her breath.

". . . always ruining everything . . ."

"Stay put, I'll be back," Claire called as she hurried down the stairs. She'd reached the first floor and already grabbed her purse, cell, and keys when she heard a pounding on the door. Relieved she threw the door open, expecting Kane, ready to fall into his arms. "I've been trying to find you, Tessa called and—"

Weston Taggert stood in the shadows of the porch. "And what?"

Fear dark as death slithered down her spine. "Wait a minute. What are you doing here?" she asked, her lungs constricting as she saw desperation in the corners of his mouth. Her knees threatened to give way.

"I think you'd better come with me," he said, his expression grim.

"With *you?* Why?" But she knew. Oh, God, with mind-numbing certainty she knew.

"Because, Claire, I've got your boy."

CHAPTER 34

Kane drove like a madman. He tromped on the accelerator and took a corner too quickly. His tires squealed in protest and an oncoming car swerved, the driver blasting his horn before disappearing into the fog. Kane didn't care. He had to get to Claire and find Sean. The minute he'd hung up from Claire, he'd started for the door and realized with chilling certainty why Claire had every right to fear for their son. Because of Weston Taggert.

Paige had admitted to being on the dock that night, of thinking she saw an enraged Kendall kill Harley for being with Claire, but it had been Tessa she'd seen and not knowing the truth, she'd held her tongue for sixteen years, protecting Kendall and doing her own quiet penance for not helping save Harley's life by taking care of their father.

But Neal Taggert had provided the real clue. The only person to have gained from his brother's death was Weston. That he hadn't killed Harley was, in Kane's opinion, just luck. The other two men who had been rumored to be his half brothers had met quick, untimely ends. Kane didn't know why Paige, the only other Taggert progeny had been saved, but it probably had something to do with Neal's will.

He nearly missed the lane for the Holland estate, but managed to make the corner, the beams of his headlights cutting through the mist and splashing against the mossy trunks of giant Douglas fir trees. If Weston truly had killed off all of his father's sons, wouldn't he also want to get rid of their sons, Neal's grandsons? Jack and Hunter had died without fathering children. So had Harley, but Weston might not think so. If he'd seen Sean and done the math, wouldn't he assume that Claire's child had been sired by Harley?

Don't even think it, he told himself, *the kid is mad, that's all, and he took off to cool off. He's safe somewhere. Probably already home with Claire.*

Barely visible through the mist and trees, the lights of the old lodge glowed warmly. Kane rounded a final corner and stepped on the brakes. He cut the engine, pocketed his keys and was halfway up the steps when the door opened and Samantha wearing a black dress, stood, backlit by the houselights. "Mom—? Oh."

"Isn't your mom here?" Kane asked.

"I don't know. She was." The girl was obviously worried. "I was upstairs getting dressed for Grandpa's party and Mom and I had kind of a fight and she went downstairs, I thought. But she's not here."

"Her car's parked in front of the garage."

"Yeah, I know."

"Are there any other vehicles missing?"

Samantha was shaking her head. "I don't think so." She bit her lip. Looked troubled. "She was worried about Sean and I think someone came here. I saw a car drive in and then leave."

"Who was it?"

"I don't know. I was getting dressed and the radio was on and, and . . . now she's gone!" The girl was getting worked up, biting her lip, looking as if she was about to cry.

Kane placed an arm around her shoulders. "Listen, I'll find your mom," he said. "Can you call someone to come be with you—no, better yet let's find someone you can stay with."

"I'll come with you."

"I don't think that would be a good idea."

"Why not?"

"Because it might take me a while to find her. You don't have any idea where she is? Or who she was with?"

"No. We were supposed to go to the party."

"What about the car . . . you saw the car?"

Samantha shook her head, then stopped. "It wasn't a car," she said, her eyes narrowing as she concentrated. Her lower lip trembled. "I think it was a truck."

"A big truck?"

"A . . . a pickup."

"What color?"

"Black . . . or real dark."

"Did you see anyone inside?"

She shook her head slowly. "It was too dark and foggy." Swallowing hard, she said in a small voice, "Is Mommy in trouble?"

"I don't know, Samantha. But I want to find her. Let's call someone to stay with you."

"But I want to come."

"I think it would be best if you would stay here." He heard the sound of a car approaching, saw headlights through the fog. "Let's get inside," he suggested, edging her over the threshold just as the car rounded a final corner.

Gravel crunched as the Volvo stopped. Miranda, wearing a long black dress, flew from behind the wheel. "Where's Claire?"

"Missing," Kane said.

"What do you mean, 'missing'?" she demanded as she climbed the steps to the porch.

"She left with someone. Samantha can tell you the story. I'm going after them."

"Who's them?" Miranda demanded.

"I'm not sure."

"Wait a minute. What's going on?"

"Samantha will fill you in. I think Claire and Sean could be with Weston Taggert."

"Taggert—why?" she asked.

"He's into this—whatever it is—up to his eyeballs," Kane said, not elaborating because of Samantha.

"But Claire called me, I think, something about Sean."

"I think Taggert's been behind all of it. From the beginning," he said so that she would understand that the situation was grave. "I think he's been systematically getting rid of anyone who is a threat to the Taggert fortune."

"But Paige—"

"I don't understand about her. Yet. But we don't have time to sit and conjecture. Take Samantha inside and lock all the doors. Then call whoever it is you deal with at the police department and have them look for a black, or dark blue or dark green, pickup. Do you have any idea what kind, honey?" he asked, looking back at Samantha. "Did you see the license plates?"

She was standing next to Miranda and her eyes were round with fear. She shook her head. "It was dark and foggy."

"Shh. It's okay," Miranda said, obviously grasping the severity of the situation. "I'll see to Samantha and I'll call the station. I've got a friend, Petrillo. He'll see that this is handled right."

"Good. Go inside. Lock the doors. You can call my cell," he said and rattled off the number as he made his way to his Jeep. The thought of Weston and Claire together made his heart nearly stop. Weston the rapist. Weston the murderer. Weston who wouldn't think twice about killing Claire or Sean.

Kane jammed the Jeep into gear and cut a tight circle. Accelerating down the lane, he decided to drive to Taggert Industries. The murders had started with men who were employed by Neal Taggert and now Weston was at the helm of the corporation.

"That's right," Miranda said as she cradled the phone between her ear and shoulder. Cooped up here at the old lodge, she was climbing the walls as she talked to Petrillo. Fortunately Samantha was in the den, wrapped in a blanket and watching television. Still, Miranda kept her voice low. "I don't care that Sean hasn't been gone for twenty-four hours, this is serious. Kane Moran thinks Weston Taggert killed Jack Songbird and Hunter Riley."

"What about his brother? Harlan?"

Miranda steeled herself. "I don't think Weston was involved in that one." Dear God, how long would she have to lie? Could she protect Tessa? And where the devil was she now? Hadn't Claire said something about Sean and Tessa being together? The phone connection had been spotty, but that's what it had sounded like. "But I want Weston Taggert brought in for questioning. Now."

"You got it," Petrillo said as he hung up. Miranda tried Claire's cell . . . again . . . got her voice mail. The damned phone wasn't turned on. So where was she? Where would Weston take her? If she's really with Weston. Samantha hadn't seen the man who lured Claire away. Had she gone willingly—no, certainly she wouldn't have left her daughter without saying where she was going. It seemed more likely that Claire had left quickly so that Samantha wouldn't be involved.

Absurdly, she thought of Denver Styles and quickly dialed the only number she had for him, a cell phone that beeped at her. Damn this part of Oregon with its high cliffs, mountains, deep chasms, and patchy cellular service. Like it or not, she'd have to wait.

She walked to the den and saw that Samantha was huddled on the couch, her overly shadowed eyes closed as if she had fallen asleep. Miranda walked into the room and the girl stirred. Battling tears, she said, "You don't know where Mom is, do you?"

"Not yet."

"Do you think something awful happened to her?" A tear slid from a corner of Samantha's eyes and Miranda's heart tore. As brave as Samantha was trying to be, the kid was scared out of her mind.

Miranda settled onto the couch and draped an arm over her niece's shoulder. Samantha was trembling. "Don't worry, sweetheart," Miranda said, hoping she was just soothing the girl. "We'll find your mom and brother."

"It's all his fault," Samantha said, choking a little as she tried to keep from sobbing. "He should never have left."

"Shh. He didn't know this would happen," she whispered and added silently, "None of us did."

"Where are you taking me? Where is Sean?" Claire demanded as Weston, careful to obey the speed limit drove along the narrow highway that snaked high above the sea. They were in a pickup with a gun rack, but the rifle wasn't clipped into the rack. It was propped beside Weston's left hand, impossible for her to reach. At the sight of the gun, she shivered inwardly. Just how desperate was this man? Where was Sean? The thought that her son might already be dead sent chills to the very heart of her. No, she wouldn't think that way. Sean had to be alive. He had to. And she had to save him. Somehow. Some way.

Tonight the ocean wasn't visible in the fog, the only way of knowing where the asphalt ended was the white stripe painted but fading along the shoulder. Face etched in stone, Weston drove continually south and though Claire couldn't see the guardrail that was often as not missing along this stretch of road, she knew the drop-off from these cliffs was hundreds of feet to the swirling angry sea.

"Where the hell are we going, Weston?"

"You'll see when we get there."

"Is my son all right? You haven't harmed him yet, have you, you bastard."

"Just shut up."

But Claire was trying to keep Weston distracted as she reached into her purse, her fingers moving silently until she found her cell phone. She didn't dare bring it out, had to fumble in the dark. Thankfully Weston had the radio turned on and was listening to the news, checking the weather report. Her fingers found the phone and she flipped it open, coughing and clearing her throat loudly as it clicked on. She could see the digital readout in her purse and with quick glimpses, she fumbled, trying to turn the volume down. Her heart was pounding a million times a minute and she could barely breathe, but she prayed she could call 911 without him realizing what she was doing.

A car bore down on them from behind. Headlights in the rearview mirror. Weston glanced at the mirror and slowed, as if hoping the guy would pass. He didn't.

"Damn it all," he ground out and saw a turnout, a vantage point overlooking the ocean on a clear day. The car behind them passed. Weston checked his watch, then eased back onto the highway. Claire saw the readout of her phone glowing in her purse. Nervously she punched out the numbers, then covered the speaker with her hand. She stared straight ahead and when she thought the connection was made, said, "Where are we going? What's south?"

"I told you not to ask any questions," he said, and she imagined she heard a female voice say, "Police Dispatch."

"But I want to know where you're taking me," Claire said loudly, over the radio. "You've got my son, Taggert, and my sister, too, so where do you think you're taking me and why? I have the right to know if you're kidnapping me." While she was talking she thought she heard a muted voice say, "Police dispatch. Do you have an emergency?"

"Where are we going? Where is Sean? I'm supposed to be at my father's party, remember. Dutch is announcing that he's running for governor tonight and if I'm not there, if any of my sisters, his daughters, aren't in attendance, he's going to get suspicious."

"It'll all be over before he knows a thing."

"Not true. Miranda's with the DA's office in Portland. They're going to hunt you down like the dog you are, Weston Taggert, and if you hurt me or my son or anyone else, they'll find you."

"Like they found out about Harley?" he demanded and then laughed. Her heart stopped. "You don't know what happened do you? All this time you thought you were protecting your sister, Tessa. Because she slammed him over the head with a rock."

Claire froze. What was he saying?

"That might've done the trick, but I couldn't be sure, now could I? Couldn't take a chance. I hated to do it, but Harley was weak and I gave up trying to carry his ass."

"So you killed him? Wait a minute, how?" Claire said, silently praying that the police dispatch hadn't hung up and was recording this, Weston's confession.

"I was there that night. I saw what happened and I dived into the water. It was instinct. At first I thought I'd save the son of a bitch and then it occurred to me to let him die."

"What did you do?" she asked, more frightened than she'd ever been in her life.

Weston slid a glance her way and she shivered for it was pure, undiluted evil. "I just helped nature along. Held on to his ankle until he quit struggling."

"But you . . . how did you breathe, I mean . . ."

"Incredible lung capacity. He'd already taken in water on the way down. I just had to wait."

"Oh, God."

His smile was a slash of white. "And do you know what my fantasy was back then?"

She couldn't answer, didn't want to know. All she could think about was saving Sean and Tessa.

"To have all of you Holland girls. I thought it was the ultimate revenge for . . ." He clammed up suddenly as he spied a turnoff, an old logging road that angled upward through the remaining trees.

"Where's Sean?" she demanded. "And Tessa."

He slid a glance her way. "Safe."

"Up here, on this old road. What is it?"

"Don't you know? This is where it all started, Claire. Up here was the first logging camp, bought by your old man. It's fitting as it backs up to Stone Illahee where old Dutch is making his announcement about running for governor. Jesus. Come on, they're waiting for us."

"Who?"

"Your son and sister for starters. I had them rounded up. That's right, I didn't do it. I have an alibi for the time they went missing."

Her heart sank as she saw that an old rusted gate was hanging open and fresh tire tracks wound up the hill . . . surely the police would be able to identify the tracks . . . or would they? Even if they did, by that time it would be too late because she was certain that Weston meant to kill them all.

Unless she could stop him.

"Did you get all that?" Petrillo asked as he clicked off the recording. Miranda clutched the telephone receiver in a death grip.

"Yes," she managed to say, fear scraping her soul. She'd heard the call that had come into police dispatch, had listened with horror to the conversation between Claire and Weston Taggert. The bastard who had raped her. Had killed Harley and let Tessa take the blame. Had killed Jack and Hunter. Her heart twisted with fear. "You have to get them safe," she whispered, hoping Samantha didn't overhear her.

"We're working on it. Figure from the clues your sister gave us that they're at Camp Twenty-Four, up along the bluff to the south of Stone Illahee. The place has been abandoned for fifty years. I've already dispatched some men."

"I hope you're not too late."

"So do I," Petrillo said and he sounded worried. "Someone better tell your father."

She glanced at her watch. It was nearly nine. About the time her father would be making his announcement in the ballroom of

Stone Illahee. Miranda's stomach contracted. "I'll see to it. Just get to them, Petrillo. Nail that son of a bitch and make sure that my sisters and nephew are safe."

"Doin' our best," he said before hanging up. She turned and found Samantha standing in the doorway.

"That was about Mom, wasn't it?"

"The police think they've found her."

"Is she okay?"

"We think so. I'll know in a little while. The best detective in the world is working on it. Now, go on upstairs, wash your face and get a move on. We need to go to the party and explain what's happening to Grandpa." Samantha was up the stairs like a shot and quickly Miranda punched out the number of Kane Moran's cell. He was in love with Claire. Sean was his son. He deserved to know what was happening.

Kane hung up the phone and glanced at his watch. He was only five minutes away from the turnoff to the old logging camp. He'd been to Weston's office and the security guard had insisted Weston was still there, evidenced by his car parked in his marked spot. But Kane had insisted the guard call Weston and when he hadn't been able to find him, they'd walked to the office. Weston wasn't anywhere in the buildings and, upon checking with a guard at a nearby lot, they'd discovered that a dark blue pickup was missing. The same truck that Samantha had seen. The same truck that Claire had climbed into. Kane didn't dare think about Claire and what could happen to her at Weston's hands. It was too chilling. But if that bastard so much as touched her, Kane would kill him.

Period.

And what good would you be to her then? What good would you be to your son?

Gritting his teeth and squinting into the night, he didn't want to think about the consequences. Right now he had to find them. He heard sirens cutting through the night, but couldn't see their lights in the fog. Nearly missing the turnout, he nosed his Jeep onto the old dirt-and-gravel road. Weeds and potholes greeted him. A rusted gate stood open. He shifted down and gave his rig some gas. He didn't know how long this road was, couldn't see over the edge of the cliff as the narrow lane switched back and forth up the mountain.

He had no weapon. No gun. Not even a knife.

But he'd learned hand-to-hand combat while he was in the military; knew what it took to kill a man.

And if Weston Taggert had done any harm to anyone, Kane would take him out. The engine ground up the hill, surely announcing his arrival, his tires spun and caught in the steep incline. He had to put his rig into four-wheel drive to keep from sliding down the hill and into the foggy nothingness.

"Come on, come on," he said, expecting with every turn to see the pickup looming in the dark. To face Taggert. To, please God, save Claire. They had unfinished business, the two of them, and now they were four. Sean and Samantha were definitely part of the deal. Which was just fine.

Where the hell were they? God, he'd climbed for ten minutes steadily and still there was no sight of . . . suddenly he was in a clearing. Two vehicles, their lights dimmed were parked between dilapidated buildings with sagging porches and broken windows. Between the dark pickup and a filthy gray van, in the beams of the headlights where fog rose like smoke, a group of people huddled. Kane's heart pounded as he recognized Claire and Tessa, very much alive and unmoving as Weston stood to one side, a rifle trained on both of them. On the other side of the clearing was a second man whom Kane recognized as Denver Styles. Sean was missing.

Heart in his throat, Kane slowly climbed out of the cab. Weston's deadly gaze moved to him, but the rifle remained trained on the women. "Look who showed up. The goddamned cavalry. Put your hands in the air, Moran."

Kane did as he was told. He only had to get close to Weston, near enough to jump him. The rifle, once it wasn't pointed at Claire wouldn't be a problem. Kane learned years ago how to disarm a man. The fog, heavy with the primal scent of the sea, would help camouflage his moves.

"What's he doing here?" Styles demanded, sliding an irritated glance at Kane.

"Trying to save the day."

"It's all over," Kane interjected. "The police know what's going on."

"Sure they do," Weston mocked, but seemed a little nervous.

That wouldn't do. The last thing Kane wanted was for the rifle to fire because Taggert was twitchy.

"Our plan will still work." Weston wasn't going to be deterred. He hitched his chin in Kane's direction and from the trees nearby an owl gave off a lonely hoot. "We'll just make sure Moran is in the accident. As soon as we find the boy."

"I told you the kid isn't important," Styles said. "He's not related to you. He's Moran's son, not Harley's."

"You're sure of that."

"Saw the DNA report myself."

How? Kane wondered. What was the deal with this guy? Was he an assassin? A killer for hire? Styles complicated things. Kane knew he could take out Taggert, the guy was getting soft in the gut, but Styles was another matter. The two men he had to disarm were standing too far apart. Fortunately Styles didn't have a weapon cocked and aimed. But that didn't mean there wasn't a gun hidden beneath his jacket.

"But the kid can make you. He saw your face."

"I'm going to disappear," Styles said. "And I'll take the heat. That way if the cops think that the accident was planned, they'll blame me. It's my van that's going to go off the road and into the sea anyway. No one will ever know that you were behind the deal. Just give me my money and I'll do the rest. You can take off, go make yourself an alibi."

So the guy was a gun for hire. Well he'd have to get close to Taggert to take the money and when he did, Kane would make his move. There was no way he was going to let Claire get in a car with either of these two pricks. His muscles tensed. He was on the balls of his feet, ready to spring.

"What about him?" Weston asked and motioned in Kane's direction with the muzzle of the rifle.

Kane froze.

Styles didn't so much as glance his way. His jaw was rock hard, his lips a thin line. "As you said, Moran gets it, too."

"You bastards, do you think you'll really get away with this?" Claire glanced at Kane.

"Shh. Don't say anything," Tessa warned and there was something about her attitude that seemed off. "Just go along."

"Are you nuts? I'm not going along! Not ever." Claire was angry and scared and Kane wanted to find a way to comfort her.

"Neither am I, Taggert. As I said, the police know just what you're up to."

"So where are they? Jesus, Styles, let's get this over with." He reached into his jacket pocket and withdrew a thick envelope. Kane inched forward. "This is most of it. You'll get the rest once the job is finished and if I find out you're lying about the kid—"

"He's not. Leave Sean out of this," Claire said. "Whatever it is." She sounded desperate. Panicked. "Sean's not Harley's son!"

She was moving forward, pleading with Weston, ignoring the gun barrel pointed straight at her chest. Kane heard a rush in his ears, saw Weston aim. "No! Claire duck!" he screamed, rushing forward. In his peripheral vision he saw Styles move.

"Now!" Styles yelled as the barrel of the gun shifted, sighting on Kane.

He leapt at Weston.

A rifle cracked.

Kane hit Taggert hard. Taggert screamed as they went down, the rifle falling to the earth. Kane pummeled the man with his fists, reached upward, intent on driving the bastard's nose into his brain. From everywhere there were shouts and from the corner of his eye Kane saw a dozen men in SWAT gear stream from the trees. Sirens sounded and he caught a glimpse of Claire, ashen faced, rushing toward them.

"Stay back!" Styles ordered, aiming a pistol at Kane. "Give it up, Moran." He pulled a wallet from his pocket and flashed a badge. "Get EMT here now!"

Someone peeled him off Taggert who was writhing on the ground, blood gurgling from his lips.

"You're hurt!" Claire cried, staring at his shirt and the bloody stain on it.

"It's Taggert's." Styles still had his weapon trained on Taggert.

"Who the hell are you?" Kane demanded.

"FBI. Undercover. Taggert was into a lot of illegal shit."

"Where's Sean?" Claire asked, and for the first time Styles smiled. "With his grandfather. I don't think Dutch is going to make a run for governor after all."

"We need life flight!" the EMT who was working on Taggert said and Styles nodded, walked to the van and barked orders into a walkie-talkie.

Kane held Claire close. It was over. Taggert, if he lived would be in custody. Claire was safe. Sean was safe. He'd finally come home. He kissed Claire's tear-stained face and sighed. "Come on, Princess," he said. "Let's go get our boy."

EPILOGUE

"So Denver Styles was with the FBI?" Claire asked. She and her sisters were seated around the outdoor table two weeks after Weston Taggert had been captured. It was near twilight. Sean was shooting baskets and Samantha was upstairs listening to the radio, some of the strains of music filtering through the thick branches of the fir trees surrounding the patio.

"Styles was deep undercover, so deep that no one here in Chinook, not even the police knew it," Miranda said, and her irritation was visible as she twirled the stem of her wineglass between her fingers.

"You thought he should confide in you, is that it?" Tessa said, as she lit a cigarette and placed one bare foot on an empty chair. "When you were a part of the investigation."

"It would have been nice."

"Oh come on, Randa, it would have compromised the entire sting or operation or whatever it's called."

"She's right," Claire added and smiled. "Admit it, the real reason you're ticked off is that you started to fall for him."

"If that's what you want to think," she said and sipped from her glass.

"That's the way it is."

"He called here looking for you," Tessa added.

"I heard."

"Did you call him back?"

One side of Miranda's mouth lifted a bit. "I'm considering it."

"Oh, for God's sake, go for it. So you were embarrassed, so what? He was just doing his job and he does have a nice ass."

"Tessa!" Miranda said, as if shocked.

"Yeah, like you haven't noticed."

Claire giggled. "Shh. My daughter might hear you."

"Oh, I'm sorry," Tessa said. "Like that's the biggest one of your problems."

"Okay, okay, you're right." Claire did have more than her share of situations that needed her attention. Even though Kane had helped save his mother, Sean wasn't certain he trusted the man who was his father. He was still stung from dealing with Paul and wasn't eager to let another man, regardless of being blood related, into his life. Recently he'd voiced his opinions about Claire remarrying.

"Are you nuts, Mom?" he'd asked while trying to perfect a skateboard jump over a retaining wall near the lake. "You just got out of one bad marriage and now you're jumping back in. Can't you give it some time? Isn't that what you always tell me to do?"

She'd argued of course, even told Sean that Kane had been her first true love. Her son had indelicately thrown Harley into her face and the implication, though unstated, was that she was fickle. She'd decided he had a point. Then Sean had pushed the issue. "And I don't like the way he calls you 'princess.'"

"It's a joke," she'd explained.

"Yeah, a bad one."

"I'm not changing that, I like it," she'd explained, and on that issue they were at a standoff. It only made things worse that Samantha thought Kane was cool. That really bugged Sean. Well, tough, he could just be bugged, Claire decided, as she took a sip from her glass.

"So you're getting married to Kane next year?" Tessa asked.

"Umm, that's the plan."

"It's not like you don't know the guy. What's it been now, sixteen years?"

"Maybe even longer, but who's counting? It's what's happening now that matters." And that was true. She loved Kane, he loved her and they could wait a little while, just let things settle down.

Tessa finished her wine. "I'm just glad Dad gave up all that nonsense about running for governor. Wouldn't that have been a pain in the butt?"

So much had happened. Weston was in custody, still hospitalized but expected to live and stand trial. Paige was now in charge of Taggert Industries and Kendall had filed for divorce. She and Stephanie had already moved to Portland. Dutch had given up his political dreams and was satisfied to spend more time with his daughters while constructing another phase of Stone Illahee. Ruby and Jack Songbird were suing Weston Taggert for the wrongful death of their son and Tessa was getting restless.

"So what're you going to do?" Miranda asked her youngest sister.

"Now that I'm a free woman, that I know I didn't kill Harley, I'm going back to California and maybe I'll try to take some art classes or something. I don't know." She narrowed her eyes on Lake Arrowhead. "Maybe I'll just hang out here a while. You don't know how good it feels to finally be free."

"Yeah, I do." Claire said. "The divorce papers came on Monday."

"Congratulations!" Miranda said, then turned as she saw a boat slicing across the lake. At its helm was Kane Moran and damn it, Claire's heart still jumped at the sight of him in his beat-up leather jacket and jeans. He'd aged in the past sixteen years but there was a part of him that was still the rebel boy whom she'd fallen in love with all those years ago.

"Are you sure you can wait a year?" Tessa asked, seeing her sister's face.

"Mmm. We'll see. I think it would be best."

"You think?" Tessa wasn't convinced.

Kane moored the boat, waved to the sisters, then hurried up the dock and headed toward the garage. He said something to Sean and with a disinterested lift of one shoulder, Sean passed him the ball. A heartbeat later they were involved in an intense game of one-on-one.

"Looks to me as if it might work out," Miranda observed just as Sean faked Kane out and made a layup.

"Fingers crossed," Claire said, smiling as she watched her son and his father vying for the ball. "Fingers crossed."

Dear Reader,

I hope you enjoyed *Whispers*. This book, set near the Oregon coast and revolving around the three Holland sisters, is one of my favorites. I loved writing each woman's story.

I'm lucky in that I can revisit some of my favorite characters.

Recently I was asked to write a sequel to *Deep Freeze* and *Fatal Burn,* two of my most popular novels that are currently being repackaged and republished in December 2015 and February 2016. I was thrilled to pen the new novel, and the result, *After She's Gone,* takes up about a decade after the first two books end.

In *Deep Freeze,* Jenna Hughes, along with her two daughters, has escaped the glam and glitz of Hollywood. Little does the ex-actress know that an obsessed fan, one with murderous intent, has stalked her all the way to the shores of the Columbia River and the small town she now calls home. Not only is she in danger, but both of her daughters, Cassie and Allie, are in the maniac's brutal plans.

Fatal Burn takes up where *Deep Freeze* leaves off. In this story, Dani Settler, a tomboy and friend of Jenna's daughter Allie, goes missing. The bloody trail turns instantly cold, and the police as well as her father are stymied. While Travis Settler frantically searches for his daughter, Dani is running out of time and must rely solely upon her wits to keep herself alive against her would-be hate-filled killer.

After She's Gone, a brand-new book, will be in the stores in January 2016. This book takes up nearly a decade after *Deep Freeze* and catches up with Allie and Cassie Kramer; both have tested the waters of acting in Hollywood with varied success. Allie, the younger sibling, is much more famous than her older sister. Jealousy and rivalry have been a part of their lives and culminate when Allie goes missing, and Cassie, never all that stable to begin with, is suspected in her sister's disappearance. Is Allie dead? The victim of her sister's jealousy? Is she part of an elaborate publicity stunt? Or is she now the victim of her own insidious stalker with his own malevolent intent? Catch up with the Kramer sisters and find out in *After She's Gone.*

For those of you who are into my Grizzly Falls series, which features Detectives Alvarez and Pescoli, you'll be glad to know that in late 2016, there will be two more books available. *Expecting to Die* takes up where *Deserves to Die* left off, with a very pregnant Regan Pescoli debating whether she'll stay on the force or throw in her badge and stay home after her baby is born. Unfortunately an old nemesis plans to take the choice away from her, and all her carefully laid plans, as well as the lives of her family, are threatened. Things only get worse in *Willing to Die,* where Pescoli and Alvarez battle a foe who is willing to sacrifice everything to extract a deadly revenge.

I think you'll like the stories. At least, I hope so.

If you'd like more information on these books or any other I've written, please check out my website. At www.lisajackson.com you'll be able to see what's new and read excerpts from upcoming as well as already published books. Also, you can like me on Facebook at Lisa Jackson Fans or follow me at readlisajackson on Twitter.

Keep Reading!

Lisa Jackson

**Please turn the page
for a very special Q&A
with Lisa Jackson!**

While *Whispers* is a novel of suspense it's also a novel about the relationships between the three Holland sisters. Was any one sister in the story your favorite?

Of course I love them all, and originally the story was set to surround Miranda, the oldest sister, but my editor wanted the story to revolve around Claire, the second sister, whom I didn't like as well. I thought she'd messed her life up too much, and as for Tessa, she was the wild child. I rewrote the synopsis, and the focus of the plot shifted a little. The end result I think was an improvement, and I got what my editor had thought: that Claire was the sister to whom the readers would most relate.

The *Whispers* is a stand-alone novel. Do you ever see yourself revisiting the Holland sisters, or has their story been told?

I probably wouldn't continue with the Holland girls' story, but might do something where they're in the background. I feel, for the most part, their stories have been told, but there's always a new generation or some black sheep in the family who might want to appear and let the sisters come forward again. I do think Miranda and Tessa might have a little more story in them.

While we're on the topic of sisters, you have a younger sister, Nancy Bush, who's also a *New York Times* bestselling author. What's your relationship like with her?

I guess "Sister Nan," as I call her, is my best friend and has been for most of my adult life (though I wouldn't cop to this or didn't believe it as a teenager when she raided my closet after I went to school for an earlier shift). Now, though, and for years, we live near each other and hang out. We raised our children together and write as a team as well as individually. We are definitely joined at the brain! (And the heart as well.)

The *Whispers* was originally published in 1996 and upon its initial publication wasn't considered a huge success. But then a few years later, when it was repackaged and republished after your success with *Cold Blooded*, it became a *New York Times* bestseller and is

one of your most successful books to date. How did that feel? Did you think that *Whispers* was the little book that could?

I think timing is a large part of success, and my career began as a slow build. When I began to concentrate on romantic suspense and thrillers, with trying to keep the reader guessing while, I hope, creating relatable (is that even a word?) characters, the book sales increased. Readers connected with the suspense angle. I think I finally found my niche, people began noticing me, and some of my older books became all-time favorites. I couldn't be more thrilled, as I love some of the older novels.

Every so often you'll take a break from your series and write a stand-alone novel. Do you enjoy writing those more?

It's refreshing to write about new people and new places, of course, and in some ways it's easier, as I don't have to keep track of the characters' lives (such as Detectives Bentz and Montoya in the New Orleans series, or Detectives Alvarez and Pescoli in the Grizzly Falls, Montana, "To Die" series), but I love revisiting old friends. I enjoy getting into the groove of their lives, but wouldn't want it as a steady writing diet. I like to mix things up. So I'm lucky that I can do both!

Of all your stand-alone novels, is there one that's your particular favorite?

Oooh. Tough. I guess I'd have to say *You Don't Want to Know,* as it's dark, moody, and has all those Gothic elements I love. I can't tell you how much I enjoyed writing Ava's story. Old, creepy house. Isolation. Family members with secrets. The feeling Ava's going out of her mind. An island with an abandoned mental hospital with a history. A homicidal maniac purported to be on the loose. What's not to love?

What makes you decide to revisit a book that you've originally planned as a stand-alone novel? For instance, your novel *If She Only Knew* was a stand-alone. Yet a few years after it was published you wrote a sequel to it, *Almost Dead.* Did you feel there was more story that could be told?

Well, often times it's fan request or editor request. Or it could be a tidbit of a storyline that comes to mind and I think, *Ooh, that would be great for Nikki Gillette or the Cahill family.* I try to keep the door open, as I do love revisiting my characters . . . so time will tell.

I hear there may be a sequel to *Almost Dead* at some point down the road. I guess the Cahills have more secrets?

That family? Of course! They're steeped in secrets. I loved writing those two books. But the right plot has to come to mind before I sit down and really get into it. So far just little snippets of ideas have popped through my head for the Cahills, nothing solid yet. But yes, I think there will be another book in the future.

Your novel *Without Mercy* is a stand-alone, and you'd always planned it that way. Yet after it was published, your readers started writing to you, asking if there would be a sequel. When something like that happens, does it get your creative juices flowing? Would you want to write a sequel to *Without Mercy*, or do you feel that story's been told and there are other stories that you want to write?

I would like to revisit *Without Mercy,* and yes, lots of readers have asked about the characters. I definitely think there will be at least a second book, but I have many others to write first, and that story hasn't gelled. The original book came to me in a flash while driving and listening to an advertisement on the radio. I'm hoping for that kind of inspiration.

Your earlier novels, like *See How She Dies*, *Final Scream*, and *Whispers*, had plots that focused around families and the dangerous secrets that they shared. But your later novels, like *Hot Blooded* and *Never Die Alone* in the Bentz/Montoya New Orleans series, and *Left to Die* and *Deserves to Die*, in the Pescoli/Alvarez Montana series, had plots that focused around serial killers. Why the shift in direction?

This wasn't intentional—just the ideas that come to mind. I like to change it up and I have. *You Don't Want to Know* is another family story that I wrote recently, for example; the same with *Tell Me*. When I write stories centered around cops, I usually want a murder or two, so yes, serial killers work their way into the plots. However, I don't ever want to be considered a "one-trick pony." I like to keep the readers wondering what will be next.

Most of your stand-alone novels, like *Whispers*, are set in the Pacific Northwest, where you live. Is there a specific reason for that?

Only because I'm familiar with the Pacific NW and I have series set in Montana, New Orleans, Savannah, and a few novels set in L.A. I tend to go with places I love or know well, as it adds authenticity to the novels. And come on . . . the Pacific NW? With all the seasons, fog, dark coastline . . . a perfect setting, I'd say, and since it's home, it's familiar ground.

What's up next on the publishing horizon for Lisa Jackson?

One of my earlier novels, *Deep Freeze,* will be repackaged and re-published in December 2015. It's one of my favorite books (as well as popular with readers). I wanted to revisit the characters in this story and catch up with Jenna Hughes's daughters who have now grown up in *After She's Gone,* which will be published in January 2016. I figured they were pretty messed up with dealing with the terror of *Deep Freeze.* Once again, it's fun to catch up with old friends, even if things haven't gone so well for them. Love it!

In this explosive new thriller, #1 New York Times bestselling author Lisa Jackson delves into the deep bond between two sisters and their shared dream that becomes a harrowing nightmare of madness, hatred, and jealousy. . . .

Cassie Kramer and her younger sister, Allie, learned the hazards of fame long ago. Together, they'd survived the horror of a crazed fan who nearly killed their mother, former Hollywood actress Jenna Hughes. Still, Cassie moved to L.A., urging Allie to follow. As a team, they'd take the town by storm. But Allie, finally free of small-town Oregon, and just that little bit more beautiful, also proved to be more talented—and driven. Where Cassie got bit parts, Allie rose to stardom. But now her body double has been shot on the set of her latest movie—and Allie is missing.

Police discover that the last call to Allie's phone came from Cassie, though she has no recollection of making it. Instead of looking like a concerned relative, Cassie is starting to look like a suspect—the jealous sister who finally grew sick of playing a supporting role. As the tabloids go into a frenzy, Cassie ends up on a Portland psych ward. Is she just imagining the sinister figure who comes to her bedside, whispering about Allie—a visitor of whom there is no record? Is someone trying to help—or drive her mad?

Convinced she's the only one who can find Allie, Cassie checks herself out of the hospital. But a sudden slew of macabre murders— each victim masked with a likeness of a member of Cassie's family—makes Cassie fear for her safety and her sanity. The only way to end the nightmare is to find out what really happened to Allie. And with each discovery, Cassie realizes that no one can be trusted to keep her safe—least of all herself. . . .

Please turn the page for an exciting sneak peek of Lisa Jackson's

AFTER SHE'S GONE

coming in January 2016 wherever print and ebooks are sold!

PROLOGUE

Portland, Oregon

He watched.

Carefully.

Paying attention to every detail as the rain sheeted from the night-dark sky and streetlights reflected on the wet pavement.

Two women were running, faster and faster, and he smiled as the first passed into the lamp's pool of illumination. Her face was twisted in terror, her beautiful features distorted by fear.

Just as they should have been.

Good. Very good.

The slower woman was a few steps behind and constantly looking over her shoulder, as if she were expecting something or someone with murderous intent to be hunting her down.

Just as he'd planned.

Come on, come on, keep running.

As if they heard him, the women raced forward.

Perfect.

His throat tightened, and his fists balled in nervous anticipation.

Just a few more steps!

Gasping, the slower woman paused, one hand splayed over her chest as she leaned over to catch her breath beneath the streetlamp. Rain poured down from the heavens. Her hair was wet, falling in dripping ringlets around her face, her white jacket soaked through. Again she glanced furtively behind her, past the empty sidewalks and storefronts of this forgotten part of the city. God, she was beautiful, as was the first one, each a fine female specimen that he'd picked precisely for this moment.

His heart was pumping wildly, anticipation and adrenaline firing his blood as an anticipatory grin twisted his lips.

Good. This is so good.

Silently he watched as from the corner of his eye, the first woman raced past him just as he'd hoped. Eyes focused ahead, she was seemingly oblivious to his presence, but, in his heart, he knew she realized he was there, observing her every movement, catching each little nuance of fear. He saw determination and horror in the tense lines of her face, heard it in her quick, shallow breaths and the frenzied pounding of her footsteps as she'd flown past.

And then she was gone.

Safely down the street.

He forced his full attention to the second woman, the target. She twisted her neck, turned to look his way, as if she felt him near, as if she divined him lurking in the deep umbra surrounding the street.

His heart missed a beat.

Don't see me. Do not! Do not look at me!

Her expression, at this distance, was a little blurry, but he sensed that she was scared to death. Terrified. Exactly what he wanted.

Feel it. Experience the sheer terror of knowing you're being stalked, that you are about to die.

Her lower lip trembled.

Yes! Finally.

Satisfaction warmed his blood.

As if she heard a sound, she stiffened, her head snapping to stare down the darkened alley.

That's it. Come on. Come on!

Her eyes widened, and suddenly she started running again, this time in a sheer panic. She slipped, lost a high heel, and she kicked off the other, never missing a step, her bare feet still slapping the wet pavement frantically.

Now!

He shifted slightly, giving himself a better view, made sure that he didn't miss a thing.

Perfect.

She was running right on target.

At that moment a dark figure stepped from a shadowed doorway to stand right in front of the woman.

Screaming, she veered a bit, slipped, and nearly lost her balance, only to keep on running, angling away from the man.

Too late!

The assassin raised his gun.

Blam! Blam! Blam!

Three shots rang out, echoing along the empty street, fire spitting from the gun's muzzle.

She stumbled and reeled, her face a mask of fear as she twisted and fell onto the pavement. Her eyes rolled upward, blood trickling from the corner of her mouth. Another bloom of red rose darkly through her white jacket.

Perfect, he thought, satisfied at last as he viewed her unmoving body.

Finally, after years of planning, he'd pulled it off.

Allie Kramer was dead.